L.A. Naylor

ROOTS BOOKS

This is a work of fiction. Names, characters, businesses, places, events, locales and incidents are either the products of the author's imagination or used in a fictitious manner. Any resemblance to actual persons, living or dead, or actual events is purely coincidental.

First published in 2019

ISBN 978 0 9547437 1 0

Typeset by RefineCatch Limited, www.refinecatch.com
Printed and bound in Great Britain by Clays Ltd, Elcograf S.p.A

www.lanaylor.com

Freedom

Blackbirds, buzzards, and doves
land on cathedrals and palaces
just as they do on rocks,
trees, and fences …

and they shit on them
with the complete freedom of one who knows
that god and justice
belong to the soul.

By Humberto Ak'abal
Translated by Miguel Rivera

Chapter 1

The earth was growing and dying, one faster than the other, but Lia was cautiously optimistic. She had looked forward to this night for so long and she wasn't about to let anyone spoil it.

A gaunt man sitting nearby couldn't get the attention of the waitress, a good thing in Lia's opinion, given the quantity of beer he had already guzzled. But he wouldn't give up and she had learned to expect trouble in life, so it was easy to duck with the kind of speed that would have made Bruce Lee proud. The ashtray shattered against the wall, jabbing a shard of glass into her mosquito-bitten ankle. She stifled a yelp and teased the prickly feel of it out.

The waitress began to apologize but Lia held a hand up and stretched her face into a smile of reassurance. The waitress turned to the idiot who had thrown the ashtray and Lia watched, amazed, as she took his order for another beer. She was streetwise enough to know the violent consequences of selling alcohol to people who were already drunk, but she wouldn't be doing the waitress any favours by pointing it out.

She looked at Richard. He was oblivious to the fact that she had just avoided receiving a serious head injury. Apart from Rafael, he was her only friend. She reached up to fiddle with her eyebrow ring before remembering that she'd removed it as soon as they'd arrived. He, on the other hand, had ignored her suggestion of removing his Rolex to avoid drawing attention. It wasn't until a very kind tourist guide had *advised* Richard to remove his watch for their safety that he complied.

Leaving London had still been the best idea she'd had in years. For the first time, she was living life on her own terms, drawn by the strange pull of her heart all the way to Guatemala to see Rafael again. She didn't know much about the country but the hopeless romantic in her didn't care. She was just happy to be here.

'Of all the places to meet, why on earth would Rafael choose a dodgy establishment like this?' asked Richard in his most condescending voice.

Lia ignored him. In the two weeks since they'd been in the country, this place had to rank as one of the least memorable, but so what? Rafael had told her he wouldn't be able to see her straight away due to work commitments. Instead, they had travelled down the highway away from the sprawl of the city to Antigua, the first of the places on her must-see list. It had been a mouth-watering taste of adventure. She and Richard had hiked up the magnificent slopes of the Pacaya Volcano to feast upon panoramic views way above the clouds. They had visited nearby market towns and been dazzled by the rich tapestry of colours and live music on display. Well, *she* had been dazzled. She wasn't sure exactly what was going on with Richard. As far as she was concerned, Guatemala had everything: bright blue skies, Maya ruins, vast lakes, beaches and the tastiest foods. They'd only returned to the city to meet up with Rafael.

A few people had been in the basement bar earlier but it had now gone 10 p.m. and there wasn't an empty table left. More people kept arriving, adding to the resonance of male chatting voices over the jukebox. Still no sign of Rafael. Lia held her breath as she counted the number of firearms in plain view. A man wearing camouflage fatigues hovered near the entrance carrying an assault rifle. Those who didn't carry guns had machetes. There were no windows to release the cigarette smoke that twirled up to the low-hanging ceiling before creeping down the walls. Naked light bulbs and electrical wiring dangled at eye level over a wooden bar in the far corner. The remains of faded blue paint peeled off the front.

'I'm still sure he'll be here,' said Lia, staring around the room again, brows furrowed.

She'd read on Wikipedia that Guatemala had originally been named the Land of Trees by the first settlers, the Maya, but here in the city she hadn't seen a single piece of foliage; just men roaming the streets who looked at her as if she had done something to upset them. The streets were paved in hard knocks and lined with bullet holes, but Lia's desire to leave England had been as strong as any religious calling.

They'd met Macy for the first time just hours earlier whilst still locking horns over Richard's Rolex.

'I've *always* worn a watch since I was about five years old,' said Richard. 'It's a part of my personality and style.'

'But you don't need to be a schedule slave now that you're out here.'

'I wouldn't mind so much if I had my phone with me, but you managed to persuade me to leave that behind.'

As Lia had glared at him, trying to think of some way she could still win the argument, for the sake of them not being mugging targets, Macy stopped by their table.

'You *could* just buy him a much cheaper watch to wear.'

She'd introduced herself and asked if she could join them for dinner, effortlessly dissipating the tension between them.

'So where are you from?' asked Richard.

'Amersham,' said Macy, with a knowing smile.

Lia studied Richard, who was staring at Macy's gorgeous long, light frizzy hair but trying not to be obvious about it. He tried again. 'And what are you?'

'Human, and you?'

Lia giggled, no doubt adding to Richard's discomfort.

'I meant where did you originate from?' he said.

'A uterus.'

Macy grinned and then grew serious. 'I'm mixed race. Half-caste. Mulatto. Biracial. A halfie. My father's from Bermuda, he's a mix of Portuguese and black African, and my mum is white British, from Amersham, which is where I grew up.'

'So you're British,' said Richard, as if he still needed some sort of clarification.

'I am,' said Macy, 'I am black, I am white, I am blended and wholesomely British. Amazing, right?'

Richard nodded. Lia was glad of the extra company. Macy was smart, funny and lovely-looking.

'You look Hapa to me, Lia,' said Macy with a wink. 'How do you describe yourself?'

'I think I like mixed race best,' Lia said after a pause. She was usually uncomfortable talking about anything race-related but she was drawn to the way Macy seemed so at ease with it all.

'So, like me, you've had it from both sides, I bet,' said Macy. 'Too yellow to be white, or too white to be yellow, right? Yada yada yada.'

'A little,' said Lia. It was like her life experience was being told to her by someone she'd never met before.

'My dad was white British and my mum was Chinese. They died when I was four and I was adopted when I was eleven,' she added.

Macy nodded, her expression neutral.

'I think it's your round,' said Richard, smiling too widely at Macy as he took in the human armoury surrounding them.

Macy scraped her chair back and stood. 'Sure, I'll get us some drinks. While I'm gone don't lull yourself into a false sense of security or anything, but please try and relax.'

She was looking at Richard when she said that. It was the kind of advice Lia's adoptive mother would offer up. *Learn to feel oneness with the whole world. Change adversity to luck. No point to have just one set of parents. You can have two, perhaps more. This is the Chinese way.*

Macy flicked tightly curled ringlets of hair back over her shoulders, retied her hair wrap and looked down at Richard as she smoothed her ankle-length denim skirt. They both knew Richard was uncomfortable by the way he slouched to hide his six-foot-plus bulk and kept cracking his knuckles under the table. His carefully creased Ralph Lauren slacks and designer shirt had obviously not escaped Macy's notice either.

'Same again? Though I imagine you'd prefer Remy Martin's venerable Louis XIII cognac, I don't think they sell that here.'

Richard grinned, oblivious to Macy's sardonic tone. 'I would prefer it, given the choice, but another locally brewed version of rum, or *ron*, as they call it here, will be just fine too.'

Macy displayed a row of perfect white teeth as she inclined her head in a gesture of acquiescence.

Not far from where they sat, a steel pot on the floor rattled and tinged as someone spat something into it. It wasn't the noise that amazed Lia, or even the sight of spit flying through the air. It was the sheer distance that it had travelled and the accuracy with which it landed in the centre of the pot. She turned to stare at the table of men, one in particular who was getting up to shake hands as the others prepared to leave.

It was Rafael. Her heart leaped as she once again took in his tousled and lustrous dark brown hair and chiselled features. She stared, trying to gauge his mood, hoping that he still wanted to see her as much as she wanted to see him. He was three hours late, after all.

She watched as Rafael grabbed the arm of the man next to him and pointed his finger towards the man's chest. The man put both his hands up, took a step back and nodded in submission. To her surprise Rafael lit a cigarette, something she hadn't seen him do before, and the three men he had been talking to left.

A lone figure surrounded by empty glasses and bottles,

Rafael now turned and caught her eye. A warm grin turned his face from handsome to downright celestial as he stood up. She raised an arm to wave.

'He's here and he's coming over!' she said to Richard and the back of Macy, who was gliding through the crowd towards the bar. To her frustration he stopped in front of the waitress, presumably to pay a drinks tab, but had to wait whilst she fumbled in her apron pockets for the total figure owed.

'Gosh, it really is true what they say about Spanish time-keeping skills,' said Richard. He glanced at his watch with disdain.

Lia frowned. 'He's Guatemalan, not Spanish, and I'm sure he's got a good reason.'

'I saw him at the bar earlier,' said Richard. 'He had a briefcase that he passed over to the barman.'

Most table occupants had finished eating, but the scent of pine needles, tobacco and floor-strewn sawdust continued to mix with the smell of roasted corn and tamales.

'So you've only known him for a few months?' said Richard.

'Yes.' As if he didn't already know. 'He taught a Spanish language course at my university and we got on really well,' said Lia. She snaked a finger over water drops that clung to the outside of her glass and wiped it around her lips. She'd never been far from thirsty from the moment she felt the sky open up beneath her as they whooshed into the airspace above London. Coming out here to find Rafael and realize their feelings for each other would surely fulfil the secret longing that she – and surely everyone else – had to love and be loved. Nearly everyone she had met at university seemed to find it easy to find a partner who wanted to be in a relationship. They attracted their partners without having to try too hard, probably because they had been born lucky. Well, she might not have been born lucky but she was on the right path now, and the fact made her what she'd always dreamed of being:

normal. She looked at Richard with no idea how to explain it all to him; that love was profound and that it didn't always follow a formula.

'I think it was my turn to get the next drinks in, not Macy's.'

'It's just a round of drinks,' said Richard.

'It's the principle.'

'I don't mind getting the next few rounds,' said Richard.

'Thanks but no,' said Lia, curling her left eyebrow upwards into a frustrated scowl. 'Let's take it in turns and stop slinging your dad's money around.'

She watched his face turn red and flustered. He wiped a sweaty palm through brand new tufts of hair that sprouted baby hedgehog-like over his head, the colour of hay and the result of three sessions of hair transplantation surgery.

Macy returned with their drinks grouped firmly between slender hands. She wiggled her hips in graceful rhythm to the jukebox music, captivating the nearby men. As they stared, she set all but her own glass of *ron* down on the table and raised it to the men.

'*¡Salud, amor y dinero!*' Health, love and money!

She was toasted back by about fifteen men who lifted their glasses in return as they sat around three tables that had been pushed together to accommodate the group.

'This is probably what working men's clubs were like in Britain a hundred years ago,' said Lia.

Macy ruffled Richard's hair with a giggle and sat back down, eyeing one of the muscled men nearby with a flirtatious smile.

'We're probably in one of the most economically deprived areas of the whole inhospitable city,' said Richard.

'There are far worse areas,' said Macy. She had fallen in love with Guatemala whilst travelling from the north to the south. That was all they knew about her. She was still looking at the muscled man who seemed to be gathering the courage to approach her.

'It won't be easy finding a paid job, let alone one that will pay you more than a few dollars a month,' said Richard as if he had become an expert on the country.

Lia rubbed her eyes. Unlike her, Richard didn't need a job and had never known what it was like to be desperate for money. All he seemed to care about were his material possessions, and in London, he had them all: the latest iPhone, a fancy drone, even a Ninebot Segway that was part robot. If he'd had his way, they'd be staying in a couple of the Hilton suites uptown, living off room service and guarded by their own security personnel. She smiled at such a ridiculous thought. By now they were on their fifth (or sixth?) drink. Her head was light with the dizzy satisfaction of being in the same room as Rafael once again. Macy was eleven years older than her, and to be spoken to with equal status was also fantastic, her age and youthful lack of alcohol tolerance kindly overlooked.

Unable to play it cool any longer, Lia decided she would go over to greet Rafael first. But then she watched the waitress walk away, and he finally approached their table.

'Rafael!' Lia bounced out of her chair and wrapped her arms around the man in a loose hug. He pulled her into his body.

'How are you, Julianne? I'm so sorry I couldn't join you for dinner, I had to wait for an important meeting to finish.'

She stepped back. He was the only person she knew who insisted on calling her by her full name. It had only been a few months since she'd last seen him but he had lost weight. He was still handsome though, even with blackened fingernails and hair that she could now see was shiny with sweat. The twinkle in his eyes was still there, lightening the atmosphere and her heart.

'Don't worry, we've had a great evening. I'd like to introduce you to my friends, Richard and Macy.'

They both shook hands and Lia wondered what, if anything, Rafael would surmise from the brief touch. Would he realize how paranoid Richard was of picking up microbial pathogens from his hand? The thought brought a giggle to her lips.

'Lia told me that you teach at the San Pedro Spanish School,' said Macy.

'*Sí, señorita.* I can teach you Spanish if you want.' He spread his arms wide as if inviting all three to embrace him in a group hug. 'Welcome to Guatemala.'

Lia grinned. 'Thank you. Richard might be interested in taking lessons while he's here in Guatemala. Macy is already fluent.'

Gwa-te-ma-lah was fast becoming her favourite word. Gwa-te-ma-lah ... the way it flicked off the narrow tip of her tongue, accompanied by a fine mist of spit if she wasn't careful. It was the most unconventional place to job hunt, which made it perfect for her. She had about five hundred pounds of misappropriated student loan to her name and that was it.

'I've never considered learning Spanish,' said Richard, 'but it may come in useful whilst I'm on the run from my father.' He fiddled with the bottom button of his Pierre Cardin shirt.

'I'm sorry to hear that,' said Rafael, turning to study Richard. His speech was slow and warm but Richard didn't look at him. After an uncomfortable pause, Rafael added, 'I hope you find what it is you are looking for.'

Both men glanced at Lia and then at each other, and Lia had the feeling they were sizing each other up like children in a playground, probably arriving at all kinds of mistaken assumptions.

Lia wished she hadn't let Richard tag along for the ride – her ride. What had she been thinking? Rafael and Richard were polar opposites. She should have realized that they wouldn't get along.

Rafael turned back to Lia with a smile and casually flopped an arm over the back of her chair. She leaned into the crook of his arm. 'It's so lovely to see you again.'

He grazed her cheek with his fingers. 'Can you imagine my

delight when you agreed to visit? Pure happiness has been radiating from my heart. Our friendship makes me feel as proud as a king on his throne.'

Richard's mouth pursed as if he suddenly smelled something unpalatable, but he remained silent.

'This lovely soul was so kind to me when I visited London,' said Rafael. 'We got on so well together.'

It was as if they had never been apart. Hearing his voice made the whole world a better place.

'We played pool in a pub and that was the icebreaker,' said Lia, although she'd already told Richard this on the plane.

'Glad you showed up, Rafael,' said Macy. She winked at Lia.

The muscled man who had been watching Macy stood up with a giddy smile. Lia thought she saw him slip something small and shiny under his hand across to one of the other men in the group, a short, stocky, moody-looking man, before sauntering over to their table.

Macy stood to meet the man at eye level with a confident smile as she introduced herself.

She glanced down at Lia and Richard. 'I'm just going outside for some fresh air.'

'Be careful, *señorita,*' Rafael called out to Macy. She turned to acknowledge his warning with a nod before continuing on her way.

'How long will you stay?' asked Rafael, turning back to Lia.

'Until my money runs out, which will be soon, but I'm hoping to find a job, like teaching English or something.'

'I might be able to help,' said Rafael. 'There is a man, *el patrón,* not far from San José Patula where I live.'

'What does he do?' Lia asked.

'He's someone I work for. I could introduce you. He may want an English teacher for his children.'

Lia's hopes soared, and for a snapshot instant she saw some kind of future laid out before her, like the myriad of night stars she once saw over London during a major power outage. What could be better than the possibility of a real job after experiencing a stream of job rejections in London?

'That would be amazing.' She turned and kissed him on the cheek.

'My family also lives there and I'd like to bring you to visit. I've told them about you.'

Rafael glanced at Richard and grinned.

'How far away is San José Patula?' asked Lia.

'From the city, about three hours by bus.'

Rafael looked down at the floor near his feet and gestured towards the bar.

'I left my bag over there. I'll be right back.'

He stood and stretched. Macy returned at that same moment to the clinking of glasses and bottles, a token of appreciation by the same men who continued to drink nearby. She announced she was going to the ladies, grabbed her bag and wiped small beads of sweat from her forehead before following Rafael into the crowd.

Lia watched as they threaded their way past standing drinkers and waitresses who were carrying the last of the dinner dishes away.

'What was that nonsense you were saying about finding it hard to get a job?' she said, turning to Richard.

'Well, if that's the kind of work you're interested in.' Richard looked away.

She turned back to search for Rafael and squinted in confusion. The throng of human bodies around them began to move as if they had been zapped at high voltage. Fear crept through her body. The babble of people escalated into the disturbed feel of a simmering riot and men ran towards the stairs, shoving past each other in panic. She heard the repeated sound of glass breaking as people dropped their drinks and others crunched over them.

She caught sight of someone who looked very much like

Rafael, except that this person couldn't walk properly and had both hands pressed against his chest and stomach as he staggered towards them. He veered left then right, as if trying to balance a water jug on his head, before collapsing onto the floor. Lia shook her head, unable to process what she was seeing. Her view was obscured once again by people running past, and she told herself it couldn't possibly have been Rafael.

Richard murmured something she couldn't hear properly. In slow motion, it seemed, the man came into view again, still lying on the floor, and in her mind she willed him to get up. She searched the faces in the receding crowd, desperate to have identified the wrong person, and hugged her knees to her chest as she prepared to wait for Rafael to come forward and tell them he was fine.

Though Richard's facial expression was austere and his courage seemed limited, he still exuded sensible principles. He pushed his chair out and yelled at her, breaking into the wishful thinking she was busy weaving around herself.

'We have to get out of here.'

Lia sprang up, propelled towards the door by the surge of people. But then she stopped. Her legs defied her. If it actually was Rafael and he had been hurt, there was no way she would leave him there.

She stumbled, pushed by the last wave of people, and then turned, determined to go back to him. Whatever had happened, she had to make sure he was okay.

Richard called her back but his demand for her attention grew more distant with each step she took, until it was easy to ignore him.

A few feet away from the man lying on the floor, she slipped in a dark puddle, unaware that it was blood. She regained her balance and stared at him. Her heart started to race and she fought the sudden urge to throw up. There was no denying the familiar contours of his face. She let her breath out then, a loud sigh of relief, because Rafael was definitely alive in spite of all the blood. It probably wasn't as bad as it looked. He lay flat on his back and stared at her. He was calm, even as he panted in an effort to draw breath, and seemed not at all surprised to see her. She wondered if his whole history was chasing through his mind the way people claimed it did when they were brought to death's door.

She gently took his calloused hand and swallowed, her eyes widening as she surveyed the dark patches of blood that still trickled from his crimson-stained shirt, soaking through her jeans around the knees.

'What happened?' Her voice was barely a whisper and she wasn't sure that he could hear her or was even able to speak. In retrospect, it was a stupid thing to ask.

'*El patrón*. Take the address from my left pocket.'

She nodded but couldn't bring herself to move. How could he be thinking about her employment needs right now? She watched his once alert eyes become dull and his eyelids begin to droop.

She forced herself to look again at his front. It was as if all of it was bleeding, from his chest to his stomach, and yet how could that be possible? She tried to think of what to do. Her head spun at the thought of touching his wounds yet she knew she had to try and stop the bleeding.

'I'll be okay,' he whispered.

'I know you will,' she replied and tried to smile.

'It doesn't even hurt,' he wheezed.

Lia stared at him. 'Who did this?'

She tried to sound firm but her voice was alien – flat and high-pitched, as if her lungs were bursting with helium.

A frown sketched itself across his withering features and he didn't attempt a reply.

Lia trawled her brain to think of something more positive.

'Someone will have called an ambulance. You'll get fixed up in no time.' She didn't know how to save him herself and the knowledge of this made her want to scream in frustration.

'I wanted to show you my country,' he whispered. The sinewy lines of his jaw clenched.

'You will.' He was one of the strongest people she had ever met.

She leaned over him and thought about peeling his shirt upwards to look underneath. She could make out two gashes but she had no idea how to stem the blood and was scared to touch in case she made everything worse.

She couldn't keep looking at his face; even in the dim light it looked as if his lips were turning blue. Her gaze dropped to the tattoos on his right arm, spreading from the inside of his wrist up to his bicep and creeping under his shirt sleeve: Melpomene and Thalia, the iconic masks of comedy and tragedy, in faded green, red and black ink. They looked to be about as old as Rafael. Next to it was a more brightly coloured tattoo depicting a purple AK-47, the stock marked by a skull and crossbones. Burial crosses were carved in red, each bearing a single word: *Panzós. Ixcán. Rabinal.*

His eyes flickered open for pain-filled seconds and an agonising sadness drew Lia down till her head was mere inches from his. Her body trembled.

'Go to the *finca* … though we live in a time … where greed is honoured and suffering ignored. Go, for the sake of the children.'

As far as she knew, Rafael didn't have any children. Had she misheard him? Her hand was now stuck firmly to his with dried blood. The barman was the only other person in the room but he remained static, shielded behind the bar. Above him a wall-mounted electrocution chamber zapped as it claimed another winged victim amongst a massacre of assorted insects.

'Have you called for help?' Lia spoke in Spanish to the man but he just stared at her, pale as a ghost, his mouth forming a perfect O. She repeated the words, raising her voice until he lifted his mobile phone towards her and shouted back.

'*Si, lo haré ahora*.' I'll do it now.

Rafael's last words were punctuated with a savage effort and Lia bent close to hear them.

'I wish I could have achieved more for my family.'

His chest stopped heaving. She waited, desperate for another movement, but there was nothing – no eyelid tic, no intake of breath. The life and soul of Rafael vanished as if he had never really been inside the mess of skin and bones left lying on the floor beside her. It was as if they had both made each other up.

Lia gasped, a vain attempt to draw breath for Rafael as well as herself. Pulling her hand away from his was like pulling Velcro apart. She didn't ever cry in front of people, but the rapidly growing lump in her throat threatened to cut off her air supply if she held it in for much longer. She wanted to follow wherever he had gone, knowing it was impossible; and even if she could have done, her legs had turned to rubber. She glanced upwards with guilt at the barman, who watched as her hand made its serpentine way into Rafael's trouser pocket. Her fingers closed around a piece of paper and something else. She pulled it out and realized she was holding a small lock knife. She dropped it and bit back the sobs that were bubbling up in her throat.

Chapter 2

The sound of approaching sirens pierced the gloom. Richard turned back to the bar entrance, spitting uncharacteristic profanities, hating the fact that he had to go back inside. He took the stairs two at a time and could immediately see Lia huddled on the floor in the middle of the room. His face glistened with sweat and froze as he took in the state of the room. She was kneeling next to someone who was obviously badly hurt.

'Right, that's it.' He grabbed her by the elbows, grimaced at the blood-soaked floor and yanked her to her feet. He saw a knife lying near the man and grabbed Lia's hand. The sight of blood always made him queasy and the sheer quantity of it was like nothing he'd ever seen before. He was determined not to look at the inert form. Lia barely registered him except to pull herself away and collapse onto the floor again with a soft wail.

He looked down and recognized Rafael, a different version, a lifeless version, and swore again. He pulled Lia up by a limp hand that this time he refused to let go of. His only thought was to get them away from the madness and all the blood and the stench of sweat and smoke and fear. He felt as if he couldn't breathe and pulled her even harder in his haste to get back outside. They clumped up the hollow wooden staircase and he felt colour returning to his face as he took a deep breath.

Macy held the door of the Volkswagen taxi open. Glancing down at Lia, he saw her face crumple as she became aware of her blood-soaked clothes under the prying glare of the streetlights. A crowd of onlookers had gathered around the entrance and, conversing in fast-paced Spanish, began to gesticulate towards them.

Judging by the state of her, they probably thought it was Lia who had robbed Rafael of his life. He fought the impulse to push her along faster as she crawled into the back seat. He got in behind her and slammed the door as the first police car pulled to a stop.

'What the hell just happened?' Richard said, as Macy fired curt directions to the taxi driver. It was the first time he'd seen Lia cry, and she didn't reply. They moved away and he was relieved to find the roads quiet at this late hour.

From the front seat Macy sang softly along to the radio.

He turned to study Lia and the messy silence that rested between them; it was the kind that bonded them together with invisible glue. There was no point in him saying anything. Not yet. It was too fresh to talk about and yet impossible not to. Was Rafael dead? He'd looked dead. Richard shook his head. He hadn't exactly taken a liking to the guy but still, how could something that horrible happen to someone? Had he been right to grab Lia and drag her away? What if Rafael had still been alive, even slightly? Could things have turned out differently? What if he'd been wrong to listen to Macy, someone they'd just met and who they knew nothing about?

He hadn't acted heroically. Macy had physically barred his entry into the taxi every time he'd reached for the door. When begging him to return to the bar and find Lia hadn't worked, she'd ordered him to go back in a voice that promised far worse if he didn't. She'd shaken him by the shoulders with surprising strength and told him that the Guatemalan police murdered and locked up innocent people every day. Even then he had hesitated until she was about to brush scornfully past him and find Lia herself. Thank God his legs had finally moved.

If Rafael *was* dead then Lia had been the last person to speak to him, and he wondered what, if anything, they had said to each other. Personally, he believed Lia was too young and naïve to really be in love with Rafael, but then what did he know about love? Nothing.

'He was hurt and alone,' said Lia, her voice breaking. She wouldn't look at him.

'You could've stayed with him too, but you ran away.'

Her accusation carried the strength of a swinging sledgehammer. Glancing at her shivery, shocked-into-sober form, he realized she was taking her frustrations out on him, and shame mixed itself into the hotpot of shock and fear, even though the feeling of being threatened lessened with every mile they travelled away from the scene. He took care to sit as far away from her bloodstained clothes as he could, and he couldn't wait to take a shower.

'Look, hanging around is not the way things are done here,' Macy intervened, twisting around in the front of the car to face Lia. 'The police could've arrested you – us – jailed you just for a bribe. There's no such thing as justice out here.'

Lia leaned back till her head rested against the back seat. She took a deep breath and remained quiet, to Richard's relief. The events of the last hour began to recede from reality safely into memory as he considered the weight of Macy's words. Justice: that ancient concept of fairness that has taunted and haunted poets, philosophers, travellers and soldiers for as long as time itself. Still, something else nagged at the back of his mind, making him uneasy.

'Macy, where did you go after you came back to our table?'

The question hung in the air and a barely discernible shadow passed across Macy's eyes before she turned back to face the front of the car.

'The bathroom. Then I lost my bag in all the shoving,' said Macy. 'It didn't have much in it … I keep my money here.' She lifted her shirt and pointed to a money belt strapped to her waistline. Her hand shook and even in the poor light Richard could see flecks of dark splatter on the shirt.

'Is that blood?' he asked.

'It was all over the place.' He wondered why she sounded defensive. 'Lia, did Rafael give you that address he was talking about?'

'Yes,' said Lia, her voice soft in contrast to her previous outburst.

'Let me see it,' said Macy. She hung an arm past the driver with a shadowy palm outstretched.

Lia hesitated, prompting Macy to sigh in exasperation. The tiny slip of paper she clutched must have felt like her last link to Rafael, his words the only part of him left that sloped forward in positive determination.

'I put my hand into his pocket,' she said after a pause. Richard sighed, willing himself to relax. She leaned forward to hand the paper over to Macy. He hoped the taxi driver didn't understand any English.

He watched as Macy took the yellowed piece of paper and angled it towards her side window, using the streak of passing streetlights to read the text. He'd been in Guatemala long enough to know that no driver in their right mind would stop at a red traffic light after dark.

'Won't we be witnesses wanted for questioning?' asked Richard. 'Won't the police be looking for us to take statements?'

'We should leave the city as soon as possible,' said Macy. 'It's not safe now. The police are corrupt and could charge Lia, or all of us, with murder.'

'That's surely not possible,' said Lia.

'You have no experience of this country and therefore no idea as to what's possible,' he retorted, 'though I could pay for an excellent solicitor if we needed one.'

Lia shook her head and rolled her eyes.

The car slowed as they neared the first drop, a dark alley leading to the budget hotel she had picked earlier that day.

'Take my shirt and put it on over yours,' said Macy. 'There's less blood on it and it should stop the lobby guy from getting freaked out. Let's meet at noon tomorrow.'

She placed the scrap of paper onto the dashboard and slid both arms out of her shirt to reveal a tight-fitting vest. Lia grabbed the oversized shirt and slipped it on. Somewhere in the darkness of the alley Richard heard scuffling sounds and wondered if they were rats or homeless people. He tipped the driver and followed behind Lia as they entered their hotel.

Upstairs in their room Richard knelt beside his bed and clasped his hands in prayer, eager to feel the peace and contentment that always came to him once he prayed. It was a reminder to himself not to worry about things that he ultimately couldn't control. God always took care of everything. He breathed in as deeply and slowly as he could and began to recite in his mind: *Today I ask for your hand upon mine, Lord, as you lead me safely through. Guide my heart, my mind and body to navigate the way forward, and when I am weak, be my strength*. Connecting to God in this way, he soon felt his mind becoming clearer and his heartbeat slowing.

'Please, God, bless and protect us as we venture into new places that I never imagined I would get to see with my own eyes ...'

'Why don't you ask God why he didn't bless and protect Rafael?' said Lia.

Richard was unaware that he had spoken out loud, but his eyes remained squeezed shut and he didn't reply. He wasn't offended. He felt protective of Lia even though she'd been rude to him in the bar and kept demanding that he dress like a gypsy. They were obviously all in shock and he didn't want to antagonize her further. He had learned a long time ago that she didn't believe in God, and so he got to his feet and padded into the bathroom, closing the door behind him. She could shower after him.

He stared into the mirror hanging above the sink. Was it essential that they leave the city straight away? Wouldn't that be some inference of guilt? And where exactly did Macy think they should go?

After minutes of indecision, he climbed out of his trousers and removed and folded his shirt, inspecting the material for signs of blood. He had managed to remain remarkably clean in comparison to the girls. His shoes were another story but he found that the blood scrubbed off without too much difficulty. Blocking everything from his mind, he concentrated on removing all traces of the evening and stepped under the shower.

Minutes later, clad in a thin cotton towel that clung intimately to his body, he opened the bathroom door. Lia stalked straight past him, and as the bathroom door slammed, he turned away, rubbing his eyes.

'We need to talk.' She spoke from behind the door, her tone grave. Richard let his bulky frame fall onto the bed. He was tired, exhausted even, but he was determined to support her in whatever way he could.

'You can tell me anything,' he called back and hugged his knees to his chest in an attempt to release the stiffness in his lower back. He stayed like that, lying on his side until he heard the shower turn off and the bathroom door open.

'It's not that I don't appreciate your company,' she began, 'but I feel like I really need to be alone. I never planned to make this journey with anyone. I'm happy to spend a few more days together while you decide where you're going to go, but then we should go our separate ways.'

She might as well have just slapped him.

'Why would you want to travel by yourself in a country where you have just witnessed the murder of somebody you were obviously very fond of?'

She stopped where she was and stared at him as the word sank in. *Murder.*

'Don't be ridiculous. I'm sure he wasn't murdered.'

Richard shuffled around until he lay flat on his back, drew the paper-thin cotton bed sheet over the length of his body and plumped the pillow under his head. Like their bed sheets, the pillows smelled of moth-eaten cotton that had flapped outside in the rain, intertwined with nights of sweat and fabric detergent.

Lia walked over to the tiny table in the room and switched on the fan before she spoke again, with a voice like ice. 'I shouldn't have left him there alone. It might not even have been that bad.'

'It looked about as bad as it can get, Li,' said Richard. He recalled the open, staring eyes and the blood. So much blood.

'But you don't know that for sure because you aren't a doctor,' she snapped. 'You had no right to drag me out of there before I'd had time to think things through.'

He sat up. 'I'm sorry, Li.'

'I didn't even call the emergency services but instead relied on that stupid man behind the bar. I don't know how to call them here.' Her voice caught in her throat and he sat up, intent on getting up to comfort her, but she shook her head, a wave of anger forming a barricade between them.

'And why the hell would we get into a car and run away from the scene of a terrible crime?' she asked.

'You heard what Macy said.'

'But she sounded over the top. Maybe a bad experience has made her paranoid.'

He sighed. 'There was nothing else we could have done to help him.'

'So do you mind if we go our separate ways then?'

Richard switched off his bedside light and lay back down. He sensed Lia pulling on clothes before climbing into her bed, which was about three feet away on the other side of the wall.

'I'm not like you, Li.'

'That's an understatement,' he thought he heard her mutter. In a world where money provided security, he couldn't understand why him having it made her so uncomfortable. He sighed, letting the frustration wash over him. He never seemed able to do anything right. Except play chess. He was great at something which was utterly useless to the human race and which he couldn't even apply in real life. This was the first country he'd ever visited outside the UK, and so far it had been one long nightmare. He was constantly in fear of being ripped off or getting lost. On his own he would also struggle to communicate with taxi and bus drivers.

'Look. I know you've had to overcome some awful experiences at a young age and I can't imagine what any of that was like. I think it's amazing how you've adapted.'

Lia responded with a hollow laugh. 'What has any of that got to do with us parting company here?'

'You got to live in different countries. Maybe all of that helped prepare you to deal with something like this.'

'*Nothing* prepares you for death.'

Richard sat up, stung by the pain in her voice. 'I'm not going back to live with my dad, Li, and I don't want to be on my own here either. I've never been on my own in a foreign country before, let alone one renowned for being so dangerous.'

He knew how pathetic he sounded but surely he had a point. Every single person who was able to speak to them in English had warned them to be careful, while the English-speaking newspaper he'd bought had been filled with all manner of murder stories. She was silent, and for that he was grateful.

'I guess we don't have to talk about it right now,' said Lia, long after he thought she might have fallen asleep. They said goodnight to each other, but he doubted he would be able to sleep.

Chapter 3

A lorry came to a crashing stop outside the restaurant below, pulling Lia out of the dead of sleep. It was only five o'clock in the morning and her neck ached, conscious of the yielding material on which her head was pillowed.

She scrambled out of bed to the nearby window. It was broken and swung open with a gentle push. Below, three men unloaded masses of Coca-Cola crates. The bottles swayed like drunken dancers, clanging together as the boxes were stacked inside the restaurant.

The early morning air was humid, dense with unfamiliarity, and she sighed. Unfamiliarity was reassuringly familiar. Vendors stood by steaming street stalls, packing away or setting up; she wasn't sure.

Lia scanned the street for signs of police and wiped sweaty palms over her T-shirt. Prostitutes beckoned from sidewalks, grouped together under street lamps. The youngest, who must have been about twelve years old, looked up as if sensing Lia's gaze upon her. She lifted a hand to point up towards the window and shouted something in shrill Spanish.

Banging the window shut, Lia swatted a mosquito from her face and fell back into bed, throwing her hair over the pillow to cool the back of her neck. Her eyes were closed but thoughts were taking over, criss-crossing themselves through her brain.

She'd watched Rafael collapse onto the floor, so obviously she wasn't crazy, because she knew it had happened; and yet today, just a few hours later, the fact that he might be dead was simply inconceivable.

Her whole life was a series of bad endings: rapid, all-consuming changes almost too fast to keep up with. Give it long enough and it became dangerously tricky to stop, to slam the brakes on, come crashing to a sudden halt and expect the dust to settle in sympathy, just because it happened that way for others.

By far the best thing that had happened to her had been meeting Rafael in her last year of university. He had taught a brilliant Spanish class and then asked her where he could go for something to eat. It had been his first evening in London. They had walked to the nearest pub where Lia treated them both to a roast chicken dinner.

Rafael enraptured her with stories of his homeland right from the start: of hunting in jungles and forested highlands, running from the acrid smoke of erupting volcanoes and fishing off the coastal lowlands.

They had discussed politics and racism in London and Guatemala; how much of it was explicit in Guatemala while often subtle in London. They also talked about land.

'In the eyes of the ruling authorities, the indigenous Maya don't own land even if we've lived on it for countless generations,' said Rafael, his voice still as clear as if he was sitting right beside her at that moment. 'Land can be sold from under our feet to anyone with money. It's happened within my own family.'

Lia couldn't imagine ever having enough money to buy land anywhere. She enjoyed talking to him though, and they had both become engrossed in each other's company. The following evening, when Rafael placed a hand over his heart and confessed that he was too poor to eat out again yet wanted to spend more time with her, Lia invited him to her flat.

The next day, at the end of class, they added together the little money that they had left between them and walked to the nearest supermarket. She laughed as she watched Rafael stroll around the aisles, marvelling at the diverse array of goods on display. He had pointed with raised eyebrows when he saw how much a pineapple – his favourite fruit – cost. They bought two plantains and a can of black beans.

'There are supermarkets in Guatemala,' he explained, 'but most of us shop at the outdoor markets because they're much cheaper.'

That evening Rafael boiled the plantains in their skins and mashed them in a bowl. He mixed a little sugar and salt into the black beans and mashed those too. Then he scooped up patties of the plantain, put a dollop of beans in the middle, closed them up and pan-fried them; and as Lia watched, she felt as if it were parts of her brain that were being mashed and fried as Rafael told her about the genocide trial of the former Guatemalan president Efraín Ríos Montt.

'This man, an army general at the time, imprinted pure terror into the hearts of every indigenous person.'

His hands shook as he rubbed the back of his neck and cleared his throat.

'When the army came, I was four years old. They tortured and killed everyone there, except my sister and me. My father told her to run and never stop and never look back. We never saw him or my mother again. My sister picked me up and ran like a jaguar.'

Lia shuddered. Outside, the wind had picked up and shaken the windows of her kitchen like lost spirits desperate to be let in. She got up and edged her way around the table until they were face-to-face and she could simply squeeze his hands. He flinched and she backed away, surprised by the tingling in her fingers and the sudden pounding in her chest. It was the cold, hard look in his eyes and the way his mouth had shaped into a snarl. He seemed so far away that she may as well have been invisible. She'd seen it before. Something had shaken him to his very core and left unhealed lacerations upon his soul.

'Do you think this Montt person will be found guilty?' she asked, once their bellies were full.

'He was convicted of genocide and crimes against humanity two years ago. Too many witnesses would not be silenced, both alive and dead. After the ruling, the Constitutional Court tried to erase the verdict but it was too late. The truth was out.'

'Why don't you move to England?' she said, surprised by the hope laced in her tone.

Rafael hadn't hesitated in his regretful response. 'My home is my land in Guatemala. I couldn't ever be anywhere else. It's the only place I belong, with my family, Lola, Marco, Favia and the rest. You should come and visit.'

Neither of them seemed willing to look away from the other after he said that. They kissed, with a powerful attraction that she hadn't known was possible. He had the softest lips that made her body melt in a way that would stay with her until she saw him again.

After Rafael returned to Guatemala, Lia threw herself into applying for jobs following her graduation but found no one willing to employ her. Throwing away utility bills, unpaid and unopened, along with heart-stopping overdraft statements right up until the bailiff came knocking wasn't a recommended lifestyle. There were a finite number of times that she could run from debt and threats, and her instincts had screamed at her to escape before London messed her up for good. If London didn't want her, then she didn't want London. Belonging, like trust, was sacred.

Three hundred university students tripping their heads off on LSD in the high-rise halls of residence bought her airfare to Guatemala with cash to spare. Lia needed a place to start again, somewhere with no unrealistic expectations of her. She'd decided this the day after she had walked around watching students merrily put their lives at risk. Some hung off balconies twenty floors up, flaunting their naked bodies while singing to their shadows; others followed detective trails of unwrapped toilet tissue around the campus and onto the road. That nobody had died that night signalled to Lia that she was being given some kind of radical choice to change her life for the better. Her main responsibility from now on would be looking after her rucksack. It was going to be her base. From it, she was sure she would grow some healthy roots somewhere, with a legitimate job and debts that she could pay.

'It's too dangerous in Guatemala,' her adoptive mother appealed down the phone in the weeks leading up to her departure. 'Why not keep trying for jobs in London or Spain? Or come back to Egypt and stay with me.'

As much as she loved her, there was no way she was going back to live with her mum, who was teaching at a school in Cairo. For too long she'd bombarded Lia with Chinese proverbs like 'To forget one's ancestors is to be a brook without a source, a tree without a root.' She was forever telling Lia to look back at her roots and the debt of gratitude she owed to those who had contributed to her success. Lately, she had tried her hardest to conjure up her parents in her mind and failed. Well, she could see them in an outline kind of way, but she couldn't feel them. Did this mean she was doomed? She was tired of trying to feel gratitude to the persons who had left her behind forever when she was just four years old.

'I have just as much chance of finding work in Guatemala,' said Lia. 'Plus I'll be safe because I'll be with Rafael.'

It was the last thing she had said to her mother. What a cruel joke.

Lia woke with a start in the humid and airless hotel room, suddenly aware of clockwork breathing that was not her own, and sat up to look at the humped figure sighing from the bed next to hers. Richard Chadwick-Hollamby, white, blue-eyed and the first born-and-bred Londoner she had met. He was twenty-four years old – two years older than her – six feet four and built like a rugby player who'd eaten one too many burgers. The light colour of his skin was a near match to the bed sheet which had slipped down to his hips.

She stared at the contours of his upper body. He wasn't fat but lacked muscle definition, and in his sleep, exposed and unguarded, he looked more like a vulnerable boy than a grown man. She had never met any girl he had dated and she almost couldn't imagine him having a girlfriend.

Richard's family lived next door to the matchbox she had rented in her last year of university. For a whole year Lia overheard the screams of Richard's alcoholic father as he flung insults at him. *You stupid, lazy, brain-dead waste of space … worthless piece of ugly shit.* His stepmother also lived in the luxury-laden house, with influential aunts and uncles scattered nearby. Lia didn't believe it, but Richard always insisted his father would be proud of him one day and magically transform into a vision of kindness.

Lia's belly gurgled, a reminder of how long it had been since she had last eaten. She felt a stab of nostalgia for the tiny kitchen she'd left behind. It had been Richard's sanctuary as well as hers. He would tap on the oval-shaped kitchen window after a beating and sit mute and dishevelled. She always sat opposite, fiddling with the tablecloth and counting the chilli oil stains while the sputtering of the kettle gathered momentum.

Before meeting Richard she had amused herself with romantic delusions, like how splendid it would have been to grow up in England with all her friends and a large family close by, and her school and favourite hangouts around the corner. Richard had blown her fairytale fantasies to pieces. The first time she entered his house, its perfectly placed antiques and period-piece furnishings had been unmarked by any signs of human contact but instead seemed to be adorned with an unhappy tension which had spread over the family.

When she'd cleared out the last of her belongings, said

goodbye to Richard and prepared to shut the door of the flat behind her for the last time, he had galloped out of his own house with the edgy energy of an escaped zoo animal, slamming the neo-classic mahogany front door behind him. He wore designer everything, from his watch to his Kurt Geiger shoes, and stopped her in her tracks. It replayed in her mind like a moment on a loop, an unseasonable August wind sweeping rubbish across the street and Lia trying her best to rush to the nearest tube station without delay.

'Let me come with you.'

'No.' Lia raised her eyebrows and couldn't believe he was serious, even as she noted the whites of his knuckles around the holdall and the steely determination in his eyes.

'You've never roughed it in your life. And how are you going to explain it to your father? He's expecting you to take over the family business.'

Above all, she couldn't imagine spending so much time with a practising Christian who had no sense of independence.

'I'm giving it up. Today. Right now.'

When she asked why on earth he wanted to come out to Guatemala and just *drift*, like a lost raft at sea, it was as if he'd rehearsed his reply.

'I need to take a risk for once in my life.' He wept tears that edged sideways across his face, pushed by a determined northern wind, and she had figured, *whatever*.

Now that they were actually here, though, it was apparent she was better off going it alone. At least she knew where she was then, and she could encourage Richard to return to London where he belonged. He had a whole city to go back to.

For a time she had mistakenly thought she might gain a lifelong membership into the world of academia, an enormous, extended family from which she could carve herself a bright future by accepting a place at the University of East London. She had kept to herself, reading all the books she could get her hands on, whether or not they were relevant to her degree in

Ecology and Spanish. Then her experiment with illicit drugs began: weed, speed and ecstasy.

Unlike most of her drug-taking student friends, she hadn't been comfortable asking her adoptive mother for money. She already owed her in so many ways. It was her mother's beliefs that had guided her towards the study of ecology in the first place. Her mother believed that upon death everyone and everything went back to the earth. She meant it not in a biblical way, but in an energetic kind of way. She believed that all souls, spirits and their physical matter simply changed form to rejoin the natural earth, a precious living life in itself. Her beliefs had sparked in Lia a passion for studying nature and the environment, and ways to protect and look after it. A degree in ecology would help her get a job in nature conservation or provide a path to a PhD, and prompted her to get her first ever job as a waitress. She'd meant to do it as a means of getting away from the drugs scene, but in reality all it did was give her a means of paying for the drugs she continued to experiment with. It was a pretty good escape from the real world.

Lia rolled onto her side. Life was all about survival. She'd survived three weeks of waitressing before throwing soup over the chef's head to stop his attempts to touch her. She'd immediately been fired, and after fifteen unsuccessful job interviews, drug dealing took over where waitressing left off.

She thought back to the last day of university and the first-class honours award for the thesis that she'd fabricated. She cringed, reliving the disappointment; how she'd started with a conclusion, a week before the hand-in deadline, and worked backwards, deciding on an imaginative set of results, a useful method and arriving at an interesting hypothesis. That's when the world of academia had been blown apart forever. She was sure she would be caught out, that her paper would have been pulled from the pile, crossed out in red and dealt with appropriately. Maybe she would have gone back and taken the whole thing more seriously. Instead, she had been rewarded with the highest possible class of degree, and with it, she'd realized that any sense of belonging there was meaningless.

Rafael – sweet, kind Rafael – had been the one person who had given her university life any kind of meaning. She swung her legs out of bed and shook her head. Now everything had changed again. They had to get out of Guatemala City.

Chapter 4

Macy squashed the last of her belongings back into her rucksack and cast her eye over the room. She would miss it, even the lopsided Jesus, faded and forlorn, nailed onto the wall in a cheap plastic frame.

She swung her rucksack over her shoulder and almost skipped out into the street past the Carmen El Bajo church. She relished the dry heat on her skin and paid no attention to the homeless waifs begging for spare change.

Propped up on the pavement, a drunk waved a bottle at her. Macy paused mid-step. The bottle was dark green and long empty, yet he seemed able to trap rays of sunshine within it and direct them at her. It was like he was trying his damnedest to shoot her down with each blinding flash of light.

Forced to blink rapidly, she studied the man, suspicion rushing through her mind like a red alert. Was that the killer? Or perhaps he had been employed to follow and record her every movement with each flash of the bottle that was really a camera. She couldn't help herself. She kicked the bottle out of his hand and watched it smash against the pavement. If she hadn't – and if it really *was* just a bottle, which now seemed likely – she was sure he would have thrown it at her once her back was turned. He swore a tirade of grumbled, bleary anger that quickly faded.

Macy shivered in spite of the heat. It was the thought of being sectioned for psychiatric care in Guatemala. She had heard horror stories about the reeking, dilapidated city building where people like her were incarcerated and medicated against their will. There was no way in hell she could go through that. It was bad enough in England. She recalled Doctor Medino's disapproving yet kindly frown when she told him she was leaving the country.

'The things that cause people to relapse into episodic behaviour are sleep problems, stress, changes in time zones, basically anything that causes major changes to your routine – like travelling abroad.'

That had been a year ago. She'd been off meds for five months, and all had been fine until yesterday. She'd let her guard down just once because she'd figured she was doing so well. She swore under her breath. At least she knew where to get more pills fast. Those were two good reasons for leaving the city.

She had managed to snatch just two hours of sleep, if that, but she was fizzing with energy in contrast to the shadows growing ever larger under her eyes. A switch had been flipped and she had every right to be furious. It was because she cared and because someone had the audacity to violently take a man's life, right next to her, as if she was invisible. But she knew she wasn't. He'd seen her and she'd seen him. Hadn't she? She'd looked into his cruel eyes and seen the same desperate look she'd seen in herself. Except she had only ever tried to kill herself, never anyone else.

Macy took a deep, calming breath and hummed as she turned over in her mind how the evening had played out.

She liked Richard and Lia. They were so radically different to each other. She felt a thrill of excitement, the dead weight of unwanted solitude lifting. She would do everything in her power to spend more time with them. It wasn't like she had that much choice anyway. They couldn't possibly know how much she needed them, to anchor herself to their reality in case her own fell down in a pathetic heap around her.

She should have known better, considering everything she'd already been through. Drinking, of all things; when had it not sent her spiralling down into hell? The more she drank, the worse it got. She knew this, but it was the first time her drinking had led to something so dreadful.

She was becoming manic. No. She was hypomanic, in the way that she could feel moments of jubilation for no good reason. No balanced person would feel joy following the night they'd just had. The sunlight made it worse, feeding the already fiery look in her eyes. She clenched her fists as hard as she could, pressing her nails into her palms until she knew she had drawn blood.

On a brisk stroll around the grid-like streets, Macy passed the central market in the Plaza del Sagrario. Stalls packed into every inch of the area were selling fruit, vegetables, flowers, weavings and ready-made street food: bags of freshly made pork crackling, cheeses, tacos, chilli tortillas and corn. She bought far more food than she needed and stuffed the excess into the top of her rucksack.

She cursed as she dropped a few coins and they all rolled out of reach, falling one by one into the gutter. At least she had managed to stick to her budget over the past few months. It was one of the ways she could tell she wasn't sick.

Macy loved Guatemala because here she was just a blank page ready to be fitted neatly over the story that was life before. The fact that she was a walking contradiction stigmatized by mental health problems no longer mattered. That she had become too ill to run the business that had made her a six-figure income in England was to no avail here. She was sailing through the market now and had to keep reminding herself not to dance to the music that played in her head. *Boom ba ba boom ba ba booom!* Instead she greeted locals in calm reply as they called out, '*Buenos días, señorita.*'

It felt like five minutes but she had walked for over an hour before she rechecked her watch. The sharp fusion of colours and smells danced around her and she couldn't wait to record all of it in her journal.

She stopped at an internet shop and stepped inside. Fifteen minutes later she was back outside with the pharmacist she had called, a tall, gangly man in his late twenties with numerous silver chains wrapped around his neck. She'd met him in a bar six months ago and they'd swapped numbers after he'd bragged that he could get hold of any pharmaceuticals under the sun.

'Pablo, I need some pills,' said Macy after they'd greeted each other. 'You said you could get me anything I needed.'

The young man looked around and then stared at her as if unsure that he could trust her.

'For you?'

She nodded.

'There was a robbery recently. I don't know ...'

'Jesus, Pablo. I have bipolar II. Do you know what that is?'

'Yes.'

She wasn't convinced.

'I was diagnosed after I tried to jump off a bridge in London. But it was way too busy with people. A group of Christmas shoppers saw me perched precariously on the barrier, crying my eyes out. They made it impossible for me to jump and held my arms until an ambulance arrived to take me away.'

He continued to stare impassively at her, making her uncomfortable. She didn't know how else to explain it to him. She hadn't wanted to kill herself really; she led a blessed, interesting life, but she'd wanted – no, needed – to make the rushing chaos stop and to still the raging thoughts that had driven her to commit all kinds of strange acts.

'Are you suicidal now?' asked Pablo.

'No,' said Macy, 'but I might be if you don't help me.'

'What do you need?'

'Carbamazepine and Lorazepam. A year's worth of five- and ten-milligram tablets, please.'

He nodded. 'Wait here while I make a phone call.'

Macy let out a deep breath and sat on the kerb, allowing herself a moment to marvel at how responsible she was being. It was all about taking precautions. It was hard to believe she was the same person, the one who had founded and been the CEO of Chatlove.com. It had started off as a blog, a place to offload the tide of words that would fill her mind and her mouth on the path to oblivion, before she'd received the diagnosis that had turned her life upside down. It was somewhere to record her feelings and let go of her failures in the romance department. The growing number of supportive responses she'd received in the comments section had spurred her to redevelop the site into a fully fledged dating website. In two years she'd grown the business to 250,000 regular users and embarked on a journey of unparalleled excess, making a substantial amount of money along the way.

Naturally, she hadn't understood the diagnosis or the seriousness of it at that point. No one did. All she knew was that she was riding at the centre of her very own tech boom, and she carried on right where she'd left off before she was sectioned the first time. There were the parties, so many parties: parties to drop in on, parties to organize, dinner parties, aftershow parties and launch parties. There was so much alcohol all the time; she stayed in fancy hotels, ate five-star cuisine, shopped like the world was ending and had lots of casual sex. Because she could.

She looked inside to check Pablo was still there. Was she trying to get her hands on too much medication? It seemed she never knew how much was too much. She'd had the best of everything just a few years ago, but had that success been enough? No. She'd decided to take it to the next level by floating her company on the stock market. It gave her a net worth of £15 million, and then she went all out on marketing, hiring staff and partying even harder. She'd had no idea that the website was loss-making. Within two months of listing, the share price plummeted and continued to head downwards at a pace that weirdly matched the energy she was still putting into the company. It was torture but she couldn't stop, not even to sleep. She didn't even remember being taken to hospital the last time. Chatlove.com posted a massive loss and was unable to raise the funds needed to keep operating. The rest was history, and that was when she had finally worked out that she had to get sober.

She shook her head, not wanting to think any more about it, or the weird buzzing that she was feeling all over her body.

Pablo appeared at the entrance. 'I'm arranging the delivery now.'

She let her breath out in a low hiss, relieved at how easy it was turning out to be to buy drugs of any kind in Guatemala. The angels were definitely watching over her. She was one of the lucky ones. After the third hospitalisation, the doctors had come up with a couple of mood stabilizers that actually worked for her. She had managed to start from scratch again, simply by surviving the long flight from the UK to Guatemala without descending into madness.

'Did anything happen to make you feel unwell?'

Macy stood up and pulled a faded, yellowish slip of paper from her front pocket. 'Do I look unwell?'

'You look tired,' he said. She loved the way he spoke, the way it was slow and deliberate and ordered.

'Well, you could say that death visited last night while I was out with friends. I can't talk about it. I don't want to talk about it. It's important that I don't talk about it. I want to forget, but I doubt that's going to be possible.'

She'd lost him, she knew. She looked across the road and took a deep breath to steady herself. Faces stared at her. They all looked like the man from last night, and then the faces blurred and she felt dizzy, as if on a sped-up merry-go-round.

She changed tack. 'Do you know this address?'

He took the piece of paper and scanned it. 'I just know that it's in a farming area in the hills north of here. It should be easy to find.'

Macy stared at him for a moment. 'Oh, I don't plan to go there.'

'Okay ...' Pablo raised a quizzical eyebrow. 'That's good, because my contact is in Cobán. You have to go there to pick up the pills. Give me one thousand quetzals now and the same again on the pickup.'

He handed her a piece of paper with a name, address and phone number on it.

Macy reached into her pocket and began counting out the notes.

The young man thanked her once she'd passed the wad of money to him and, in spite of the bright sun, opened his eyes wide as Macy brought her face up to plant a kiss firmly on his lips. He lifted his hands to her shoulders and gently yet firmly pushed her away, to her acute embarrassment.

Chapter 5

They were having breakfast not far from the Carmen El Bajo church, a safe distance from the brimming, wildly painted chicken buses that belched clouds of dark fumes as they lurched past.

Richard waved Lia off to a table and walked to the counter to order. She watched as he shifted from one foot to the other, trying to count out the correct change. The currency might have changed but he still had the annoying habit of arranging the coins in order of size with the smallest coins on top, all facing the same way.

Both sides of the street were lined with faded pink, blue and green buildings, shuttered and barred shopfronts flanked by vendors selling everything from street food, shoelaces, fabrics and newspapers to antibiotic tablets. Disheartened, once-neon signs jutted out into the road, advertising an abandoned time from long ago.

Richard walked over, laden with two cups of black coffee and a basket of assorted bread. All morning Lia had analysed every last drop of conversation with Rafael. She'd replayed his emotional state, his body language and the way he'd been with the people she saw him with. Nothing had seemed out of the ordinary. He'd seemed fine, right up until he'd left them to get his bag. Her mind refused to remember anything beyond that point except his tattoos. Did Rafael have an association with the theatre? And why would he have a tattoo of an assault rifle? It made no sense.

'I'm going to the address he gave me,' she said through a mouthful of dry toast.

'Every hour that we're here I think that's more of a crazy idea,' said Richard.

'Rafael's family live around there and I need to find out what's happened to him.' Mentally she detached from the ache that saying his name caused. 'And I came here to find work, too.'

'Then let's all go together,' said Richard, his expression hopeful.

She turned away to study the street, giving him no sign that she was considering his suggestion. She watched an old man polish the shoes of a suited businessman who was reading a newspaper by a dry fountain; a barefoot child wandered alone, selling tortillas from a colourfully woven basket.

'Rafael wasn't what I was expecting.' Richard's tone dropped an octave. 'He was rather … scruffy.'

Lia glared at him. 'He's been doing manual labour. His teaching is seasonal. He does other jobs to supplement his income. You've never needed to take multiple jobs in your life before. Money has always just been there. You've never had to make choices between the likes of food or electricity, knowing that you can't pay for both.'

'He had the money to visit London,' said Richard.

'It was part of a once in a lifetime exchange trip funded by a university,' she retorted. 'He worked very hard and was paid very little.'

'Maybe he was mixed up in something else.'

'Like what?'

'Something he shouldn't have been. Something that got him killed.'

Lia sat up straight. What did he mean?

'You're actually suggesting that if he's dead, it might be his own fault?'

'I saw him have a pretty heated conversation with the barman before he came over to us.'

'What conversation?'

'I couldn't hear. But I did see him pointing his finger like he might have been warning him, before he handed his briefcase over.'

'Really?' she stared at him. 'Are you sure?'

'Yes, and I keep hearing how drugs are big business here. Could he have been involved with drugs?' Richard shrugged. 'I'm just saying that it's a possibility.'

As far as she knew, Richard had no knowledge of her own foray into the world of Class As. Luckily. She had no intention of him ever finding out and no intention of dealing ever again.

'One thing I do know, Richard. Look around. The darker your skin, the more basic your job and living standards. The outdoor vendors and street cleaners are brown. The bankers are white. What does that tell you?'

'You're alluding to colonialism? A natural process from long ago which has no bearing on what happened last night.'

Lia spat a mouthful of coffee over the remainder of the bread. 'What is natural about robbing, raping, enslaving and murdering indigenous people on the basis that they all happen to have darker skin?'

'Then why have so many nations partaken in it?' asked Richard.

'Greed, and an evil superiority complex.'

She visualized waving goodbye to Richard as soon as she got the address back from Macy. A waitress stopped by the table with a fixed smile and offered them a free coffee refill. They both accepted.

'I do understand that centuries of exploitation aren't magically reversed overnight. I just don't understand what that has to do with Rafael,' said Richard.

'And I don't understand why you think he might be involved with drugs,' hissed Lia.

Richard sighed. 'I'm sorry. That was a callous suggestion to make.'

The will to fight left her body as quickly as it had come. 'He is ... was ... is a really wonderful person and I am having real difficulty accepting that something terrible has happened to him.'

'It could be dangerous to go to that address. Why don't you think on it some more? We could visit a museum first.'

Lia looked up from the depths of her coffee cup. She broke off a piece of sweet bread, dipped it into her coffee and nodded. They both needed a fresh perspective.

Richard relaxed the corners of his mouth and sat forward, shading the nape of his neck which the sun had already burned. He downed the last of his coffee and gave her a puppy grin of exuberance.

They made the half-hour walk towards the National Palace along sidewalks seething with people. Traffic was congested and horns blared as if the aim was simply to outdo each other in volume. A warm breeze threw dust from the road into their eyes, wrapped in the smell of hot vehicle exhausts.

At one point Lia stumbled into the road, unaware of how close she was to being clipped and dragged under an old lorry until it roared past, inches from her ear. A man on a bicycle had turned onto the road in front of them, and from behind he looked exactly like Rafael. His hair was the same and he was dressed in the same clothes. It had to be him. She broke into a jog behind and shouted out.

'Rafael!'

As soon as the man's head turned, she knew it wasn't him. She took a shaky breath, stopped running and felt a hand on her arm. Richard pulled her back up onto the pavement.

'You're going to get run over,' he said, his cheeks red from chasing after her.

'I must be losing my mind,' she said, tears pricking her eyes.

'You're not,' said Richard.

Tatty restaurants and shops lined the street and still she couldn't stop herself from scanning the crowds in search of Rafael. They passed an empty McDonalds. The shiny red and yellow canteen stood in stark contrast to the surrounding buildings that were dirty, with cracked, dusty windows and broken doorways. A morose, sleepy-eyed boy stood outside wearing a dark brown uniform with the now familiar AK-47 propped on his shoulder.

Every few minutes someone on the street held out an open palm as they walked by. Most often it would be a woman clutching a baby, wearing indigenous clothes: multicoloured *huipiles* with neon-bright embroidery and hand-woven ankle-length skirts. The further they walked towards the regiment of imposing buildings that included the National Palace, the more claustrophobic and hot the crowds grew, rushing past one way and then the other. Police stalked the streets, protected by black bulletproof vests, in close vicinity to army patrol units where soldiers with red berets lined up under a massive flag. Lia tensed as the crowds hemmed them in. Like yesterday night in the bar, she smelled the swell of humanity, a cluster of body odour and cheap cologne. Panic started to rise in her chest. She looked up at the wide, open sky and forced it down, willing herself to get a grip.

They entered the plaza square and pushed their way through the crowd. Some people waved placards that attacked government corruption: *¡No más corrupción! ¡Gobierno mafioso! ¡Fuera ladrones!* Some of the signs were in English: Out with the robbers! Enough is Enough!

'No wonder so many shops and businesses were closed,' yelled Lia. 'They've all come out here to protest.'

They became surrounded by people playing drums and dancing whilst others waved flags. There were uniformed health workers, students and office workers on the square, with more people joining in all the time.

'Why are they protesting?' shouted Richard.

A man turned to them with three young girls who must have been his daughters.

They had painted the blue and white colours of the Guatemalan flag on their cheeks and the youngest was blowing a whistle.

'We are demanding that the president steps down because he has stolen a lot of money. We have been here for the last few months and we will stay until he goes.'

Lia nodded, wishing that Rafael was with her. She imagined him smiling reassuringly as he talked history and politics to her, watching while the police fingered their guns.

She pointed to the National History Museum, not far from the National Palace where a throng of tourists waited patiently to be allowed inside, and led the way to the entrance.

'Charming structure,' Richard said, looking up in awe. 'So eclectic, combining colonial architecture with French and neo-classic influence like this.'

Lia tuned out his words. She took a few steps inside and stopped, drawn to an exhibit about the K'iche' Maya people of ancient history.

Artefacts sat on incandescent display: pottery in the shape of bowls, cups, plates and small clay whistles called *ocarinas*. Leaning closer, she saw they were carved or painted with symbols full of animal imagery.

Ahead, a doorway invited entry into another exhibit, the Maya World Tree. Like Rafael, his ancestors had weaved their lives around and worshipped the natural world. She stifled a sneeze in the dusty air.

An old voice whispered behind her, startlingly close.

Crouching under the shadows of a narrow table he looked like a ghost, with ringed eyes and thinning white hair, albeit dark in complexion.

'You,' he called again, standing and pointing a spindly finger at her. 'You have it, that look. I know that look.'

'What?' She stared at him, wondering if he was a tour guide. He was too shabbily dressed to look the part. More likely an apparition brought on by too little sleep, she thought.

'*Desanimado* – dispirited – by the violent loss of a loved one.'

How could he possibly know that?

'Christmas, 1981, midday. A group of men, *chafas* armed with Israeli Galil rifles, unleashed their anger. Shackled our hands and made us walk. They tried to kill me.' She allowed him to pull her closer.

'Look where they sliced me.' He drew two fingers from his left ear, under his throat and over to the right ear so she couldn't help but look at the scar.

'My blood flowed. Somehow I escaped to Mexico and I stayed there a long time, but we K'iche' people, we so love the land that we come from. I had to come back.'

'Who did that to you?' she asked.

'They are the same today as they have always been,' he whispered, looking past her and pressing up against the wall. His words became more urgent.

'Violence killed my spirit and now I live just to pass the time, day to day. It might be too dangerous to do anything more because in the end, nothing is achieved.'

'Why are you telling me this?' she implored him.

'Whatever you start you must finish,' the old man said, pointing a finger close to her face. 'You can do this. What they want to forget, they destroy.' He pointed over to the World Tree exhibit. 'Even there.'

He stopped and shrank back from her like a wounded animal as two uniformed men pushed Lia aside and grabbed his arms.

'Stop right there,' she demanded. 'This man is talking to me.'

She may have been young but with her head held high and an acid tongue, she was used to fooling people. Not so with these men. They ignored her and proceeded to drag the scarred man away, not towards the exit as she'd hoped but towards an elevator held open by another uniformed man.

'Stop!' she yelled again but she was merely shoved back against the wall. Tourists stopped to stare but no one did anything to help, and Richard was nowhere to be seen.

The old man twisted around towards her as the elevator doors began to close.

'This soul you lost. He's in the underworld but it is not a bad place. He's just waiting for the darkness to change to light.'

The doors sealed together and she found herself alone again.

A soft tap on the shoulder made her jump. She turned to find Richard beside her.

'We have to leave if we're going to meet Macy on time.'

Lia shook her head. 'This poor man has just been strong-armed into that lift by two brutes.'

'What man?'

'In here.' Lia repeatedly pressed the call button of the elevator.

Richard's expression changed to bewilderment as he waited. Five minutes passed and the elevator didn't show any sign of returning. Finally, he pulled a crisp new ten quetzal note from his wallet and gestured to her to follow him as he dropped it into the donation box on his way out.

Chapter 6

Richard sat on a cracked step outside the hotel, his forehead and cheeks glowing pomegranate red in the late morning sun. Lia had walked to a shop to buy drinking water. In the museum, she had continued to press the elevator button, ignoring him as usual, even though it was obvious the lift was broken. He assumed Lia thought she had seen Rafael again, her brain once more trying to deny what her eyes had witnessed. At least she had followed him outside a few minutes later. As soon as they reached the hotel, she asked him to watch their rucksacks; not to spare them from unnecessary carrying, he was sure, but to get away from him. They had walked past a small church on the way back from the museum and he'd made the sign of the cross. Lia had snapped like a crocodile trying to take his head off and her words still rang in his ears, but it had been the look in her eyes, the mockery, that he couldn't stand.

'Five hundred years ago Pope Alexander VI instructed Christian European leaders to capture and kill Maya people unless they agreed to convert to Christianity,' she sneered. 'They were told they had to work for free and give away their land. Put *that* in your religious pipe and smoke it.'

The force of her words shook him. He started to reply but she had rudely cut him off and told him to google something called the Inter Caetera Papal Bull, whatever that was. So he'd remained silent, determined not to inflame the situation further.

He couldn't relax, and he felt worse when he saw the three men, boys really, across the road. They made him even more worried about their predicament. They were doing nothing, but it was a nervous kind of nothing, a nothing filled with something. They leaned against the front of a black Nissan truck parked opposite the hotel, in silence, their eyes shifting left and right. They were tattoo-stamped and black-vested with muscular arms, looking as if they were pretending not to watch him but really were.

He sighed. He was worried about his father, about Lia and about the possibility that they were headed down some kind of snake trail of atrocity and disaster. In the two weeks they'd been here, all he'd learned about Guatemala was that it was a country that specialized in death, either by war, malnutrition, murder, mudslides or earthquakes. His own short experience of the country proved it.

Whilst waiting in the hotel reception he'd watched a CNN crime report about members of the Mara Salvatrucha 13, one of the most renowned gangs that had originated in El Salvador and now operated across North and Central America, with a prominence in Guatemala. It claimed gang members were being trained to become teachers and businessmen, investing money made from drugs and extortion rackets into legitimate businesses. Tattoos used to be compulsory, but the reporter had interviewed a former gang member who had been told not to get tattoos on visible parts of his body, to more easily avoid identification. As a result of the gang's growing sophistication, gang leaders were even able to access and recruit members from student populations.

He couldn't understand why Lia didn't see it: the tattoos, the briefcase, the knife, and even the fact that he was a teacher. Rafael was obviously some kind of knife-wielding, drug-toting recruitment gangster who had likely brought about his own demise due to incredibly bad decision-making skills. As he went through these possibilities in his mind, he liked Rafael even less.

He watched Macy walking up the street towards him and screwed up his eyes against the sun to study her. He appreciated the fact that she was on time and waved in welcome, but when she saw him she stopped and stared back with such a rigid, unsmiling intensity that it made him look away. What was the matter with her? He didn't get up off the dusty step to greet her, worried that if he did, he would find himself lurching off balance under her gaze.

Macy set down her rucksack, took a pack of cigarettes and a lighter from her back pocket and sat inches from him.

'How's Lia?'

'Upset, but that's to be expected, isn't it?'

Macy nodded.

'We should go to Cobán for a few days,' she suggested. 'It's north of here; there are waterfalls, caves, mountains and forests.'

'Have you got Google maps?' he asked. 'You can show me where it is.'

She smelled of cloying citrus, whether from mosquito repellent or perfume he had no idea but he found himself drinking it in until she lit a cigarette. She offered him the packet and he shook his head. He had declined her offer of cigarettes at least three times the previous evening.

'I don't bother with a smartphone any more. It stopped me sleeping, and I became a social media addict. I'm off all of it now.'

'Well I miss my iPhone,' said Richard.

'Yes, you could retreat into your online world now to avoid having to talk or even look at me. Take it from someone who knows; being out here without your phone is the best thing you could do for yourself.'

He risked a sidelong glance, wondering if she was right, and changed the conversation.

'You're lucky your skin can take the heat out here.' The sun was threatening to burn his face to a crisp. She inhaled deep into her lungs before breathing out a perfect smoke ring.

'You're lucky your skin means you'll never be labelled a terrorist or be told to get over slavery.'

It took a second or two for what she had said to sink in.

'Quite a shy kipper, aren't you?' She didn't look at him.

'Kipper?'

'Kid in their parent's pocket.'

'Not any more,' he replied after a brief hesitation. He was beginning to realize how leaving home had been the most liberating move he could have made, even if he had no idea what he was doing in Guatemala. He no longer had the sensation of being trapped or of feeling worthless. He thought about maxing out his Visa cards in case his father had them frozen. Freedom had become his drug, and for all his worries, he wanted to fully experiment with it.

Lia rounded the block, and with a sigh of relief, Richard jumped to his feet and took a bottle of water from her. Macy also got up, wrapped Lia in a loose hug then drew back.

'We ought to ring round the main hospitals if you've not done that already,' she said, producing a mobile phone from her back pocket.

Lia nodded, her face lifting with gratitude.

'I thought you said you didn't carry a phone any more,' said Richard.

'It's an old-fashioned flip phone, not a smartphone.'

Richard wished he had thought of calling the hospitals. Lia needed rational proof of Rafael's death, which would hopefully bring her some closure in time.

'There's a café less than five minutes from here on the way to the bus station.' She pointed down the road and they hoisted their rucksacks up onto their shoulders.

'I was saying to Richard we should visit Cobán,' she said. 'It's an area of unforgettable natural beauty that will take your mind off everything. We could all do with it, once the shock has worn off a bit.'

Lia didn't reply. Richard preferred to wait outside with the rucksacks, while Macy accompanied her inside the tiny café. He bought a packet of sweet bread and biscuits from a vendor and then looked back over his shoulder with the same disquiet, sure that they were being followed. The three young men and the black pickup truck they had been leaning against had gone, but when he looked back down the road, a very similar truck pulled to the kerb not far behind him, as if waiting to see where they were going next. The blacked-out glass meant he couldn't see who was inside. He told himself he was being paranoid after watching the CNN crime report and tried to wipe the thought from his mind.

Lia came out of the café with Macy in tow, and his heart sank as he saw her wipe a tear from her cheek, her face scrunched with frustration.

'I'm so sorry, Lia,' he said, and moved to place an arm around her.

'They wouldn't confirm if he was there or not, or dead or not. We tried three hospitals and they all said the same thing.'

She sniffed noisily and Richard wished he had a tissue to give her.

'Why?'

'Protocol. Waste of bloody time, more like,' she huffed. 'I just need to know for sure, for definite …'

Macy looked chastened. 'I'm so sorry, I had no idea they would be like that.'

They picked up their bags and walked on to the bus station. Like their accommodation, the bus tickets cost virtually nothing, and they were told that the journey would take five hours. At this sun-high hour the roads were busy with a single file of hot, battered vehicles moving steadily in both directions, bumper to bumper.

They boarded the bus, stowed their luggage and were soon moving north. Grey, multistoried, ramshackle buildings gradually gave way to smaller, quaint housing, while traffic on the roads eased. The driver took this as his signal to accelerate, with no caution for blind corners so long as there were cars to overtake.

Richard stretched his legs out into the aisle. He wondered if the same black truck was following them and then dismissed the idea as the musings of an overtired mind. Half-formed thoughts bunched around his mind, jostling each other for attention. Coffee and banana plantations appeared and disappeared between his thoughts; snapshot images of his father about to lose his temper, of Macy hugging Lia and of Rafael collapsed on the floor in the grotty bar they had finally left behind.

Lia stared out of the window. He took a breath, determined to file all his thoughts deep into his subconscious, and tore open a packet of biscuits. He watched the landscape unfold into a sharp sequence of greens and blues. They were the colours of hopes and dreams. He finally relaxed.

Hilly land fell away to reveal gaping cliff drops. Treetops of rainforest canopy formed a platform thousands of feet below and eagles circled above. Every ten minutes or so the bus jerked to a stop. As the bus expelled its standing occupants, more were sucked in through the front.

Sitting directly behind, Richard watched Macy converse easily in Spanish, responding to curious smiles with conversation while sharing her tacos with two giggling young girls. He was grateful for her charismatic energy, even if she was at times intense.

The higher the bus climbed, the more the landscape melted from tropical jungle to pine forest and misty mountains. By the time the bus was less than half full, Lia had slipped into an exhausted sleep. Her head lolled against the dirt-blotched window, her hair forming a kind of spider's web. A dung beetle made slow progress as it burrowed its way ever deeper into her hair until Richard, unable to watch its clumsy antics any longer, leaned over to cup it in his hands. He threw it out the top of the open window, somehow wishing Lia could have witnessed how calm and unafraid he had been. Lia didn't stir. He thought about running his fingers gently through her hair, but his hands knew better and returned their grip to his book.

He was trying to read *Birdsong* by Sebastian Faulks but he kept re-reading the same sentence over and over again: 'This is not a war; this is an exploration of how far men can be degraded.'

Richard put the book down and again watched Macy through the gap between the seats. She muttered to herself, mouthing words as she scribbled in a notebook. He wondered again if they had been right to put their trust in someone they barely knew. He recalled the blood that had been on her shirt, which was surely strange considering she was meant to have been in the ladies' bathroom. And wouldn't it have been far more prudent to stay and give statements to the police?

'That man was *murdered* and we've just run away from the scene.' He spoke quietly behind her.

She slapped her notebook shut and turned to give him a hostile look.

'Are you snooping?'

'No,' he retorted.

She paused. 'I seriously doubt the police will be looking for us.'

Richard spoke to the back of her head. 'But you made it sound otherwise last night.'

She turned back to him with one eyebrow raised.

'You said the police were corrupt,' Richard continued, 'and might even charge Lia with murder. That's the main reason we agreed to leave the city with you.'

Macy looked as if she was picking her next words carefully.

'I'll tell you what I know about the city morgue, shall I?'

He didn't want to know and shook his head in reply, but she continued anyway.

'Vultures constantly circle it because the police hardly ever investigate the bodies that turn up there.'

She took a swig from her water bottle. 'I've heard that body parts can be bagged up for eight months or more and the place is overflowing with dead people. That man obviously wasn't rich so he will likely spend the next year or so rotting in that place.'

Richard wrinkled his nose.

'So we probably are safe,' hissed Macy swiftly. 'But having said that, why take the risk?'

Richard sat back and turned away from her in an effort to put a stop to her sudden fast-talk. She was being too intense again. He watched clumps of tree trunks loom and fall away behind them. Until two weeks ago he'd never been on a plane, and his life had consisted of buying and selling stock for his father's antique business, living off his money and doing everything he was told. What did he really know about anything else?

Macy turned to him again, this time with a smile. She gestured to the vacant seat beside her. 'Come and sit here for a bit, please.'

He was relieved to stand and stretch his body even if he couldn't stretch to full height. He sank down next to her, blaming the lack of shock absorbers on the bus for the steadily growing ache in his lower spine.

'You and Lia are lovely. You make a fine couple.'

'We're friends, but that's all.'

'Well maybe you should be more than that, because I reckon Lia might fancy you. I can tell these things, you know.'

Richard looked doubtfully at her. Did she know something he didn't?

'I really don't think so.' Just the idea of it released a mass of sticky odour from under his armpits. 'She wants to continue travelling on her own, actually. She'll probably go to that address, look for that man's family and try and get herself a job while she's there.'

Macy's forehead furrowed into two vertical lines running between her eyes. 'You're just going to let her go?'

'She's got a mind of her own; hardly any money to her name, but that's never stopped her in the past. She doesn't even have a return ticket back to London.'

Macy's mouth dropped open. 'This is Guatemala, not London!' As if he wasn't aware of that. 'So should she be going off into rural areas on her own? Especially given what's just happened? Can't you persuade her to stick with us?'

'Us?'

'*I* believe you have an expendable quantity of cash,' Macy ignored his probe.

'Why do you say that?' He was finding it hard to follow her train of thought.

'You could offer Lia a modest monthly amount for being your travel companion.'

Richard was too bewildered to reply.

'She sounds like she needs it.' Macy looked pleased with herself.

'Travel companion? Isn't that just an old-fashioned word for an escort girl?'

Macy's face clouded and a shiver crossed her features before she composed herself. She reached down to her bag for another small bottle of water.

'Look. Whatever "arrangement" you have now doesn't have to change. You're essentially offering her money to let you stick around for a while. And yes, it's been done before for sex services, but that's not what I'm suggesting here.'

Her openness caught him off guard and he hunched his shoulders as he shrugged. Maybe she was right. Perhaps she had an instinct for these kinds of situations. She might even be the answer to his prayers.

'It's really quite simple,' said Macy. 'If she doesn't need money then she doesn't need to go to that address with the notion of trying to get a job.'

'Why are you so against her going there?'

'I'd like to travel around with you both and get to know you better.' She glanced at him with a look of dread and swallowed. 'And I think I saw the man who attacked Lia's Spanish teacher, friend, whatever he was. Worse than that, I think he might have seen me, and the thought of it is making me ill. I just don't think it's safe to go to San José Patula.'

Richard stared at her, his heart racing. 'Would you recognize him again if you saw him?'

'I don't know.' She looked wildly around and it was then that he noticed the dark circles under her slightly red eyes and that up close, her hair was a mess.

He shifted uncomfortably in his seat and thought of the young men in the truck who might be following them.

'Tell Lia what you've just told me.'

'No.'

'You've got to tell her.'

'I want to forget it. It's really stressing me out.'

'Tell the police, then.'

'Maybe he *was* the police.'

Richard chewed on his lip. 'You think the attacker might be somehow connected to the address.' He shook his head without waiting for her reply. 'We've got to persuade Lia not to go there.'

Macy shocked him even more as she began to laugh, a gentle guffaw that accelerated in euphoric depth until she was rolling around in her seat, clutching her sides and weeping. She glanced at him and convulsed again. Was she experiencing some kind of delayed shock? Whatever it was, it gave him the creeps.

'Old-fashioned advice is not a good alternative to experience where Lia is concerned,' said Macy at last, wiping tears from her eyes once she'd brought herself under control.

She was laughing at him and it grated. Lia was the most independent female he had ever met in his life. She didn't seem to need anyone, let alone an ex-neighbour who fancied himself as some kind of strange employer, paying her for her company.

'You might be able to convince her,' said Macy, but she looked at him as if she both doubted and pitied him.

'Why do you think Rafael was attacked?'

'Probably because he was part of a gang and into drugs.'

'That's exactly what I thought,' said Richard. They were united on this, at least, and it made him feel better.

'This country is pretty much controlled by drug dealers and the military; it's a legacy from America and Israel and their forthright foreign policies of breeding murderers.'

'I saw him hand a case over to the barman,' said Richard.

'Oh, you saw that too? I've been wondering who does that late on a Saturday night in a bar. Got me suspicious straight away.'

'Me too!' Richard couldn't help feeling pleased that she had also seen it.

'And why would you keep a female friend waiting,' she went on, 'someone visiting all the way from the UK? Imagine if she'd been on her own. Not very gentlemanly.'

She shrugged. 'You didn't like him, did you?'

She didn't give him time to reply and continued, 'I don't know anything about San José Patula except I read that the narcotics police recently found 120 kilos of heroin at the airport and it was apparently bound for a shell company there.'

'Bloody hell.'

'Hell, shell, well, it was in the papers,' she said with another shrug.

Richard nodded uncertainly.

'The worst thing about this country is the way rural people are *still,* five hundred years on, exploited by Guatemalan oligarchs and multinational companies for the natural resources on the land. Slaved by the depraved and sold for gold, they plead and fight to be freed, but the West's greed for a dime and a nickel makes triple the ripple, so they're kicked off their land and banned from everything but hunger, whilst the multinationals and corrupt governments still plunder ...'

'Where's that from?' asked Richard.

'Just came to me now,' said Macy. 'I love rhymes, good times, not crimes, look for the signs.'

'Wow.' He was impressed but he was also thinking Macy was acting a bit strange. Again, he put it down to delayed shock.

Macy smiled and then her expression turned hostile again. 'I'd like to continue writing. Do you mind?'

Their conversation over, Richard returned to his seat, mulling over her words. Lia hadn't said a single word since getting on the bus but Macy hadn't seemed to notice. She had babbled like a nervous child, until he'd known that Lia couldn't bear it any longer and had closed her eyes. He knew she was suffering and yet it wasn't as if Lia and Rafael had actually been in a proper relationship.

He sighed heavily, feeling the need to pray. It always helped. God would remind him that they were all going to die and cross over but that some went sooner than others. God had their best interests at heart. He dismissed the doubts that crept into the back of his thoughts: if God was in control, why such a violent death? He repeatedly told himself that everything was going to be all right.

They'd been travelling for four hours on a properly surfaced road that now turned to potholed gravel as they climbed higher through thick forest. Shacks dotted the roadside and pigs and cows wandered free, forcing the bus to slow. Richard felt a sense of claustrophobia as frowning clouds swirled overhead, sweeping the light from the sky.

Macy got up to stride up and down the emptied bus aisle. Every few minutes she would stare his way with a scowl that reminded him of an irritable old school teacher.

He wondered what would be worse: going back to England, where life was ordered, clean and he knew what to expect, or staying in Guatemala with its dirt, crime, chaos and so many poor people everywhere. The idea of going back to his father's house was bleak.

It came to him then, a startling sense of realization so simple he was amazed he hadn't figured it out till now. The girls were far more lost than him because neither of them had Christ in their lives. It was up to him to be the pillar of support who they could turn to. It was no good merely praying for himself; he had to pray for them too, with humility, love and patience. Was that why he was in Guatemala? As he was thinking about this, the first roll of thunder crashed around them. Lightning flickered across the sky. They drew up to a bus terminal whose faded sign announced their arrival in Cobán. The bus stopped and a torrent of rain began to fall, pounding down the windows of the bus, erasing the outside world into one contorted smudge.

Chapter 7

The Monja Blanca hotel boasted old-fashioned, colonial rooms around a courtyard garden filled with pine trees, orchids, moss, ferns and bromeliads. Butterflies floated around the mini jungle and the smell of the moist greenery, mixed with banana leaves and wood smoke, had Lia sinking into one of the hammocks strung out on the porch.

The rain, Macy had informed Lia, seemed to be a permanent feature of Cobán but had turned to a barely visible curtain of drizzle accompanied by the hushed sounds of water rushing through gutters. A dark-haired mongrel with pendulous teats lay a few feet away, undaunted by the light sprinkling of rain upon her.

Five siblings ran the hotel. The oldest, Miranda, had introduced them all during check-in. Her long, wiry hair was plaited into two braids that didn't require any hairbands to keep from unwinding. She spent most of her time in the kitchen, sweeping the floor, patting and twirling tortillas or chopping onions until she had to wipe the tears from her face. As she showed them to their rooms, she apologized for ambling with an unsteady, rocking gait, the result of being attacked by paramilitary forces twenty-five years ago.

On the far side of the porch, Richard and Macy swung in hammocks, shielded from the rain by a huge old pine tree that had seen better days. Thick and scaly bark had peeled off and the needle tips looked as if they had been dipped in brown paint.

A feeling of unease gripped Lia as she watched them. Richard whispered urgently to Macy, who pressed the heels of both hands to her temples, shaking her head.

'Are you guys okay over there?' said Lia.

'Sure!' Macy forced her mouth into a grin but it never reached her eyes.

Macy whispered back to Richard. He swung both legs out of his hammock and crossed the porch to Lia in a few long strides. Macy's full attention was now anchored back on Lia.

'What?' Lia prompted.

Richard hesitated. 'I'd be honoured if you would consider being in my humble employment for the next six months. You're short of cash and I'm short of a travel companion. It would mean I'm not left on my own here and you aren't in danger of being stranded in Guatemala.' He coughed, flushing a humid pink.

She didn't know whether to be angry or just laugh. It *was* kind of funny. 'Do I have the necessary qualifications?' Lia exaggerated a wink and a nod.

Macy walked over, looking way too serious. Something bigger was coming and it was clear they'd rehearsed it.

'Macy saw who attacked Rafael,' said Richard.

She had blocked out the memory but in an instant she was back in the bar with Rafael as he lay on the floor, the vitality leaking from his body. Lia took a deep breath and forced her eyes tight shut for a second.

'Why didn't you tell the police? The bar was packed ... there must have been other witnesses.'

Macy laughed in a way that made her feel young and stupid. 'The police could well be implicated in his death.'

Lia looked at Richard but he wouldn't meet her eyes.

'We could tell the British Embassy; someone might come with us to the police,' said Lia.

Macy lit a cigarette with shaky fingers. Grey tendrils of smoke uncurled from her mouth and nostrils, winding towards Lia. 'I'm getting a headache just listening to this.'

'But we might be Rafael's only chance of getting justice.'

Macy threw her arms up and shook her head. 'This is Guatemala! Over here powerful people do what they want! Anyone poor, indigenous or dead is devalued like a cheap currency. They don't get justice. Justice means nothing for them. Look around you. It's taken thirty years of campaigning to put one single mass murderer on trial here.'

'And that mass murderer was convicted of genocide,' said Lia. 'In his own country! I don't think that's ever happened in the whole history of the world before.'

'But then the court overturned the conviction.' Macy turned to Richard. 'Told you she wouldn't listen.'

Richard stood closer to Macy and, to Lia's amazement, placed an awkward arm around her. 'It might not be safe to go to the police or to San José Patula, which is why I am offering you the job of a lifetime. Explore the most beautiful areas of this country and actually get paid to do it. We would have our own separate rooms … in case you were thinking …'

'Tell me what you saw,' she said to Macy. She kept her voice as level as she could.

'It all happened so fast,' said Macy. 'A man about as tall as me who stood really close to him and pushed a knife … I think it was a knife … into him. I think. More than once. That's it. I got out of there.'

'What did he look like?'

'Roughly my height, dark, with thick, bushy hair and eyebrows that joined up. That's it, I honestly can't remember anything else. It's all a blur.'

Lia shook her head. Macy's vague description set her nerves on fire. 'And you don't think it's important that the police are told any of this?'

'C'mon, Lia, we've already been through this,' said Richard.

'And I think you're being irrational,' she said, her voice almost a whisper. She was rigid with restrained fury. 'Give me the piece of paper with the address on it.' She hoped Macy still had it.

'But I really don't think you should be …'

'Give it to me.' she demanded, raising her voice. The dog lifted its head and whined.

There was something about the situation that Lia was beginning to find intolerable. Something nameless was stirring within Macy, a shape-shifting, dangerous metamorphosis that had resulted in unblinking, magnified and depthless eyes.

Macy pulled the crumpled address from her front trouser pocket and threw it onto the floor. Lia leaned out of the hammock and snatched it up.

Springing forward, Macy's fingers encircled Lia's smaller wrists with surprising strength as she breathed a coffee-laced warning into her face.

'They could be following us right now,' said Macy.

'Who?' said Lia.

Macy changed tack. 'If you go there then you are linking yourself to that man's death, and this country is as corrupt as they come. Extortion, kidnappings and murders are everyday events and *you* are getting involved.'

It was a total invasion of personal space and an unwanted reminder of how empty her life now felt.

'I loved him!' Lia yelled. 'And *that man* has a name. Rafael.' Lia yanked her wrists out of Macy's grip and tipped herself out of the hammock.

'Stay the hell away from me, both of you.'

She slipped her trainers on and placed a shaking hand on the curve of the dog's belly. The dog licked the back of her wrist.

Lia stood and set off around the garden path, retracing the route they had taken from the bus terminal, close to the forest edge. She passed the same dusty canteen sporting a Gallo

Cerveza beer sign, the bright yellow-painted grocery store and a small collection of shacks.

A brood of feral chickens tiptoed across the road. The cheeping of the chicks dissolved the remaining enmity coursing through her body. When she noticed the dog jogging at her side, a half smile lifted her lips.

She knew it would be dark soon and the rain caressed her face, but there was no way she was going back for a jacket.

A truck roared past, loaded with labourers carrying cutting and digging tools: machetes, picks and hoes. To her left, the rainforest ran green, interrupted by rusty barbed wire fencing that was gnarled and cut in places. She kept up the pace until she saw a clearing in the trees and realized that she had reached the entrance to a park, marked by a locked wooden gate.

She looked over her shoulder, saw no one watching and launched herself over. The dog scrambled underneath a loose piece of wire.

Along a path leading away from the roadside, she followed the shoosh of running river water and revelled in the spongy bounce of the earth. The trail narrowed as it became more overgrown on each side by vegetation that reached out with giant arms to encircle her willing body in its embrace.

A piercing call cut through the fading light somewhere over her head. Tracing the sound to its source, she stopped to admire an owl perched in a tree hollow. It stared back, one eye wide open, the other closed.

Further into the forest, her ears sharpened to new noises: caterwauling, hooting, cooing and barking. The dog appeared intermittently, sometimes swallowed by a jumbled mass of head-high ferns, vines and palms.

As she walked there was the sense that it didn't matter where she went; whether it was the city or the jungle, this was a country that could take her life in a single breath, on a whim if it so chose. But who cared? Nothing much seemed to matter. Then she frowned. It was unlikely but still possible that if she could find Rafael's family, she would find out that he was hurt but alive. It *was* possible. She was starting to breathe heavily and brought her hand up to her chest. She shook her head as her thoughts accelerated, conflicting. All she could see were Rafael's open eyes, motionless. And blood. Too much blood.

She gasped as her breathing became more rapid. She was going to faint. She couldn't get enough oxygen and so she tried harder, panicking as she made her ribs heave, until the whole jungle around her was spinning and she bent down, hands on her knees. It still didn't help. As the sounds of the jungle receded to a strange silence, she felt herself fall to the wet earth where she curled up in a ball to meet the blackness.

Lia became aware of something moving across her face and shivered. Where was she? She opened her eyes. The dog was licking her face. Clouds of mosquitoes were attracted to her sweaty skin and had turned it bumpy and itchy. She sat up and whirled her arms around her head to protect her face, but it was too late.

The dark came suddenly even though she had been aware of the fading light. Feeling stronger, she stood up, resisting the temptation to scratch her face. She continued walking as if the last twenty minutes hadn't happened. The air high above began to fill with throaty howls, non-stop, a cacophony of bone-chilling vibrations.

The hairs on her arms and the back of her neck stood to attention. Her eyes adjusted to the dark and she saw a shape about a foot and a half long, slinking through the undergrowth towards her. She blinked and the dog burst out of the shadow and leaped up, dropping down in a pounce, jaws snapping. The squealing animal didn't have a chance.

Lia's heart threatened to break out of her chest, but at

least the treetop howling moved further away and became less coherent. The dog tore the head off something that had once resembled an oversized rat.

She forced herself to walk on, unwilling to watch the dog drooling with elastic guts and yet reluctant to step further into the night without the security of the canine. At least she could see again. An enormous full moon bared its soul, floating above the tree line, ghostly, a grinning globe of yellow that multiplied in puddles of water below. The rain had stopped but she could still hear the gurgle of moving water.

She came out into a clearing where a handful of wooden crosses could be seen sticking out of the ground. Glass bottles filled with fresh flowers surrounded them. She was walking through some kind of gravesite and she stopped to stare at the flowers, each one a solemn assurance to someone that they wouldn't be forgotten. A tranquility settled over her as she considered the invisible presence of those departed and what she would do next with her own life.

Behind, the dog continued to gnaw on her catch. Lia took one last look and rounded the corner of the path alone.

A massive body of flat, silvery water greeted her, stretching away in a shimmering zigzag and cradling the moon in its centre. She saw wood cabins not far away but no other signs of life.

Lia took her time treading forward, anxious to avoid being seen. She came to the water's edge, tempted to drink from it, until the sulphurous smell put her off.

She sat on the grass at the foot of a mahogany tree and took off her shoes and socks, rolling her jeans up as high as she could. The water was a balm on her mosquito-bitten ankles. She stood and walked along the water's edge. The dog stood tall, paw-deep at the water's edge now, watching her. She beckoned and whistled. The dog remained as rooted as the mahogany tree behind her.

Lia splashed the dog and it dropped into an instant play

stance, ears flattened, rear end in the air, wagging her tail. As Lia splashed her again, the dog dashed away as quick as a startled bird and then came back, arching away with grace to dodge the droplets.

Her ankles were slick with mud. Lia strolled back towards her shoes and socks, wiping a wet hand over her face. Her stomach cramped and she wobbled on her feet, momentarily light-headed as frogs bounced around her.

The dog ran up and snuffled her nose against Lia's hand before vanishing back into the shadows. She stooped to pick up her socks, reluctant to put the damp material back on. The moon hid for minutes behind a pack of clouds, turning the night sky darker than black, and the forest lit up with fireflies, tiny flashing lamps offering the path back. She leaned against the magnificent tree and rested both her hands on the bark, letting pieces of it crumble through her fingers, resigned to facing Richard and Macy again.

She sighed. All trees and animals were sacred. According to her adoptive mum, trees and animals were more sacred than human life because they provided all the oxygen, food and shelter that humans needed and absorbed the spirits of the ancestors. It was incredible to think that humans had destroyed so much of the nature that kept them all alive.

Lia shook her head, determined to remain positive. She certainly didn't need Richard or Macy telling her where to go or how to live her life. Going back to being a burden on her mum was out of the question. At that moment she felt more at home in the forest than she did around people. The idea of home, she realized with a jolt, wasn't a place on a map. It was a string of people with a nasty habit of dying on her. It was a loudspeaker in her ear, telling her that she didn't belong around people.

She breathed in the calm and peace of the open breeze, able to think with fresh clarity in spite of her hunger. Perhaps Macy was right; the powerful would always win over the little guys.

Even so, there was no way she could go wandering aimlessly around Guatemala as if Rafael had never existed.

The dog appeared beside her and sank onto her haunches to watch as Lia put her trainers on. Their eyes met, solemn, inches apart. Lia smiled. The jungle grew soft and quiet as if it accepted and approved her choice. She knew what she had to do. She got to her feet and started back down the path.

Chapter 8

Macy sat with Richard at the breakfast table, buttering hot toast. She had emptied the entire contents of her rucksack onto the floor the night before, rummaging through her belongings until she had been rewarded by the discovery of a stray sleeping tablet, lost at the bottom of one of the side pockets. She had clapped her hands together like an excited child, swallowed the pill and proceeded to fill her notebook with the avalanche of words that poured from her mind.

With the help of the tablet she had managed to sleep for about an hour, but she wasn't stupid. She knew it wasn't anything like enough and that her mind and body were lying to her. At least she could collect her newly ordered tablets that day. She was definitely hypomanic, one tiny step before manic, her mind on the verge of exploding out of control.

Lia dropped her rucksack and slid into the chair next to Richard. She smiled at him and he smiled back, but not once did she look at Macy, and it hurt because she wanted Lia to know that she was determined to keep the peace today. She had tried to wait up for Lia, to make her understand that she could trust her, but had fallen into bed and finally closed her eyes just as the sun had reared its head behind the thick fog of dawn steaming over the hills.

Macy glanced at Lia again. If she had her rucksack on her now, ready packed, it could only mean one thing.

'Where did you go yesterday?' asked Richard.

He patted Lia's rucksack and stared at the swollen mosquito bites on her face.

Macy couldn't wait any longer.

'Lia, I am so sorry for being such a pressurizing idiot yesterday. I wasn't myself.'

'It's okay. I'm sorry too. I don't want you to do anything you're not comfortable with.'

As Macy took a bite out of the toast, Lia puffed out her chest and looked braced for another confrontation.

'I'm going to San José Patula. Today. On my own.'

'That's good. Have some tea,' said Macy, her mouth full. She knew she wouldn't change Lia's mind but at least there was still Richard. She scraped her chair back and got up to turn the extra cup over, wiping it clean with the bottom of her T-shirt.

'Thanks,' Lia replied.

Macy sat back down, grateful that Lia was still talking to her. She tried to ignore the urge to move her legs which had plagued her all night, a creepy-crawly type of feeling as if there were a million ants running riot inside them. She settled for tapping each foot alternately under the table where she hoped no one would notice.

Miranda stood in the kitchen doorway. 'Something for you to eat, Lia?'

'Eggs, refried beans and toast, please.'

'You went inside the forest last night,' said Miranda.

'Yes, it was beautiful. Your dog accompanied me.'

Miranda nodded and hobbled over, passing Lia a leaflet entitled 'Laguna Lachuá National Park'. Pictures of monkeys, jaguars, cougars and swamp snakes leaped off the page.

They continued to eat in heavy silence until Lia spoke again.

'Richard, give me two days on my own and then meet me at San José Patula if you want.'

Richard froze in mid-bite. 'Are you accepting my offer?'

Lia nodded with a curt glance his way. 'Condition number one: I get to say where we're going. Condition number two: don't get any ideas about *us* because I do *not* fancy you, okay? I'll leave you a copy of the address.'

Richard blushed a fiery red and said nothing. Macy kept her eyes on her plate, determined to remain quiet, although she was now thinking about how rude Lia was when she ought to have been thanking Richard for offering financial assistance.

'Have you got a pen I could borrow?' Lia asked. Macy pulled one from her shirt pocket, kissed it – a serendipitous moment whereby she could spread some positivity and light to Lia without making a big deal out of it – and passed it to her.

Lia spoke the words out loud as she wrote them down on a cream-coloured paper serviette: EL PATRÓN, FINCA SAN ISIDRO. KM 46.5, CARRETERA, CIRCA SAN JOSÉ PATULA, JUTIAPA.

'Do you know how to get there?' asked Richard.

'Not yet,' said Lia.

'Are you going to go to the police?' he asked.

She shook her head and handed him the serviette.

'*El patrón* means "boss" in Spanish,' said Macy to Richard, eager to be helpful. She hadn't asked to come to San José Patula and Lia hadn't invited her. It hung in the air between them like a wet blanket. Lia's words were an obvious attempt to push Macy to a safe distance. It was clear she didn't want to see her again, and the knowledge of it was like a sharp slap.

'Well I'm going to Semuc Champey for a few days to empty my head,' said Macy. It sounded like she had a plan; no, she did have a plan now, even if some divine being had just decided it on her behalf and kindly planted the idea in her head. She had a plan, she had energy, and she would damn well carry on doing things the way ordinary people did. She smiled brightly.

'Where is that and what is it?' asked Richard.

'It's not too far from here; it means sacred water and there's a massive limestone formation with beautiful, crystal-clear pools of water and waterfalls.'

'I'd like to join you if that's okay,' said Richard.

Macy jumped up, knocked her chair back, ran around the table and hugged him tight around the neck before becoming aware of Lia staring at her with raised eyebrows.

'That would be so so great,' said Macy. She picked her chair up and sat back down. 'It's remote, full of wildlife and a wonderful place to rebalance the senses and—'

Richard stood up. 'So I won't be joining you, Lia.'

'Okay, but … I mean, it's fine if you do.'

'Look, I haven't meant to irritate you the way that it seems I have. I'm more than capable of making this journey on my own … or in the company of others.'

Richard bent to kiss Lia on the forehead. Macy was surer than ever that she was being guided by a higher force. It served Lia right for treating him badly; plus he was the kind of guy who wouldn't put up with her own bipolar drama and inadvertently feed off it. He was kind and there was something solid about him, and he was choosing her over Lia! She bit her lip to stop herself from dancing on the breakfast table and bounced her legs harder underneath it until she became aware of the *thud thud thud* and forced herself to stop.

'Take good care,' Richard said.

He left, presumably to return to his room.

Macy sat back, watching Lia eat, as she searched her pockets for a lighter. 'You didn't even wish him well.'

Lia frowned but had the good grace to look guilty.

'Miranda, how do you get to San José Patula from here?' said Lia.

'Take the bus back to the *ciudad* then go to Calzada Roosevelt 5 road, which is in Zone 3, and wait there for the bus northbound. San José Patula is a *pueblo* about two or three hours away.'

'Thank you, I'll be checking out after breakfast.'

'Looks to me as if you and Richard have separation anxiety and you're not even dating,' said Macy with a straight face.

'Couldn't be further wrong,' said Lia. 'I'm glad you guys will be travelling on together.'

Macy shrugged, unable to comprehend Lia's thinking.

'My brother will give you a lift to the bus terminal,' said Miranda. It was raining again and soil from the garden peppered the water as it flowed into the street.

Lia stood to say goodbye. After a brief hesitation she wrapped Macy in a quick, loose embrace.

'It was good to meet you.'

'Liar,' said Macy and looked away, scratching her forehead. 'Like I said, I'm truly sorry for my oafish behaviour. I think I might be—'

'It's fine. I just need some time alone.'

'It's not fine,' Macy whispered, suddenly desperate to explain. But how was she supposed to tell anyone, let alone a virtual stranger who already disliked her, that she didn't need to sleep any more and that the whole world, Lia included, seemed to be slowing to a sinister snail's pace?

'Don't worry about it,' said Lia. There was a warning tone in her voice that Macy didn't appreciate. She gave up and turned away.

'Good luck on your travels, Lia,' she muttered.

Chapter 9

Lia stepped out of the car and landed ankle-deep in a swirling mass of muddy water. Miranda's brother chuckled at her discomfort as he waved goodbye. She waded towards the scruffy ticket kiosk.

Another criss-cross of lightning zapped the sky. Ticket in hand, she ran inside to find the terminal crammed. People sprawled on all available chairs and floor space, chased inside by water and mud. A thin, ageless mother sat on the floor with two babies and held a hand out for change. The bottom of her ankle-length skirt was cemented with dirt. Lia bent to hand over the meagre change left from buying her ticket but regretted doing so as wet, bedraggled children surrounded her, palms up. With nowhere to go or sit, she stood there, jostled as children shoved each other to get as close as possible.

The bus arrived on time and she stepped over fingers, toes and sprawled bodies, eager to hand over her rucksack and find a seat.

The conductor thrust a baggage ticket at her and pointed to a queue by the entrance. She was grateful for the breeze that diluted the smell of poverty.

The bus wasn't as comfortable as the last ride had been but it was cheaper. She sat next to a family of two adults and three children who had squeezed into the two seats adjoining hers. Other than a baby who was trying to catch her eye with each wave of a chubby arm, she was ignored. Then she felt a tap on her shoulder and turned around as best as she could without elbowing the baby in the face.

A handsome man with thick, curly hair stuck his arm over the top of her seat, waving a bag of plantain crisps in front of her. He immediately had the attention of the baby, who climbed onto Lia's lap and stretched for the packet. The mother pretended not to notice.

Lia gently extricated the packet from the baby's fierce grip and pulled out a crisp for him, eliciting a vague yet approving smile from his mother. She helped herself. They were salty and crunchy. She handed the packet back and the baby crawled back to the safety of his mother, sucking on the crisp.

'*Gracias, señor.*'

The man placed a crisp into his mouth, thrust the packet back to her and gestured for her to take more, which she did.

'You could pass for Ladino or one of us Maya,' he remarked with a smile, 'until you open your mouth.'

'I love the Spanish language. I'm going to learn to speak it like a native,' she said, suddenly cocksure of herself.

The man introduced himself. 'My name is Casiano and I come from Rabinal in the highlands.'

She frowned, pushing away yet another unwanted image of Rafael in the bar. Rabinal had been one of the words tattooed on his arm, marked with a bright red burial cross.

'Over twenty different languages are spoken by the Maya here in Guatemala, not just Spanish. In Rabinal we speak Achí. Of course, during colonial times we weren't permitted to learn Spanish. Our oppressors thought we would pick up information that we could use against them. Then, for a time, there was only Spanish. But today, all my children attend a bilingual school. Children are reading and writing in Achí for the first time since the sixteenth century.'

In the time that she'd been in Guatemala this had to be the first good thing that she'd heard.

'Where are you going?' he asked.

'San José Patula.'

'I know it well. I used to work there in a *maquila,* an American-owned clothes factory. It almost killed me. My job was to maintain the sewing machines. For eleven years I was paid one dollar a day. I worked fifteen hours every day and had to ask permission to go to the bathroom.'

She shook her head. 'Was the company shut down?'

Casiano laughed. 'No, no! I was fired for taking time off when my wife was giving birth.'

Her ears burned with what he had told her and the inkling that looking for paid work in Guatemala might be about as foolish as looking for the sun at night.

She pulled out the address from her pocket and passed it over the back of the seat. 'A friend of mine said I could find work, on a farm here, a *finca*. Do you know it?'

Casiano scanned the paper. When he looked up at her, it was with a deep sigh that flared his nostrils.

'Did you come to this country expecting to lead a quiet life?'

She shook her head. 'No.'

He looked thoughtful. 'I don't know this particular finca but you may not be safe there.'

'Why? The civil war is over. It's been over for twenty years.'

'It was a racial war, not a civil war. It's aim was to kill us indigenous people, and the military forces were supported and financed by American and Guatemalan government elites. The real question is, why was there a war?' He had a hard, distant look in his eyes. 'Violence doesn't fall from the sky. A few international corporations and landowners had reduced us to landless slaves from whom riches could be made. We rebelled. So they ordered the army to kill us. Now the war is over, but these criminals haven't magically gone away.'

For the hundredth time she wondered who would want to kill Rafael. Why had he handed a case over to the barman?

For safekeeping? Or could it have been some kind of drug deal gone wrong? She yanked off her wet trainers and socks and lifted her knees under her to swivel around until she was sitting cross-legged in front of him. She noticed a tattoo on his shoulder of some kind of Maya glyph.

Casiano scratched his stubble as he noticed her looking. 'Tattoos are a sign of courage. We have drawn our history onto our skin for centuries.'

He sighed. 'I love my country dearly, but it will not be safe until we take care of the past. People must face up to the war crimes they committed or we will never end impunity. And I worry about the situation sliding downhill.'

They were both silent, as if two strangers again and their dialogue had been nothing but a piece of Lia's imagination floating through the air. She swivelled round to face the front of the coach.

The bus continued to roll through thick, jungle-like terrain. The road was narrow with a steep drop on one side, and hundreds of feet below, a soft blue river could be seen twisting through farmland. She thought she imagined the scraping, high-pitched whine coming from somewhere below until she was thrown out of her reverie by the bus slewing into the middle of the road. It continued towards the cliff edge as if propelled by an invisible superpower.

Passengers were tossed to one side. Lia grabbed the metal bar at the back of her seat just in time to avoid slamming into the baby. Somehow she was able to take the weight of a standing couple who fell against her. She thought her arm would snap like a twig and the baby would be crushed under their combined weight, but the bus finally came to a stop and they eased off her aching limb.

Lia stared out the window into grey nothingness. The edge had eroded with rainfall and might still give way, taking them all on a death slide.

The baby whimpered. Advising everyone to stay where they

were, the driver stepped down from the bus. Rain continued to tap on the windows and the bus shuddered as if scared of being tipped over by the wind.

Two men sitting near the front jumped down with the driver. Lia slipped her socks and shoes back on as fast as she could and filed out with everybody else, rubbing the throbbing muscles in her arm.

They sheltered under a giant tent of trees that diverted the rain over an umbrella of foliage. The driver crawled under the bus and disappeared from view. The mood was tranquil; perhaps people were simply happy because today, everyone had stayed alive.

Lia wiped lank strands of sweat-soaked hair from her face and watched bright green and red beetles fly past, inches from her nose. She wanted to sit down but the sight of giant ants scurrying across the gravel deterred her. The driver finally walked over, splotched with engine grease.

'The drive shaft has broken and the bus must remain here until we have a new one.'

'How long?' she asked. A rapid exchange of Spanish followed.

'Three hours, maybe more,' said Casiano. Lia shook her head in alarm. Most of the group had run out of drinking water. The driver shrugged and lit a cigarette, sucking on a filter that was soon swathed in oil.

'Don't worry, we'll get a ride before then,' said Casiano.

As he spoke, a dented black Nissan pickup rounded the bend and stopped. Three young men in black vests and sunglasses got out to talk to the driver. They agreed to take as many people as possible on to the next town. Casiano moved away to spread the news before jogging back towards Lia.

'There's room for you. Get your things.'

She thanked him and headed back to the baggage compartment of the bus, squeezing past baskets wrapped with multicoloured rope and cardboard boxes of wilting fruits and vegetables. She dragged her rucksack out and it was passed up into the back of the pickup. She climbed in after it to settle beside the same family of five that she had sat next to on the bus. The baby dismissed her with a loud wail and fell asleep.

Casiano passed Lia a worn, brown leather suitcase, and he too climbed up into the pickup and sat down. 'It is best that you are dropped at the next town. A stopping bus leaves for the city in two hours.'

The first twenty minutes had everyone laughing alongside Lia's own amusement. They all knew she was a foreigner, and acted as if they did this kind of thing every day and as if foreigners never usually got caught out like this.

An hour into the ride the atmosphere turned sombre. Every inch of Lia's body ached. It must have shown because she was offered extra clothing to sit on but she declined, determined that nobody would be forsaking comforts on her account. She lost count of the number of times she was slammed into the side of the truck or bounced into the air as they travelled over bumps and potholes. But anyone getting off was treated with care and offered hands of help. There was always a smiling face to pass down the bags and everyone waved goodbye like old friends. She was relieved to be away from Richard's paranoid thoughts of being followed.

They eventually reached the next town – hardly a town, more like a sleepy, run-down cluster of buildings and shacks through which the main road widened and continued. Lia was dropped off, dizzy with a raging thirst, but every building in sight was shuttered or barred and there was nowhere to buy water.

A chicken bus appeared against the skyline and Lia hoped she wasn't hallucinating it into existence. Proud and stoic, it had been lovingly repainted in every multicolour possible, with the name *Gabriela* painted on the side. The front grill and bumper were mirror-shiny chrome, and the sound of mariachi music rose in volume as it drew near.

She squinted, trying to work out if the driver planned to stop. The sun pulled out behind the last wispy clouds, which had no choice but to evaporate like a dream. She wobbled, light-headed, and focused all her attention on not fainting by the roadside. Just as she thought the driver would pass by in spite of her wild arm-waving, a conductor appeared on the steps, and in one swift motion, grabbed her by one arm and her rucksack by the other, pulling both up behind him into the crowded aisle.

The bus began to pick up speed but Lia froze, staring at the conductor. It was the old man from the museum who had been dragged away by guards.

'You!' she shouted in Spanish over the engine's roar. 'You're okay! What did they do to you?'

He ignored her, balanced her rucksack on his head and forced his way down the aisle towards the back of the bus. He opened the rear door and climbed a ladder to the roof, even though the bus had reached at least seventy miles per hour. He returned minutes later to collect her fare, eyeing her with suspicion before shouting her destination back at her. Was he was an omen of more violence to come? After another five minutes of staring, she finally concluded that it was someone else and she had the good sense to look away. The scar running across his throat had tricked her.

She was anxious to get the rest of the trip over with. All the seats were taken and she found herself squashed between people again, this time standing. She listened to the onomatopoeic sounds of dialects spoken by people who were shorter and more colourfully dressed than everyone else, and was careful not to trip over a rooster that stuck its head out from a cardboard box and clucked in warning.

Luckily, vendors soon boarded, selling drinks, nuts, fruit and ice cream. Lia bought two bottles of water and a banana under the watchful eye of the conductor. He nodded in understanding once she'd torn the plastic cap off one of the bottles and glugged for minutes at a time. People left in dribs and drabs, and before long she was sitting down, satiated and heavy-eyed. She tried to stay awake but it was impossible.

The bus pierced the heart of the city at eight o'clock that evening. The light had faded and Lia was the only passenger left as they pulled into the dimly lit terminal building. Even the bus conductor had got off before her.

Lia mumbled her thanks to the driver, a smile carved into her exhausted face. She hoisted the rucksack over both shoulders and ignored the hunger and aches that coursed through her body. An armed guard escorted her until she was outside the bus depot and then she set off to search for a hostel.

The bus had passed numerous budget accommodations a couple of streets away, and she took up a brisk pace, giving the impression of knowing exactly where she was going. She took the first left that she came to and then crossed into the middle of a traffic circle that had grown crowded due to a taxi breaking down. Crossing to the other side of the road, she entered the Ojau hostel.

Once she handed her passport over it took less than five minutes to check in and be shown to a room. She dropped her rucksack like a stone and spent the next ten minutes under a cold shower. Within fifteen minutes she was dressed in clean clothes and back out on the street.

Marimba music played from a nearby restaurant and Lia headed for it, pushing open the door to find a large, open-plan room with over fifty tables and easily a hundred people inside. The smell of Chinese food squeezed her stomach tight. Those seated nearest stared her way. She stared back and subconsciously held her breath as once again she saw how many guns were carried in plain view.

Two men dressed in fatigues stood at the bar close to the entrance, drinking shots. They paused mid shot to reach for the guns propped against the bar but quickly changed their minds once they'd looked her up and down. Lia kept her face neutral.

The two men resumed drinking their shots. Lia wondered what it felt like to be provided with such power over who got to live and who died. Was it addictive, in the same way that heroin, porn or shopping could be? People began to eat and talk amongst themselves again. A waitress came over and with a friendly smile, showed her to a vacant table, shoving a greasy menu her way.

Lia relaxed as she saw other women seated, drinking alcohol, eating and enjoying themselves. She ordered a bowl of noodles with mixed vegetables, which, upon arrival, was mountainous. It was a welcome change from rice and beans, and with her mouth full, Lia almost forgot the sobering fact that people in the restaurant could shoot her dead if they chose to. Red lanterns lit the room, providing a warm, peaceful glow.

Occasionally, a barefoot woman would skulk inside, carrying a basket containing chewing gum, nuts and sweets, and she would implore people to buy something. A few people dropped coins into the basket without taking anything in return.

Just as Lia finished eating, three young children entered the restaurant. Their bones jutted out and they were shoeless and dirty. They hovered like bewildered moths by the door. Their eyes flitted towards the security guards, and they waited until their backs were turned before darting over to the nearest table where a couple sat.

The oldest child was perhaps eight years old. He wore a ripped pair of trousers with a broken zip and a torn shirt, missing buttons. His hair was matted and patchy. The couple had finished eating, with food left on their plates. The oldest child pointed to it and the man graciously nodded. The child scooped up morsels and fed the youngest girl, taking the occasional mouthful for himself. The second child shovelled as much food as she could fit in one go into her mouth, scarcely giving herself time to swallow before scooping up another mouthful. Their wide-open eyes shone like marbles, swivelling the room as they ate, looking for the next table to go to and keeping a wary look out for reprisals. The couple stared miserably away.

They moved swiftly from table to table, sticking close together. Every waitress acted as if the children were invisible but not everyone allowed them to eat. A group of men waved the children away with derision. Lia shook her head as she saw how much food they had left over. The oldest child hesitated, eyes wide at the sight of chicken legs, ribs of pork and noodles. One of the men raised a fist above them and he flinched before grabbing his siblings by the hands to tug them away. Lia regretted eating the entire contents of her own meal, uncomfortably bloated whilst the children risked being hit for a few mouthfuls of nourishment. With the security men alerted, they left as quickly as they had arrived, devoured by the night.

Lia paid her bill and was about to leave when a hush spread over the tables. A waitress switched on a large, wall-mounted TV and asked everyone to listen. The room grew quiet as everyone turned their attention to the screen. Lia strained her ears to hear the news report being broadcast. It seemed to be about protesters in the plaza and the president, Otto Molina. Had she heard correctly? Was it possible that he had just resigned from office and was being taken to jail, where he would face corruption charges? The actual president of Guatemala?

A collective roar erupted through the restaurant, drowning out the TV and shocking Lia with its intensity. Everyone stood to cheer, their arms thrown up in victory, hugging, shaking hands and patting each other on the back. Some of the customers, grown men included, started to cry.

Lia was about the only person who remained seated, her stomach taut at the sudden change of mood. She swallowed, ignoring the nausea that came from overeating, and continued to watch as fresh bottles of beer, rum and tequila were opened and chinked in jubilation.

'To the future of Guatemala!'

'Victory to the people!'

'Down with the government!'

'We did it!'

She was suddenly aware of a group of three men and two women standing near to her table, watching her.

'You are not Guatemalan, are you?' one of the men said to her in English with a wide smile.

'No, I'm from the UK. Just visiting.'

'You've come here at a historic moment. Do you understand what has happened?'

'The president is going to jail?'

'That's right!' replied the man. 'Because he wasn't fit to govern. He stole millions in funds from the people and this is our response to what is happening in Guatemala today.'

'I've heard Molina was an army general in the 1980s.'

He nodded grimly. 'He was one of those with hidden powers, someone who could do anything without fear of arrest or prosecution. Imagine that.'

The room still crackled with sporadic applause and cheers and the chink of glasses, and she had to lean closer to the man to hear him.

'Please. Join us and celebrate the good news.' He raised a bottle of tequila and a shot glass her way.

Lia thought of her aching body and her sudden desire for privacy. Macy had told her it was impossible to fight corruption and injustice in Guatemala. Well, she'd just been proved wrong on the grandest possible scale. She ought to celebrate, and yet she couldn't seem to persuade her stiff, bruised body to move much.

'I'm sorry, I can't stay. I've had a crazy journey—'

'Very well, very well. Be careful out there tonight.'

She thanked him and got up to leave. Her forehead beaded

with sweat as a wave of anger washed over her, which, if nothing else, at least gave her energy. Rafael should have lived to see this day. She imagined the happiness and pride that would have shone from his face, and she felt like pounding the table with her fist because she just couldn't shake off the ridiculous sense that he had deserted her as soon as she had arrived. What if he really had been smuggling drugs, as both Macy and Richard seemed to think? She shook her head.

At the exit, she pushed the door open and was startled by the scene before her. A crowd had gathered outside: people hugged and kissed, others raised and clenched their fists in a power salute. As they walked past the restaurant, people waved, beckoning her towards them. Some banged on drums, their faces painted in patriotic blue and white to match the waving flags. She hesitated before stepping forward. They were heading the same way she was. It was unbelievable that people had come together at this late hour. A woman walked past as if in a trance, eyes fixed, clear but wet, with a steady stream of tears flowing down her cheeks. Others cried through swollen, bloodshot eyes, with snot streaming and sobs that vibrated through her.

Her chest began to ache and she tried as hard as she could to swallow it away. She reminded herself that she had absolutely no idea who these people were; she hadn't lived through the tortures and terrors that everyday Guatemalans had been forced to live through, and she wasn't plagued by the kind of memories that had haunted Rafael.

Lia took a deep breath. Perhaps what they did have in common was simply a converging of paths, because hadn't they all lost people who were precious? How different her life might have been if her birth parents hadn't died. There was no doubt that her adoptive mother loved her and would do anything for her; but for all that, it was strange to know that there wasn't a single person alive on the planet – that she was aware of – who was genetically related to her.

Other people rallied round and she found herself draped in the Guatemalan flag as someone gently squeezed her shoulders. She felt strangely liberated and there was a moment of unity so profound that it left her both upset and jubilant at the same time, for how was it possible that she could be in closer proximity, both mentally and physically, to these strangers gathered around her than to her actual friends and family? How was it possible that out here in the dark, late at night in one of the most dangerous countries of the world, she had never felt safer?

That night somehow offered her back a missing part of herself, in an unexpected celebration of life and a remembering of lives lost. It was a cathartic release, such that by the time she neared the entrance to her hotel she was no longer sure whether she was moving of her own free will or whether she'd been guided spiritually by loved ones on a journey to her own redemption.

Chapter 10

As soon as Lia left, Richard felt as if someone had punched him in the gut, and yet he knew she needed breathing space. She was one of less than a handful of friends in his life and he was genuinely concerned for her safety, but there wasn't anything he could do other than let her go.

The day had passed slowly into evening but according to Macy, who was acting more and more strange, everything seemed to have become part of a bizarre, rhythmic pattern: laughter, rain, wind and crickets, but also numbers, colours and language. She told him they were intertwined by connections that people like him just couldn't see. Everything had a reason and a moment for itself – awkward had become easy; black was white – and Richard had no idea what to do about it.

He found her in the common room that afternoon, dishevelled and barefoot. Richard had rarely gone barefoot in his own house, let alone a communal space that had to be shared with strangers, and the thought of it horrified him.

'I'm going to meet a friend today,' she said in a hushed voice. She looked away, biting her bottom lip. She was too preoccupied to listen to anything he had to say and could be meeting with the devil for all he knew.

On the wall in front of him, a dark green house gecko peeked out from behind a colourful painting of an indigenous woman wearing traditional dress, disappearing before he could place it in full vision. Macy filled his vision instead as she leaned close and squeezed his cheeks hard between damp palms. He smelled coconut face cream and coffee breath and thought for a second that she was going to kiss him.

'Okay, how long will you be?'

'This is so *mild*, darling. The higher I get, the harder it is to calm down. But don't worry, because I'm going to pick up the medication to control it before things get out of hand.'

She released his cheeks and sobbed, gulping air like a fish. 'I'll take big doses to begin with and all my thoughts will be stolen from me.'

'What exactly is the matter?' he probed. He was as disturbed as she was fragile. She had seemed so charming and self-assured when they had first met.

'Let me stay with you while I try and fight this ...'

'Fight what? I thought we were going to that place with the waterfalls.'

'I can't now,' said Macy.

He inwardly cursed. Perhaps she was suffering from a bad case of nerves, which he could fully relate to. But where should they go instead and what should they do? He didn't have the Lonely Planet guidebook that he'd seen most other travellers leafing through at one time or another. Perhaps that was what gave them such an air of confidence. He was a city boy, a Londoner; he ought to be able to handle all this and more. He definitely didn't want to spend another night in the hotel, mingling with the travellers that were staying there, with their baggy yoga trousers and beaded plaits. He wasn't like them and he wasn't trying to be like them; but still, each sideways glance in his direction jarred. He didn't care for any more travel stories either, whether it was from the two Australians who were held up at gunpoint on the bus to Puerto Barrios, or the German who was lucky enough to survive malaria and amoebic dysentery, holed up in the jungle for three months following a divorce from hell.

Most of the travellers they'd met were gorgeous and not afraid to flaunt it. It made him uncomfortable. He was reminded of himself as a child, the awkward, lonely nerd with a terrible haircut and an obsession with books. At least the church group that he'd started going to at the age of fifteen made up for it, making him feel welcomed and genuinely liked. He'd forgotten about his loneliness and the fact that he could never measure up to his father's expectations. His parents hadn't approved of the religious zeal that carried him to the Protestant church every week, but as far as he was concerned, Christianity had saved him in a world which he'd found to be, more than anything else, cold and cruel.

He'd thought Macy was different. She'd been warm, funny, generous and accepting of his foibles. Now all he wanted to do was google her rapidly changing behaviour: manic, intense, distraught, passive-aggressive and selfish. He shook his head. He needed her, regardless of her state of mind, or rather he needed her Spanish speaking skills. A crazy idea was forming with beautiful clarity.

'We have to go back to the city,' said Richard.

'Okay, I'll come with you ... can't be on my own right now ... anyhow, take a bow, just until I'm better,' she said.

The weird wordplay thing again.

'Tell me what's wrong,' said Richard.

'What is wrong is that one in every four people will experience mental health ... issues ... but I don't want Lia to know,' she replied.

He stalled and then figured she was being dramatic and dismissed her words as he returned to his idea.

'If we asked around in that city bar, we might be able to find out for sure why Rafael was attacked, what happened to him, and if our opinions of him can be substantiated by other people, it might help Lia come to terms with what's happened.'

The more Richard thought about it, the more he liked the

idea, so long as he could convince Macy to go along with it. It would give him a good, valid reason to see Lia again. It would show Lia that he cared about her. He frowned. Placing Rafael in a bad light didn't feel like a very Christian way of being but it was all he could think of right then.

'I don't *want* to go to that bloody finca,' said Macy. She sniffed and the words tumbled out faster and faster. 'What if the murderer's there and recognizes me? But I want Lia to like me. I like her. I like you. Do you *know* how lovely it is not to be stigmatized, especially by people who are younger than you? I have to get the pills first. Fast. Or there'll be a bomb blast. Now. Then I'll get down to the same level as you again. I know where to get them. Took the last ones yesterday.'

She fixed him with a hostile stare and then sprang up, striding out through the garden without a backwards glance.

Richard stared after her. Pondering their predicament, his mind kept returning to the ridiculously insignificant fact that she had left the house still barefoot.

Eventually he stood up to make more coffee. He had to believe she would feel better once she got hold of whatever medication it was that she needed. The dog, peering up at him from under the kitchen table, looked unconvinced.

Macy returned over an hour later, still intense but armed with a plastic bag full of boxes that he assumed contained her pills. He repeated their reasons for going back to the city, trying to ignore the feverish glitter in her eyes. He wasn't going to take any chances with the accommodation this time around either. Of the twenty-five sprawling zones that made up the city, he'd already booked them into the Holiday Inn in Zone 10.

'Does it sound like a crazy idea?'

'Not at all,' Macy replied. 'We can find out if the barman knew Rafael or if he knew what was in the case he handed over. He'll remember me.'

'Exactly!' Richard was relieved they were on the same page.

'If we're careful, everything will go smoothly and we can meet up with Lia and travel on together.'

'The girl can't think straight.' Macy shook her head. 'I know she's upset and she has every right to be, but she wants some kind of justice or closure or something for her friend and doesn't understand how unrealistic that is.'

'Well, I just want to see what we can find out to help her with the closure part,' said Richard. He'd seen how the men in the bar had responded to Macy's charms and he was sure they would do so again. He just had to make sure she ate a good dinner and slept well that evening. Based on the whispered comments made by other guests staying in the hotel, she had barely slept the night before. She had hardly been able to sit in one place for more than a few minutes at a time, let alone sleep. He'd been treated to her singing, accompanied by a guitar-playing, tie-dyed American, and over eight hours of indiscriminate, non-stop chatter, first to him and then to anyone still awake in the hotel. Tonight, he was sure, would be different. There wasn't much a good night's sleep couldn't fix.

Chapter 11

By nine a.m. the next day, Lia sat on another bus, her clothes already damp with sweat. She'd waited at the bus stop for an hour, surrounded by stinking street rubbish and flies. The city was a different world in the daytime but today was especially unusual. Crowds passed by, singing, chanting, banging drums and cheering as the party vibe warmed up to a day of celebrations. Fireworks were set off and people honked their car horns in noisy approval; entire buses and shops had been draped in massive national flags.

Squawking chickens and packages of all shapes and sizes were strapped onto the roof of the bus. Everyone else managed to squeeze inside except a few young men who clung like vines to the outside, from windows and railings, confident that they would not fall off.

They passed through a heaving bus terminal. Inert men lay coffin-ready on the side of the road whilst the next street drew pimps, prostitutes and drug dealers together. The stench of garbage, booze and death trapped the unfortunate inside. Fresh graffiti was sprayed over old. *SIN JUSTICIA NO HAY PAZ*. No justice, no peace.

People stormed the bus from all directions as it crept through the central market, and paid no attention to the fact that this was a road with moving traffic. Men, women and children thrust their wares through the bus windows, shrieking prices; the air filled with the scent of sweet mango and guava as people bought drinks and snacks and kept a steady stream of coins gravitating towards eagerly outstretched palms. Everything was sold here: Rolex watches, sarongs, sinks, alarm clocks, fruits, vegetables, beans and fly-bathed meat swinging from rusty hooks. Lia settled on two bottles of water and a banana.

Past the market, the bus crossed into a smarter area and picked up speed. A huge shopping mall nestled amongst rows of department stores. Young couples and groups of young people strolled round in Levis, shiny Kickers and designer tops. Girls wore make-up, hair clips and flashy jewellery while the lads wore Ray-Ban shades and chunky watches. The buildings were sparkly, modern, and the cars were mostly tinted four-by-fours.

Passing quickly through this area, the outside view melted back into shabby hardship, and the only signs of abundance were in the number of barred windows and layers of razor wire. They touched the city outskirts, climbing steadily higher, and Lia turned around for a last look. Sticking out of the hillside were hundreds of shacks made out of cardboard boxes that formed a domino structure. A woman breastfed, dogs snoozed and two toddlers played with an empty water bottle.

The winding road continued upwards into rocky and barren hillside marked by clumps of cacti. After another hour they pulled into the small town, the *pueblo*, of San José Patula.

The houses here were mostly small and simple, made of breezeblocks and painted in faded pastel colours. Mountains framed the town. Dogs, cats, chickens, pigs, oxen and cows roamed freely.

The main road continued through the town in a straight line with potholed tracks forming a gravel network around the town. An unglamorous church painted sky blue stood by itself across from the bus stop, by far the most looked-after building.

Next to the church, a park was fringed by hedges and a school where uniformed children poured eagerly out of its doors.

Lia stepped off the bus. All the boys and men, Ladino and Maya alike, from the young to the old, wore cowboy hats, plain white shirts, old jeans and machetes. A few of the younger women wore western-style dresses but most wore the traditional multicoloured *cortes* and *huipiles*. She wondered who to ask for directions.

'*¿Puedo ayudar?*' Can I help you? a young man called out.

'*Sí,*' she replied. '*¿Dónde está* Finca San Isidro, *por favor?*'

'*Ah ... de* Miguel Cana.' The man scratched his nose and turned to the group that was beginning to form around her. He spoke in a kind of half-formed Spanish, too fast for Lia to catch, and others joined in until an older man spoke above the rest, addressing her in a booming voice. The finca, she learned, was an hour's walk away, and he pointed in the same direction that the bus had followed. He spoke slowly, saying that someone in a black pickup truck would be leaving the pueblo in one hour and would take her with him. Lia thanked him.

Under the scalding sun Lia squinted at a nearby canteen and headed towards it, eager to remove her rucksack. Flies buzzed around the small, square room and a cockroach scuttled across the wall. Her T-shirt was pasted like glue to her back. Marimba music played from an ancient wooden radio that crackled with interference every few minutes. There were five square tables in the room, one of which was taken by two old men. They sat in silence and watched Lia without the slightest acknowledgement of her smile.

She ordered a room-temperature Sprite, all that seemed to be sold from behind the bare counter, and waited with growing nerves. The men continued to stare and she fought the temptation to eyeball them back. The woman behind the counter remained busy cleaning out a cupboard, occasionally humming to the radio.

Ten minutes before the hour was up Lia waited once more

in the heat, convinced that her rucksack had gained an extra twenty pounds. Some of the locals greeted her, tilting their hats or nodding to her. She was about to ask again if anyone knew how she could get to the finca when a black Nissan Navara pickup pulled up abruptly beside her.

A man jumped out and asked gruffly, '*¿Me voy a* Finca San Isidro *con usted?*'

'*Sí, gracias.*' She nodded immediately and he beckoned for her to get into the front passenger seat. She placed her rucksack in between them and climbed in.

'*¿Como te llama?*' she asked politely. '*Me llamo Lia.*'

The man, who she would later come to know as Rodrigo, merely grunted and ignored her. Lia choked in a whirlpool of dust as he completed a jerky three-point turn.

They pulled away from the side of the road and were soon cruising through the town. Passing the church, Rodrigo made the sign of the cross. Richard would like it here, she thought. He was only an inch or two taller than her but stocky and muscular, with bushy black hair hanging in a scruff over his eyes and a thick beard that was shiny where sweat had dripped into it. A permanent sneer emphasized thick eyebrows that met in the middle. It was obvious from the start that he didn't like her, and she wondered what Richard would make of her getting into a strange man's pickup, as casual as could be.

They left the town behind, weaving around bleak hills and empty rock faces, higher and higher until they rounded a sharp corner and were looking down on the pueblo and its ant-like movements.

Lia asked Rodrigo how far away the finca was. He breathed a dismissive grunt in her direction. Irritated, she repeated the question, aware that he'd heard her perfectly well the first time. She was answered with a growl and he glanced at her with open contempt before replying that he didn't understand. Sensing her discomfort in the awkward silence, he smiled with satisfaction.

She forced a smile back and said in English, 'You have the manners of an arrogant arsehole.'

He ignored her and remained focused on the road ahead, for which she was grateful as it folded into steeper and narrower gradients, each twist demanding a cool head, firm hands and reliable brakes. She reminded herself that she had a legitimate reason for travelling into the middle of nowhere with this man. She refused to be intimidated and decided she could easily outrun him if it came to it.

After a quarter of an hour, they passed a farm that had constructed large canvas coverings under which grew foot-high saplings. The sweet scent of jasmine drifted into the car before they turned right, off the road onto a rough track with grass waving from either side of tyre marks. A sign hung from rusty hinges. On sun-bleached wood, it read 'FINCA SAN ISIDRO'.

Rodrigo stopped and slammed the gear stick into four-wheel drive, the thudding movement perfectly synchronized with Lia's beating heart. They began to traverse down the track, rocking from side to side on the uneven surface.

Lia had given no thought to what she would say to the patrón once they arrived, but at least he had known Rafael and would be able to introduce her to his family.

They passed through a gate, opened by a young boy who ran barefoot back into a nearby shack. On both sides of the track, the fenced-off fields contained horses grazing. Lia counted eleven horses. To their right, at the bottom of the flowing expanse of grass, a small stream gleamed, running for as far as she could see. The thick arms of ancient trees hung down over the track and smacked the roof of the truck as they scraped by, as if to test the mettle of the occupants within.

Rounding another bend Lia hoped they wouldn't meet any oncoming traffic; the road was barely wide enough for the pickup and she didn't fancy their chances of reversing back down the hill. A few minutes more and they reached the hilltop. Lia got her first view of the house as the car rolled up the driveway and stopped.

It was the kind of place she imagined some of the wealthiest country folk in England to be living in. Made of red brick and plastered in pastel shades, the building was framed by white Romanesque pillars and decorated with latticed windows containing intricate stained-glass designs. A dark blue antique carriage rested on its poles beside the house, next to a red Ford Model A Coupe. The pathway was neatly paved and hedged in by hundreds of small, multicoloured flowering plants. On the opposite side, an old, beaten-up, open-top Volkswagen 181 Trekker was parked, guarded by a solid length of pine trees that stretched up at least five times as high as the roof of the house.

Rodrigo stopped the car and beckoned impatiently for Lia to get out. He leaped out himself and called out in a sullen tone, '¿Patrón?'

He turned back to the truck and threw Lia's rucksack onto the floor beside her. She picked it up, unwilling to bear the antagonism emanating from his eyes and yet unable to look away. She thanked him with an over-pronounced '*Gracias*' laced with sarcasm.

A pair of muddy riding boots lay strewn against one side of the main door, preventing it from slamming closed. The air was cooler, with a sweet-scented breeze – a welcome relief from the muggy humidity of San José Patula.

A grey-haired woman appeared in the hallway and hobbled over. Upon seeing Lia she half turned her head away and called softly, '¿Patrón?'

Chapter 12

Macy had taken a double dose of the new pills but she was still hypomanic, waking frequently during the night. She had vivid dreams that she couldn't remember, and she even woke Richard up after calling out in a panic with no recollection for the briefest of moments of where she was. He hadn't seemed to mind too much. When she was like this she was still quite easy to love, in the way that she wanted to be helpful wherever possible. She really did want to help Lia come to terms with Rafael's death and even thought about shocking Lia and Richard by figuring out by herself who had killed him. She knew she was more than capable – endowed as she was with an almost euphoric understanding of the unique energy flowing through and around her – but in the same vein she wanted to make Lia beautiful art, buy Richard presents and basically spoil them both with platonic love.

She pushed her way out of the taxi and stood by the entrance to the bar. She looked left and right, and hesitated with Richard beside her.

'Wait here for me,' she said, barring his way to the door.

'What? I don't think so. I'm coming in too,' said Richard.

'No man is going to talk freely with you breathing all over him like a wannabe policeman.'

This wasn't the way they had planned it but it made far more sense. Besides, he wouldn't understand a Spanish conversation anyway. Before he could say anything more, she was through the door and down the basement stairs. She didn't believe for a second that they would find out much else about Lia's teacher friend. As if a complete stranger would admit to looking after a bag of drugs or money. As if a complete stranger would talk to them at all. But if it meant not being deserted by Richard then she was happy to try. The barman *would* probably remember her and that was a bonus.

It looked as if the bar had only just opened for the day and she was the only person odd enough to be chasing a drink at this hour. There he was, the same barman she had chatted up the other night, with his spidery body, black T-shirt and black leather trousers, reminding her of the dancing and endless rounds, the tips and flirting.

'*Buenas días,*' she said, with a wave of a hand. She heard herself talking as if from a distance away. The barman remained expressionless.

'You remember me.' She framed it as a statement. Everyone remembered her.

Still the barman ignored her, wiping a cloth over and over the bar as if she were a stain that he could wipe away. Did he hate her? Had she offended him that night? She took out a cigarette and offered the man one. He took it and she lit up for both of them. Still he said nothing, and in the silence she listened to the sound of the cigarette paper crackling as it crept down towards her fingers. She looked around the room, pausing at the exact spot where Lia's friend had been stabbed. She turned back to the man and pointed to the tequila bottle behind him.

'One for me and one for you.'

The man finally looked at her. Aha, she thought with a smug grin. Got your attention now. He smiled a shark-like smile and poured them both a generous measure. She ignored the faint alarm bell going off in her head as she smelled the tangy liquid. Her doctor would be sorely disappointed; she could hear him now, telling her that she was simply asking to be destabilized. There would be no going back from this one, with or without the meds. The alcohol would banish the effects of the meds she had travelled so far to get, and she would wind up in a nuthouse, or dead, with no recollection of how she had got there.

He swirled the liquid around the glass and she lifted her own, conjuring up the feel of the liquid fire rushing down her throat. The way her moods were going, the way her 'brain chemistry', as Dr. Medina would put it, was feeling so explosive, it would be enough to push her into full-blown mania – she was sure of it. She'd start to talk and allow the millions of perfectly formed words to spill out of her mouth and they would have a wonderful time and he would think she was fabulous and tell her everything and anything she needed to know.

Macy passed more than enough money over to cover the drinks.

'My friend is heartbroken since her friend was attacked in here. Is there anything you can tell me about that night, please? It would be in the strictest of confidence and is just to help her come to terms with what happened.'

Her heart began to speed up with anxiety at the thought of leaving the bar with no useful information.

The man shook his head and she glanced down once again at the liquid fire calling her name.

'He was a good man. I don't know why he had to die,' he said.

She smiled, relieved. That was something at least.

'We saw that he had a case that he passed to you that night. Do you know what was in it or what happened to it?'

The man shook his head with a scowl. 'You should be careful asking so many questions, *señorita*. Why do you care?'

She held the glass to her lips, desperate to shoot the liquid down and make the task so much easier, but forced herself to put it down again.

'I don't care.'

Was it her imagination or had his tone changed to something altogether more nasty? It didn't once occur to her that she might be in danger. He leaned closer and suddenly the smell was overpowering, like wine mixed with tequila, beer – and urine? It repulsed her.

'Maybe you can be nice to me, *much* nicer to me, and I can tell you more?'

She sighed. She didn't want to return to Richard none the wiser. She looked once more at the glass and lifted it to her lips.

A noise behind her made her turn. It was a couple, or a hooker with a man; she wasn't sure. The man sat with his back to her and the woman looked drugged but it didn't stop her from yelling for a beer. Her raucous laughter rang out around the empty bar, fake and hysterical, until her companion slapped her into silence.

The barman leaned in to kiss Macy but she wasn't through talking. A sudden, overwhelming sorrow came over her and tears welled up in her eyes. She made no effort to hide them.

'Do you have *any* idea who attacked Rafael?' she heard herself asking and immediately felt better, cleaner somehow by using his name, as if it was some small act of defiance on her part. She surprised him even more then – oh yes, she'd always be a step ahead of the likes of men like this. She grabbed him by the back of his neck and held on much harder than was necessary, pulling him towards her but aware that she had closed her fingers around two delicate pressure points. She kissed him so hard that their front teeth clinked together, and then she leaned away from him and held him at arm's length, and waited.

The barman shook off her hold, rubbed his neck and switched on an old black and white TV before taking two beers out of the fridge and opening them for the couple sitting behind. He took the beers over and then took up his place behind the bar again.

'Rafael was a good man, a better man than me. Now drink your drink like a good girl.'

She picked up the glass, brought it to her lips and then let go, watching as it dropped to the table and bounced once on its side. The anticipated but non-existent sound of glass shattering was an anticlimax, but the barman didn't even seem to be annoyed with her as the transparent fluid spread across the surface between them.

'There are rumours he was involved in drug trafficking but somehow I don't believe it.' He grinned then, nodding to the other man as if they'd shared a private joke.

His reluctance to provide her with firm answers irritated her, as did his insistence on pouring her another massive shot of tequila.

'But who in their right mind hands over a briefcase in a bar, late at night, right?' she replied. 'I mean, come on!'

'I don't know what was in the case. It was lighter than a feather,' said the barman, 'as if it was empty.'

Out of the corner of her eye she noticed the other man getting up and heading over to the bar with what looked like an envelope in his hand. She tensed. Perhaps he thought he was being subtle or he expected her to look the other way, but she continued to watch as he slid the envelope under his hand towards the barman, who received it with barely a nod. The man was covered in tattoos, from his hands up his arms to his neck, and even over his bald head. Now that she was so close to him she could see that he was practically toothless. A lonesome yellow front tooth was framed by a black gum that reminded her of a congealed lump of raw chicken liver. She finally understood.

The toothless man turned to her then, just as the warning bells started to sound, and she told herself to get out of there while she still could.

'If he was one of us, we would have avenged his death by now, *señorita*.'

She nodded in dreadful acknowledgement. All she wanted to do was find Richard and escape. She glanced back at the girl who was swigging her beer, her face a merry red where the man had hit her. He was taking an unreasonable age to return to his table.

'Search her,' the barman whispered with a savage hiss.

Toothless man didn't need to be told twice and reached out suddenly, taking her by surprise as he yanked her off the bar stool. Fear dampened her forehead and lifted the hairs on her arms. It was an old, familiar fear that she felt shooting up inside her body, twisting around her ribs and stroking her with layers of anxiety. How could she honestly expect to help Lia and Richard when she'd proven so completely, time and time again, that she couldn't even help herself without falling apart or having a nervous breakdown?

'You really have no good reason to do this. Please,' she begged.

She'd been completely sober for a year, right up until she'd met Richard and Lia. She'd been on the longest stretch of sanity she could remember, sleeping perfectly, eating perfectly with the perfect amount of energy to take her through the day. The last episode she'd experienced had scared her and scarred her enough to stay away from alcohol; and yet she'd begun to feel bored. Meeting Lia and Richard had been wonderful and good for her, so why was she here now? Why? Did she have any useful information for Richard? She tried to remember but her thoughts seemed to distort and evaporate just before she could take hold of them. The distortion began to gather pace, faster and faster, spinning around her head, louder and more persistent as the disgusting toothless man groped her through her back pockets. Macy had had enough. She grabbed the shot glass and tipped the contents into her mouth, swallowing with a satisfied grunt.

Chapter 13

A greying, fair-skinned man strode up to the doorway. He was slim with a neat moustache, cashmere jumper and dark blue jeans. Ignoring Rodrigo, he addressed Lia.

'Can I help you?' He spoke perfect English.

'I hope so, I—'

'Wait a minute,' he said, and fired numerous orders in machine-gun Spanish at Rodrigo, who nodded moodily and walked away.

'One day that man is going to be the death of me,' he said, gritting his teeth as he stared after the retreating figure. He pushed up his sleeves to reveal tanned skin.

'Come in, come in,' he beckoned. She pulled off her trainers and followed him into the hallway. To her right was a dining room with a large wooden table and eight tucked-in Victorian oak chairs with claw feet.

'Please, have a seat.' He pointed to a chair and then almost ran over to pull it out for her. She jumped as he yelled, 'Faaavia!'

The old woman appeared and he nodded to Lia. 'Would you like a drink?'

Without waiting for her to reply, he turned to Favia and asked for two glasses of lemonade. He glanced at his watch and huffed. 'Would you excuse me for just a few minutes? I have to make a couple of phone calls.'

Lia looked around. On one side of the room, eight worn but well-kept saddles hung from wall racks. Most were English saddles but there were a couple of larger rodeo ones. A zebra skin adorned the wall, with a silver candleholder on each side. Wax had dripped onto the floor to form mini stalagmites. Children's riding boots littered the floor, along with an old car battery.

Black and white photos lined the opposite wall, of uniformed military men and horses, blank-faced and part of a long-gone era. There were no pictures of smiling children or a partner. A crooked, dog-eared image of Christ pegged to a cross was framed between two bay windows behind an antique Chesterfield.

The man returned.

'Sorry about that. Let me introduce myself. My name is Miguel Cana and I own this place.' He looked with pride at Lia and then smiled. 'And you are?'

'Lia Nightwood.'

'And what can I do for you, Lia?'

'I'm looking for work. Some locals told me that you might be interested. I could teach English, for example, or help out with administration. I have a CV that I can show you.'

She waited, trying to appear far more relaxed than she felt. Miguel fell into deep thought.

'Why Guatemala of all places?'

She hesitated. 'I love the Spanish language and I want to learn much more. My friend Richard, well, he plans to travel around the whole of Guatemala. But he has a larger budget than me—'

Miguel clapped his hands together like an excited child.

'It's a popular place for Spanish language students. Much cheaper than learning in Spain, right? Well, it may be destiny that you ended up here!' He stood up and started pacing around the table.

He paused dramatically. 'I've lived here for fourteen

years with my wife and children. I was fortunate enough to come across a small fortune in the days when I was running an insurance company with my sister. She put me in a very compromising situation though – screwed me up completely – and we finally agreed to sell the firm. I bought this place and moved with my wife and, at the time, my only child, Raul, out of the city. It was the best day of my life. I hardly speak to my sister now. Or that monster of a president who happens to be my sister's best friend.'

Speechless, Lia stared at him as he continued to pace.

'Do you know that the president was finally forced to resign?' He laughed, a hearty laugh of pleasure. 'Who would have thought it possible here in Guatemala?'

'I heard,' she replied. 'But what exactly did he do?'

'*¡La Línea!* It was a long-running scheme in which businesses paid bribes to avoid paying import duties through customs. Apparently he made millions off it.'

'Who will run the country until the next elections?'

'As the vice president was also arrested … But really, the way it works here, there are about twenty-five, thirty families in Guatemala and together they run the economy. Most of them are family friends, either through my wife or mother, or business ties. You should stay for lunch and I'll show you around.' He stopped to look at her. 'You don't have to go right now, do you?'

Lia shook her head and Miguel sat down beside her, drumming his fingers on the table.

'My wife and I don't get on these days. She's become a religious fanatic.' He looked at her as if he expected advice from her position of being another woman.

She took a deep breath. 'I think people usually turn to religion or become more religious when they're looking for solace … or when a situation has them isolated or scared.'

They stared at each other. Miguel looked as if he was trying to make up his mind about something. Then he let his breath out with a deep sigh, and Lia dropped her shoulders as she became aware of how tense she had been.

'Where are you from, Lia? You sound British but you don't look it.'

'I'm totally British,' said Lia. 'English on my dad's side and Chinese on my mum's.'

'Oh,' said Miguel, 'a Madame Butterfly.'

Lia stared at him with a quizzical eyebrow raised. She knew the story but there were far better comparisons to be made.

'Actually, no. Madame Butterfly was Japanese and my dad never abandoned my mother.'

'You're half-caste though.'

'Like Gok Wan, that TV presenter, or Jessica Henwick, the actress from Game of Thrones, which, believe it or not, I haven't seen.'

She didn't speak Chinese, had never been to China and barely knew any stories about her family there. Having spent more than half her life away from England, either culture felt wrong even if it was her actual background. She was like some kind of racial impostor, but she wasn't about to tell Miguel that.

'I have three beautiful children,' said Miguel as if she hadn't spoken. 'I'm running out of money and losing my wife but I have three beautiful children.'

Favia appeared with two glasses of lemonade on a tray and Lia got up to take the glasses.

'No, let her bring them.' Miguel waved her back down. 'She's used to it. Her name is Favia and she helps me. Before I was born she lived with my mother and she's looked after me all my life. When I moved here my mother sent her to come with me. She hates the city anyway and I treat her fairly. Favia *es mi amiga*, Lia.'

Favia smiled warmly at Lia, dark eyes twinkling as Lia pondered Miguel's use of the word *amiga*. She was even shorter than Lia. Her hair was worn in a loose middle parting in two wiry plaits that reached below her waist. A blue, short-sleeved shapeless dress finished below her knees and over it she wore a red knitted cardigan that lacked buttons. Her arms were freckled and saggy.

'*Con mucho gusto.*' Favia turned back to Miguel and smiled again before excusing herself.

'Who are they?' Lia asked, pointing to the pictures on the wall.

'My family.' Miguel stood and went to stand beside them. He pointed to one of the unsmiling men. 'This was my very strict father. He came from Germany and married my mother in Spain. Some time after the Second World War they moved to Guatemala. He's dead now and my mother lives in the city.'

They had just met but Miguel proceeded to tell Lia more about his family life. He asked Lia a couple of questions but mostly talked about himself. He came round to the subject of his wife again and asked Lia if she was religious.

She shook her head. 'I follow my own ethics and try not to make them my excuse for hurting anyone.'

He looked at her for a moment and nodded. 'Yes, I totally agree. Would you like to look around the finca?'

'Oh, yes please.'

Miguel's schoolboy enthusiasm returned. 'You can stay if you want. It's no problem at all. Favia can make the necessary arrangements. I'd like you to teach my children English and help them wherever you can. I'll show you what I'm doing, and maybe you can help me too.'

Miguel got up to put his boots on and Lia followed suit, delighted yet uncertain as she slipped her trainers back on. He hadn't insisted upon seeing her CV or even asked about her work experience, but he seemed friendly enough. She had the strongest feeling she was destined to end up here, and the thought of it somehow brought her closer to Rafael.

Chapter 14

Half an hour passed and there was no sign of Macy. Richard was doing his best to quell the negative thoughts but it was hard. What if he had inadvertently sent Macy to an early death? What if he found her, as he had Rafael, sprawled out on the floor in a puddle of her own bodily fluids? It would be his fault.

He burped, trying to keep his lunch down as he breathed in the overwhelming smell of open drains. He had almost given up on the idea of coming back to the bar as he'd tried to get them out of the hotel earlier. All Macy had been interested in was trying on all the clothes in her rucksack and then throwing them on the floor. She'd recited or made up some obscure poem about time, laughing with misguided triumph as she raced around the room. But then she'd seemed to focus and they'd agreed to go ahead with their plans. His plan. It had been his idea, he reminded himself.

His shirt was damp with sweat and his hands shook as he wiped them yet again down his trousers. He considered leaving her there. He could hail a cab, fetch his luggage and head for the airport. Leave Macy a note. *So sorry I let you down. I made a colossal error of judgement.* It sounded lame even for him. In his head he repeatedly asked God what He would have him do but God was curiously silent on the matter. Usually he'd hear an internal voice that would help him weigh up the pros and cons of whatever decision he had to make. There was no doubt that Macy was vulnerable, had asked for his support and he'd agreed to give it. What kind of person other than a coward would walk away?

Richard paced the street one more time and then turned, his mind made up. He scanned the street one last time and pushed open the door leading to the bar. He stopped and listened, hearing raised voices: a man and woman having a disagreement? Resigned to whatever awaited him, he let the door swing shut behind him and propelled himself down the stairs.

He saw three people. A large, overweight man he hadn't seen before pinned Macy against the bar. She was protesting but the barman had grabbed hold of her hair and pulled her head back, keeping her there, whilst the large man searched through her pockets. Macy managed to slap the man's fat hands away with a wonderful display of strength but he came right back to grope her chest as she fought to break loose. It was another woman he had heard from upstairs. She sat at a table nearby, shouting in Spanish, her voice shrill but having no effect on the men.

Both men looked up, and when they saw Richard, the barman let go of Macy's hair and the large man also stepped back.

'You took your sweet time,' said Macy, her hair unkempt. 'Look how badly behaved these boys are being.'

'Let's go,' he replied, trying to make his voice demanding and powerful.

Macy took a step towards him and at the same time, the barman dropped an arm out of sight and then lifted it back up to reveal a gun clasped in his hand, which he rested on the bar top, pointing at them.

Richard froze and Macy must have seen the change on his face because she too turned back to glance at the barman, and then the gun.

'Bloody hell. I cannot believe this is happening,' she said.

He felt disbelief and part of him wondered if he was dreaming, until he imagined being slumped against the wall with blood gushing from his wounds. His heart rate accelerated. The pastors in his church had taught him that the minute a good person died, everyone who had ever been loved by them would be there waiting at the gates to heaven, and he'd accepted this teaching without question. Now he suddenly saw the fallacy in this thinking, because everyone and everything that he'd ever loved was still here on the earth, vital and alive. He thought of Lia and wondered if she was safe. It suddenly dawned on him that he loved her, whatever that might mean. He twisted his watch round and round his wrist until he felt as if he might spontaneously combust with the knowledge that everything in his life at this moment was entirely out of his control.

'This was your stupid idea, Richard,' Macy said, her voice icy with rage. 'Pathetic and probably genetic.' She began a tirade of abuse, obviously aimed at him but in Spanish for the benefit of the men, who burst out laughing. She'd seen the gun but was still looking at him with crazed eyes, eyes that were weirdly devoid of fear. Even though he couldn't understand the words, the weight of her helpless rage was enough to break him down, and he felt himself blushing with shame. He was ashamed of himself for getting them into this mess – what had he been thinking? Was this who he was? Someone who endangered the lives of others for no good reason other than a complete lack of common sense?

He was about to put his arms up in the universal gesture of surrender because he figured that panicking wouldn't help them avoid being shot, but Macy seemed to get angrier and angrier as he stood there, helpless, until she was erupting like Mount Etna before his eyes, yelling at him for all she was worth. She was beyond crazy. Her face contorted into an expression he'd never seen before and never wanted to see ever again.

Perhaps at this point she had lava running through her veins rather than mere blood. In one swift movement she picked up a bar stool as if it was a twig and, to his horror, raised it over her head. She turned and brought it down as hard as she could over the barman, who collapsed with a grunt out of sight. The other man took one, two, then three steps back towards the table where the other woman was sitting and Macy reached for another stool. She let out a primal noise, somewhere between a roar and a scream, and stepped forward towards them. To Richard's relief the large man raised his hands in defeat and started talking to Macy in a soft, placatory tone while the woman looked on in stunned silence. He understood then that her rage, unharnessed, was their ticket to freedom.

'Macy! Macy! Let's go!'

She blinked once, twice, as if it was an effort to recognize who was calling to her, but then she threw the stool down on the floor, still with a superhuman strength that belied her stature. Chunks of wood smashed apart into numerous pieces, and Macy walked calmly to his side like a robot.

'The case. It was taken by another man that night, someone with a gun. We don't know who he was.'

It was the other woman who spoke, in heavily accented English. Richard whirled around to look at her, momentarily amazed that he could understand her, and then, finally galvanized into action, he grabbed Macy's hand and they ran.

Chapter 15

The finca sat on twenty-five acres of land. It was bordered to the west by a poultry farm and to the east by a wall of thick jungle that was strangling the four-foot-high fence surrounding the territory.

Lia enjoyed breathing the fresh, earthy air as they kicked and crunched their way through leaves and detritus. To their left, an area of fenced-off land sloped downward, thick with coffee bushes.

'In a few weeks I'll hire workers to pick the coffee and it'll be dried on the roof of my house.'

Miguel pointed to their far left. 'There are bananas and avocados over there. The plantations were growing long before I bought this land. They've had years to mature and really are exquisite.'

'You're so lucky you can just live off the land,' Lia said, sweeping her arms wide. She felt calmer than she had in days, as if there was some ancient energy in the roots of the trees, reaching from her body into the earth beneath her feet and grounding her. This place was surely everyone's dream.

He shook his head. 'It doesn't pay enough. I also cut and sell wood to a man called Carlos. He has the men, the trucks and the oxen to do the job. Come, I'll show you.'

They strolled down the hillside and came out onto a track of crispy, cracked mud. The air was sweet, heavy with birdsong, and Lia felt herself breathing in the scent of pine as if drunk. Below, all around them and stretching away into the horizon were thousands of thick, gnarled old trees. Vines snaked around trunks almost as wide as cars; rainbow-coloured wild flowers and shrubs hugged sprawling roots; birds spun and hovered in the golden light. The sun glittered above but the air was still cool as it caressed her hair and arms. She felt a sense of peace, realising how weary she was of concrete views and man-made smells. Perhaps she had belonged here in another life even. Miguel spoke again, his voice slicing through her thoughts.

'The thing is I'm running out of wood. I used to have other forms of business but I mainly cut wood now. My sister took a position in the government after we sold the insurance business and I haven't spoken to her for over six years. Let's just say I've extricated myself from political affairs.'

His face seemed to alternate between shame and sadness.

'The police take fifty per cent of my income because I haven't got a permit to cut wood. At this rate I'll be flat broke in a couple of years.' He turned to look at Lia and ran an agitated hand through his hair before gazing out over the land again.

'I don't really care about myself; it's my children this is all for. I want them to be secure and my oldest loves this place. He would hate living in the city.'

She heard the rhythmic beat of paws before she saw three dogs sprinting towards them. They disappeared into dense foliage on the other side of the track.

'Raul's dogs. They're all fine except the big one. Lobo. Half coyote. He has bitten before so be careful.'

As if such a minor detail could ruin her mood.

They came out into a valley clearing where the land had been stripped of trees for as far as she could see. A man used a stick to smack the hides of four oxen pulling a tree trunk towards an old Mercedes truck. On the opposite hillside, tree stumps covered the earth and women hacked away at them with machetes. It was an ugly reminder that anything beautiful and precious could be stripped away.

'Those are K'iche' and Q'eqchi' women collecting *ocote*. It's a type of firelighter used for cooking. I sell that too.'

As they approached the truck, Miguel shouted a greeting.

'Carlos, *¿cómo estás?*'

'*Bien, bien,* Miguel.'

He looked directly at Miguel, his body upright, his stature the opposite of the subservience displayed by Favia and Rodrigo. He offered his hand to Lia to shake before climbing with agility into the truck.

Miguel turned to Lia again as Carlos waved and moved away. 'Do you like horses?'

Without waiting for her reply, he continued along the track. She stared around again at the razed land and the workers on the hillside. The oxen stumbled past with their ribs jutting out, ears and eyes drooping as they dragged their wooden load. They were harnessed together by a lump of wood tied behind their horns. Flies swarmed round a bloody, seeping wound on the neck of the ox closest to Lia. A skinny boy with only one arm urged them on. He nodded to Lia and she nodded back before breaking into a jog to catch up with Miguel.

'I love horses. They are my one real passion in life,' said Miguel. 'I started with four and now I have twenty-six. You can ride them whenever you like. That's another thing about my wife. She's never really loved living here in this beautiful wilderness and she won't ride the horses. I've never understood.'

'Who's the boy with the amputated arm?'

'That's Aapo, Carlos's boy. Lost his arm in a wood-cutting factory. But he's fine now.' He dismissed the topic with a flourish of his hand.

'The brown ox has a wound on its neck,' Lia said.

'Vampire bats. The boy will ask Favia for garlic.'

Lia shuddered. 'Do they bite people?'

'Just the horses and oxen. You can see them flying around at night. The only danger *you* have to worry about, apart from the Indians' – he broke off to smile briefly at her – 'are the bees. Last year they killed my donkey.'

'What can you do to protect yourself?' Lia asked.

'Remain absolutely still until they go away.'

'That's it?' She raised her voice in surprise.

'They detect movement and that attracts them. That's how the donkey met its fate. Usually you can hear an electrical buzzing sound before you see them. Get inside and close the windows and doors.' He mimicked the sound and smiled again, a boyish grin of amusement. She grinned back and realized she had almost forgotten how good it felt.

'The quickest way to make a friend is to smile at a stranger,' he muttered softly before walking on.

They crossed a small bridge made of two planks of wood. Miguel pointed to a shack with different-sized pieces of aluminium tacked over it. In the yard a few chickens pecked at the bare surface whilst a bony dog slept fitfully beside them, sprawled out in the sun.

'That's Marco's house. His wife, Lola, might be in.'

Lia startled as she heard the names of Rafael's family.

Miguel called out and a barefoot woman with a small frame opened the door. A little boy with a lazy eye popped his head round the doorway and drew closer to his mother. Miguel introduced Lia and she waited expectantly for some kind of recognition from the woman, something to indicate that her name rang a bell, but Lola wouldn't even look directly at her, much less say anything. Lia bent down to introduce herself to the little boy and was about to tell Lola that she was a friend of Rafael's but Lola abruptly excused herself and pulled the child back inside, closing the door. Lia stood, flushed with embarrassment, but Miguel didn't seem to notice. Had Rafael really told his family about her?

They turned to go and Miguel pointed to another shack.

Barbed wire ran between wooden posts to form a fence on one side, upon which rags of clothing dried in the sun.

'That's Rodrigo's place, the man who drove you here. He lives like a pig; he's a violent alcoholic and beats his wife and children. His wife is pregnant again but he drinks his wages away and his family is always going hungry because of it. Rodrigo runs errands for me but he can be lazy. He takes avocados and lemons to the pueblo to sell and helps around the finca.'

He pointed to a slightly larger house a hundred or so feet away. It was made of stone and fenced off with a much bigger backyard.

'That's where José lives, my chauffeur. He takes my children to school and collects them in the afternoon.'

'Do these houses come with clean running water?' She stared at the shacks and pictured his house on the top of the hill. 'Do the children go to school?'

Miguel nodded. 'All the properties on my land are supplied with clean well water, the same water from which our drinks were made.

'José's children go to school.' He turned to face her. 'I can't keep up with them all. Marco and Lola once had about twenty family members living in one room and it was truly disgusting. I told him either some of them go or they all go, including him. It was unbelievable.'

Lia was too shocked to reply.

'Most of the families were already living on this land before I bought it.'

'You bought the people along with the land?' Lia was incredulous.

'No, I bought the land! There was a period of adjustment and they're glad to receive wages working for me now. I didn't make them leave and at least I pay them. Some of the other landowners round here are terrible when it comes to parting with money.'

Lia was silent, turning over his words. It was hard to believe that this was the man Rafael had imagined her working for. She thought of the dwindling amount of money she had left.

'If you accept a position here, it's best you stay in my house for a few days. There are five spare rooms. I'll show you another little house that you could move into but it needs to be cleaned first.'

He moved on and Lia leaped down the path after him, unsure if she had heard correctly. Did he really just offer her a whole house of her own to live in? Miguel pointed to a small brick cottage in the distance.

'It'll be perfect. We just need to change some of the window panes, fix the doors a little and move some furniture in.'

He stared at her again with a half smile. 'I think you're like me and my son. You have a spirit that is only truly fed and nourished by nature.'

She looked around them again, charmed by his perception of her.

'It's so peaceful here,' she remarked, 'away from the crazy pace of the city.'

They reached the house and he pushed open a front door that was supported by only one hinge at the top. Inside it was dark and musty with clouds of cobwebs smothering the wooden-beamed roof. Lia forced herself to walk inside. The few intact windows were too dirty to see through. The tiny cottage consisted of a rectangular room with two doors leading off to the right. Lia pushed at one of the doors and it fell inwards, slamming heavily onto the floor with a boom that shook the house. A cloud of dust rose to blanket the room, intensifying the smell of old cellar. There was nothing inside except a stack of old paintings propped up against the wall, mostly of horses. Lia coughed on the dust and backed out.

Miguel smiled at her, half doubtful, half eager. 'This can be one room, and next door there's another just the same.'

She stared at the rickety door. 'Is it safe here?'

'Oh yes, the civil war ended twenty years ago, you know,' he said with a laugh. 'It's completely safe; well, on my finca anyway. No one will bother you here.'

He tailed off, suddenly distracted, and looked at his watch.

'I have a meeting in a few minutes. You know where the house is. Have a think about it and then please join me for lunch.'

He didn't wait for her to reply but turned on his heel and left. Lia watched, deep in thought, as he strolled away up the field.

Chapter 16

Until that last day in the city, Richard had never really felt terror and he'd never known that he possessed the kind of legs that would lift him so effortlessly up a steep flight of stairs, two at a time, and out of the city. The next twenty minutes were a moving nightmare in which the ground blurred below, and all he could hear was the regular thump of his feet merging with Macy's beats. He imagined himself falling forward against the pavement as a bullet lodged itself into his spine or his buttocks, and the thought drove him on faster as they whipped past shuttered shops, open pharmacies and endless people.

'I can't run any more,' Macy gasped, tugging on his hand, increasing her resistance with every stride until they were jogging and then walking. He couldn't see anyone following them. He had no idea where they were and jumped in alarm at the crack of fireworks going off nearby. His head throbbed.

'We'll get a taxi,' he gasped, waving at a car. The first driver he signalled performed a rapid U-turn and pulled up beside them.

'Holiday Inn Hotel, *por favor*.'

The man nodded and seemed impervious to the fact that both he and Macy were trembling like frightened deer.

'There's a car following us,' said Macy as she stared out the back window. 'It's them.'

Richard's heart missed a beat and his skin crawled with

renewed, itchy sweat. He turned to look but there was no car immediately behind them and the nearest vehicle was just turning off at the last intersection.

'I think we're fine, Macy,' he tried to reassure her and took her sweaty palm in his, sensing that he needed to calm her, but she pulled away as if he had tried to touch her inappropriately.

'It's still there, Richard,' she said, frowning at him. 'When are they going to stop the Nazi machine?'

'Nazi machine?' She sounded paranoid.

'Don't you know? That imperialist one. You don't know much considering people are trying to kill us.'

Her eyes were wide open and he could see the whites all around her irises. He had to try and keep her calm, but he was spooked by her demeanour and still smarting from the tirade of abuse she had thrown his way.

'What did you manage to find out?' he eventually asked.

'About what?'

'Rafael. What did they say about him?'

'Who?' She had begun to swat imaginary insects from around her face.

Richard sighed. 'It's the whole reason we're here.'

'And you, my dear friend, are a very sexy person when you're hot and bothered. But don't think I don't know exactly what's going on. Invisible people with their sadistic greed. I think I used to be one of them. Do you know I used to order sex on the internet just as easily as pizza?'

'What do you mean?'

'I can hear them talking to me. Voices chatter-chattering in my head, telling me about things, all deceits and falsehoods. I get it!' She waved her arms wildly around her head, nodding up and down.

She wouldn't stop moving around next to him, fidgeting as if she'd overdosed on caffeine, and she wouldn't stop talking.

'Everything has gone wrong here, it's really terrible, and to think I used to be one of them too, a corporate-climbing moron who didn't stop once to think about anything real. I had the best of everything, Richard, just like you, and then I lost it all.'

They were pulling up to the hotel entrance but Macy was oblivious and continued to chatter, almost as if to herself.

'Wait here,' said Richard, interrupting her flow. 'I'm just going to get our bags and then we can ask the driver to take us on to San José Patula. It'll be quicker and safer than a bus.'

'You're not leaving me here alone,' she whispered, grabbing his shirtsleeve.

'I'll be back in a minute,' he promised.

She shook her head. 'I'm coming with you.'

'It'll save us from having to find another taxi if you can just wait for me,' he said.

'You're trying to abandon me and I thought we had a deal,' she said, on the verge of tears.

Richard sighed in bewilderment. He had always found it difficult to make friends. So when he did, he wanted to keep them, preferably for life; and yet he was beginning to resent Macy for making everything so much harder than it needed to be. It was rare that he made a connection with someone so fast, but this person sitting beside him bore no relation to the girl he and Lia had met just a few days ago. He shook his head. Even so, there was something about her spirit, an authenticity that he didn't want to pass up. He didn't want to unfriend her. He wanted to try to make up for the danger he was guilty of placing her in.

The taxi driver was watching them in the rear view mirror and lost patience.

'*Pague ahora, por favor.*'

'I'll pay him,' said Macy. She rummaged through her pockets, passed a few notes over and slipped out of the car behind him.

In the hotel, Richard pointed Macy to a sofa and grabbed an English-version newspaper, thrusting it towards her as if it would help her blend in to their surroundings, before heading off to the luggage storage room. He handed in their ticket number and retrieved their bags, relieved he'd managed to get his shaking hands under control.

In less than five minutes he was heading back towards reception but stopped, his head swivelling as he searched for Macy. She wasn't where he had left her. He searched the lobby of the hotel but there was no sign. He dropped their bags and ran outside, searching up and down the street. It was impossible to miss her standing in the middle of the road. It looked as if she was bowing to passing cars, unperturbed by the blasts of car horns trying to move her out of the way. She saw him and waved. She still had the newspaper he'd handed her rolled up in her hand.

'Everything is divine, Richard. I want everyone to know that they are simply divine,' she shouted over the traffic, narrowly avoiding a pickup truck that swerved to miss her.

'Watch out!' he yelled.

'It's a revelation!'

'Come back here, please, before you get yourself killed!' The fear was like a knife in his gut as he pleaded with her. There was no more denying it. She was mentally ill. It was serious and her mind was starting to fail.

'This is my unfabricated true nature, Richard,' she offered by way of explanation.

'You need to rest,' he said.

'I need to stay blessed,' she said, 'until we all have the sense to protest at the way poverty and need is trumped by greed.' She pointed to the hotel and at him, as if to indicate the greed around them.

Richard stepped off the pavement as soon as it was safe to do so and grabbed Macy by the arm, dragging her back with him to safety. Several pedestrians had stopped to stare, building a small crowd next to the hotel security guards who were also watching with growing suspicion. He was anxious not to give them any further reason to congregate and tried his best to reassure the guards with a nod.

'You could have got yourself run over.'

'So now you're my knight in shining Armani,' she replied with a wink.

'Where are the pills you got from Cobán?'

'In my rucksack where I packed them, silly.'

'How many do you take?'

'Two of each. Why not, hey?' She frowned. 'Goodbye Macy, hello boring, dull, numb, unsexy nobody.'

They were back in the lobby now, hovering by their bags, with Macy still clenching the newspaper in one hand. She pointed to the side pocket containing some of her pills and he wasted no time in getting them out. He unscrewed a small bottle of water and handed it to her. She took the pills without complaint and nodded to him as their eyes met, a silent acknowledgement that she was prepared to let him help her in any small way that he could.

'Now we take a taxi to that finca place in San José Patula and find out what's happened to Lia. But I need you to tell me what happened in the bar, so please, Macy, just take a deep breath and think.'

She acted as if she hadn't heard him. He wouldn't risk letting her out of his sight again and guided her with him, one hand wrapped loosely around her arm.

The receptionist, her face etched into a polite see-no-evil, hear-no-evil, told them to sit down and said that there would be a ten-minute wait for a taxi due to developments in the city.

'What developments?' he asked.

'The president of Guatemala has been taken to jail,' she said with a bright smile.

'No!' Macy exclaimed, leaping up from her chair.

The receptionist nodded and turned to serve someone else.

'Oh my holy batshit!' said Macy, turning to Richard. 'This is a sign.'

'Does that mean that there is currently no one in charge right now?' said Richard, keeping his voice low, desperate to keep Macy from getting more agitated. 'Let's have a look at that newspaper, please.'

To his relief Macy sat back down next to him and unrolled the paper, straightening it out so that they could both read it. But Macy didn't have the level of focus required and soon gave up after turning a few pages. An article caught Richard's eye.

Guatemalan man stabbed to death in the city

GUATEMALA CITY - Another adult male has been stabbed to death in a bar in the Guatemalan capital, authorities say, bringing the total number of murders to over 6,000 since the start of the year. No one has been arrested in connection with Monday's incident, a police inspector told the Guatemala Times.

Rafael Roldan was alleged to be part of a drug cartel with ties to the Mara 18, an internationally renowned gang engaged in murder, drug dealing, kidnap and the trafficking of people. It is believed a rival gang competing for control of the neighbourhood killed him with a knife.

According to sources in San José Patula, where Roldan originated, he moved to the city and joined the Mara 18 in a bid to escape poverty and an unstable, abusive family.

In a country that has taken centre stage in the global drug trade, Guatemala has become a thoroughfare used by many drug trafficking organizations. The Mara 18 has expanded their influence amid the disarray following the 36-year civil war, and the murder rate in Guatemala is now higher than it was during the country's civil war.

In a nation of 17 million people, Guatemala's criminal organizations are the most sophisticated and dangerous in Central America. Transporting illegal drugs comprises the bulk of their activity.

He put the newspaper down just as the receptionist informed them that their taxi had arrived, but he kept what he had just read to himself. It was here, finally: proof that Rafael had been up to no good, and precisely what he needed to show Lia that he had been right all along.

'Let's go, Macy,' he said.

'Finally! Get up, then. Because you're just sitting there and I'm trying so hard to come down to and be at your level, you know, I'm synchronizing down, but I also feel like I might be of a higher intelligence because I can talk and read so much faster right now.'

She jumped up and span 360 degrees on her heels, and with one last look at the receptionist who was walking back to her desk, Richard ripped the page out of the newspaper, folded it and pushed it down into his shirt pocket.

Macy bent closer to him.

'Rafael wasn't a drug dealer or a gangster, Richard. He wasn't like the guys in the bar at all. He was actually one of the good guys.'

She turned again and headed for the exit. Richard got up, hoisted her rucksack over one shoulder and then picked his own bag up to head after her. She was clearly nuts and no longer knew what she was talking about. At least the rest of their journey would be simple, he thought to himself. All they had to do was get in the car and let the driver drive.

Chapter 17

The men were already drunk by the time Lia returned to the main house. Miguel was seated with two guests in the dining room, reaching for the Johnnie Walker bottle, when he saw her removing her shoes at the door.

'Come and join us, Lia. I would like to introduce you to my friends: Gary Davis, who works at American Business Services, and Nelson Morales from the Ministry of Agriculture.'

All three men were reddened from the alcohol and she realized she'd interrupted a lively conversation. She said little but once Miguel had introduced her as someone who would be working with him, they were pleasant enough. The conversation returned to politics.

'I've been let down too many times by people I trusted,' said Miguel, pouring whisky into a tall glass. Her stomach flipped at the generous measure.

'About two years ago I won a large sum of money on a lottery-type thing, and at the time, the Minister of Interior owed me a lot of money, seven hundred thousand quetzales to be precise. I was getting into my car when a plastic bag was put over my head and I was taken away – kidnapped – for fourteen hours. This is my country and I still don't know where they took me.'

He paused. 'Then they took me to jail where I stayed for two days. My chauffeur, José, was with me. We were scared to death. Terrible things went on inside that place.' His face crumbled as the memories returned. His guests were silent.

'After two days I was taken to another room and told to sign a piece of paper to say that the Minister of Interior had paid back the money he owed. I had a gun to my head. Of course I'm a coward. I just wanted to get out of that place so I signed it straight away. My chauffeur was incredible. We were stuck together for forty-eight hours, you know, and my family came to see us when they heard and brought money and cigarettes which we gave to the others so they'd leave us alone. José was so scared, he even cried. What we saw in that hell reduced him to a wreck ...'

Miguel got up and paced the length of the dining table. 'And you know what? The Indian was loyal to me. Loyal! He could have easily joined the other Indians in there and would have been in a safer position. He could have left me on my own to get beaten, raped or stabbed. But he didn't. He probably saved my life. People like me don't go to prison, you know ...'

The tension in the room was palpable and Lia sighed inwardly, wondering where it was leading.

'I cannot trust anyone on the finca. That's the bottom line, Lia. And I can't go on like this. When I need to be sorting out my affairs in the city I need someone here to oversee things. I need help.'

'But the way you have the business running now, it is not possible for you to be granted a felling licence,' Morales interjected. 'You don't meet the criteria.'

'What are the specific criteria?' asked Davis, slurring his words over the table as he reached for the bottle.

'Reforestation,' said Morales. 'If you are willing to invest in reforestation of up to seventy-five per cent of the land that has been felled, I can get you a licence.'

'It's a huge job and I keep telling you I cannot afford the workers. Neither will it bring immediate returns or benefits to my family,' said Miguel.

'Isn't that where Davis comes in?' said Morales, prodding the man in the ribs. 'Your company was set up to help businesses achieve export success and you sit there, telling us how you want to buy the wood. Perhaps you can advance a loan to enable Miguel to start reforesting?'

Davis grunted and shook his head. He was about to speak but Lia got there first.

'I've got a degree in ecology and I could put together a team of volunteers. This is such a beautiful place that if you – we – were to offer food and accommodation in return for labour, I think you'd get a steady stream of gringos coming through to help reforest. I could put up flyers in the city.'

A smile spread across Miguel's face. 'Do you really think?'

'Of course!' said Lia. *What* did she just say? The words had slipped out without warning and she bit her tongue, hoping she wasn't being overly ambitious.

'Okay, fine. If you can provide the labour force, I'll support it.'

Morales stared at her with appreciation bordering on lechery. 'Not just a pretty face, I see.'

Davis continued to prop himself up by the elbows against the table, eyelids drooping. Miguel looked at the man with distaste, something that Morales was quick to spot.

'I think we'll be on our way, Miguel. Thank you very much for your kind hospitality as always. Come to my office once you have this project mapped out in detail.'

Morales stumbled as he got up but was quick to recover.

'You won't stay for lunch?' said Miguel.

Morales shook his head, reached over to Davis and placed a hand on his shoulder. 'Let's go.'

Miguel shook hands with Morales but ignored Davis, who pulled himself with sluggish difficulty out of his chair. Lia remained seated as Miguel walked them out.

Favia limped through the hallway, laden with plates of

food, and Lia got up to help, taking the dishes and placing them down on the table. The aroma of steak filled the dining room and Lia's mouth watered at the sight of meat, tortillas, salad, potatoes and *chiltepe*, a homemade chilli sauce oozing the scents of mint, lemon, onions and tomatoes.

Moments later Miguel sat back down and invited her to start eating as Favia returned to the kitchen. '*Buen provecho*.'

She realized she was ravenous and helped herself to generous portions, eating with gusto whilst Miguel picked at a plate before getting Favia to take it away.

'Aren't you hungry?' Lia asked.

'I'd rather have another drink,' he replied, pouring the remainder of the Red Label into his glass.

'I want you to meet Don Chema, my foreman, and Tomás later today.'

She looked up from her plate and agreed.

'Don Chema's responsible for measuring the wood after a tree has been cut. But he can't write. So he measures the wood, calls it out and Tomás writes it down. Tomás can barely write. They're all illiterate. I did have someone, but sadly he won't be coming back.'

Lia frowned. Was he making a reference to Rafael?

'Did someone leave? Or—'

'Yes.' He took a sip of whisky. 'So I'd like you to measure the wood and write it down. Cut Don Chema and Tomás out the loop.'

'Replace them?'

'They receive a weekly wage off me that won't change because there's always so much to do. They get thirty quetzales a week but I'll happily pay you two hundred per month.'

'Thank you for the offer.' Lia needed time to think and reached for more food. 'The wood logging at the moment is actually illegal?'

'I suppose it is, yes.' Miguel grinned as if to reassure her. 'But the police won't do anything if I keep paying them.' He sobered. 'If you can help me with the reforesting, I could get legal and stop paying them.'

Lia swallowed another large mouthful of the delicious steak. 'How do the workers use wood? You mentioned that *ocote* was used to start fires.'

'They need it for cooking, fixing their houses, making tools. They can buy it from me cheaper than anywhere else.'

Lia nodded.

'I'd like to have a meeting with the local community to put our ideas to them and ask for their feedback and suggestions.' She took another swig of the whisky and realized her head was spinning in spite of all the food she was eating.

Miguel threw back his head and laughed. 'You don't need to ask them anything. You're going to have to get used to telling them what to do if you work here.'

'Oh, I just thought, you know, consulting would—'

Miguel stood up and circled the table. 'Where are you from?'

She hesitated before replying. 'London.'

'Well, our worlds are very different, granted, but in both countries things are done according to breeding and class. I know what London is like, I spent years there. Different places and different times, but don't be so naïve to think that London does not thrive on its own underclass of unconsulted servants.'

'I don't think I'm naïve,' Lia replied, suddenly hoarse. 'Why are you so against a process of consultation?'

'They would demand things I can't give them.' He spoke as if she were a child.

'More money, more free time, more time to drink alcohol. They'd hold a machete to my throat with their demands. I just want to live in peace.'

Lia watched Miguel reach for the bottle and then stop midway as he remembered that it was empty. At last Lia changed tack, painfully reminded of the violence with which Rafael's life had been taken.

'I'm sorry,' she said. 'I've been in Guatemala for less than a month and I guess I just don't understand as much as I'd like to think I do.' She produced a lopsided grimace that she hoped would pass for a smile.

He smiled, his eyes softening, and pulled the chair next to hers closer and sat down, leaning forward to take her hand.

'I want you to feel welcome here and to be a part of my family. I want you to feel safe. I'm offering you a place to live, first-rate food, a wage, my horses to ride and part of my land to reforest.'

She couldn't hide the delight in her eyes as she stared back at him.

'Thank you, that's truly generous.' She couldn't believe her luck.

Miguel glanced at the antique wall clock hanging above her. 'You can use today to look around. I'll show you to your room afterwards and get Marco and Tomás to start cleaning and fixing up that house.' Lia nodded. There seemed no point in mentioning Rafael yet. Miguel got up to leave the table but then paused.

'I want you to know that I treat the workers very well compared to the other landowners round here. I know how to say please and thank you.' She reached for a tortilla, wrapping it around the remainder of meat on her plate.

After she'd finished, he called Favia to remove the dishes and show Lia to a bedroom. Seconds later she heard a car start up and drive away.

The room was large with marble flooring, an en-suite bathroom and flowery wallpaper. A quick inspection of the cupboards revealed women's clothes in the hundreds that Lia guessed belonged to his estranged wife.

She sat on the edge of the bed and flopped backwards. The bed was springy and the covers smelled freshly laundered. She had got what she wanted and far more. She had landed a fantastic job in the most beautiful countryside she had ever seen. She had a roof over her head, great food to eat and she felt safe. But she couldn't explain the gnawing emptiness in her chest. Part of her couldn't believe she had made it to the finca without Rafael. Anger and frustration began to bubble deep inside her and then she thought of Richard and how awful she had been to him, no doubt driving him away for good. Her anger dissipated. She would accept the job offer. But she would also try her hardest to befriend Rafael's family and see if she could find out why his life had been destroyed.

Chapter 18

Macy no longer knew if it was day or night. Perhaps this was what it felt like to be born, or maybe she had actually died and started a very long journey to her own private hell. Anything was possible. She would never be able to recall how they had ended up in a taxi just outside Finca San Isidro. By the time she left the bar with Richard she was malfunctioning like a virus-infected computer, seeing killers everywhere and unable to understand why her body, in particular her arms, ached so much.

Snatches of memory played tricks on her. She remembered them running for their lives and getting into a strange car. All had been well until Richard had tried to get rid of her, and then they'd somehow ended up back at the hotel again. Her brain had continued in meltdown mode and she had no idea how to stop it. Another car ride.

She had tried to talk to Richard but heard her voice as nonsensical gibberish. Somehow he had convinced her to take more pills. It was a crude and dangerous form of crisis management but she was immensely grateful. She admired Richard for not leaving her alone to get swallowed up by Guatemala. People she'd known for much longer had washed their hands of her both during an episode and afterwards. She would never forget her ex for as long as she lived, the one person she'd loved romantically with all her heart and who'd loved her back, for a time. But she had never once blamed him for leaving because she knew he'd done it to save himself.

Given how little Richard actually knew her in comparison, she owed him a debt of gratitude. Perhaps he was the reason she was still alive, if that was what this was. Richard, the anti-hero.

Once she'd taken the pills he had bundled her into another car and continued to talk, repeatedly telling her to keep calm and quiet to avoid them being turfed out and left in the middle of nowhere, so he said. He reminded her that they were going to find Lia. Were they planning to rescue her? She surely didn't need it. Lia was one of the most pig-headed people she had had the pleasure of meeting recently, too damn proud to accept help from anyone. Unlike her! Macy knew she had to concentrate on getting herself well – though at times there was nothing better than losing her mind. Touch was sensual, colours were brighter and clearer, and ideas abounded in her head. But she was no fool. No. She was a goddess. She remembered seeing his mouth move but not being able to hear what he was saying. She had the vague sense that they were moving again and Richard was looking down at her, his face huge and round and worried. The pills had started to kick in. His voice had bitten painfully into her skull until she had the sense that she was gliding underwater, deeper and deeper, with a weight as heavy as the world pressing down upon her head and shoulders. Even so, her heart insisted on slamming against her ribs, fast and furious, annoying her with its insistence when all she wanted to do was silence it forever. The world was an ugly, scary, nonsensical place and she decided there and then that she wanted no more part of it.

Perhaps the thing that saved her from herself was that somewhere in the depths of her mind she already knew that she had bipolar. She had been through it before and accepted the diagnosis in another lifetime. So when Richard produced a bag of chilli-coated chips out of nowhere and forced one into her mouth, she didn't struggle. She felt as if she had no teeth with which to chew and she ate with the speed of a very old tortoise, taking an eternity to swallow, but she did eat something. Her hands shook too badly to feed herself but Richard wouldn't give up on her, and the fact that he was still there, trying to help her, moved her to tears.

'You've got to eat, even if it's just one mouthful. The heat of the chillies is going to help blow this illness out of your mind and body,' he said.

Had he really said that or was she making it up? Had she smashed a wooden bar stool over someone's head or not? If she had, didn't that make her a danger to herself and others? Coming to terms with the degradation of being sectioned three times in England and meeting other crazies – nut jobs – freaks – she hadn't ever wanted to believe that there was anything of herself lurking in derogatory terms like that, but it was what most people thought when they learned that she had a mental condition. Richard had assured her that she hadn't killed the barman or Rafael. Unless he was lying, she had struck gold in having him for a friend, and she didn't understand why Lia couldn't see how amazing he was. He was down to earth, sensible and loyal. He radiated kindness and honesty.

Macy also knew she was one of the lucky ones because her bipolar episodes were mild compared to those of some of the people she'd met in hospital. A week, two weeks, maybe even three would go by, and then she would start to feel better. Her head might feel as if it was one big rock and she wouldn't have a clue what day it was, but eventually she'd regain the togetherness required to get up and stay up, out of bed, and she would give herself no choice but to face living again. That's if she could get to a bed in the first place, something she couldn't take for granted.

It didn't help that right now she was drowning as the pills kicked in, unable to fight unconsciousness any more. The last thing she remembered about the taxi ride was the worried, scared look on Richard's face as the driver announced that he wouldn't take them any further and told them to get out. Of course, Richard wouldn't be able to understand what the driver was saying and would take his sweet time, irritating the man even more, who would repeat his nervous hand-pointing gestures.

She was exhausted from trying to understand what was happening and all the questions from Richard about Rafael. Who the hell was Rafael? Was he a drug dealer or wasn't he? And who cared? Did it even matter any more if he was dead? That was the moment she finally passed out.

Chapter 19

'Wake up! Go and tell Favia what you wish to eat. After you've had breakfast I'll show you some of the work I want you to take on,' said Miguel.

His voice was muffled as the hollow echo of his knuckles rapped on the door. It was six fifteen.

Lia opened the door with a bright smile, relieved that she had forced herself out of bed so early. She had slept well and already showered, and she was determined to climb mountains, swim oceans or whatever it would take to make her new job a success.

'Good.' He smiled back in approval, turned on his heels and she padded after him down the corridor, turning into the kitchen whilst he headed in the direction of the study.

'*Buenos días*, Favia,' she said, pulling a chair out and sitting at the dark wooden table. There were all the amenities you'd expect to find in a modern kitchen, including a large coffee machine and a dishwasher. The welcome smell of coffee perfumed the air.

'*Buenos días*,' said Favia. '*¿Qué quiere comer?*'

She asked for scrambled eggs and toast and then stood up to help, but with no idea where to find anything it was soon apparent she was just getting in the way. Favia took her hand, the beginnings of a smile lifting her lips, and tugged it back towards the chair.

'*Este es mi trabajo,*' she kept repeating. This is my work.

Lia sat back down and Favia nodded in approval. They lapsed back into silence as she laid a place setting and filled a mug with coffee.

Lia sighed.

'*Soy una amiga de Rafael,*' she murmured. I am a friend of Rafael.

Favia stiffened. The mug she carried trembled, spilling hot liquid down the sides. She placed it down next to Lia, opened her mouth and Lia was sure she would have spoken if Miguel hadn't entered the room just then. Instead she resumed the passive expression Lia was becoming familiar with.

'I trust you slept well?' said Miguel.

'Yes, thank you.'

'When you've finished I'll take you to my son's room. The computer's in there.'

He took a seat opposite her and was soon engrossed in a newspaper, while Favia paid no further attention to her.

Raul's room was decorated in Arsenal memorabilia and a life-sized poster of Ronaldinho. It was very tidy for a typical fourteen-year-old boy's room and big enough to play football in.

The graceful Georgian Chippendale desk housing the computer looked out of place, but the work was easy. She simply had to input all the tree measurements written in a flimsy, tattered notebook over the last year into a computer database in the form of length, breadth and width, arriving at figures in square feet. Each square foot was then valued depending on the type and quality of wood that had been cut down.

'Is the computer connected to the internet?' she asked.

Miguel shook his head. 'Out here we have enough trouble just keeping the phone lines up, I'm afraid.'

She caught a whiff of Old Spice mixed with minty toothpaste when he rested a hand lightly on her shoulder. 'My children will be back soon so you'll get to meet them.' He patted her shoulder and left.

On the wall above her hung an out-of-date Miss World calendar. A little more than two weeks away from England and already so much had happened. She wondered what Miguel would do if she got any of the numbers wrong. Would he yell? Fire her? She went through the figures, double-checking that she'd input them all correctly.

At 11 a.m. Lia closed down the computer and got up to stretch. She decided to walk around the same patch of land she had covered with Miguel the day before and stop at Lola's house again.

She slipped on her trainers and headed down the grassy slope at the back of the house. All she wanted to do was offer her sympathies and share with Lola how she had known Rafael. She crossed over the small bridge and tried not to think about how Lola had virtually slammed the door in her face when she'd been introduced by Miguel.

She knocked twice, able to clearly hear the muffled sounds of someone moving around inside, but there was no answer. Perhaps Lola was too upset with grief to open the door. She lowered her head with a sigh, resisting the temptation to lean against the door. The last thing she wanted was to be seen as some kind of pest. She kicked a small stone across the ground and turned on her heels, planning to return later that day.

Raul's dogs were lying across the path just before the makeshift bridge. She walked towards them, eager to make friends, but the dog-coyote gave her a bad feeling, staring at her with its lips drawn back. She stopped. It got up and began to charge towards her. How could she fend off a 120-pound animal intent on mauling her? She had no hope of running away.

Lia braced herself for the attack but it never came. The animal looped around her and snapped at her hands, which she dug deep into her pockets. She stood upright like a monument, her pulse thundering through her ears. The other two dogs approached, tails wagging, tongues lolling, and she remembered to breathe. The dog-coyote seemed to look at her with disdain and then trotted away as if she'd imagined its deadly intent.

She struggled to release herself from the vice-like grip of her fear and then made a fuss of the other two dogs before walking back the way she had come. She wondered how she would be able to do anything constructive whilst sharing the land with such an unpredictable beast.

Back at the front door of the main house she took off her shoes again, and doubts, old and new, began to creep into her consciousness. The locals weren't friendly like she had imagined they would be, though Rafael had always spoken about his family with love and affection. What if one of them had killed him? Or recognized her from the bar that night? What if they just refused to cooperate? What would happen if the dog-coyote bit her the next time? What if she put signs up in the city's hostels advertising for volunteers and nobody came?

She stood up, wondering what to do next, and noticed a middle-aged, dark, thin man watching her from the dining room where he was wiping a damp cloth over the table.

'*Buenas tardes,*' she said. There was something creepy about the way he had been watching her.

The man mumbled something under his breath and shook his head.

'*Mi nombre es Lia,*' she added.

'*Soy Tomás,*' he said after a pause.

'*Con mucho gusto.*'

'*¿Por qué está usted aquí?*' Why are you here?

'*Quiero reforestar algunas de las tierras.*' I want to reforest some of the land.

Tomás turned to go. She wondered if he'd understood her.

'*¿Es una buena idea?*'

'*Habla con* Don Chema, *pues.*' Speak with Don Chema.

He made a show of wiping every last inch of imaginary dirt off the table before he moved past her, out the front door, leaving the cloth on the dining room table.

She retreated to the kitchen and the comforting thought of freshly percolated coffee.

Favia wasn't there and the house was silent, as if holding its breath until some dreadful revelation came to pass. She padded over to the coffee machine and began to fill a mug, pausing halfway as two people came into view stumbling up the drive. She leaned up against the worktop to peer through the window and almost dropped the mug.

His head was down, eyes fixed on the ground, but she could tell straight away it was Richard. Her heart lifted: something she hadn't expected. Behind him drifted a ghost, its hands clawing at Richard but missing with each step. Macy.

She frowned. Richard was carrying Macy's rucksack in addition to his own bag. She realized that Macy was about to collapse.

Lia banged her coffee cup down on the tabletop and dashed out of the kitchen, skidding down the hallway and out onto the drive. She grabbed Macy's rucksack from Richard and looped an arm around Macy's waist, straining into the taller girl's yielding weight.

'I see your plans changed,' puffed Lia. She dropped the rucksack by the door, cast an eye over the bowed form of Macy and pointed Richard to the dining room chairs inside the house.

Lia left them sitting in exhausted silence and took her time as she walked back to the kitchen. She couldn't bear the thought of calling upon Favia for every little thing in the way that Miguel did. She opened and closed cupboards until she found two glasses and filled them with ice-cold lemonade. She wondered why Macy had come to the finca when she had been so against the idea. On the other hand, she now had two people to help out. Their arrival somehow validated the ideas she had swarming in her mind and made the tasks seem less monumental.

She gave them five minutes to rehydrate and rest, and then couldn't contain herself any longer.

'I've been offered an amazing job and there's room for you two to get stuck in. You'll love it.'

Neither Macy nor Richard replied.

'What's wrong with Macy?' Her eyes were almost closed and her lips chapped. She laid her head over her arm on the table and didn't reply. Lia placed a hand on Macy's forehead but she wasn't feverish.

'Macy's very ill but she's got medication for it and should be fine soon. Right now she really needs a bed and sleep.'

He was being deliberately vague.

'But what's wrong with her? She looks drugged up to the eyeballs.'

'And we aren't staying,' said Richard. 'I just wanted to tell you that Rafael was definitely a drug dealer and part of some criminal fraternity.'

'Keep your voice down,' Lia hissed, looking behind her. 'The owner of this place speaks perfect English. Tell me you haven't come all this way just to insult the memory of my friend? Again?'

Richard thrust the newspaper article into her hands and fiddled with his watchstrap as he waited for her to read it. She took a deep breath and scanned the paper.

'You can't believe everything you read,' she said, although in her heart she was no longer so sure. She thought of the open hostility with which Rodrigo had treated her. Lola didn't want to talk to her and even Favia avoided being alone with her, as if she had some awful contagious disease. It made no sense if Rafael had told his family about her as he had claimed to.

She read the piece again and then gave it back to Richard with a shake of her head.

'Miguel, the landowner, has offered me a really fantastic job.'

'So did I,' said Richard with a frown.

'He's offered me a *real* job,' said Lia. 'A job that can help sustain the raw beauty of rural life around here. Planting trees. If successful, it would soak up atmospheric pollution, rebuild an ecosystem and help to counter flooding. Miguel is cutting down the trees on his land.'

She stared at Richard, wondering if there was anything he wanted so badly in life that he would be willing to risk everything for it. What was he willing to suffer and struggle for? That was the real question. Their journey had got off to the worst possible start, and somewhere in the back of her mind she had assumed he would simply book a return flight back to the UK. She realized she had underestimated him.

Macy groaned deep within her throat and looked as if she might slide off the chair onto the floor.

'I really need your help, Richard.'

'We're not interested,' said Richard. 'It's up to you if you want to stay and join a drug cartel. I just felt it was my duty to warn you. I really want you to leave with us.'

Lia scowled. The thought of Richard and Macy leaving her alone on the finca was almost unbearable.

'You can't leave with Macy like this.'

Richard nodded. 'I know. Though how safe are we if some murderer is running around who recognizes her, or all of us?' He paused. 'Macy has been going a bit crazy with all the stress.'

'Help me get her to my room and she can rest.'

For now, their choices were limited. Lia was glad, not that Macy was ill but that it gave her time to sell the idea of reforesting to Richard and rope them both into helping.

They got up and stood so that Macy was between them, grabbed her under the arms and encouraged her to stand.

Macy groaned but did as they asked. Lia tried to reassure her in a hoarse whisper.

'I'm sure Miguel isn't selling drugs or part of a gang. He owns fruit and coffee plantations and cuts wood for a living. Everyone else around here works for him.'

Macy smacked her lips together but her words were incoherent. They half dragged, half carried her past the kitchen, down the hallway and into the bedroom. Lia hoped Miguel wouldn't have to meet her like this.

'She was … highly strung, but perfectly okay when I left you guys,' said Lia, turning back to Richard.

'She got worse,' said Richard. 'Insomnia, hallucinations … I don't think I helped.'

Lia shook her head. 'Poor Macy.'

'Poor me!' said Richard, but he said it with a smile. 'You have no idea how embarrassing it is to have to pull someone off the road who insists on bowing to moving cars.'

'Has she taken acid or some other kind of drug?'

'I don't think so,' said Richard, shaking his head. 'She's got mental health issues and doesn't want you to know.'

'You can't just stay here and not get involved,' said Lia once they'd left Macy draped over the bed and returned to the dining room.

'I'm happy to pay for our accommodation and meals,' said Richard. 'But there's really no point in getting involved if we're leaving as soon as Macy is well again.'

'Miguel won't see it that way and paying in cash isn't an option. I promise I will leave with you and Macy if you'll just stay for a while and give me time to figure out what the hell happened to Rafael.'

Richard stared at her. 'What happened to him is written in that article.'

Lia shook her head. 'Maybe so, but I need to find out for myself. Please. Would you please simply volunteer instead? I promise I will leave with you and Macy at the first sign of trouble.'

Richard looked away into the distance.

'Look. After that night in the city, I no longer felt like me,' she said. 'It shattered my whole sense of reality and I am so sorry for the horrible way I treated you. I was in shock.'

'We went back there,' said Richard, 'to the city, to the bar. Asked a few questions.'

'You what?'

'Macy went down there by herself and almost got herself killed. Through no fault of her own. It was all my idea, the brilliant thinker that I am. When we got out of there she had this breakdown going on, but she had been heading that way before that. I just didn't know what it was.'

Lia bowed her head. 'You were both trying to help.'

Richard put his arm around her and pulled her towards him. 'Okay, I'll help out for a while, but just till Macy gets better.'

'Thank you.' She swallowed. For the first time since arriving in Guatemala she was glad to have Richard there with her. She turned her face towards the sky, grateful for the gentle warmth of the afternoon sun as it hit the dining room window.

Chapter 20

Richard unbuttoned the top of his shirt as he waited in the hallway, trying not to bite his fingernails. It was late afternoon and Lia had just announced Miguel's arrival. He was convinced he was about to be introduced to some kind of crime lord, and nothing Lia had said had managed to persuade him otherwise.

He watched the smart yet casually dressed man step out of the pickup and stroll towards them.

'Miguel, I'd like to introduce you to Richard, our first volunteer,' said Lia with an energetic smile.

'Delighted, and thank you so much for coming,' said Miguel. He gripped Richard's hand in a firm embrace and welcomed him like a long-lost brother, pumping his arm like a piston.

'Do please join us for an early dinner,' said Miguel. He disappeared briefly and could be heard talking on the phone in another room.

'What's he saying?' whispered Richard, unaffected by Miguel's charm. He wouldn't be as easily taken in as Lia had been.

'I don't know, I'm not into snooping on people,' said Lia with a shake of her head.

Minutes later Miguel returned, and they were invited to feast upon a Spanish roast as if they were old friends reunited, with more chicken, chorizo and potatoes than he had thought was possible to eat in one sitting. Everything was delicious, and he couldn't help feeling more at ease with every swallowed mouthful.

'Are there any foods that either of you absolutely won't eat?' asked Miguel. He placed his knife and fork together to indicate that he had finished and gave the tiniest belch of contentment. 'I'd like you to tell Favia if that is the case.'

Richard looked at Lia and shook his head.

'Not really,' said Lia, 'although I won't eat tripe.'

Miguel chuckled and nodded in agreement.

'We don't buy beef more than once a week but I like my children to eat it. I will typically make *bistec*, which is grilled or fried steak. And what are your go-to comfort foods then, Richard?' asked Miguel. 'Mine has got to be roast chicken with greens, potatoes and homemade gravy.'

'That'll do me anytime, particularly with Yorkshire puddings,' said Richard with a grin. He found himself warming to Miguel, as much as he didn't want to.

'By the way, there's another volunteer,' said Lia, as she accepted a small glass of whisky. 'Her name is Macy but she's come down with the flu so it might be a week or two before she joins us. She's resting in my room.'

'Oh dear,' said Miguel. 'I'll get Favia to make up another room.'

As Richard ate and continued to study Miguel, he thought that perhaps he had done something right by coming to the finca with Macy. For once Lia had been happy to see him and Miguel was turning out to be pleasant and sincere. He had a refreshing sense of humour, a far cry from the gangster Richard had imagined him to be. He was undoubtedly the man in charge but even so, he was casual almost to the point of disorganized and he seemed to find them agreeable in return, in the way that he gave them his undivided attention. He had even given Richard a guided tour of the house once he learned about his father's antique business, pointing out the impressive crystal chandeliers and bronze horse sculptures that he had imported from Germany.

As darkness fell, they were invited to stroll around the finca and Richard relaxed even more. Soon Macy would be well again and they could all be on their way, together again, perhaps headed for the Caribbean coastline of Livingston or Lake Atitlan. All the tourists seemed to head that way.

Miguel interrupted his evening reverie upon their return to the house.

'I'm afraid I need to go out to meet with a solicitor friend and I won't be back till late. I'd like the three of you to make yourselves at home, and if there is anything at all that you need, please ask Favia.'

He left in the black pickup, buzzing with energy compared to Richard and Lia who were trying not to yawn every few minutes.

'I'm going to turn in for the night,' said Richard. He looked forward to being silent and motionless.

Lia nodded, her eyes almost cat-like with tiredness. 'Me too.'

They said goodnight. Richard decided against checking up on Macy again. He had poked his head around her door an hour earlier and she had been fast asleep. Instead he made his way to the kitchen in the dark, intent on bringing a glass of water to his room.

He didn't see the shadow until it was too late. It screamed, clawing at his face as they collided.

'Macy?'

Whoever it was didn't recognize him, and it was only when he stepped backwards that the screaming reduced in intensity, but it wouldn't stop.

He turned and ran, banging on Lia's door as if it might offer him a refuge. When he returned with her, seconds later, they found Macy stripping her clothes off on the hallway floor, still screaming. It was too much. The truth was that he couldn't take any more of Macy for one day, and his patience snapped.

'Shut up, Macy!' he yelled.

It crossed his mind to slap her across the face the way they did in the movies. He had already fought her for the first hour of their fateful taxi ride to San José Patula, something that he had neglected to mention to Lia. Macy had opened the car door and behaved as if she was planning to jump out of the moving vehicle. He had been forced to grab her, using a shocking degree of force to keep her in the car until the driver had brought them safely to a halt and, after much deliberation, locked them inside with the child locks activated. He had driven them through San José Patula and nearly to the finca when Macy kicked off again, swearing at the driver until he felt he had no choice but to make them get out. Richard had given him a huge tip but he still wouldn't change his mind and take them the rest of the way.

Richard fumbled around the wall until he found the light switch whilst Lia tried to wrap a blanket around Macy. The noise had woken Favia but by the grace of God there was no sign of Miguel. Macy wasn't taking kindly to Lia's attempts to cover her modesty, but it seemed Favia knew what to do. She made no attempt to cover Macy but simply spoke in a soft voice and stroked Macy's hair. After a couple of minutes Macy grew quiet and still, save for the trembling of her chin, and Favia led her like a docile lamb, back to her room, whilst Lia and Richard followed.

'I will stay with her until the morning,' said Favia. She went into the bedroom with Macy and shut the door.

'I don't think we could have coped without Favia,' whispered Lia, shaking her head.

It didn't bear thinking about. They remained standing outside for a few minutes, listening for any further upset, and hearing nothing, they returned to their rooms.

* * *

Richard yawned, hours later, as he stood outside Macy's room again, waiting for Favia to come out. Was Macy still asleep? He realized he was in deep trouble if he was expected to look after her and he dreaded how the day would unfold once she was awake.

As the bedroom door opened, relief seeped through his body. She was still asleep. Lia appeared beside him with a steaming coffee in hand and addressed Favia.

'*Ella estaba un poco loca ¿no?*' She was a little bit crazy?

Favia stopped in her tracks and stared from Lia to Richard and back again, shaking her head.

'*No, ella esta más cuerda que ustedes.*'

'What is she saying?' asked Richard.

Lia faltered and took a sip of coffee. 'Favia reckons that Macy is more sane than we are.'

Richard chuckled as he rubbed his eyes. 'Yeah, right. Well, the minute she wakes up I'm going to get those pills down her because I think my own sanity depends on it.'

Favia stood like a guard by the bedroom door and pursed her lips once she saw the pills Richard held in his hand.

She shook her finger at him. '*Ella tiene una herida en su alma, no hay nada mal con su cuerpo. No drogas ella.*'

Lia sighed. 'She said something like Macy has a wounded soul and that because there is nothing wrong with her body, you shouldn't give her the medication – not that she even knows what's in the pills.'

He didn't know what was in the pills either, Richard thought to himself.

'*¿Cuál es el problema con ella?*' asked Lia.

'*Los espíritus están hablando con ella,*' Favia replied.

Lia paled. 'She reckons spirits are talking to Macy.'

Favia spoke again. '*Está en otra realidad, pero no está loca.*'

Lia translated again. 'She says that Macy is in another reality but that she's not crazy.'

Favia headed for the kitchen. '*No te niegues estas realidades sólo porque no puede verlas.*'

'Don't deny these realities just because you can't see them,' Lia murmured as she followed.

'Well pardon me for having a hard time with that, but she wasn't around when Macy tried to jump out of a moving car yesterday,' sniffed Richard.

They walked single file to the kitchen and found Miguel seated with a coffee and newspaper, looking bright and cheerful.

'Good morning,' he said. 'I hope you slept well.'

They looked at each other and nodded, although it was a lie.

'What time did you get in last night?' asked Lia.

'Oh, I stayed at my friend's house in the end,' he replied. 'I came back about an hour ago.'

Richard put the pills down and helped himself to coffee.

'What are those for?' asked Miguel. He grinned. 'Anything I can get high on?'

'They're Macy's medications,' said Richard, 'except Favia says I shouldn't give them to her.'

Miguel dismissed Favia with a wave. 'You can't expect too much from her. Favia took years to learn to cook the simplest of dishes from my mother. She won't know anything about modern medications.'

Favia made herself busy preparing their breakfast.

Richard nodded. 'Before we got here we met an indigenous family who had been attacked during the genocide, in the 1980s and '90s. Wouldn't Favia have been targeted during that time?'

Miguel wiped his mouth on each side with a cloth napkin and threw it down on the table.

'Indigenous people were not targeted! That is a false claim. You have to understand the context. In the 1980s the Sandinistas controlled Nicaragua. El Salvador was on the verge of falling to the guerillas and so was Guatemala. Personal security was non-existent, and kidnappings and assassinations happened all the time.'

It was Lia's turn to speak. 'But the Truth Commission report proved—'

'Look,' said Miguel. 'There were some abuses but they were minimal. The army had to use force. That so-called Truth Commission judged the military very harshly and it was written with huge bias.'

'But the evidence even implicated the CIA who trained and equipped that army in methods of brutality—'

Miguel shook his head to silence her. 'Most people don't have any idea about this, but did you know that the American government deported thousands of Germans from Guatemala during the Second World War? Including my father? He wasn't a Nazi either, let that be known, and it wasn't about Nazis; it was about the Americans going after our economic interests in Guatemala. We were the primary competitors for resources here and my father's land was expropriated whilst he was interned at Camp Kenedy in Texas. They let him go and sent him back to Germany once they knew that he posed no threat.'

Lia stared at Miguel with a kind of rapt attention, but before Richard had time to think about this more, Miguel got up and announced he was going into the city.

'Have you got a busy day planned?' Richard asked, more to break the intensity with which Lia was still studying Miguel rather than because he was genuinely interested.

'A family engagement followed by lunch.'

'I'll take the tree measurements,' said Lia.

'Great, thank you, Lia. Don Chema, my foreman, will be here soon,' said Miguel. He pointed out of the window to a lone figure making his way up the driveway and waved. Don Chema tipped his hat. 'I'll introduce you. He lives in the pueblo and usually hitches a ride here.'

'Richard, if you could oversee everything? We're slaughtering a pig in a few days and I'd like you to supervise that. Make sure no funny business goes on, such as cuts of meat disappearing.'

Richard smiled, confident that he would find a good excuse to avoid having to do such an awful job.

Chapter 21

Lia trod down the hillside path towards the old milking barn dominating the area like a rusted monster looking down at them. A few days of staying on the finca and she still couldn't think of anywhere else to house volunteers. There were bales of hay stored at one end but it was otherwise disused as far as she knew. From the outside it didn't look ideal. The walls were covered in black decay and reminded her of some kind of corpse rotting from the inside out, with the nails rusting slowly away until one day there would be nothing to hold it together.

Further down the path she saw Rodrigo and Don Chema deep in conversation. As she drew level, Rodrigo glared in her direction with a shake of his head, hawked up a lump of phlegm and spat it noisily a few feet from her. He nodded to Don Chema before striding away.

Don Chema greeted her with a deadpan expression and tipped his hat. He was around sixty or seventy years old with short white hair and he dressed in a tracing paper-thin cream shirt, stained slacks and old Doc Marten boots. Wrinkle lines framed his dark brown eyes. Miguel had introduced him as his foreman and described him as a Ladino community leader who was both Spanish and indigenous by descent.

'Why does Rodrigo hate me before I've given him a reason to?' she asked in Spanish.

Don Chema stooped to stroke one of the dogs that appeared beside him and Lia jumped, her heart pounding as she thrust her hands deep into her pockets and searched for the dog-coyote. It was nowhere to be seen.

'He's a difficult man and he has many problems.'

He looked away from her towards Rodrigo's retreating figure and swiped off his hat, wiping the back of his hand across his forehead before replacing it. A gentle breeze blew the earthy scent of chickens, hay and perfumed flowers across Lia's face.

'I really don't want to cause anyone problems around here,' she said.

At least Don Chema was talking to her, she thought.

'Are you serious about reforesting this land?' said Don Chema. He was softly spoken and looked at her as if he wanted to believe her but didn't.

Lia nodded. 'One hundred per cent.'

'Have you reforested before?'

She shook her head. 'I have an ecology degree from university but no idea what to do. Miguel thinks my degree has earned me the right to lead this project and tell everyone else what to do, but the truth is it taught me nothing relevant to being here.'

Her honesty brought a smile to his face and then he shook his head and let out a surprising chuckle that made his eyes water.

'I learn fast,' she said. 'Would you help me? Please?' Lia asked the question lightly but she knew full well its significance. She needed his knowledge of the land and his respected standing within the community if the project was to stand a chance.

Don Chema looked towards the malachite-green mountains in the distance.

'Seedlings take a minimum of three months before you can plant them. They have to be about so high,' he said, indicating with his arm the height of about a foot.

'I really don't want to have to wait three months before I can plant a tree,' Lia exclaimed.

Lola, Marco and Tomás headed up the path towards them laden with canvas sacks that brimmed with avocados and lemons.

'There's a finca nearby where you can buy baby cypress and pine to start a first batch of planting. Clear the land first. It has to be free of weeds to give the saplings the best chance of survival. Plant them about eight feet apart.'

'Okay,' she agreed. 'Do we have to take the tree stumps out of the ground?'

'Leave those. They help give food to the soil and will protect the baby trees in the rainy season.'

Lia sighed with relief.

'Pick the seeds from the strongest and healthiest trees on the finca. You can buy the tools you need from the pueblo.'

'Thank you,' said Lia. She imagined the razed hillside studded with thousands of tiny trees and her body quivered with excitement.

Don Chema scratched his chin and turned to go, but then he hesitated.

'Favia told me that you knew Rafael.'

Lia sighed. 'Yes, we—'

At that moment Lola, Marco and Tomás reached the path beside them. She studied the contours of Lola's face, the first time she had really seen her properly in the light, and saw aspects of Rafael in her features. They were obviously related and the fact made Lia all the more eager to make friends, but once again she never got the chance. They ignored her presence, forming a human barrier between her and Don Chema as they turned their backs to her. They bid Don Chema a good day as if she was invisible.

'He never mentioned you,' said Don Chema, and as he turned away she realized that she had been dismissed. Her cheeks flushed with shame as she was excluded from any further dialogue, and she couldn't understand what they were saying anyway. They weren't speaking in Spanish but in another dialect, probably K'iche'. They had closed ranks and it couldn't be clearer that Rafael's family wanted nothing to do with her.

She clenched her fists and took a deep breath, unsure what to do. She didn't like it but she had to consider that all this time she had seen Rafael through rose-tinted glasses, whilst the truth was that he had lied to her. She took a step closer but then stopped.

Lola's face was downcast, lined and relined with grief and hardship; her eyes were watery and bloodshot, devoid of inner peace. Lia wondered how long she had known about Rafael and how she'd found out. How could she honestly expect Lola or anyone else to trust her, a fair-skinned stranger, in a land known for oppression and violence against its indigenous people? She was suddenly more aware of the colour of her skin than she had ever been before.

Lia bit her lip and turned away. Who was she to pile her grief on top of theirs? They didn't deserve it.

She was about to continue on her way to the barn, determined to refocus on the task of sorting out accommodation for volunteers, but it seemed Don Chema, Lola, Marco and Tomás had decided to go that way too. So she hung back, knowing that they wouldn't want her tagging along with them, and sat down on the path alone to retie her trainer laces as slowly as she could.

Breathing in the fresh air was in itself a tonic and she ran her hands through the soft green grass, closing her eyes and listening to the melodies of birds. She had made it to Rafael's homeland and now, outside and alone, she was sure she could feel his presence, as if he was nearby even if just out of reach. She opened her eyes and as the daylight flooded back in, she felt gratitude for the nature around her. When she got up to continue to the barn it was with a renewed bounce in her step and her head held high, comforted by the warmth of the sun.

At the barn entrance a line of sweat ran between Lia's shoulder blades and down her back although the air had grown cold and stale. The smell reminded her of fish guts, or cheese that had lain in the back of an old fridge for too many months. Inside the milking stalls, rusty pipes hung from dirt-crusted machinery and there were the cracked remains of concrete feeding bins. For no explicable reason she imagined blood and pus in the milk, aborted calves and cows with weeping sores. She knew Miguel hadn't kept cows for years, ever since they had died of an unnamed disease, but he had said that the stench of the barn remained the same, as if they were still there, like a curse that no one had the power to lift.

She looked up. Millions of dust particles danced within the beams of light streaming between the worn wooden floorboards above her. The light fell onto old windowpanes that lay smashed on the floor and she heard the sound of Don Chema's voice above her.

'Where is José?'

There was silence.

'The police are still not telling us anything more about what happened to Rafael other than to say it was drug related.'

'I don't believe it,' someone muttered.

Tomás spoke next. 'I don't trust José any more. He has become too close to Patrón since they were in jail together.'

There was a murmur of assent.

'Rafael and José were like brothers.' It was Lola's voice. 'He would not do something like this.'

Lia saw a ladder leading up to the first floor and, as quietly as she could, she climbed up the first three steps, careful to avoid crunching on any broken glass. As slow as a turtle she risked poking her head up until she could see into the ample open floor space above. She was mostly hidden from view by a haystack that lay across the floor, close to the hatch.

Don Chema spoke. 'Favia has something to say about the gringos.' He nodded to Favia to encourage her to speak up.

'The young girl, Lia, told me that she was a friend of Rafael.'

Lola's gasp was the only audible sound. No one else stirred.

'What friend of Rafael would live under the same roof as the patrón and not declare themselves to us?' said Lola.

Lia felt her heart rate quicken as she listened.

'She is always moving things, washing things, and soon she will try to cook things,' wailed Favia, wringing her hands. 'She may want my livelihood, all that I have left in this life. I have nowhere left to go if the patrón sends me away.'

Don Chema shook his head in disagreement and was about to speak but Marco got there first.

'Don Chema, my friend, you do your best to keep the community together but you don't live here on the finca. Once your hours are filled you can leave, unlike us who remain at the beck and call of the patrón. We see more.'

'I am sure no one will be sent away,' said Don Chema. 'Favia, you've given loyal service to that family for over fifty years.'

Tomás spoke next, his voice gentle. 'And us? What about our years of loyal service? Patrón has already given the gringos some of our jobs. Where will it end?'

Rodrigo growled, kicking up dirt and hay as he jumped up to speak. 'They are fools and they shouldn't have come here.'

Lola scowled, making no effort to hide her dislike of Rodrigo. 'What about you? I saw you arguing with Rafael before he went to the city. What were you fighting about?'

Rodrigo glared back. 'Nothing that matters any more.' He leaned back against the wall, placing his hands behind his head in a false gesture of relaxation.

'Then tell us, you drunk oaf,' said Lola, and she stood up as if she planned to strike him if she didn't get the information she sought. 'You were even in the city that day of all days. What are the chances?'

Don Chema also stood up and put his hands up in an appeal for calm. 'Rodrigo did not do this.' He paused and Lia wondered how he could be so sure when Rodrigo said nothing to defend himself. 'I will meet with Patrón and get an assurance that our wages are still secure.'

Lola sat down and put her head in her hands. 'This news will kill my mother. She keeps asking for him.'

She looked up at another man who had remained silent all this time. 'Julio. You have only been with us for a year. It was Rafael who took us in after my father died. He encouraged us to come back here and build a new life when we thought everything was over forever. He repaired our house during the rainy season and brought us food whenever we were running low.' She gestured at the group with one arm. 'He encouraged you all to rally round us while we grieved for my father. Rafael protected us. He protected all of us.'

There was a general murmur of agreement. Don Chema lit a cigarette as he stared at the floor and sat back down. Favia twisted the few remaining buttons on her cardigan. Rodrigo muttered under his breath as he drew aggressive circles in the dirt with a stick. Marco put his arm around Lola. Tomás, with his hair greased back in a failed effort to look smart, was fidgety, his hands breaking pieces of hay into a mound at his feet. Julio was the only person who managed to look relaxed, if sombre, with his thick, short hair curling around his ears; or perhaps it was just that he was years younger than everyone else there.

'The girl told me that she intends to plant trees back in the earth where Patrón has taken them,' said Tomás.

Don Chema smiled for the first time. 'I cannot see how two gringos could achieve such a tremendous task.'

Marco stood up to speak and cleared his voice. 'The burial ceremony will be held on the weekend at the Iglesia San Andrés. Close friends and family only.'

Lia startled and almost fell off the ladder in her haste to

get down. Rodrigo had stood up and stumbled as he pushed past Lola and Don Chema to leave. 'You are all fools,' he barked.

Lia dropped to the floor and sprang away, her natural instinct to find somewhere to hide. But then she stopped. She wasn't guilty of anything other than listening to a group meeting. She also had the right to try to discover for herself what had happened to Rafael. So she stayed where she was, standing in the old milking barn, as he came down the ladder and stopped, near enough for her to smell the rum on his breath. He looked as if he might spit again, quite possibly in her face this time, and she shrank back. He shook his fist at her, amused by whatever he saw in her face, but that was it. He passed by and was gone. The others came down the ladder and she waited there, no longer assuming they would acknowledge her. Neither did she want to cause Favia or Don Chema or anyone else any discomfort by greeting them.

In the end she simply mumbled, '*Buenas tardes*. I would like to look upstairs to see if the room could be used to house reforestation volunteers.'

No one replied to her except for the younger man, Julio. He wasn't like the others at all and when he saw her, he tipped his hat with a friendly smile and introduced himself before leaving the barn.

Once they had gone Lia climbed up the ladder and out through the hatch until she was standing in the room. It could easily be partitioned into at least ten good-sized individual spaces, although with what materials, she had no idea. There was no bathroom but the cottage facilities were only a few minutes walk away and Miguel had a spare cooker that he said would be moved there.

She walked the length of the room, wondering how long it would take to empty and clean or if it let in enough natural light. Richard would probably say no way. He had no idea about building things, but then neither did she. They couldn't use the spare rooms in Miguel's house because he was expecting his family to return.

Walking back towards the ladder, deep in thought, she froze. Rodrigo had come back. He watched her through the hatch, wearing the malignant expression that he seemed to save especially for her. In seconds he was on his feet and walking towards her.

Who would hear if she screamed? Would anyone help her even if they did hear? It dawned on her then that far from the violence of the city, the countryside had its own brand of wildness and that here too no one would particularly care if she lived or died. The thought made it difficult to breathe.

She backed away from him towards the far end of the barn and the stacks of hay piled up against the wall.

Chapter 22

Macy threw the bedsheets off as soon as Favia closed the bedroom door behind her. She returned to her place by the window and stared at the distant mountains, wrapped in the thickest greens and made even more multifarious by the shadows of the travelling clouds above. She tried to remember snippets of her last conversation with the short indigenous woman. Perhaps it was her kind eyes or her reassuring voice, but there was something caring and intimate in the way she treated Macy that she wasn't used to. Favia had taken her to the window yesterday and pointed to the trees and insisted that she would grow into a new shape of being just like the forest over there, rebranching, rerooting and growing ever stronger and more beautiful than she already was. She was sure she had laughed hysterically in Favia's face, because how could one honestly feel beautiful in the kind of no-man's state she was presently trapped in?

She couldn't remember when she had last taken a shower and she was sure that the incongruous smell of stale tobacco, rotten egg and something else that lingered around her was in fact just the scent of her unwashed body. She bent to pick up yet another piece of paper filled with scribbled words that she had written but was now completely unable to read.

Macy dropped the sheet of paper and watched it sail to the floor as she recalled something else she thought Favia had said: that she could become a spiritual healer. Macy's doctor in London would have locked Favia up himself if she'd come out with something like that! Favia had told her that she was connected to the mountains over there and to the land of trees and the river that flowed beyond. Had she dreamed it or had Favia actually taken her over there last night? Macy shook her head, confused by the strange circumstances she found herself in. She couldn't remember anything for sure. Dreams leaked into reality and reality became just like a dream, something that disappeared from her memory just when she needed it the most. Frustrated, she turned away and was about to lie down again when she saw it, poking out from under her pillow. A stick. A wooden stick. It all came back.

Favia had led her outside and they had walked for what felt like forever until she thought she would collapse with the effort required. It had been quiet, dark and starless. She'd folded her arms across her chest and forced herself on as eerie shadows shifted along the path. Then Favia had told her to keep still and listen. To be at ease with the trees and the grass. She told her to pick up a stick or a root or a rock, anything from nature that called to her. To her amazement it had really been there. She had talked to a stick, she was sure of it now, and heard it speak back to her. All at once she had understood everything. She had been euphoric and she wanted that feeling back again. She'd seen something celestial in Favia's eyes as well as the trees and grass. It had surrounded them. The natural world alive. That was it! It had been a revelation at the time. She vaguely recalled returning to her room with the stick grasped tightly in her palm.

Macy shook her head in wonder and picked it up. It was just a stick. She put it to her ear. Nothing. It had been nothing less than magical last night, something that Favia had described as being of the utmost importance, and she was sure it had spoken to her. She thought of snapping the stick in half now. Maybe two sticks would be better than one. She ran her hand along the length of the stick and intrinsically felt it was the wrong thing to do. She suddenly remembered an earlier time when she had been a very small child; how she and her friends had loved picking up sticks to play with. They had been the source of her favourite games, whether it be making dens, drawing in the dirt or simply playing hide and seek in the Chiltern Hills. Macy frowned. It had probably been twenty years since she had last been to the Chiltern Hills.

Last night, once they had returned, she had been too scared to get into bed. Hadn't she and Favia stood together in the dark by the window as she'd told Favia what had happened to Rafael? How they'd returned to the bar and asked about Rafael and the missing briefcase. She remembered sobbing like a baby as she'd told Favia how she hated having a mental illness that no one could make sense of.

Favia had shaken her head, slowly but firmly, and told her she wasn't sick; just sensitive. Wasn't sick! Something about being gifted to communicate with the spirit realm? *Entidad espiritual*, learning to be a bridge between the two worlds. Macy hadn't believed her, but as Favia gently held her face in her hands, her whispered words had eventually reached her. Macy remembered placing the stick carefully under her pillow, climbing into bed and having no trouble falling asleep.

She put a hand on her chest and tipped her head back onto the pillows. Whatever Favia had said or done, the fear and the incessant voices in her head that didn't belong there had lessened. She was one of the sweetest, kindest people she had ever met; and that in itself didn't make sense, because if Macy had been in the UK, she knew that she would have been sectioned by now. She would be in a place where the nurses were the opposite of Favia. No matter how in need of support she might be, they would literally ignore her; no matter how scared or frustrated she was, they would be going on with their own conversations as if she wasn't even there. Or they would physically overpower and then overmedicate her to the point that she could no longer open her eyelids. She understood that exercise and eating healthily were important, but her experience of mental hospitals was of warehousing and lockdown, with precious little to do, no place to go and certainly nothing that resembled healthy food. For the most part they were places of violence and repression … so incomparable to the room she found herself in today and the loving care Favia, and even Richard and Lia to a much smaller extent, had given her. She sighed, making no effort to wipe away the tears that fell down her cheeks. She put the stick back under her pillow, exhausted from thinking about it all.

Chapter 23

The slaughterhouse door opened and Richard followed Don Chema into a room that was lined with hay. It was impossible to avoid the stink of manure mixed with ammonia or the dread that sat in the pit of his stomach. In the centre a huge pig lay on its side with three men surrounding it. The men chatted as if they were old friends, and for a moment he stood alone and invisible, his mind numb as he stared at the animal. He was unsure of what to do until he heard his name and realized that Don Chema had introduced him and the men were nodding politely. He recognized Marco, Rodrigo and Tomás, and walked over and extended his hand, feeling everyone's eyes upon him.

The pig didn't seem able to stand and Richard lacked the language skills to ask why. He watched in growing dismay as the men heated their machetes over a fire and then shaved the animal. It squealed in distress, trying but still unable to get to its feet; and then, without any warning, Rodrigo took hold of an axe and struck the pig in the chest. He missed his target, the heart, and the pig was so frightened that it managed to stand for a moment before being struck again and again. It died over the next ten to fifteen minutes, squealing and thrashing around as Richard silently cried out for it to be over.

The men proceeded to carve the animal up, removing its skin before sawing its head off. Richard tried not to show his shock as he watched the men toil over the carcass, disembowelling, sawing and chopping for the next three hours, but he wasn't fooling anyone. He couldn't bear to help them and no one offered him a machete so that he could join in.

As he stood there, he couldn't stop his mind from struggling with a question that had kept returning ever since Rafael had been killed. If God was real then why did he allow horrendous things to happen? He looked down at the spatters of blood, skin and fat covering the floor. Had he pulled the wool over his own eyes for all these years, helped by those who had read far too much into a god that never really existed?

As he watched the men start to bag up the slabs of meat, the words of Genesis 9:2 came to him: *The fear of you and the dread of you shall be upon every beast of the earth. Every moving thing that lives shall be food for you*. If God had made this the norm, then what kind of being did that honestly make him? He imagined what Lia's response would be and shook his head, determined to rationalize his thoughts in a way that would keep his faith intact. He had a more immediate worry: that the smell of the animal remains would cause him to throw up. Luckily the men announced that the job was finished, and he followed them out of the room of death and made his way back to the main house, breathing as if his body had been starved of air.

Once under the shower he let the sensation of the steamy water calm him as it massaged his head. Twenty minutes later he was dressed in clean clothes and thinking about whether to check on Macy or not. He doubted she would be awake. For the past week she had slept past lunchtime. He listened for a minute outside her door and knocked.

'Come in.'

She sat up in bed with a sheet over her legs, looking out at the pine trees. He'd followed her instructions and brought her pills – sedatives and anti-psychotics – at 5 p.m. every day, even though Favia had made it clear that she didn't agree with what he was doing. The problem was that when Macy wasn't sleeping she had a tendency to chat at what felt like two hundred words per minute, jumping from one idea to another. But at least she'd mostly stayed in her room, pacing, crying, laughing and voicing jumbled thoughts in German, Chinese, French and Russian. Macy had told him that Favia took her out into the pine forest sometimes in the middle of the night, and he humoured her to her face but he didn't believe her. Regardless, in the last couple of days she had become calmer and more at ease with herself and her surroundings. Fingers crossed she was getting better.

So far, Macy's bizarre behaviour hadn't attracted unwanted attention. Miguel had a routine that involved travelling into the city early every day and only returning after dark once Macy was no longer able to fight the effects of the pills.

'I'm surprised you're awake,' he said.

She didn't answer. He came in and sat on the end of her bed.

'How are you feeling?'

A couple of days ago she had slept for twenty hours solid and woken confused and agitated, but he hadn't ever stopped hanging on to the hope that it was just a matter of time until her senses rebalanced. Her moods had ranged from irritable and abusive to over-excited and gleeful, and she had asked him so many questions about politics and war and whether they – him and her – were actually part of the world or lived outside of it all. If only! He had tried to follow her dizzying thoughts as she'd spoken of cosmogony and parables but it was impossible; so he'd tried to divert her thoughts instead before she became too overwrought and tried to slap him or shout at him. It had become a kind of crisis management that Lia had been too busy learning her way around the finca to engage in. Luckily for her.

There was none of that kind of energy now. It helped him place his own trauma of the past few hours behind him.

'I feel like I'm blind and deaf,' said Macy. Not even her eyes moved. 'You should go.'

'Are you hungry?'

'No. Just disappear. I wish I could.'

'I wish I could too,' Richard agreed, getting up off the bed. 'But Miguel is staying here this afternoon and wants to hang out. When Lia's busy he seeks me out like a bloodhound, and unlike you I've got nowhere to hide.'

For a second there was a ghost of a smile as she turned to him.

'What's he like?'

'Lonely, and his marriage is breaking down, but he's also generous and friendly. Lia's spent a lot of time with him in the evenings. She seems to get on with him.'

He smiled ruefully.

'Does he mind me being here?' said Macy.

'Not at all; and you should have seen him greeting me like his long-lost best friend and thanking me for any assistance I could offer. It makes it all the more difficult to offer no assistance at all.'

'Does Lia mind me being here?' said Macy.

The way she was framing the questions seemed to signal the first sign of her recovery. There was a new air of self-awareness about her, even if it brought with it a sense of being subdued. His heart leaped at the thought that she might be getting better and he was careful not to say anything that would derail her.

'She's thrilled you're here. She's started a reforestation project, which sounds wonderful, good for the environment and an excellent reason for the landowner to treat us well.'

She looked at him. 'But?'

'The locals aren't exactly friendly or helpful. She's got a massive job to do with virtually no help. I told her that you and I were leaving as soon as you were well again.'

'I feel as if my eyeballs have been taken out and put in

backwards,' said Macy with a yawn. 'My head is pounding and my whole body aches.'

She curled up on her side into a ball and pulled the sheet up to her eyes.

'I think you might be turning the corner from this ... this thing you've been going through.'

Her eyes glistened with tears. 'I'm so sorry for all the awful things I've said or done. I'm coming down from a manic episode and you're very kindly holding the ladder.'

'You're going to be fine, Macy. Give it a bit more time.'

She nodded, making no effort to wipe the tears that were spilling out onto the bed sheet.

'Richard?'

He raised his eyebrows and handed her a tissue.

'I want to do some work here, with Lia and Miguel. I need to thank them, and Favia, for giving me this time, this *chance*, to get well.'

His smile died. Apart from Macy not getting well, this was the worst outcome imaginable.

'Them? They're not a bloody couple, you know. We only came here to warn her off.'

'Yes I know and we're still alive and it sounds like she's found an amazing job but could use our help.'

She sat up and slowly got out of bed, emitting a loud groan. 'I'm grateful to you too, but right now I need a reason to live; otherwise there's no point to anything.'

He couldn't bring himself to disagree with anything she said, not when she had just found some kind of balance, so he got up to leave. Perhaps he could change her mind in a few days.

'I'm going for a walk,' said Macy.

'If you're sure.'

She still looked awful, with bleary eyes and greasy hair, and her hands shook as she picked clothes out of her rucksack, but the air of calm was still there and for that he was grateful.

He himself had slept badly, woken during the night by the dogs howling and again in the grey dawn from a nightmare in which he had felt himself bleeding out of a hole in his chest. For the first time in his life he thought about becoming a vegetarian.

In the kitchen Favia kneaded dough at one end of the table. She stood up as he entered and asked what he would like to eat.

'*Tostado con queso, por favor.*' He was delighted at how much Spanish he was picking up and he relished the newly found sound of a rolling *r* in his throat.

She nodded and turned to the sink to wash her hands.

Outside, the dogs began to bark. He looked out the window and saw Miguel standing in the drive as the dogs paced up and down. A car pulled up with José driving. A woman and three children piled out; the children ran up to Miguel and surrounded him in a group hug. The woman stood awkwardly next to him, making no physical contact.

The young girl came bounding through the kitchen door first. She stopped in surprise as she came face-to-face with Richard and tried to race straight out again, bumping into her two brothers. Her chestnut hair hung in a stylish bob about her cheeks and the unblemished innocence of her face gleamed pink. Miguel entered the room behind them.

'This is Sofía, my nine-year-old.' He glanced with pride at her. 'This is Alfredo. He's twelve, and this here is Raul, who's fourteen. Please speak English to them. They're taught English at school but they need to be encouraged.'

Raul stepped forward to shake Richard's hand. He was tall for his age and stocky. His hair was cut in an all-over grade two that emphasised a round face, and he had inherited his father's charm.

'Hello, I am pleased to meet you. How are you today?' Raul spoke in heavily accented English.

'I'm very well, thank you, and delighted to meet you too,' said Richard.

Miguel's wife was tall and elegant, with a swan-like neck emphasized by cropped hair. She stepped forward to introduce herself.

'Welcome to Finca San Isidro. I'm Clarisa.'

José stumbled into the kitchen next, laden with food shopping, and Clarisa turned away to unload the contents into cupboards. Richard's offer to help was immediately dismissed.

'Let's go into the dining room and talk,' said Miguel.

The children remained in the kitchen, with Sofía and Alfredo squabbling over a rubber ball whilst Raul chattered to his mother.

Miguel cleared his throat. 'The workers didn't give you any trouble today?'

Richard swallowed and shook his head. 'They worked extremely hard without taking a single break.'

'Good. I'll reward each man with a generous cut of meat. And I'm delighted with the computer database that Lia has been working on.'

'Have you seen her today?' asked Richard.

'Yes, yes. You know, if we bought sophisticated wood-cutting machinery and got rid of Carlos, we could cut down on as much as forty per cent waste?'

'Really?' Richard looked back at him, eyes wide, feigning enthusiasm.

'I looked at prices in the city. I may even be able to pay for what we need with a lump sum of uncut wood. It's much more valuable cut into *tablas*, of course, but we have to start somewhere.'

He walked over to the nearby cabinet and extracted two crystal glasses.

'I think this calls for a celebratory drink.' He chuckled to himself.

Richard watched as the glasses were filled with Miguel's

drink of choice, Johnnie Walker Red Label. Something about the measured confidence that came with having money and power reminded him of his father.

'I was just about to eat.'

'You can eat and still enjoy a whisky with me,' said Miguel. He pulled up a chair opposite Richard and they both sat down.

'Where is Lia?' asked Richard.

'She went down to the barn. She thinks that maybe the top floor can be converted into accommodation for volunteers.'

Favia appeared with a plate of cheese on toast and a coffee and set it down in front of Richard.

He thanked her, picked up the toast and took a bite.

'I've got the head honcho of a biofuel company visiting today. Imagine: I've had more than five requests to sell some of my land in the past few years from big, foreign-owned companies.' Miguel laughed. 'Some of them think there might be nickel and silver below ground. The man coming today wants to see if he can persuade me to let him grow biofuel crops on my land, either sugar cane or palm oil, to sell to the EU.'

'Would you consider doing that?' said Richard.

'Maybe, I don't know. If the price was right. And only once we had the reforested pine and cypress trees in place.'

'What would happen to the workers?'

'They'd probably be evicted.'

'I guess you could leave some land out of the deal for the families here.'

'Give land to the *Indios*?' He smiled as if indulging a silly child and then his face grew serious again. 'This finca is already small compared to those of my friends.'

'They'd be made homeless,' said Richard. He took a tiny sip of the whisky.

'No, they'd find jobs if they tried hard enough. Julio, my horseman, was evicted from a finca not far from here along with about two hundred families. The land was sold to a international palm oil company a year ago. He found another job.'

'Did Julio get any money for having his family's land sold?'

'It wasn't his land, so no, of course not.'

'Were the two hundred families renting the land, then?'

'No, they were just there, doing whatever it is they do. Growing corn? None of the families legally owned the land.'

Richard looked doubtfully at Miguel. 'What happened to the families?'

Miguel shrugged. 'They would have found jobs elsewhere, just like Julio. A lot of them go to the city. No one should get special privileges,' he said. 'That's why previous attempts to give land to the poor by land reformists in governments have failed so badly. If the government gives land away to people just because they are poor or dark, then they should also give computers away to all writers, or schools to all teachers. You think all carpenters should automatically get a workshop and a lifetime supply of wood?'

Richard shook his head. 'No, but when it comes to a certain standard of living—'

'I'm not responsible for poverty and inequality in my country; rather, I've helped generate employment,' said Miguel, waggling a finger at Richard. If I gave my land away I would be condemning my children's futures whilst failing to raise the standard of living for the Indians. It wouldn't help Guatemala develop. And what about drought? Agriculture is a high-risk sector. So all this talk about the land and the poor and the exploiters that you may hear, well, people don't understand. The poor have to be responsible for their own poverty.'

'Does Guatemala have a minimum wage?' asked Richard.

'I don't pay it,' he replied. 'I pay off the labour inspector to get my certificate of labour code requirements.'

Richard thought he might be joking. 'Seriously?'

'Everyone does it,' said Miguel with a grin.

Richard shook his head.

'Look,' said Miguel. 'There shouldn't be special laws that divide and undermine Guatemalan society. There shouldn't be special privileges or advantages.' He got up to pace the length of the dining table. 'We all have the same rights, which are to contribute to the country's development: invest, create jobs, produce. That's our role. Let the politicians stick to politics and let the churches stick to pastoral work. Roles are predetermined and the status quo should not be questioned. At the end of the day people have to respect the constitution of the Republic.'

'Is drought a major issue for Guatemala?'

'Certainly in parts of the east where the climate has changed. There hasn't been a rainy season for the past few years. It just stopped. Rivers have dried up, crops have died and temperatures keep going up. It's a case of migrate or die over there.'

Richard froze at the sudden appearance of Macy poking her head around the hallway. She shuffled past them, silently mouthing that she was going for a walk outside. He prayed that Miguel wouldn't turn round at that moment and see her.

'I'd like you all to accompany my family and me to afternoon mass soon,' said Miguel.

Richard looked back at him, feeling his shoulders and his spirit lift.

'Thank you, that would be wonderful.'

He could do with the sense of order and stability that church always gave him. The thought of singing hymns and sharing prayers was the perfect antidote to his mood. He smiled, relieved. Lia would hate the idea, but he needed the comfort and peace that going to church always gave him.

Chapter 24

Rodrigo wasn't carrying a machete, but as Lia stared at his fleshy hands and imagined them wrapped around her throat, she knew he was a dangerous adversary. Since arriving on the finca she had tried not to aggravate the man or get in his way, even when he had been rude. Telling Miguel about his off behaviour would get him into needless trouble or just provoke him further, so she had kept quiet. She had considered returning his verbal abuse, word for word. Perhaps he wouldn't have seen her as such an easy target. Now she understood that none of that mattered because there was a good chance that he was Rafael's killer. Lola seemed to think it was possible. He was short, stocky and his eyebrows joined in the middle. He matched the person that Macy had described in the bar that night.

She stared out of the open double doors on the far side of the barn and considered jumping. It was about fifteen feet to the grass, and if that didn't kill her, she figured the dog-coyote would happily finish off whatever was left. She realized that she had been scared of anything that moved in her peripheral vision in case it was the dog-coyote coming to bite her. She'd been worried about getting too close to Macy because she didn't understand the illness. She'd been nervous about failing at the massive reforestation job she had set herself. So much fear and so many worries, and yet what was the point if it all came down to this?

Her eyes narrowed and she shook her head. Enough was enough. She was sick of carrying around a knot in her stomach. She turned round and kicked an old can of paint as hard as she could in Rodrigo's direction. It landed and rolled a few feet from him. She looked around for something, anything, that she could now use to protect herself.

Dozens of empty chemical containers and tools lay scattered in the hay. She picked up a long, rusty screwdriver. Looking more closely at the two nearest containers, she noticed that they still contained liquids. One had a black cross on the label while the other had a skull and crossbones. She grabbed the latter in her spare hand, unscrewed the lid and began to advance back towards Rodrigo.

To her surprise his reaction was to smile – something she had thought him incapable of – and as if waking from a trance-like state, he turned and left the barn as quickly as he had arrived, disappearing without a backwards glance.

Lia sank to her knees and closed her eyes. She let go of the improvised weapons, vaguely aware of the screwdriver rolling away. How had she not connected the dots before now? If Rodrigo was guilty of murder, then he had a motive for coming after her. But why hadn't he just got rid of her when he had the chance, in the truck on the way to the finca? And why wasn't he treating Richard badly too? Why just her?

'Are you okay up there, Lia?'

Lia looked up and took a deep breath. Macy. She'd climbed halfway through the hatch, and Lia's first thought was that she had spoken clearly, without slurring.

'You actually do look pleased to see me,' said Macy, screwing up her eyes in mock disbelief.

'I am.' Given the choice she would pick Macy over Rodrigo any day; but still, the last thing she needed was Macy ranting about the destruction of the earth or accusing her of being the cause of her suffering. 'How are you?'

'I'm still alive.'

'Do you think this would be the best place to house volunteers? I just don't know how we could divide the space up into private rooms.'

She decided to keep the ongoing conflict with Rodrigo to herself rather than put additional stress upon Macy, and if she told Richard, he would once again pester her to leave – or worse, leave without her.

'Welcome to my forte,' said Macy, pulling herself through the hatch. 'With all the wood lying around this place I could build beams to frame each room and even bedframes and bedside tables. It wouldn't take too long. Ten rooms at least.'

'You reckon you could do that?' Lia asked, trying not to look doubtful. Macy hadn't even brushed her hair, which stuck up in uncombed lumps. 'Are you feeling better?'

'Over the worst. Getting to work is the therapy I need now. I speak seven languages but I'm a carpenter to boot.'

Lia stared at her. 'Wow.'

'The easiest thing for the walls would be to buy rolls of palapa, which are woven palm leaves made into a kind of matting. We can buy it from the market in Zone 4.'

Lia recalled the bustling, shrieking area from her last bus ride.

'What would they sleep on?'

'Miguel said he had plenty of blankets, and travellers often have their own sleeping bags.'

Macy carved the floor up into ten rough spaces by kicking a slow path through the dust.

'We have to get rid of all this junk before I can get to work in here.'

'I'll start emptying it tomorrow,' said Lia. She met Macy's eyes and her brow furrowed. 'I don't want you to exert yourself too much, though.'

There was an awkward silence and Macy looked away.

They climbed back down the hatch, Macy first, and tramped over the grass in the direction of the main house.

'Are you planning to stay for a while?'

Macy sniffed. 'Do you want me to?'

Lia hesitated. She needed to be honest. 'Richard has refused to tell me what's happening with you.'

She knew it was some sort of mental illness and wondered if Macy had grown up with it like others grew up with a stutter or a lazy eye.

Macy sighed, a distant expression on her face. 'I was diagnosed with mild bipolar six years ago. I left England after the last time, once I'd recovered … couldn't sleep for weeks, literally; lost my business, ran my credit cards up and drove my friends away. *So-called* friends,' she added.

'My house got repossessed. I was awful to be around, so I can't really blame my friends and family. I was hostile and my mind was racing with so many thoughts at once. Eventually I was hospitalised, and I got better.'

'You started to get ill again here, didn't you?'

'After what I saw in the bar …' Macy's lips trembled.

Lia shook her head. 'Let's not talk about it if it's going to make you ill again. And I do want you to stay, if you want to.'

Macy wiped her eyes. 'However hard I've tried in the past, this is the only place I've been able to recover without going into an institution.'

She rested one hand lightly on Lia's shoulder. 'I want to be here as much as you do.'

They started up the hill path and stopped halfway up for Macy to rest.

'What's it like working for Miguel?' Macy puffed.

'He's respectful and kind.'

Perhaps she was also a welcome distraction from his family troubles, although she didn't mention this. She also resisted the temptation to tell Macy everything she'd overheard from the locals. There was no doubt in her mind that Rodrigo had been involved in Rafael's death and she was sure Lola knew it too. Perhaps Macy would even recognize Rodrigo once she saw him.

She turned to look behind them at the green camel humps of the distant mountains. Macy blew her nose on a tissue and fumbled around in her pockets until she located a cigarette and lighter, but her hands shook so much that in the end Lia lit it.

The glow of the cigarette end matched in perfection the fireball of sunset forming before them. It wrapped the sky in a blaze of reds, purples, pinks and oranges and bathed the girls in its glory. They watched in humble silence as the sun dipped lower. It was only when the cooler breeze began to caress her face that Lia was reminded of how the golden entity of warmth, light and life would soon give way to darkness once again.

Chapter 25

Richard stood on the driveway with Tomás, loading the back of the black Nissan pickup. His clothes were filthy but he felt a mental load lift from his shoulders as he saw Macy and Lia making their way towards him.

'Where have you been?' he panted, hauling a gas cylinder up into the back. 'I was getting worried.'

'Working out where volunteers might be able to stay,' Lia replied. Though darkness was upon them he could see how exhausted Macy was in the way that she dragged her feet through the grass and kept leaning on Lia.

'Have you heard them?'

'Who?'

'Miguel and his wife, they've been yelling at each other for the past hour,' said Richard. 'The children can probably hear everything.'

Raised voices continued to echo from the kitchen. Richard and Lia carried furniture and crockery as quickly as they could from storage inside the main house to the pickup: three single beds, two electric lamps, a grotty cooker, small fridge, wooden tables and chairs in need of repair, mismatched crockery, pots, pans, the computer from Raul's room and food supplies.

Two pickup journeys and a few hours later, the cottage resembled a functional home. Macy had taken her tablets for the first time unbidden by Richard and fallen into a deep sleep, ensconced in one corner of the tiny room that she and Lia had agreed to share.

'Damn it. I've forgotten my rucksack,' said Lia once the shower was free.

'I'll get it; you look like a walking corpse,' said Richard with a grin. He had been about to close the door to his room and then remembered they needed to return the pickup.

'Thank you very much,' she smiled back, throwing him the car key.

He was on the verge of telling her what a good team they made but changed his mind. He was just pleased the tension between them seemed to have dissipated in the days they'd been apart. She no longer treated him as if he was somehow to blame for everything. If he was honest, he also didn't want Lia going up to the house alone at this time of night. In the past week he'd seen Lia and Miguel grow more familiar with each other, and something about it made him uncomfortable. He'd watched Lia become increasingly drawn to Miguel's sharp, grey eyes and the way his hands could move with nimble speed to saddle up a horse. There was an unspoken bond that had developed between them, perhaps because through some strange quirk of destiny, the immediate directions of their lives were now dependent upon each other. He was paying her wages and he was her boss, but he didn't seem to put up the professional working barriers that he did with everyone else.

He opened the door and stepped outside. The air was still and heavy, as if it might rain, and it was the first night upon which he couldn't see any stars. The darkness was complete, perfect for hiding all his flaws. As his eyes slowly got used to the dark, his steps were soft and soundless on the grass, his senses heightened. He got into the pickup as quietly as he could, listening to the occasional hoot of a hidden owl.

He found Miguel brooding in his study.

'My wife is going to leave me and take the two youngest

children.' His speech slurred and there were two empty whisky bottles on the desk.

'I'm sorry to hear that,' said Richard.

'It's only a temporary separation for now,' he added.

Richard nodded.

'I'm glad you're beginning to settle in here,' Miguel's voice softened.

'While my wife was away, I made the big mistake of bringing a prostitute to the house. I'm fed up with having a wife who hates me.' He sighed. 'And I deliver the funds to run this household so I have the right to play around. Unfortunately she found out. I felt the most intense shame and guilt.'

Miguel leaned towards him and made as if to reach for his hand. Richard took a step forward to shake his hand but Miguel's arm instead fell back onto the desk with a thump. He looked vulnerable and sad.

'Will you stay and have a drink?'

Miguel had obviously had enough for one evening, Richard thought.

'No thank you.'

He raised the empty whisky bottle towards Richard. 'It's rude not to accept hospitality from your host.'

'I'll join you once the girls have got the adverts for volunteers up in the city,' he promised. 'We'll have an excellent reason to celebrate then.'

He wasn't sure if Miguel heard what he said as he was distracted by the appearance of Tomás. Miguel lifted a third bottle of whisky out of a box that he had stashed under the table. He opened it and poured a glass half full of the Red Label and watched Tomás swallow it down in one go. Richard wondered if the entire finca community might be raving alcoholics. At least he hadn't seen any sign of drugs. So far.

'*Gracias*, Patrón,' Tomás mumbled, looking keenly to the remainder of the bottle and then back at Miguel, with the glass still in his hand. He hung around in the hope of being offered more. Miguel shook his head.

Tomás hung his head and disappeared with the empty glass.

'You know, it's not easy for me living here,' said Miguel. 'When I'd only been here a few months, I drank him unconscious after he waved his machete at me, thought I'd be scared. Thought I might run away from here! Instead I feed him, drink with him, clothe him and pay him to work with me.'

He wrapped an arm around the bottle, looking more forlorn than defiant. Richard wanted to leave, yet Miguel was the kind of man to whom it was hard to say no in spite of how tired he was. He had the same ability to reduce him to feelings of powerlessness that his own father had. He wondered if Miguel might have been involved in Rafael's death but quickly dismissed the idea as ludicrous.

'Tomás was extremely drunk but calmed down as soon as I threatened to kick him off the property. He's fathered thirty-one children, you know. What do you think of that?'

Richard swallowed and blushed. 'I take it he hasn't been taught the value of family planning.'

Miguel laughed at his discomfort. 'Condoms are taboo here. The pope forbids them and the Vatican has a big hold over the poor. It's a big part of why they're in such a wretched mess.'

Even as a practising Christian Richard couldn't argue with that. He had simply disobeyed church teachings in this area of his life. He immediately thought of Sarah, one of the first girls he had met at his church group and with whom he'd had his first real relationship at the age of nineteen. It had lasted six months and would have lasted longer if she hadn't left with her parents for a new life in New York.

'Do you ever feel lonely?' Miguel asked.

Richard shook his head. 'Not really.'

'Not scared of death or dying alone?'

'No.'

Miguel leaned under his desk to grasp something. He brought up a shotgun and pointed it at him.

'What about now?'

Richard's legs threatened to buckle as he took a step back. The shotgun wobbled as Miguel lowered and placed it down on the desk, laughing. A minute drizzle of spit frothed onto his bottom lip before he licked it away and took another swig of whisky.

'I'm only joking. I want you to take it with you.'

'Is that thing loaded?' He was suddenly aware of the fact that every moment of his life was simply a microcosm of the universe and that the present moment was all that he and any other living person ever really had. Life unfolded – or folded – in the present. Too often he had let the present slip away, wasting precious seconds of his life as he worried about the future or fretted about the past. In the moment, right then, he felt incredibly still and calm.

Miguel pointed to the trigger. 'Safety catch is on. But now that you've moved down to the cottage, I can't guarantee your safety.'

'Safety from what?'

'An *Indio* was killed in the city and there have been problems around here ever since. His funeral is tomorrow.'

Richard stepped forward again, ears pricked, all the while wondering if the more times one had a gun pointed at oneself, the more desensitized to it one became. Miguel grasped him by the arm and thrust the gun towards him, trying to get him to take hold of it. Richard took the gun with both hands although it was the last thing he wanted.

'Who was he?'

'Someone who worked for me. There was a confrontation between some of my workers. I'm too busy to keep up with the politics, but most of the premature deaths around here are caused by illegal drugs, gang-related violence and a heavily armed population.'

He was sure he was referring to Rafael and was about to ask more when Raul walked into the study. Miguel beckoned to his son and his face softened.

'Come and give me a hug, my dear son. I'm so, so sorry that I could not reconcile with your mother.'

Raul looked upset. Richard put the gun down as quietly as he could next to Miguel's briefcase, but it didn't escape Miguel's attention.

'Take the gun.'

Miguel's voice was firm. Richard stared at the length of metal and thought about storing it under his bed. Did he have it in him to shoot someone? He shook his head, his cheeks burning.

'I can definitely speak for Lia and Macy when I say thank you, but no.'

'Keep it for protection.'

Richard shook his head again, unusually determined to assert himself. 'No thank you.'

He wondered if he was making yet another error of judgement as he placed the truck key down on top of the briefcase beside the shotgun, said goodnight and left.

Chapter 26

Miguel jogged out of his house onto the driveway, followed by two men dressed in suits complete with wide-brimmed hats, cowboy boots and leather belts with massive metal buckles. One had a moustache that reminded Macy of Yosemite Sam, arch enemy of Bugs Bunny.

'Before you go I'd like to introduce you to two colleagues of mine,' said Miguel.

Macy made an effort to smile, wondering how she would muster the energy to talk, let alone climb into the back of the pickup.

'This is Jorgé Castaño, a candidate for mayor of San José Patula, and Alejandro Miejo, a member of congress.'

'Hello,' said the men, one after the other. Already she couldn't remember their names, and with the briefest nod in their direction, she took a few steps closer to the pickup.

Lia shook hands with each man, not seeming to mind the way they lingered over her, wrapping her hand completely in theirs, giving the illusion of warmth and honesty that politicians liked to convey. One of the men stared brazenly at Lola as she walked from the main house down the hill and Macy decided she didn't like either man. She knew her lack of enthusiasm peeved Miguel but she didn't care. A year ago she would have fallen over herself trying to impress men like that, but that wasn't who she was any more and she was glad.

They left as soon as she'd hauled herself into the pickup and barely sat down. She gripped one side and grunted as she swerved to avoid the overhanging branches that threatened to knock her senseless. Today they were on their way out of the finca after what felt like an eternity of days spent sleeping the world away. Her head was still foggy with the drugs, her coordination hit and miss, and as soon as they passed the entrance to the finca she wanted to turn back.

José was running city errands for Miguel and had agreed to give Lia a lift. Macy couldn't think of a good enough reason to stay behind, particularly when Lia had virtually no money and no idea about the tools and materials they needed to buy.

He dropped them off in Zone 1 and shoeshine boys immediately trailed them where a throng of scruffy backpacker hostels had sprung up alongside a colony of shops. The contrast to the wide, green, quiet space and sweet finca air made Macy widen her stride in her haste to get back, until Lia, virtually jogging along, grabbed her by the shoulder.

'Slow down, it's not a race.'

'Sorry.'

'Are you okay?' said Lia. Always the concern. She tried not to let it irk her.

'I just think it's a little early to be advertising the project,' said Macy. 'I need to build the accommodation first.'

'Miguel said that the first couple of volunteers can stay up at the main house for a week or two.'

'Oh.' Macy forced a smile. Now there was no way she could allow the tools they bought to sit idle. She would have to get to work as soon as possible.

They were allowed to put up flyers in all six of the hostels that they visited, so they pinned up one A4 printed document in English and Spanish that read:

FOOD & ACCOMMODATION OFFERED IN RETURN FOR WORK ON A REFORESTATION PROJECT NEAR THE BEAUTIFUL TOWN OF SAN JOSÉ PATULA. CALL 249-1957.

After, they took a taxi to the bustling market that formed part of the seedy bus terminal in Zone 4. An old man directed them to the woven matting shop, deep inside a dizzying maze of dark and narrow stalls that reeked of eye-watering spices and fish. Macy shrugged off the feeling that she was walking through the recesses of her brain. She hustled a hard bargain for fifty rolls of matting while Lia wiped sweat from her face and watched, wondering out loud how they would get the matting out from the shop and into the car. Macy couldn't blame her for doubting her. That was what mental illness did. It refused to inhabit places of trust, preferring to centre itself on the doubts and fears and suspicions of 'normal' people.

'Can you hold two rolls at a time?'

Lia nodded and stuck one roll under each arm. Macy did the same.

'Let's go,' said Macy.

She led the way out, through the tunnels of alleyways until they were back on the outskirts of the market by the side of the road. They still had ten minutes before José was due to meet them.

'Let's sit here. When José comes he can help us collect the rest,' said Macy. She concentrated all her attention on tracing the pattern of the palapa matting with her fingers, thankful to be able to sit somewhere, in silence, but wondering if she would be able to find the strength to get up again. Lia sat beside her.

'It's Rafael's funeral today.'

Macy barely acknowledged Lia. It felt like they were running around, expending all this energy, and every day the world just kept on getting worse. Dr Medino said that she always suffered from declinism at this stage of her illness – the belief that society was trending towards decline or failure – when actually the 'evidence' suggested otherwise. She wanted to talk to Favia about it. Humans had killed off over half of all the world's wildlife and trees. With air quality on the decline, ice caps melting and plastic rubbish literally everywhere, the evidence was plain to see.

'I should be there.'

Macy still gave no response.

'I should have got the address and just gone, and to hell with everyone else,' said Lia.

'You've got to know which battles are worth fighting,' said Macy with a yawn. She had battled the effects of her pills to make sure she was up in time to catch a lift to the city with Lia.

'Are you sure you can't remember anything else from going back to the bar that day with Richard?' asked Lia.

Macy scowled. She'd already told Richard everything she remembered, even if it wasn't much. Retrieving information was almost impossible when her body refused to function properly. Her thoughts were jumbled and there were empty spaces between her memories, or tricks of the mind. That was the problem with Lia and the whole world. Telling the truth when you were shoved into a box and labelled mentally ill. Nobody wanted to believe her. How could she expect Lia to be any different? She craved a smoke but preferred to go without than feel Lia watch her shaking fingers, judging her and then worse, lighting the cigarette for her. She hated the side effects of the medication.

'It's all a blur.'

She didn't tell Lia about the horrible memories that had come back, like standing in the middle of the road as cars roared past in both directions.

They sat on the kerb with their feet in the road, the only

stillness in a swirling cacophony of movement as another bus passed and was attacked on all sides by vendors.

'They're keen,' said Lia.

'They're not keen, they're desperate,' said Macy with a blank stare in her direction, 'because they're starving.'

'They're not starving; their bones aren't jutting out and their bellies aren't distended,' said Lia.

'See that child over there?' Macy pointed to a little girl picking up empty plastic bottles from a rubbish heap. 'How old do you think she is?'

'Seven or eight.'

'She'll be eleven or twelve years old but she's stunted; undeveloped, physically and mentally, because she can't get enough of the right things to eat. It's a slower, deeper kind of starvation that's been building for decades in this country.'

Lia shook her head.

'You know what the saddest thing about that night is for me, Lia? That I can't even remember what Rafael looked like, let alone anyone else who was there.'

'When we were in Cobán you said you saw the killer and you described someone who looked just like Rodrigo.'

Lia jumped to her feet as José pulled up next to them.

Macy shrugged. 'Sometimes if I forget someone and then see them again, it jolts my brain into having a recollection, but I'm pretty sure I never met or saw Rodrigo before.'

Lia sighed. 'I'm going to get a friend to mail me out a photo of Rafael and I'll give it to Lola.'

She threw the palapa rolls into the back of the pickup and held a hand out to pull Macy up from the pavement. Macy begrudgingly accepted.

'Lola already hates me, so it's not like things could get worse,' said Lia.

'She doesn't hate you, she just doesn't understand what we're doing here, turning up out of the blue and working for someone like Miguel. All the locals are suspicious.'

Lia looked away.

José agreed to help them carry the rest of the palapa to the truck. Trailing one behind the other with the matting stacked in their arms, they made what felt like a hundred more trips back and forth to the shop. Then he led them to another stall where they bought hammers, nails, a saw, spirit level, tape measure and portable radio. Their last stop was at an agricultural warehouse selling huge sacks of animal feed and garden tools, where Don Chema had told them to buy ten hoes.

Macy slumped against the back of the truck as soon as she'd climbed in, exhausted but happier once they were climbing up into the rocky hills again. In this respect Favia was correct. There was a calming effect on her nerves and in her mind whenever she turned to study the tree life interspersed with so many different species of plants, all living in harmony.

Back at the finca Macy saw an acorn on the grass and felt compelled to pick it up and place it with her stick, which she still kept under her pillow in the cottage. She felt a profound sadness and a lethargy which she couldn't explain but which always followed a manic episode. Favia had said it was a visiting ancestral spirit trying to make contact with her own indigenous soul, tempting it away from all things earthly. She didn't know what to believe but she found the words comforting.

There were no cars in the drive and only the three dogs to greet them. The front door of the main house swung open as soon as Lia tried it, to her visible relief as she hurriedly put distance between herself and the coyote-dog.

Everyone, including Favia, had gone to San José Patula to attend the funeral. They found a note on the dining room table from Miguel, who had accompanied his wife and children to the city where he would drop them off, with the exception of Raul, to stay with his mother-in-law.

'Let's drive the pickup down to the barn to unload,' said

Macy. There was no way she was going to haul fifty rolls of palapa on foot anywhere.

They hurried back out to José who was turning the vehicle round.

'Can we please take the palapa and tools to the barn?' she asked.

He shook his head. 'I must go back to the pueblo now. We'll do it later.'

He revved the engine and, without waiting for them to reply, took off down the drive, leaving a cloud of dust behind him.

'He'll be going to the funeral and we probably made him late,' said Macy, staring after the truck.

Lia sighed. 'What now?'

'Lunch, then you can help me clean the barn out.'

Macy turned back to Lia, a small smile playing on her lips. She had just remembered something else from that night that she believed was important.

'What?'

'The briefcase. I remember the barman telling me that Rafael's case was as light as a feather, like it had nothing in it.'

'So it wouldn't have been full of drugs or money, which would have weighed more.'

Macy nodded.

'What do you think was in it, then?'

Macy shrugged. 'That, I don't know.'

'Thank you,' said Lia. She looked thoughtful but didn't say anything else.

They had lunch in the main house, helping themselves to a selection of cold meats, bread and salad and washing it down with a pint of water. She watched, amused, as Lia folded two pieces of meat into a small plastic bag and stuffed it into a trouser pocket, part of her ongoing effort to win over the coyote-dog.

It didn't take them long to find a cupboard full of cleaning tools. They took a couple of floor brushes and a roll of bin liners and set off for the barn.

First they threw all the old cans, tools and plastic containers out through the double doors at the end of the barn. When the floor was finally clear, Macy rested while Lia swept the worst of the dust out and then bagged up the rubbish they'd thrown. Keeping Lia busy was the only remedy for missing Rafael's funeral. They left the haystacks where they were, piled like brickwork high in the far corner, and Macy scribbled down the measurements she needed for each room with a growing eagerness to get started. She was fed up of staring at a wall of grey nothing as if some twisted doctor had removed her heart and soul. It was time to listen to Favia and get off her meds. Starting that evening she would cut her dose by half.

Chapter 27

They had been living on the finca for a month. Richard had shaved for the first time in a week and dressed in his best clothes, admiring the way his trousers once again creased down the front of each leg, thanks to Favia. It was Sunday and he couldn't wait to sing hymns and be in the presence of a holy man as his prayers washed over him.

José slowed the car in front of the church, searching for a parking space, and Richard continued to ignore the banter that was still flowing like a bad wine between Miguel and Lia. It wasn't a particularly beautiful church but it was exactly what he needed; old and stern, it brought with it a sense of ordered peace.

He wished Macy had come with them, but she had been the only one able to persuade Miguel to let her carry on working. Lia had tried but he had refused to listen to her. Macy worked in the barn every day, stopping only for lunch when she would share with them her ongoing vision for the barn, blissfully unaware of how unrealistic it sounded. He couldn't imagine one person overhauling an entire barn, even with her consistently late evening appearances after being isolated up there all day. She would return to the cottage with her hair matted with sweat and dust and her hands covered in nicks.

It was different with Lia and her oh-so-amazing friendship

with Miguel, he thought, scowling. He'd told her how Miguel had pointed a loaded gun at him and she hadn't batted an eyelid. He didn't understand how she could spend so much time in his company. They were also being insensitive to Clarisa and the children, who were sitting in the car with them after José had picked them up earlier that morning.

'Take God into your heart before it's too late,' said Miguel, staring at Lia with a smirk as he teased her.

'I can't, because he doesn't exist,' said Lia, rolling her eyes in mock protest.

'"The fool hath said in her heart there is no God. Corrupt are they and have done abominable iniquity: there is none that doeth good." Psalms 53:1, King James Version,' said Miguel with a grin.

'Morality, goodness or whatever you want to call it doesn't require religious belief,' Lia replied.

He chortled in a way that annoyed Richard further. He glanced at Clarisa and believed Miguel was simply using Lia to irritate his wife. She was already upset from being asked to forego their usual attendance at a catholic church in the city, as a favour to Miguel. Today they were headed for a Protestant church in San José Patula because there was someone he needed to see there. Richard didn't mind, given that he'd attended a Protestant church himself for the last ten years.

'I have read and studied this nonsense, you know,' said Lia. 'Romans 8:28, "God causes all things to work together for good, to those who love God, to those who are called according to his purpose." Well, how do you explain paedophilia in the church?'

'Sexual abuse happens all over the world, not only within the church,' said Miguel.

'But does God really allow the torture of children on earth by divine reason?'

Miguel shrugged and glanced at his wife. Like Richard, she

was trying to ignore the conversation. Raul was possibly the only child listening in on their small talk and Richard felt like telling Lia to shut up.

'Is that why he won't lift a finger to stop massacres and disasters? If he won't stop them then he must be some kind of psychopath; if he can't stop them, then what makes him a God?' said Lia.

Clarisa leaned forward, her cheeks pale. She placed a hand on Lia's shoulder.

'Lia, we cannot possibly know all the reasons why bad things happen. Just know that God has a purpose with everything that happens, good or bad, and he has a plan for each of us.'

Lia shook her head. 'I'm sorry but I can't believe in something simply because I'm told to or that I'll go to hell if I don't.'

Clarisa smiled. 'Jesus never said that non-believers are going to hell.'

'But you believe that religion is merely used to control the masses and to keep the poor ignorant, right?' said Miguel.

'And oppressed, yep,' said Lia. 'Christians, Islamists, Buddhists or Judaism; the ones who take themselves too seriously are all the same.'

She turned away. 'Clarisa, Richard and anyone else who finds this conversation offensive, I am really sorry.'

At least she apologized, thought Richard. He got out of the car and headed for the church entrance, eager to keep out of the sun before he sweated through his clothes.

Inside, he sat in a pew near the back and watched the congregation begin to fill. Many of the members turned to stare in curiosity, and he in turn couldn't help staring at the tiny old women who were half his size and the children who were directed to sit in the front, dressed in velvet waistcoats and oversized baggy trousers.

Lia spotted him straight away and made her way over to sit next to him, followed by Clarisa and the three children.

Miguel made a big show of greeting several well-dressed men before sitting a few pews in front of them.

'I won't be able to understand the sermon,' Richard whispered to Lia. He picked up a hymn book and flicked through pages of Spanish. It was such a good feeling to be there that he decided he didn't really care what language the sermon was held in.

'I'll translate if you want,' she whispered back. He saw a glint in her eye.

He shook his head and was about to request that she say nothing more until it was time for them to go, when a priest stepped forward from a side door and announced the first hymn. José was the last person to slip through the main doors and close them behind him. He sat on the end of the pew in front of Richard, who was surprised to discover that the church, now virtually filled to capacity, consisted of an even mix of indigenous and Ladino people.

They stood up to sing. In front, Miguel whispered to a man, unaware of the church proceedings because they both remained sitting down far longer than everyone else. Richard watched as Miguel dug deep into his pocket, pulling out a handful of notes that he thrust into the other man's outstretched hand. The man took the money and abruptly left the hall. Miguel ran a hand through his hair and Richard thought he was going to follow the man out, but instead he joined them, nudging Richard to move down the pew to accommodate him.

'I wonder what that was about,' Lia whispered under her hand. 'Looks to me like Miguel just got bribed right in front of us.'

Richard didn't care. Didn't want to care. Couldn't she see that Miguel was standing right next to him? All of a sudden he was struck by a worry he never thought he'd have. What if the church couldn't provide him with any of the answers he was seeking? Like why he was drifting further and further away from his relationship with God? He suddenly had a sense that he had been in this exact church before, even though it was impossible. And the lesson he'd already learned was that all humans carried on their business, whether in the sanctity of church or outside it. The walls made no difference.

The sudden quiet of the hymn ending and the shuffling movement of bodies kneeling for prayer pulled him from his thoughts. The priest spoke in a loud, rich voice that seemed to ooze self-adulation. Richard shrugged the thought away.

He turned his head at the sound of the door opening. Three women in indigenous dress stood at the entrance, unkempt and hesitant. They looked tired and frightened. He waited for the priest to notice them.

Miguel shook his head at Richard and leaned closer. 'He won't let them in. Never does.'

The priest marched up to the women with all the authority of a police officer. He shook his head at whatever they were appealing to him for and spoke firmly before turning them around and pushing and prodding them back through the door.

'Who are they?' he asked.

'Homeless,' said Miguel. 'Definitely not church members. He told them to read the bible and pray.'

Richard took a deep breath and the room span. He blinked rapidly and the priest returned to the pulpit, frowning at the children in the front row as his voice filled the church. Some of the children started to sniffle, looking around for their parents before breaking down in tears. Richard avoided Lia's eyes. Was this why his dad had always frowned upon his religious beliefs and tried to stop him from attending the church group in London? It was different there. But perhaps he had simply wanted to protect him from the likes of the priest in front of him. For the first time since being in Guatemala he felt like calling his dad.

He had looked forward to this morning so much and it was turning out to be nothing but a farce. At the same time, it helped him finally understand what the hell he was doing in

Guatemala. It was Sunday, yes, but this church was the last place he could expect to find salvation of any kind. If anywhere, it was to be found in his everyday life, in the actions he took to help his fellow man on the finca or on the street and in the way he chose to live his life every day. He waited for the sermon to end, with a new sense of impatience. He couldn't profess to worship God in church yet not express love for his neighbours. It was where he had been going wrong, and why he felt so guilty. Just because his neighbours happened to be on the other side of the world, he had been nearly blind to their common humanity.

Richard had money in his pocket. He rose to his feet, intending to leave the church and give it to the women who had so obviously been in need. In the same instant Rodrigo burst through the entrance. His bloodshot eyes locked with Richard's and he drew his machete from where it had been hanging by his side.

Richard drew in his breath and sat down again. Rodrigo charged towards him wielding the metal. Was God about to test him for a higher purpose just as he was learning to live here?

Lia grabbed him by the arm and tensed but Rodrigo stopped in front of José, not them. He yelled something indecipherable and the whole congregation fell silent, including the priest who made no effort to intervene.

Richard could smell alcohol on Rodrigo's breath as he spat angry words at José and pushed him further against the bench with the pointed end of his machete. José was by far the bigger of the two but made no effort to defend himself other than to shake his head. The blade glinted in the rays of sunlight coming through the stained glass above them, pointed inches from his neck.

'*Es tu culpa.*' Rodrigo continued to repeat these words.

Lia turned pale, still clutching Richard's arm, her body quivering.

'What's he saying?' said Richard.

'He's blaming José for something,' whispered Lia.

Miguel shook his head in disdain, eyes narrowed. 'This is the kind of behaviour I have to put up with regularly.'

Rodrigo swung his machete high above his head, and something within Richard snapped like a rubber band.

'Wait!' he yelled in English.

Everyone in the room turned to stare, including Rodrigo. Even the priest was watching him, tucked safely behind his pulpit.

Richard pulled away from Lia and stepped out of the pew, moving until he was between the two men, forcing Rodrigo to take a step back. For the millionth time he wished he could speak more Spanish.

'Lia, help me out, please,' he said.

Lia paled even more. 'He already hates me,' she whispered. 'He's not going to listen to anything coming from me.'

'Let them fight it out,' said Miguel, his voice quiet. 'Lia, stay where you are or you'll endanger your life.'

Lia stared from him to Richard, her face anguished. She nodded at Miguel but began to edge out of the pew towards Richard.

'Rodrigo, *no te lo culpes o José*.' The way she spoke exuded confidence, warrior-like, until he looked into her eyes and saw how scared she was.

'*Cállate*.' Shut up. Rodrigo's voice was like thunder and although he was almost as short as Lia, he was built like a bison in comparison. Richard risked a glance at Miguel and was surprised to see him down on his knees, eyes tightly closed as he prayed. In spite of everything he had said in the car, it seemed the man believed in God after all. He hoped Miguel was praying for their safe return to the finca.

'*Vamos a descubrir la verdad*,' said Lia, raising her voice to match his. It sounded persuasive, whatever she had said.

Richard tried to convince himself that Rodrigo wouldn't

actually harm anyone inside of a church, but it was futile. He wasn't even that scared, which made no sense under the circumstances. He felt no sense of panic, probably because he'd already been there too many times in recent weeks. Perhaps he had become numb to fear. And while Lia was terrified, at least she refused to be silenced. He wondered what she had said.

Rodrigo surprised all of them by lowering his machete and staggering from the room. Almost as quickly as it had started, it was over. People in the congregation began to talk among themselves but stayed seated.

'Are you okay?' he asked Lia as he turned to walk back to the pew. She remained standing in the aisle, even though the priest had now resumed the service in a louder than necessary voice, determined to regain everyone's attention as quickly as possible.

She stopped and turned to him. 'I'm *not* religious.'

She made it sound like he had accused her of being so.

'I think I know that by now,' he said. He felt an overwhelming desire to pull her to his chest.

'But I've no right to insult whatever you believe in,' she whispered. 'I'm so sorry for all the rude and horrible things I've ever said.'

'It's okay. You raised some valid points.' He smiled, put his arm around her stiff body and drew her back into the pew, acutely conscious of her body relaxing against him. He couldn't remember the last time he'd made the sign of the cross to bless himself, or anyone else. At the museum in the city he'd read about Guk'umatz, a feathered serpent deity held sacred and worshipped by numerous tribes for thousands of years until after the Spanish conquest. According to the ancient K'iche Maya people, Guk'umatz was the originator of all knowledge and transporter of gods. He had created humanity, and yet today he was long forgotten, nowhere to be found other than in the occasional museum. What if he was slowly losing his own faith and there was nothing he could do to bring it back?

The thought that he might be left with nothing but a cavern in his mind where his faith had once lived perturbed him even more than Rodrigo did.

They journeyed back to the finca in stony silence. Miguel refused to speak to anyone, including his wife and children, building tension in the car until they were less than five minutes away.

Finally he turned around.

'You have no idea what these people are capable of,' he began. 'If you don't want to put your life in danger, or mine, you need to respect those boundaries or get off my land.'

'I'm so sorry,' said Richard. Lia remained silent. It seemed ludicrous to think he had come between José and Rodrigo whilst Rodrigo had been armed and drunk, or that he might have placed Lia in danger.

'You know one of my workers was killed recently. There are rumours that José or Rodrigo or both of them were involved.'

Richard nodded. He couldn't think of a single motive that José would have had. Rodrigo, on the other hand, had just proven how unstable and violent he could be.

'Why don't you call the police?' said Lia.

'The police are already investigating, but as yet they have no proof.'

'Have they questioned Rodrigo?' asked Lia with a trace of optimism. 'Surely he'd incriminate himself. Have they questioned José?'

Miguel rolled his eyes.

'Look, Lia, I heard what you said to Rodrigo. Let's find out the truth!' He mimicked the high-pitched voice of an annoying child. 'Well, I'm warning you for your own safety. Leave it alone. I can't have you endangering your lives or the lives of my children. As much as I want to know the truth, just like you, if anything like this happens again you're all out of here.'

Richard looked at Lia. Just because she hadn't talked about Rafael recently didn't mean she had forgotten her hare-brained idea of finding out who was responsible for his death. Lia's cheeks flushed as she lowered her head.

Miguel dismissed her with a shake of his head, turned to his children and asked them how they were finding life in the city. Their one-word, sullen replies did nothing for his mood.

Richard stared at the field of waving grass as they drove through the entrance to the finca. He realized he had no idea what was more important to Lia: keeping a job that she already loved with all her heart, or disobeying a man who was used to maintaining order his way, and taking the consequences that came with that.

Chapter 28

The sound of hammer strikes echoed from the barn across the land, pounding out a brutal routine to which Lia and Richard readily aligned themselves each day as they laboured under Don Chema's supervision. He showed them how to clear the land with the primitive use of hoes, cutting the weeds just below the soil surface. The work was slow and difficult but they left Macy alone to work in the barn, respecting her wish for solitude.

Lia met with Miguel regularly to plan the day ahead and the progress they were making but in the days since the church incident, their relationship had cooled. He stopped requesting her company, preferring to eat and brood by himself in the main house once he'd returned from the city. With the locals still refusing to speak to her unless they had to, Lia began to wonder if she would ever find out anything more about Rafael's death.

Today though, Miguel had requested she meet him at the main house and they were discussing the logistics of moving a batch of plants from the nearby finca down to the area of land where they were needed.

'Tomorrow morning you'll meet my horseman and ride with him down to the valley,' said Miguel.

'Great. Will you join us?' said Lia. She had been waiting for the opportunity to ask him how he had heard that Rodrigo or José or both of them had been involved in Rafael's murder.

'I'll be in the city,' he replied, without looking at her.

She glanced at the mass of papers overflowing out of his briefcase. 'Need a hand sorting those papers out?'

'No,' said Miguel, and proceeded to shove them back inside the leather case as if she had threatened to burn them. Perhaps she was trying too hard.

'I don't think Richard has ever been near a horse in his life,' she said, determined to keep the lines of communication open between them.

'You'll need the horses to carry the saplings and tools. All the cars will be in use and my wife has taken the pickup.'

He bid her a good afternoon in a frosty tone and indicated with a flick of his wrist that she should go. She got up, fed up with his sulky demeanour, and bent to put her shoes on by the front door. She decided she would walk to the barn to see how Macy was getting on before returning to the valley and joining Richard for the rest of the day.

Lia was a quarter of the way down the hill when Miguel called out from the driveway.

'Lia! Two volunteers have just called and spoken to Favia! They've left the pueblo and are on their way here. Wonderful news! Well done, Lia!'

He waved to her with a broad grin and lingered for a moment, staring with what she could only interpret as forgiveness, before he disappeared back into the house. Lia continued on her way, hopeful. Once she explained that she had known Rafael he would understand why it was so important that she find out the truth.

She hoped Macy hadn't been overstating her abilities to turn the old, decaying barn into basic accommodation. She had been too tired at the end of each day, having spent hours in the heat digging up weeds, to see for herself what Macy had actually been doing.

At the entrance to the barn she heard music playing above. She climbed up the ladder and her eyes widened.

One half of the barn was unrecognizable, infested with Macy's new-found energy. Logs had been cut, moved and placed upright as if by magic, forming the corners of new rooms that were joined at the top and bottom by freshly sawn wooden beams. The barn carried a fresh, sweet pine scent that was warm and welcoming, and there were already six square rooms in place.

The matting they had bought formed new flooring and paper-thin walls for the new rooms that were eco-friendly and sustainable, although they did nothing to provide any soundproofing. The rooms were left open at the top, protected from the sun but probably not the rain by the much higher and leaky-looking barn roof. The first two rooms were larger than the others and Macy had already built a double-sized bed frame in one. It had no mattress or other furnishings. Three more rooms contained a hammock slung diagonally across the pine beams and nothing else.

'Hey,' she called out to Macy who was locked in concentration as she nailed more of the palapa matting into the wooden beams.

'Would you hold this up here while I hammer these nails in?'

Lia did as she was asked and told Macy the good news, but Macy didn't stop hammering until the last sheet of palapa was up. Then she put down the hammer and turned down the radio.

'Well, the place isn't ready yet,' said Macy at last, wiping a line of sweat from her forehead. 'I've got loads more to do. I haven't even begun to make shelves or cupboards.'

Earlier they'd agreed to house volunteers in the barn, away from Miguel, his drinking and his family problems.

'And I was going to make this area into an open living room space with bean bags and a big table and chairs.' Macy spread her arms wide. 'You get the full benefit of the natural light here.'

But there wasn't even a lock on the trap door to provide any pretence of security. The threat of Rodrigo following her up into the barn was still fresh in her mind and Lia doubted they would be able to convince anyone to stay in such basic conditions.

'Let's show them what we've got and people will decide for themselves whether they want to stay or not,' said Lia.

'I'll take a quick shower and go and wait for the volunteers at the house then,' said Macy. She walked back to the far side of the barn and was about to turn the radio off but instead stopped and focused on the news which had just come on.

Lia turned to leave.

'Wait.'

Something about her tone made Lia uneasy. Macy turned the radio up but it was over before Lia could make sense of it.

'Someone's died?'

'I think it was one of those guys Miguel introduced us to the other morning. The mayoral candidate for San José Patula,' said Macy.

'Jorgé Castaño? He's dead?' said Lia.

Macy nodded. 'Shot yesterday morning. They're linking him to drug running.'

'No way! What else did they say?'

'That was pretty much it.'

'I wonder if Miguel knows.'

Macy shrugged. 'Probably.'

They looked at each other and Lia felt as if they were discussing someone who had lost an argument or a bet, rather than their life.

'Why is it that people associated with this finca keep dying? Do you think Miguel could be involved?' asked Lia.

'He was trying to make up with his wife again yesterday morning,' said Macy, 'and I can't imagine him doing anything that would put his kids in danger.'

'And he's so open,' said Lia. 'The way we've all got free run of his house and land. He's not secretive like he has anything to hide.'

'How about José, then?'

'He's just so passive and quiet and always seems to do what he's asked without making a fuss – unlike Rodrigo,' said Lia.

'They say it's the quiet ones you have to watch out for,' said Macy. 'Rodrigo obviously blames him for something serious.'

'Apparently he *was* in the city that day,' said Lia with a sigh.

A noise somewhere between a cough and a huff made them turn. Lia jumped as she saw Rodrigo standing on the bottom rungs of the stepladder with his head poking up through the hatch. He announced that he had two people with him. Lia turned to Macy, willing her to just recognize him. Whatever Macy did or didn't remember, Lia still believed that Rodrigo was most likely responsible for Rafael's demise.

Macy shrugged her off with a look of bemusement and shook her head. Her eyes lit up at the news Rodrigo had brought, as if she hadn't dared believe the same information coming from Lia.

'*Gracias*, Rodrigo,' said Macy. He acknowledged her with a nod, neither friendly nor unfriendly.

Macy wiped her hands on her trousers and strolled over to Rodrigo. She introduced herself, shook his hand and thanked him for bringing the volunteers over. Rodrigo disappeared back down the hatch and Lia couldn't believe he had been so polite.

'Leave your rucksacks down there for now,' Macy called. 'I can bring them up in a minute. Come on up.'

A young man was the first to pop his head up through the hatch. His name was Pavel, he was Russian and twenty-five years old. He climbed up beside them and then bent to lower his hand to Liz, his girlfriend. Standing side by side, she was about a foot taller than him. She was Dutch and twenty-two years old. They both spoke rudimentary Spanish.

'So, the accommodation isn't finished, as you can see,' said Macy. 'I plan to build pine beds and get mattresses up here but you could sleep in these hammocks just for a few days or on this bed once we cover it in blankets.'

She led them to the room with the pine bed frame in it and talked faster as if to ward off any attempt the couple might have of announcing their departure back to the city.

'The way the rooms are built, you've blocked out any natural light so they are quite dark,' said Pavel. He walked across the floor, looking into each room.

'You're right. But they're really just for sleeping in and you have no curtains to draw.' She smiled. 'As soon as you step out here you're hit by a marvellous spectrum of fresh air and glorious sunshine through the biggest window you've ever seen in your life.' She pointed to the double doors at the end of the barn.

No one spoke for a minute and Lia watched Macy fidget with her fingernails.

'It's a good thing you're an electrician,' said Liz, winking at Pavel. 'Maybe you can put a light bulb or two in each room.'

He smiled and Lia pressed her hands together in relief.

'I'll show you around the finca and the reforesting area if you're ready,' said Lia.

'Are you guys hungry?' said Macy.

'We ate in the pueblo before we left,' said Pavel. 'We'd love to see the reforesting.'

'I'll show you the cottage first as that's where the kitchen, shower and bathroom are. You're welcome to hang out at the cottage as much as you want,' said Lia.

'Who owns this place?' asked Liz.

'A guy called Miguel,' said Lia. 'He's an interesting person with a fascinating history.'

Macy's eyes narrowed. 'He's a landowner of European descent and the place is quite feudal, as you'll see if you stay here a while.'

'While we were travelling around Ixcán and the Western Highlands, we met indigenous families whose water source on their land had been poisoned, or they had been forced to sell their plots to palm oil companies,' said Pavel. 'They were left completely destitute.'

Lia frowned. 'That place you mentioned. How do you spell it?'

Pavel spelled it out as she had suspected. It was another of the words that had been tattooed on Rafael's arm, marked with a bright red burial cross: Ixcán, Rabinal and Panzós. They were all the names of places in Guatemala.

Lia shook her head. 'Well at least Miguel is willing to reforest the areas he's chopped down and he does actually pay the people who work for him, even if it's not a huge amount.'

'Any idea how long you intend to stay?' said Macy.

Liz and Pavel looked at one another and shook their heads. 'Not really. The longer the better if the project is good. Time will tell.'

It was Lia's turn to smile. Even if Macy hadn't identified Rodrigo as the killer she believed him to be, things were looking up.

Chapter 29

Macy bustled around the kitchen, humming as she beat eggs in a bowl before pouring them into a frying pan and spreading butter over thick pieces of fresh bread. Favia sat at the table next to Lia and Richard. Their daily routine usually involved Favia making breakfast and washing up, but with Miguel and his family away, Macy had persuaded her to sit and relax with a cup of tea while she cooked. They had attached a gas canister to the oven at the cottage and it was easy to make breakfast there, especially now that Liz and Pavel had joined them, but today Macy wanted the opportunity to reverse roles.

'I don't want your job, Doña Favia,' she repeated in Spanish. 'I just want to thank you for your kindness towards me.'

After a half-hearted protest during which Favia kept glancing out the kitchen window, no doubt to check that the driveway was still clear of Miguel and his family, she accepted a plate of steaming scrambled eggs and toast and Macy watched with pleasure as she ate. Somehow they had swept the entrenched social class barriers of Guatemalan society to one side, if only for an hour. There was no expectation on Favia to wait for everyone else to finish eating and leave the kitchen before she herself was permitted to eat anything.

'Don Julio *está llegando*,' said Favia. She turned with a half smile, pointing at the dark figure sat upright on a majestic black horse that swished its tail as it cantered up the hill. He led three more animals: two dark brown horses and a sleek grey with striking black spots, who pawed and danced behind him. Macy hurried outside to greet him, followed by Lia and Richard.

'*Hola. Soy* Julio *y esto es* Negra.' He patted the horse before jumping off its back and thrust the reins of all four animals into Richard's reluctant hands. He seemed to derive amusement from Richard's immediate discomfort, but Macy liked his cheerful energy and the way he was quick to smile.

Richard introduced himself and the girls, and Julio beamed even more as he shook hands, nodding at Lia who he had already met. Liz and Pavel had eaten breakfast at the cottage and already returned to the barn where they were helping for the day. Macy agreed to accompany Lia and Richard on horseback to the reforesting site, keen to see the rest of the finca for the first time since her arrival and to help carry as many saplings to the reforesting site as possible before she returned to the barn.

Lia told Macy about the church incident and made her promise to keep out of Rodrigo's way. She'd only agreed so that Lia would leave her alone. With every passing day Lia became more adamant in her belief that Rodrigo was responsible for Rafael's murder, even though she was no closer to finding any real evidence to back up her claim. It made Macy all the more glad that she had managed to avoid going to the church. That Rodrigo hadn't actually harmed any of them suggested to her that he didn't recognize them and therefore hadn't been in the bar that night, which meant he was innocent. The more Lia built such an immutable idea in her head, the more it seemed to increase the hostility between her and Rodrigo. Macy sighed, wishing her memory hadn't betrayed her just when she needed it most. However much Lia disagreed, she was still sure Rodrigo wasn't the violent man she had seen in the bar the day Rafael had died.

Julio shouted a jolly greeting to Favia, interrupting Macy

from her thoughts. Favia stepped into the hallway and pointed with mock disapproval at the mud he'd brought in on his boots. He smiled at her with affection but refused to take them off, looking around the room with undisguised contempt. Handsome and dignified, he strolled with confidence over to the saddles. Macy trailed behind as he pulled one of the saddles down from the wall and handed it to her.

'How long have you worked here?' asked Macy in Spanish.

'Just a year, not long compared to the others.'

'Do you like working here?'

He sniffed as he slid another saddle off the rack.

'It's a job.' He was reluctant to say anything more but his eyes blazed with obvious discontent.

Macy followed him back outside where he proceeded to saddle up one of the horses. He took the saddle from her and placed it on one of the smaller horses.

'Why did you come here?' said Julio.

She told him about the reforesting, leaving out any mention of Rafael.

'It would give the community a longer supply of wood.' He paused. 'When you kill the trees you kill the people. The air turns dirty. Plant a tree and you plant life and hope and respect.' He spat onto the grass verge of the garden.

'We want to work together with the community so that everyone prospers,' said Macy.

This time Julio stifled a laugh. 'Miguel wouldn't let you unless his life depended on it.'

'Which is maybe why he's already agreed,' said Macy, 'and now we even have two volunteers to help.'

Julio stared at her, unconvinced.

He instructed Lia and Macy to ride Kosheela and Xavier, the smallest and sturdiest of the four horses. Richard would ride Negra and he would ride Canela, the flightiest and youngest animal. Macy saddled her horse under Julio's watchful guidance, self-conscious of her unsteady hands even though she had significantly reduced her medication intake. It took another fifteen fumbling minutes before they were ready to go.

Xavier's fur was shaggy, soft and clean, and Macy dragged her fingers through his mane, revelling in it. She had last ridden a horse as a moody adolescent. The three dogs appeared out of nowhere, bounding playfully around the horses, and there was no hint of aggression from the dog-coyote.

They waved to Favia and headed off at a walking pace down the drive, following Julio in single file towards the greenhouse containing saplings they had purchased from the neighbouring farm. They loaded a saddlebag each with twenty pounds of saplings. Julio also carried three hoes, a machete and a shovel that he placed across his lap, riding with one hand holding the tools and the other grasping the reins. They turned the horses around and left the gravel path to pad down a narrow trail of dry, cracked mud.

The sun glittered like gold, filtering through the tree cover in a yellow haze. Macy inhaled the cool, fresh air and stared wide-eyed at Richard's back as the cool air hit her lungs and her body harmonised to the balance and rhythm of the horse's body.

Julio whistled as they journeyed. He showed them another route to the valley that Richard and Lia had not known about and he kept the pace slow, allowing them to admire the mighty pine trees and dancing leaves as the horses disturbed the path. Macy had the sense of being surrounded by every kind of life here, from beetles and rodents to birds of all colours and the untold movements of animals that were smart at hiding from the likes of four humans. Some of the trees were ancient, with roots that twisted unevenly over the forest floor before disappearing underground.

She watched Lia and Richard as their horses walked companionably beside each other. Richard said something to Lia and, to Macy's surprise, she giggled like a schoolgirl. At least they were getting on now, Macy thought with a smile.

She urged her horse on faster and passed Richard and Lia to catch up alongside Julio.

'Where did you work before here, Don Julio?'

'My family own land about a hundred kilometres from here – many generations of my family have been there – but the government sold it to a multinational company where no one is responsible for their actions. We grew maize, beans, potatoes and other things but it was all destroyed in the name of rural development and turned into sugar cane. They use it to make biofuel for cars in Europe. My family and many others were left with nothing. The whole province doesn't have enough food to feed its children.'

Macy shook her head as she met his eyes.

'I'm so sorry. Is your family trying to get it back?'

'Of course. At first we refused to leave but they burned our houses down and called the army in. My father said it was no different to being in the war. You know we live in the stables here? That building is meant to house horses, not my elderly father.'

Macy felt her insides curdle, with guilt or disgust she wasn't sure. She wondered why Miguel hadn't moved Julio and his father into the cottage that she, Lia and Richard were now living in. Did the locals resent them for it?

She'd thought about it before but today was the first time she really worried about it in the depths of her bones: what if corporate greed was ruining the world faster than the activists could save it? She had always been on the periphery of activism in London. She had met numerous people campaigning for human rights, animal rights and environmental rights but she had never attended a protest or a march. They'd sort of faded in and out of her consciousness over the years as she'd focused on making money. It helped explain why she felt so ridiculously pleased to have built the new structures in the barn, even if they were primitive. It was the first time in her life that she had done any hard work for anybody else without being paid for it, and it felt good and meaningful in a way that her internet business never had.

In the brief silence that followed they heard a sequence of sharp cracks and then the creaking and groaning and muffled *whump* of a tree falling to the ground. As the path snaked around the trees, Macy sensed a larger separation between the trees and an increase in sunlight falling on them. Minutes later they came out into a clearing to find Don Chema and Tomás sitting on a tree they had felled. She counted the total number of casualties: seven.

As soon as Tomás saw them he leaned backwards to drop something behind the log they were sitting on and crushed the half-smoked butt of a cigarette beneath his foot. He tipped his hat in deference and scarpered away up the path they had just descended.

Don Chema stood up and stretched a tape measure across the breadth of the fallen trees, waiting for Lia to write down the measurements. She pulled a piece of paper and a pencil out of her pocket and jumped down. Richard and Julio trotted on ahead, forging a gentle path up the hillside to the clearing they had started days earlier.

Macy wondered what it was that Tomás had dropped and so quickly run away from. It looked like a stick. Lia had also spotted it and she leaned over to pick it up. When she realized what she was holding she nearly dropped it.

It was a wooden cross, about two feet long, with the name RAFAEL carved across and the half-finished carving of a wild animal, perhaps a jaguar. She watched as Lia ran one hand softly over the wood and bowed her head.

'You are doing his job now,' said Don Chema with a deep sigh. Lia's horse must have sensed an emotional shock going off in Lia; she tugged her head up, jerking the reins out of Lia's hands, and backed away with a snort. Lia let the horse go and the mare settled a few metres away, bending her head to graze.

Don Chema stood up and gently took the cross from her.

'Rafael was the only one of us who could read and write. He was always carrying papers around with him. Wasn't scared of anyone so long as he knew he was right.'

Lia took the tape measure and started measuring the next fallen tree. They worked in awkward silence. Macy imagined the easy banter that would have passed back and forth between Rafael and Don Chema. She remained on her horse, watching an uneasy but much-needed dialogue unfold between Don Chema and Lia.

'What was he like to work with?' Lia blurted the words out as if they would choke her if she held them in any longer.

Don Chema stopped, the tape measure suspended in mid-air, and stared at Lia.

'Rafael was a wonderful, funny and intelligent man. To us he was a hero of kindness and strength. He was also a little crazy, but he would help anyone.'

'That's the Rafael I knew!' said Lia.

'How do you mean, he was crazy?' asked Macy, curious at his choice of words. Don Chema continued to measure and call out numbers to Lia.

'He was too brave,' said Don Chema after a pause. 'He spoke about things, places, that many of us were too terrified to think about any more, including me.'

'Like what?' pressed Lia.

Don Chema looked into the forest and seemed agitated, as if he could hear something far away that worried him. He paced up and down a few times, glancing uncomfortably at them as Macy wondered what he was up to. Eventually he stopped and proceeded to hide the cross under a pile of sticks and leaves. She suddenly understood.

'We won't tell Miguel,' said Macy. His back was to her and she wasn't sure if he had heard her. Lia picked up her reins and prepared to climb back on her horse, and he turned and tipped his hat.

'When it is finished we will place it deep inside this forest, the place Rafael loved with all his life,' called Don Chema. He cleared his throat. 'I will show you.'

'Thank you,' said Lia.

'If the police come here in the next few days, be careful. Don't accept a ride to the pueblo from them,' he said, looking into the forest again, his brow furrowed. 'There are *narcos* nearby, and ears and eyes are everywhere. People are killed around here and nothing ever happens after.'

Macy shivered at his words, wondering if this meant they were beginning to gain the trust of the *campesino*.

He turned away from them and took the same path Tomás had, just as the beat of hooves announced someone else heading towards them. There were four people on four horses: Miguel, his son Raul and two people she'd never met, who forced Don Chema off the path with barely an acknowledgement of his presence as they cantered past and pulled their horses to a rough stop next to Macy and Lia.

'Good morning!' said Miguel.

His words were repeated with youthful enthusiasm by Raul.

'This is Enrique and Adolfo,' said Miguel. 'They are police officers investigating the tragic death of my friend and colleague Jorgé Castaño who was recently killed.'

Macy and Lia glanced at each other without a word and the two men greeted them with smiles, looking as if they were enjoying the opportunity to ride the horses much more than the chance to investigate. Together they followed the path that Julio and Richard had taken to the reforesting zone and Miguel brought his horse up to ride alongside Lia.

'Raul got sent home for fighting at school,' said Miguel. 'So I had to change my plans. But I'm also very keen to see what's been going on here and to show it all off to these gentlemen.'

As Lia rode ahead and continued speaking with Miguel, Macy studied Raul, a shorter and less assured but far more handsome version of his father. He noticed her looking at him and waved. It was obvious he thought the world of his father. They rounded another bend and she saw Richard.

'Thought you were never going to get here,' he panted from the clearing where he was working alone. He looked pleased to see everyone, especially Lia. His face was bright red and dripped with sweat, and he stretched his lower back with a grimace before stumbling towards them, dragging the hoe behind him. Julio had gone, taking Richard's horse with him, and the saplings lay neatly in rows where they'd unpacked them, ready to be planted.

Lia dismounted and unloaded the saplings from one side of the saddlebag whilst Richard emptied the other. She removed the saddlebag, saddle and bridle from Kosheela and left her to graze, picking up a hoe to carry on working alongside Richard. Macy dismounted to empty her own saddlebag.

'Lots of people wouldn't consider such gruelling work unless they owned the land,' said Miguel, looking down at Richard. Macy climbed back on her horse, aware that she had already spent enough time away from the barn and the new volunteers.

'People define their whole lives by what they think they own,' said Lia, 'but they usually own less than they realize.' She swung the heavy weeding tool and missed entirely, cutting through nothing but the warm air.

Miguel sat straight on his horse and smiled down at her with the same benevolence with which he had treated her until the church incident.

'Well, you're welcome to treat this land as your own.'

Lia stopped what she was doing to smile back. 'Thank you, Miguel.'

Macy rolled her eyes. Could Lia not even tell that he was flirting with her for the benefit of his companions?

The earth wasn't soft and pliable, as she had expected it to be. It was dark brown, rock hard and filled with a jigsaw of roots and greens that all had to be broken up with the hoes and removed with their bare hands. Working in the barn was hard work but she didn't envy Richard and Lia their task here. Sunburned in the raw sunlight, they desperately needed a hat or shades and had forgotten to buy either, screwing up their eyes instead as they heaved the hoes across the ground and bent to throw the undergrowth to one side.

As Macy watched, the earth seemed to move beneath Richard and Lia's feet. At first she thought she was imagining it, and then she realized they had disturbed an ant nest, oblivious to the mass of scurrying movements over the earth until the unmistakeable burning caused by a multitude of bites climbed up their legs. They threw the hoes down to slap at their legs, hopping from one foot to the other.

The corner of Miguel's mouth twitched but he managed not to laugh outright.

'Don't worry, the pain only lasts for a few minutes,' said Macy. The ridiculous image of Richard and Lia performing in *Riverdance* came to mind. Even the birds seemed to jeer at them, calling *look-a-look-a-peep-peep* to each other whilst others clacked and seemed to laugh at them.

'I wouldn't mind owning land and property like this,' said Richard once the ants had dispersed. She admired him in that moment, the way he underplayed his own pain. He insisted he was weak but there was something impregnable within him, something so reasoned and utterly devoid of conceit. Lia let loose a tirade of swear words and leaned briefly on him to replace a shoe. Macy glanced back at Miguel and thought she saw a hint of jealousy in his eyes.

'Well, it will certainly keep you fit,' said Miguel. 'And let's face it, Richard, you could afford to lose some weight.' He turned to Raul. 'Isn't that right, my son?'

Raul hesitated, for an instant uncomfortable, but when his father nudged him with his knee, he nodded and laughed, a forgery that had nothing to do with his bright white teeth.

The two men also sniggered but added nothing to the conversation.

Richard said nothing and continued to work in deadpan silence. It was the first time Macy had seen Miguel take pride in mocking someone and it took all her willpower not to applaud him with a sarcastic clap.

'I'm only joking with you, Richard,' said Miguel, winking at Lia. 'Back to business. Is there anything you need before I go?'

The two policemen were already turning their horses to go back the way they had come, unwilling to keep still for more than a couple of minutes.

Lia kept working, swinging her hoe again and making contact with the earth this time. 'We're going to need an area of land to grow seedlings on and about half an acre to grow vegetables on for the volunteers.'

Miguel nodded. 'Use the flat land closest to the barn, and when you've finished here today come up to the main house and let's have a drink.'

He seemed to be inviting Lia directly rather than the three of them. 'That's one way in which I do pay, you know, for choosing to live here, isolated from people. I've no one to talk to. The Indians don't know about anything.'

Macy looked from Miguel to Raul and back again, unable to keep quiet.

'You talk as if they aren't human.'

Miguel spoke without hesitation or surprise. 'Because they aren't like you or me. They're dirty. They don't bathe. They're not educated – I'm sorry, but you can't have a decent conversation with someone who is not educated.'

She expected Lia to say something at this point, like how it was Don Chema and not her university degree that had taught her the methodology they were using to reforest the land; or Julio who had made them aware of the global growth of biofuel and the displacement of families by people working in the industry. To her surprise, Lia kept quiet, and everything went from bad to worse.

'What's that joke you told me from school today, Raul?' said Miguel.

'I don't remember, Papa,' said Raul. If she wasn't mistaken, Macy thought she saw embarrassment darken Raul's features as he took in their shocked faces. He would prefer not to have his joke repeated in front of them given the choice, which he wasn't.

'How do you keep an Indian out of your backyard?' said Miguel with a grin. He leaned towards Lia, pointing a long, narrow finger at her, and winked. 'Move your trash cans to the front!' He burst into laughter that echoed across the clearing.

'Never trust an Indian even if he helped you once,' said Miguel as if dispensing fatherly advice to them all. 'He will be happy to rob you the next day.'

'Don't you think that's racist?'

Diplomacy had never been her strong point and the words shot out before Macy could bite them back.

Miguel sat up higher, rigid on the Arab stallion he was riding, and frowned at her.

'I see the situation in my country is beyond your comprehension. I give you a place to convalesce, my house to live in and my horses to ride, and you sit there accusing me like I'm the devil.'

'And what do you think, Raul?' said Macy, turning to the boy with a curious lilt of her head, her face carefully devoid of all judgement. 'That you can't trust Favia even though she's looked after you and your family her whole life?'

Raul didn't say anything, but in the split second before his father intervened, his eyes spoke of guilt and shame.

'Look,' said Miguel, 'the Indians may respect me but they don't like me.'

'Maybe it's because everyone around here is reduced to such servitude,' said Macy. 'I was taught to respect and help my elders. Favia's the elder and yet *you're* the one *she* looks after – and not just when you're ill.'

Macy glanced at Lia and Richard and couldn't believe that neither still had anything to say. They were swinging the hoes again with vigour as if the present conversation wasn't even happening. She had thought far more of both of them.

'What do you think I should do?' said Miguel. 'Take my children out of school, stop their education and unclothe them? Give all my money to the Indians instead? You think that would help solve the country's problems?'

Raul stared open-mouthed from his father to Macy and back again.

'I'm heading back to the barn,' said Macy. She was afraid of getting herself into something she wouldn't be able to get herself out of and which would impact on Lia, just when they had become friends again. It was not the place for her to explode with unrestrained fury or to debate. She shot them all a scathing look instead and turned her horse towards the path.

'Favia would be dead without the job that I gave her,' Miguel shouted after her.

Macy bit her lip and felt her tongue soak in the taste of blood. She didn't believe him for a second.

Chapter 30

Richard swore as he attempted to hand-wash a shirt over the *pila,* a large outdoor sink made of concrete, usually reserved for use by women. He had filled one side with water and wondered how he would empty it out as it didn't have a drain. To make it worse he had slept badly, kept awake by the girls bickering for half the night, and even though it was only lunchtime, he was already tired.

'Get a bucket, fish some water out and use that to wash your clothes on the other side of the sink,' instructed Macy.

He did as she suggested and once the shirt was wet, he scrubbed it up and down the corrugated side of the sink until he accidentally rubbed his knuckles raw on the stone and stopped to hop around in painful frustration.

Lola happened to be walking past the cottage at the same time. The sight of a grown white man trying and failing dismally to wash his clothes must have been so incongruous a sight that she burst out laughing until tears rolled down her face. He didn't mind. He grinned and returned to the sink, determined to finish the job. When he held the shirt up to inspect it he saw that he had torn a hole in the material, through which he turned to eye Lola in defeat. Lola's laughter spilled out once more into the sunshine from deep in her chest, and he threw the shirt back into the sink, dissolving into a puddle of laughter that instantly connected them. He understood enough by now to know that this wasn't how things were done in a machismo society. Somehow it set them at ease with each other, even if he could barely communicate beyond clumsy hand gestures and reading directly from his Spanish phrase book.

Lola eventually took pity on him.

'*Lo haré por ti,*' said Lola. I'll do it for you.

She offered to do his washing in exchange for a few quetzales and Richard responded by shocking the local community, forming a collective whereby each week a volunteer washed the clothes with her. The fact that men as well as women willingly became clothes washers under Lola's paid management baffled the class-conscious community but also served to make them more approachable. Through this interaction Richard began to form a friendship with Lola.

'Macy, would you help me carry the washing to Lola's, please?' he asked, more to stop the girls arguing than because he really needed it.

Macy appeared in the doorway. 'Sure.'

'You're going to Lola's house?' asked Lia, appearing behind her. She stalked past Macy to join Richard.

Richard nodded.

'Can I come?'

'I'd rather only one of you came if you can't be civil towards each other,' said Richard with a stiff shrug.

Macy came out and stood next to him. 'I'm coming.'

She turned back to face Lia. 'And all I'm saying is that Miguel is a racist, and us continuing to stay here makes us complicit in supporting a colonial, racist system. I'm not sure how much longer I can justify working for someone like that.'

'Well at least he's not a killer,' said Lia. 'It's Rodrigo that I won't make any effort for. That's evil right there.'

'But he had no motive ...'

They went on and on, both of them getting on his nerves. She just wouldn't shut up about Miguel and Lia wouldn't stop in her insistence that Rodrigo had killed Rafael. He gathered up the clothes in his arms, left a similar-sized pile for Macy and started walking towards Lola's house. Macy soon caught up with him.

'Look,' he said, 'the one thing we can surely all agree on is that regardless of the unethical means by which Miguel obtained this land and his racist attitude, if we can reforest a significant proportion of the land, it will afford future generations – Ladino, indigenous, whoever – a healthier and more sustainable environment.'

Macy nodded. 'I guess.'

'There are other reasons for keeping the peace. The local workers, except for maybe Rodrigo, all approve of the reforestation project and want it to go ahead.'

At first they had watched from a distance, shaking their heads, no doubt amused by the sight of such unwieldy tools in unblemished hands, but their scepticism changed to quiet surprise as they witnessed the land coming to life again, tree by tree.

Everyone took a lunch break at 1 p.m. Afterwards came the easier job of planting the saplings and admiring each new life that stuck up out of the earth in an ever-growing patch. After weeks of back-breaking toil, Richard was losing the spare flesh he carried and his skin had toned to match his expanding muscles. His body was starting to sculpt itself and he was able to work for more than fifteen minutes at a time without feeling as if he was killing himself. He was even beginning to enjoy it.

'I guess I do feel committed,' Macy admitted with a sigh. 'Liz, Pavel and I have finished fencing off and planting about half an acre of corn, tomatoes, carrots, spinach, onions and potatoes.'

'That's great,' said Richard.

'But I don't see why I should apologize to Miguel.' Macy shrugged.

'Well, whilst we're here I guess we should all try and stay on good terms with him,' said Richard, 'for all his flaws.'

Yesterday morning Julio had joined them and picked up a hoe. The shift in energy had encouraged Lola, her husband Marco, Tomás and Favia to come forward too, individually, during a spare moment, to exchange friendly news, advice and banter. Richard's hands were lumpy and sore with blisters but the harder they worked, the more enthused the locals became and more help was offered whenever possible. In the afternoons after school, and in the absence of his siblings, Raul joined them. His curiosity led to an eagerness to join in and then a friendly competition to see who could plant the most trees.

Richard knocked on the door to Lola's house and she opened it almost instantly. He blinked as he took in the bare walls, dirt floor and lack of electricity and furniture, unconsciously tightening his grip on the clothes. She invited them to sit on the floor whilst she took the clothes and put them into a woven basket. Her sickly mother, who was Rafael's sister, lay under a blanket in the far corner of the room, breathing heavily as she slept.

He enjoyed listening to the Spanish passing between Lola and Macy with its melodic otherness, even if he couldn't follow much of what they were saying. Every few minutes he rolled a couple of marbles back across the floor towards Lola's children, who were taking it in turns to aim them at a plastic cup.

Lola prepared to feed the two children. She rearranged sticks on a rudimentary stove made out of three stones placed next to a soot-covered wall. Reaching into the waist pocket of her skirt, she pulled out a few pieces of *ocote* that she had taken from the hillside. She lit the *ocote* and bent to blow on the fire. She coughed and Richard wondered how the family were able to tolerate the smoke day after day.

The expression on Macy's face brought him back to the present. She was glowering and every time Lola said something, she seemed to get angrier.

Lola gave the children a tortilla each. She divided the beans left over from the morning so that each child had an equal share. It was barely enough and Richard hoped that she and Marco had food for themselves.

'What are you guys talking about?' said Richard. His memories of Macy's illness were still fresh and he got nervous whenever she displayed anger or frustration.

'Lola just told me that she was eighteen years old when Miguel moved here and built his house. She remembers it well because her family were told to give up their *milpa* fields and work for him. If anybody refused, they were told to find a new place to live, and there wasn't much anybody could say or do because he paid the local police to enforce his wishes.'

Richard gasped, appalled. He was finally beginning to understand how Lola's agreement to live like this must have been an act of desperation resorted to in a time of crisis: a clear-cut choice between survival and total ruin.

'They wake up at 4 a.m. to do household chores. At 6 a.m. everyone aged five and above starts work. For Lola and her children this means collecting *ocote* on the hillside. On a good day they can pick up to 130 pounds, tied in a sack around Lola's waist. It earns her the pitiful amount of three quetzals.'

'Her children don't go to school?'

Macy shook her head.

As he listened to them talk, he heard Rafael mentioned by name, and *la ciudad*, the city, and realized that Macy was telling Lola about the things that had happened to them before they'd ended up on the finca, things that they had said they would keep to themselves. Lola clapped a hand over her mouth. Then it was Lola's turn to speak and he realized that he simply didn't want to know what she was saying. It had been easier to think of Rafael as a gangster. He didn't want to know that he had in fact been a wonderful man who had always helped others, or that he had been adored by everyone who had known him. Perhaps death made saints of them all, he thought with a sigh.

Even he had stopped entertaining thoughts of leaving though. The longer they stayed on the finca, the happier he became. How could he be so happy? It was hardly the safest place – police and civil patrol units ruled the streets with impunity and were easily bought off. Don Chema repeatedly warned them to avoid any contact with the police. He had been earnest when he'd told him that on the occasions when the police *were* able to locate a kidnap victim, rather than take them home they would place the victim in custody and say, 'Okay, we saved you. Give us two thousand dollars or we'll shoot you ourselves.'

For all this, here on the finca they seemed to live in a trouble-proof bubble. London had become a tiny, irrelevant speck in the back of his mind, where washing machines, TV and concrete ruled, and happiness was expected to come with it like a 'buy one, get one free' offer in a bargain sale. At least here people were frank about life. No one believed or even pretended to believe that the police could be trusted or that the courts were just, even if the president had been impeached, and it was to this level of honesty that he found his spirit awakening and becoming addicted. He was falling in love with the wild, green country, just as Lia and Macy had done before him.

'I'm going up to the main house,' said Richard, standing up to leave.

'Why?'

'Miguel kindly said I could use his phone to call my dad.'

'I'll come with you.'

'*Muchas gracias*, Lola,' said Richard. In faltering Spanish and helped by Macy, he agreed to return the next day to help wash the clothes.

His father picked up on the first ring. He gripped the receiver and tried not to sound nervous. Macy hovered outside the office door, trying to look unconcerned.

'Hello, Dad … how are you? I'm so sorry I haven't called all this time.'

'Hello, son. Are you coming back?' The voice was familiar yet softer than he remembered.

'No … sorry, but no, I won't be coming back any time soon.'

'I know you're in Guatemala. I've wanted to speak to you since you left, to say sorry for every awful thing I ever said or did to you.'

Richard remained silent on his end of the phone, almost unable to believe his ears.

'I'll be putting money into your bank account and you can still take over the business from me, if and when you come back.'

What could he say? 'How did you know I was here?'

'I got the police to trace your Visa card.'

Stunned, he muttered his thanks, said goodbye and placed the receiver down.

'Are you okay?' asked Macy.

'For years I've asked God to help make my father go easy on me,' said Richard with a wry smile. 'Turns out all I had to do was move here.'

He had longed to hear his father apologize, and yet when the words finally came, they had little emotional impact. Perhaps they had come too late or he had moved too far away in his head to really care any more.

Yesterday he had privately embarrassed himself whilst attempting to pray to God for the first time in weeks. He'd asked that God show him a way to get Lia to fall in love with him. It had felt foolish before he'd even knelt and he cringed at the memory. Either God wanted nothing more to do with him or being a Christian now felt as outdated as the antiques his father collected in England.

The more he thought about it, the more it seemed a false source of authority. He'd donated money – often – into a pot that was constantly on the move through the congregation, for various causes. But the detail and the struggle behind the money? Or where that money went and how it was spent? He hadn't ever given it a second thought. The pot was like a debt that never got paid but kept getting bigger the more money people put into it and the more time went by. The fact was that churches didn't supply the social services required by those in need. The homeless weren't housed and the hungry weren't fed. It seemed the further from church he got, the more empowered and capable he became of making a positive impact on the world around him.

They could hear Miguel talking to Favia in the kitchen and Macy rolled her eyes.

'I'll speak to him now,' she promised with a grimace.

'I'll come with you.' These days she was totally back to her old self. Not that he had known her for long, but her eyes were clear and her demeanour relaxed. She was down to half a pill a day, a fraction of what she had taken when they first got to the finca. They made their way to the kitchen.

'Miguel …' began Macy, her expression suddenly so contrite that Richard had to hide his amusement.

'I apologize from the depths of my heart for yesterday's outburst.'

She glanced at Richard and he knew her well enough to realize that she felt no remorse at all.

Miguel sighed and looked at her as if he was trying to make up his mind whether to embrace her or not.

'Thank you, Macy,' he said. 'That means a great deal to me. The evening before I met you all on the horses, I saw Rodrigo and Julio fighting near the stables. I ordered them to stop. It drives me crazy and they wouldn't tell me what it was about. I'm Libran!' He threw his hands in the air as if this explained everything. 'I just want peace and harmony in my life. So I get frustrated. It's why I spoke so disparagingly about the workers the day after.'

Macy nodded. 'I understand.'

They turned to go but Richard paused. He was thinking about Julio and how he was different from the others. It was the way he wasn't afraid to strut about. He didn't fawn over Miguel like Favia, Tomás or even Don Chema did, and Richard knew that he had only been working on the finca for a short time.

'You don't think Julio could have had anything to do with the death of your worker?'

Macy shook her head in startled disagreement, frowning at him. He knew Macy thought highly of Julio but he felt he had to ask anyway.

Miguel raised his eyebrows in surprise. 'I hadn't considered it,' he said with a deep breath. 'It's possible, but I doubt it. He's a popular face around here, gets on with everyone. As far as I know they were good friends.'

Richard nodded and turned to go.

'Please,' said Miguel. 'Try not to worry yourselves about this any more. It was such a nasty business and a terrible shock to everyone here. I'm sorry you've been exposed to it. Oh, and you're all more than welcome to use my phone again any time,' said Miguel.

'Thank you,' both Macy and Richard chorused.

'It's Rodrigo that bothers me,' he added. 'He should be delighted with the fact that he has a roof over his head, his lovely wife Lidia and another child on the way, but he's a complete drunken mess.'

As they walked back towards the cottage, Richard found himself thinking about the shotgun at Miguel's house and he hoped once again that he hadn't made a terrible error of judgement. He wondered what the two men had been fighting about and whether Lia had been right about Rodrigo all along.

Chapter 31

Macy high-fived Pavel and Liz as she stood up. They made a striking couple. Pavel's small frame made Liz look bigger than she was but his strength more than made up for it.

'You are two of the most self-sufficient and energizing people I have ever had the pleasure of meeting,' she said.

'Likewise,' said Pavel.

'What brought you both out to Guatemala?'

They had just finished upholstering an old sofa in the barn and she planned to walk up to the main house to get a couple of pounds of freshly ground coffee for the cottage.

'I left the Russian army.' Pavel sighed, wiping sweat from his forehead. 'I signed up for a year's draft and survived the six-month-long induction, but on a transfer to St. Petersburg I got into a fight. I refused a stupid order to make someone coffee.'

'God, I'm so sorry,' said Macy.

'Armies will always produce some people who will do whatever they are told, with no thought process of their own,' said Pavel. 'So I escaped to preserve my mind, not just my body.'

'And that's where we met,' said Liz with a wide grin. 'I finished my nursing degree and was on a six week voluntary exchange placement and I found Pavel trying to break out of the same hospital. After a few days we made a plan and left together.'

'I love you guys,' said Macy, 'and I am so grateful that you ended up here.'

News about the project spread as volunteers came and went and before long, thousands of small trees studded the land. Some only stayed a few days to a week, and others, like Pavel and Liz, stayed for months. Some of the volunteers were little more than teenagers whilst others had been in their forties and they came from all over the world, united by an opportunity to plant trees.

The walk up and down the hill took Macy mere minutes now and she no longer experienced calf pain or breathlessness. Foremost in her mind was the concern that as more time passed there were more and more aspects of finca life that they kept secret from Miguel.

Once Marco and Julio discovered that Pavel was an electrician, they requested that he connect their living quarters to the electricity grid, and Pavel happily complied. They didn't tell Miguel and it felt as if they were beginning to lead double lives.

She walked past the vegetable garden which had recently yielded a large batch of organic produce for the community and, unbeknown to Miguel, caused a whole day of celebrations. The sight of stalks of corn towering over the weeds had stirred long-buried emotions. She hadn't really understood it until she watched Marco enter the garden one morning and stroke the bright green leaves when he thought no one was watching. Now she was sure the corn stalks were a reminder of the days when the locals could call the land their own.

She found herself thinking about Rafael again, surprised that Richard had openly asked Miguel such an outrageous question about Julio. Could Miguel be the perpetrator of a crime such as murder? Surely, unless her mind was still playing tricks on her, he was capable of anything – if his history was anything to go by. He was racist at heart and just happened to be Rafael's last employer. But what motive could he possibly have had? Rafael had worked with Miguel for years, and if he had problems with him, surely Miguel would have just fired him? She had no regrets telling Lola how they had returned to the bar that fateful night, trying to track down Rafael's long-lost briefcase. It was just a shame that they hadn't been able to find it.

She was so deep in thought she had almost reached the top of the hill before she saw Richard.

'Clarisa has just arrived back with the children,' he said. 'She and Miguel are trying to reconcile again.'

'That's great news,' said Macy. 'We can show them the reforested area.'

At that moment Sofía came running down the path towards them so fast that at first she thought the girl would run straight past.

'Hi, Sofía,' called Macy. 'It's good to see you again.' In the time that Sofía had been away her hair had grown and covered her eyes and she looked as if she had lost weight.

Sofía stopped but only because she could see Pavel and Liz coming up the path in front of her. She turned to face Macy.

'Go and sell tomatoes in the market, Indian,' said Sofía, and she spat at Macy with her hands balled into fists.

Macy froze, but Sofía hadn't finished. 'Why were you people able to live here with my father and my brother while we had to go to the city?'

Pavel and Liz had caught up with them and Pavel tried to intervene. 'Hey, that's not nice. We're working with your father to enrich the land for future generations, and that includes you.'

'It's not fair,' she yelled. No one knew what to say and her defiant nature made it difficult to comfort her. Macy could see the hurt in Sofía's eyes but she couldn't suppress the revulsion she also felt towards the girl.

'Leave. I hate you. This is my home not yours, *Indio*,' Sofía hissed, and again her words seemed to be aimed directly at her and her brown skin.

'It's a damn shame you don't know any better.'

She tried not to take the racial slur personally but couldn't help thinking that this was where they had gone wrong with Miguel. She looked at Richard and a familiar frustration bubbled up inside her. Did the words of Miguel's youngest child really bother Richard when they weren't directed at him? Wasn't that why racism still persisted into the current day? Because it was minimized or ignored by people like Richard?

Richard stared from Sofía to Macy in silent surprise but he said nothing. It was just as she thought.

'Have you got treacle in your ears, Richard?'

'I don't know what to say to her,' he replied, turning his hands palm up.

She suddenly felt limp, the adrenalin leaving her body as quickly as it had arrived. Perhaps the time away and constant aggravation between her parents had left an indelible mark and hatred was really all that Sofía had left, to be passed like a mantle from one generation to the next.

At that moment Sofía saw Iker, Lola's six-year-old son. She jogged towards him until she was close enough to pick up a pine cone and throw it at him.

'Hey *tonto*, go back to your dirty house and your dirty people,' she taunted him in Spanish.

Iker stayed where he was and dodged the first two flying pine cones as if he was playing a game of dodgeball. Unable to hit his agile body, she lost patience and ran towards him, pushing him over and kicking down on his arms, which he wrapped around his face, curling up on his side in the grass.

Richard and Liz, who were nearest, were quick to intervene, restraining the girl in a bear hug whilst Macy and Pavel checked the boy for injuries.

With watering eyes and her lips pressed tight, she jerked away from them and ran.

Macy sighed, watching as Pavel hoisted a still cheerful Iker up onto his shoulders and headed for Lola's house. She continued on her way to the main house. It wasn't just this incident that gave her the prickly feeling that they were all heading blind towards something terrible. It was the growing number of things they were keeping secret to avoid Miguel's disapproval; from Favia secretly rearing baby chicks under her bed in the main house, to Don Chema joining them for dinner at the cottage before he left to return to the pueblo. As the months passed, the age-old barriers of race and class had crumbled further between the volunteers and the locals, but Miguel had no sense of it. He was just delighted to see little trees growing on his empty land.

The back of her neck was wet with sweat. Her shirt clung to her and she realized they had reached the sweltering peak of summer. The air was hazy and hot to breathe, but even if she dripped sweat from head to toe, she was also thriving in it, keeping well and sleeping a regular eight hours.

She reached the entrance and listened for the sounds of Miguel and his family, but the house sounded deserted. She took off her shoes and headed for the kitchen. Favia was there, mopping the floor. She smiled when she saw Macy, the lines around her eyes crinkling as she gestured for her to sit down.

'Would you like a cup of coffee?' she asked. 'I've just made some.'

'Yes, please,' Macy replied. She sat with an unintentional thud.

'Something on your mind?'

'Lots of things,' said Macy, but nothing she could easily verbalize. Compared to Favia, whom many white people in Guatemala probably believed halfway between human and animal, her own life was a bed of roses in this racially illiterate society. She sighed again.

'Favia, why did everyone around here think Rafael was a little crazy?'

Favia sighed and looked away.

'I know he was a good man,' added Macy.

'He wanted all of us to protest the land theft,' said Favia, her voice barely more than a whisper. 'It's no secret what happened here, but it was a long time ago.'

'Did you?' said Macy.

'Of course not,' hissed Favia, staring around her at the walls, as if worried they might have ears.

'Why not? If it was wrongfully taken?'

Favia turned on her and she was shocked at the depth of anger in her eyes. 'What happens when you are simply too afraid to protest? Does that make you a bad person?'

Macy shook her head. 'No, of course not.'

'We grew up during a time when the army or the police would beat us, cut us and kill us for no reason. Every day we lived in total fear. To protest anything meant certain death.'

Macy nodded. 'But look what happened in the city recently: all those people protesting against the president, and now he sits in jail like an ordinary accused criminal.'

Favia's hands trembled at her sides but she refused to sit down.

'When I heard about those protests I felt utter terror,' she admitted. 'That people would even bring their children ...' Favia's face drained of colour as she shook her head. 'I wanted to scream at those people and tell them to run before the military gunned them down.'

Favia touched Macy lightly on the shoulder. Her eyes were huge and shiny as if she was holding in a thousand tears, and her breathing shallow. 'I had a family too,' she whispered. 'I'm the only one left. Surviving has been my greatest act of resistance.'

A wave of regret washed over Macy.

'God, I'm so, so sorry,' said Macy. 'I don't ever want to upset you.'

She got up to hug Favia who turned her back and walked to the other side of the kitchen. She remained there for a minute before returning, her face freshly composed.

'Protesting takes money,' she said. 'Money for buses, money for food and water ... and what about the lost wages because you aren't doing your job, or tending to the family, or to the crops? So people like us, we cannot easily find a way to protest anything.'

'Rafael would have been in that crowd in the city, wouldn't he?' asked Macy.

'Yes,' said Favia. Her face broke into a distant smile.

'Where is Miguel?'

'He took Clarisa down to the forest.'

'Raul must be happy to have his mum and siblings back.'

Favia nodded, her eyes twinkling. 'He poured me a cup of water. That boy is growing less like his father every day.'

Macy smiled. 'He spends most of his free time with the volunteers and is really hard-working.'

He'd grown up almost overnight compared to his siblings, she thought. There was nothing Raul enjoyed more than driving the volunteers to the pueblo and back in the old Volkswagen Trekker. He was a good driver, too. Liz had asked Raul what the police would do if they stopped him for driving under age without a licence. He had smiled and pulled a fifty quetzal note from his pocket to show her. Whenever they all squashed into the car to journey into the pueblo, machismo heads would turn and mouths would drop open at the sight of Pavel sitting on his girlfriend's lap and a fourteen-year-old boy driving the car.

'You've all got to be more careful,' said Favia, turning to look out of the window. Her voice was so soft that Macy could hardly hear her.

'Here come Miguel and Clarisa.' She turned back to Macy

and swallowed. 'The rainy season is just a few weeks away and then your time here will be over.'

She wasn't imagining it, then; Favia felt it too. Maybe Richard and Lia had reached the point where they simply refused to see or feel any more negativity even though the stench of it was all around them. They had learned to live amid a feudal system that bred extreme inequality. They slept soundly between clean cotton sheets whilst Julio and his father slept under a dirty blanket in a corner of the wooden stables. Snakes and mice passed through gaps in the walls of Lola's house whilst a breeze passed through the holes in the roof of the barn. Both homes were rustic but better than sleeping in the stables, which were full of blood-sucking ticks. They showed Miguel nothing but respect, attention and even friendship, and they had learned to look away each time he limited the potential of his workers for his own gain. How naïve they were to imagine that this could be any kind of a stable situation.

Macy grabbed the sack of coffee that Favia had put aside for her, laid a hand softly upon Favia's arm and left before she would have to see Miguel and Clarisa.

Chapter 32

Lola, Favia and Lidia, the women on the finca, took much longer to accept Lia. Perhaps it was because she was so much younger than Macy and yet found herself in a position of authority, or maybe it was because Macy had shown herself to be more vulnerable and therefore human. When the locals had initially shunned her, Lia had simply succumbed to the invisibility they inflicted upon her, but they had been unable to keep it up once the project picked up pace and she stopped spending as much time with Miguel in the evenings. Slowly, they began to treat her differently, eventually going so far as to invite her into their houses.

Today Lia was using her lunch break to drop off a box of aromatic rice and chicken that she had cooked the night before. Lola's initial refusal of food gifts had been met with equally stubborn resistance, and when she whipped the lid off the first box and the aroma had enveloped them, Lola reluctantly accepted it.

She knocked on the door and waited. Lola had even become comfortable enough to smile indulgently whenever Lia pronounced a Spanish word wrong and then took the time to correct her, as she did with Richard. She had taught them some of the slang they used amongst themselves, a mix of K'iche' and Spanish, and when they began to use it, her face lit up with pleasure.

The door opened and Lola invited her in.

'*Buenas días*, Lola, *¿cómo está?*' said Lia.

Lola smiled. '*Bien.*'

She took the food box and gestured for her to sit on the bench that ran the length of the room inside the house. She was about to make herbal tea, freshly picked from José's garden, when Lia took the photo from her pocket and thrust it into Lola's hands.

'I asked a friend in London to send it.'

Lola took a sharp breath. She touched the man in the photo, her face at once tender and shocked.

It was a picture of Rafael, a living, breathing, smiling Rafael with his arm looped around Lia's shoulders.

'Taken in London, where we met.'

Lola stared at Lia, still uncomprehending. Her face clouded over. 'He would have told me about you. He told me he met a Mark and a Stanford and somebody called Julianne.'

'That's my full name. No one but him has ever called me that.'

Lola was silent again, but it was a fertile silence of fresh awareness and new thoughts.

'Why didn't you tell me?'

'You, I … we all needed time to grieve,' said Lia.

Lola sighed. 'What does this all mean now?'

Lia shrugged. 'Nothing. I just wanted you to know, and to have the picture. You can cut me out of it.'

Lola hugged the picture to her chest, her eyes shiny.

'You should know you meant a great deal to him.'

She surprised Lia by placing her arm around her and squeezing her shoulders tight.

'Everyone around here liked Rafael, especially Raul.' She smiled and swatted a fly away from her face. 'In many ways he was like a baby brother to Rafael.'

'He's a good brother to Alfredo and Sofía, trying to keep them out of trouble,' said Lia.

Raul would sometimes bring a football down to play with Iker, in spite of Sofía and Alfredo's sullen refusal to join in. He had also taken to spending the night in the barn on occasion, in one of the spare hammocks, appearing with his dogs late at night when he could no longer bear hearing his parents fight.

The tears spilled out now, as Lia had known they would, mingling with the lines on Lola's face. She twisted her hair through her fingers as her mind returned to the last night in the city when she had been with Rafael.

'I couldn't help him,' she whispered. The guilt came rushing back without warning.

Lola nodded. 'Macy told me you were all there that night. It wasn't your fault.'

Lia closed her eyes for a second, willing the images away. 'Don't you want to know who *is* responsible?'

'Just know this: that a butterfly waits, growing inside its prison until one day the time comes to fly free.'

Lola picked up the machete she had been using on the hillside earlier that day and sharpened the blade against a stone, focused upon the small sparks that glittered against the floor with each grate of metal.

There was an urgent rap on the door. They weren't expecting anyone else – Marco and Rodrigo were in the pueblo and Richard and Macy had gone on ahead to the reforestation zone with the volunteers.

'*Buenas días*,' said Julio, uncharacteristically flustered as he pushed open the door, removed his hat and came in.

'Lola, I don't know what to do any more,' he confessed. 'I asked the patrón for a pay rise. I told him about my father and how I need the money for the doctor and medicines.'

Lola gestured for him to sit on the bench beside Lia. She took his hand, gave him the box of food and bent down to reach for another box under the bench. She took thirty quetzals from it.

'I can give you this.'

Julio shrugged her off as she tried to give it to him, and shook his head with a frown. He stood up and paced the room.

'He told me to look for more work in the pueblo.'

Lola sighed and looked down to the floor.

Julio scowled. 'He's never liked me because I refuse to be a pet animal to him in the way that Tomás and José let themselves be.'

'Richard can help your dad,' said Lia.

He had already paid for the doctor for Lola's mother. He'd found Lola kneeling in the garden behind Miguel's house, picking out the herbs that would help bring her mother's fever down whilst listening out for the car that would herald Miguel's return. Lola knew all about the wild plants and herbs, which ones to eat for food when crops failed and which ones made good medicine. She'd told Richard that she refused to get into more debt with Miguel for the sake of a few plants that grew unbidden, free to root and flourish as they pleased. Richard had insisted on driving the doctor to her door the next morning and he covered all the costs on one condition: that nobody told Miguel what he had done. Lola's mother was now well enough to travel into the pueblo and spend the morning there, catching up on gossip with old friends, and Richard had been delighted with the outcome and strangely empowered at seeing how a small amount of money could make such a difference to someone.

'*I* should be providing for my family, not you,' said Julio. 'I earn my money, I don't want handouts.'

'I know,' said Lia, 'but we just want to help.'

Julio rounded on her. 'You think I want to live only at the whim of others? Shouldn't *I* be the one to determine my own life and my father's?'

'Yes, of course,' said Lia, a flush creeping across her cheeks. She cleared her throat.

Lola put her hand on Julio's shoulder. 'It's okay, Don Julio.'

'It's demeaning,' muttered Julio. He thrust the box of food

back at Lola and shook his head. 'Keep that for your children. We should have a fair wage, Lola, the money that we've earned.'

'Sit down and have some tea,' said Lola, taking the box and handing him and Lia a small tin cup of tea each.

Julio sighed and did as he was asked. He saw the photo that Lola had placed on the bench and picked it up.

'So good to see you again, my friend,' he said softly. He smiled at Lia then and visibly relaxed before turning back to Lola.

'The patrón was even late paying Carlos. In another few days his oxen would have collapsed without food. Then what would he do?'

'Hire someone else,' said Lola. She shook her head in dismay.

They sat in silence, Julio studying Lia, making her uncomfortable.

'You should just tell her,' said Lola.

'Tell me what?' said Lia.

There was an awkward but brief silence.

'I thought I could start a riding school here,' said Julio at last, with a shy smile. 'Teach the volunteers, the children and anyone from the pueblo who wanted to learn about animal care and riding, for a small fee.'

'That's a fantastic idea!' said Lia.

'But I don't know how to speak to the patrón about it. I would divide the fee with him and we would both benefit.'

'I would be happy to raise it with him. I'm supposed to report to him in the next half hour anyway,' said Lia.

Julio picked up the photo of Rafael and Lia again. 'I miss him.'

'So do I,' said Lia.

She stared at Julio and wondered how much she could trust him. She stood up, trying to think of a way to tell them her worst fears without sounding small-minded or crazy.

'About Rodrigo … he's violent and I think he did something to Rafael,' she spluttered, the words coming out all at once. 'He threatened José when we were in church and he's always been aggressive and nasty towards me.'

Lola and Julio stared at her, their eyes wide in surprise.

'Nobody likes this awful man,' said Lola, as if she'd just drawn this fresh conclusion.

'What were you arguing about with him recently,' she asked Julio, 'when Miguel came by and saw you both?'

Julio shook his head. 'Nothing much. I just told him I would kill him if he ever hurt his wife again.'

Lia felt her scalp prickle. He still held the picture of Rafael and her in his hand and she wondered if he knew more about Rafael's death than he was letting on. Could he have been involved too? She quickly dismissed the thought but felt a strong urge to leave Lola's house.

'You should talk to Rodrigo and ask him where he was and what he was doing that day,' said Julio.

It was what Macy had been saying for months.

Lia shook her head. 'I'm sorry, but he's violent and I've heard how he abuses his pregnant wife. I'd rather keep away from people like that.'

'Then how will you find out the truth?' said Julio in a gruff voice.

'I don't know yet but I'm working on it,' said Lia.

Unless she had imagined it, a secretive glance passed between Julio and Lola, and Lia had the feeling that she had said too much.

She swallowed the rest of the sweet tea and opened the door to leave. She couldn't rid herself of the butterflies in her stomach as she went on her way, alone, up to the main house.

Cars parked in the drive signalled that Miguel hadn't gone into the city. Lia kicked off her trainers and noticed Macy's shoes beside the door. What was she doing there? She walked past the dining room and kitchen, taking a deep breath. As she approached the study she saw Macy standing with her back against the wall and a sheaf of papers in one hand. She put a finger up to her mouth to dispel any doubt she might have had that she was eavesdropping.

Lia heard the unmistakable rumbling voice of Nelson Morales, one of the men she had met on her first day at the finca, in deep conversation with Miguel.

To her horror she felt a sneeze forming; she managed to clamp the inside of her arm to her mouth but an *ah-mmp* still came out, muffled but audible.

Miguel appeared at the door.

'Good afternoon, how lovely to see you both.'

She mumbled a greeting to both men and Macy thrust the latest logging measurements into Miguel's hand. Lia mouthed a silent 'Thank you' at her, realizing she had forgotten to pick them up from the cottage.

'Morales, I don't think you've met Macy before,' said Miguel.

'Hello Macy, how lovely to meet you.' He stood up to appraise her and then offered his hand. She looked at it as if it were something she found mildly distasteful but to Lia's relief she stepped forward and offered her own, shaking his hand vigorously and for longer than necessary.

'And where are you from?' asked Morales.

'England.'

'I mean your parents?'

'Bermuda and England.'

'You look Afro–Mestizo.' Morales smiled at Miguel.

'Yes,' said Macy, 'And I could pass for Garifuna, the mixed-race descendants of the African slaves who were exiled by the British after repeated rebellions and ended up along the Caribbean coastline of Guatemala.'

'I only meant that you don't look English,' said Morales.

'No?' She winked at Lia, obviously enjoying herself. 'Have you been to England?'

'Not yet. I would love to visit.'

'You should. You'd learn that lots of people look like me there.'

Her brash mood made Lia wish Macy had stayed at the reforesting zone with the others.

'It's a lovely day to be in Guatemala too,' said Lia, clearing her voice. 'I had the most amazing fresh bread made by one of our volunteers.'

'You remind us that society is not as black and white as we like to think,' said Miguel, as if she hadn't spoken. He took a sip from his glass and placed it carefully back down onto a coaster without looking away from her.

'Good!' said Macy.

Were they staring each other out or did Lia just need to relax a little? She sighed, wondering whether to admire the way Macy could so casually overrule his assumptions. She closed her eyes for a second and let the distant coo of a pigeon fill her ears.

'I've just seen Julio,' said Lia, 'and he came up with the idea of earning you more income by starting a riding school. He's got the brains and ability to make it a huge success, don't you think?'

Miguel returned to his desk and sat back down. His face had been impassive but now his lips curled in disapproval. He and Morales were already drinking though it wasn't even noon.

She thought she heard Morales snicker with his mouth pressed up behind his glass.

'A riding school!' Miguel repeated, as if the mere thought of it was ludicrous. 'Julio is a K'iche' Indian. He's not destined to make money and if I did give him the opportunity, he would drink it away.'

'Okay,' said Lia, 'but what if you're wrong? The volunteers alone are willing to pay to learn to ride properly.' She was ready to leave it at that, preferring to bring the subject back up once Morales had gone, but Macy stepped out in front of her. She pulled a cigarette from her packet and lit it with steady fingers.

'If it didn't work then you would have proven your point,' said Macy, her eyes cool and unblinking as they swivelled from Miguel to Morales and back. 'But it deserves a chance.'

'He's smart, yes,' said Miguel. 'Look how he's used you to get to me. Not a chance in hell.'

Macy shook her head, expelling tendrils of smoke towards the men, which Lia knew would annoy Miguel who was a non-smoker. 'Actually, this is the first *I've* heard about a riding school, but I think it's a brilliant idea.'

'Give the Indians a taste of money or business and I could have a revolution on my hands,' he snorted. 'No, keep the Indians in their places. Start to trust them and they'll get you when you're not looking.'

'Okay, fine,' said Lia, suddenly desperate to leave the room before Macy went so far as to drop ash over the floor. She shot Macy a warning glare.

'And don't spend too much time with them,' he warned. 'Remember you work for me, not them.'

'Of course,' replied Lia.

Macy turned to look at her with raised eyebrows that only Lia could see and eyes that blazed with scorn.

'Right, well, we're going,' said Lia. 'Thank you, Miguel. It was lovely to see you again, *señor*.'

She felt the eyes of both men burning holes into her back as she retreated, pulling Macy along with her.

Chapter 33

'Yes sir, no sir, three bags full sir.' Macy said, as soon as they were out of earshot. 'The longer we stay here, the less I like that man.'

'Were you listening in on them?'

'I was trying to prove my theory that Miguel is the most likely person in this whole sorry set-up to have knocked Rafael off.'

'And did you hear him incriminate himself?'

'No,' admitted Macy. 'But I think we should all leave this place soon, regardless of what we do or don't find out.'

'We can't,' said Lia, her tone pleading. 'Rodrigo was involved and I think Miguel knows it too.'

Macy stared at her with half-amused, half-pitying eyes.

'Do you honestly feel that strongly?'

'I still believe in what we're doing here,' Lia whispered, but it sounded like a lie.

'You mean lining the pockets of some fascist landowner with free labour and a fresh supply of trees whilst unwittingly promoting his racist ideology?'

'Of course not,' said Lia.

'Then why are we here, working in a place where the indigenous – the family and friends of Rafael – are treated with so little respect?'

She looked away in frustration. Why wouldn't Lia just answer the question?

The pine trees towered around them, fallen acorns all over the grass. They dropped away with the ground, and between the coffee and banana plantations Macy noticed another steep path curving beneath them.

She looked back at Lia. She had always thought of her as having a strong sense of integrity, someone who would always rise above dishonour and deceit. Had she been totally wrong?

'You said it yourself, ages ago.' Lia rounded on her then, nostrils flared. 'The rich and powerful always win because there's no justice here. We agreed that—'

'I was wrong. The Guatemalan president is in jail, after all,' said Macy with a shrug.

'Rafael would want us to plant as many trees as we could,' said Lia. Rafael. It always came back to him. 'The workers support us too,' she said, as if she could read Macy's mind. 'All except Rodrigo.'

'But they aren't going to benefit from any of the trees we put in the ground.' That was one of the things she was finding harder and harder to accept with each passing day.

'How tight do you have to be to even make them pay for the tiny bit of *ocote* needed to light their cooking fires!'

They stood in brief silence beside the fenced-off garden of vegetables. The branches of trees shivered gently in the breeze, and looking up to the sky, Lia also trembled. Macy was tired of trying to understand her.

'Would you just come with me to the stables?' said Lia.

Macy finally relented with a sigh. 'Okay.'

'Don't you feel a real sense of belonging here? That has to count for something,' said Lia in a small voice.

'No I don't, not particularly. I think you have to be enough for yourself,' Macy muttered. 'You have to choose to belong wherever you are, whether it's in between two worlds, on an aeroplane heading somewhere new or back to a landscape of already-lived experience.'

Her words were lost on Lia, who had visibly tensed. Julio stood by the entrance to the stables, talking to Rodrigo as he brushed one of the horses down.

'*Buenos días,*' Macy called with a cheerful wave.

The men nodded to her but became silent as they approached, until Lia was near enough to pass the rolled-up notes to Julio.

'Hello, Julio. Please. Take this from Richard, just this once.' she said. 'It's for your dad.'

He paused and then took the notes with a sullen nod. Rodrigo watched the exchange, as did Macy, but Lia wouldn't acknowledge him. Although Macy knew better than to say anything, she was still totally convinced that Lia was wrong about him.

Back at the cottage, sitting on the bed in Richard's room, Lia brought up the possibility of giving the locals an equal share of funds. Outside, the dark was absolute, with the usual spangled glow of stars hidden by dense cloud cover. It was the first evening in weeks that they hadn't laid out on the grass, enjoying relief from the heat of the day and looking skyward as they listened to crickets chirp and talked about their home lives or the weirdest foods they'd tried during their travels.

'Except Rodrigo,' said Lia. 'We don't need to give a murderer anything.'

'How on earth can you say that?' Macy threw her arms in the air. 'You have absolutely no proof to back up your claims.'

'It's not my fault your mind went completely blank after that horrible night in the city,' Lia shot back.

Richard stood up. 'Okay, let's keep it calm. The point is that Miguel pays pathetically small wages to everyone, so we're not going to single anyone out or make one family suffer for no reason.'

'I cannot believe you just suggested giving money out to everyone,' said Macy, sitting up straight. 'Since when did the issues here become yours to fix? And what on earth makes you think *you* know what's best?'

Richard sighed. 'Well, it's not my money, it's my father's really, and he's got too much of it. We'd just be redistributing it more fairly.'

'My toothpaste is running out and no lie, I'm beginning to think that when it's finished, I should be too. I should just leave,' said Macy.

'So you're against the idea?' said Richard.

'I'm against you feeding your ego whilst unconsciously reinforcing the pernicious assumption that brown-skinned people need fair-skinned people to help them,' said Macy.

Richard stared at her. 'You're welcome to use my toothpaste.'

Macy grinned but then grew serious again. 'Doing something like this would imbue *you* with a sense of pride and satisfaction, but what would it do for the locals? Have you even bothered to ask them?'

'It would mean they could access healthcare,' said Lia.

'Wealthy westerners coming in to rescue the poor,' said Macy, the sarcasm dripping from her voice.

Richard nodded. 'You're saying it's like financially, we're really just supporting the structure that keeps everyone browbeaten?'

Macy's eyes narrowed. 'Exactly, and also it's self-serving, because in the long term, are you helping this community fix any of the real problems they have?'

'So how about if we asked Don Chema to talk to everyone else about setting up a fund? They could vote for it, and if approved, they decide how it gets used.'

Macy sighed. 'That's a slightly better idea.'

Lia stood up. 'And I don't want to leave. I feel at home here, and that's a big thing.'

'You're basically saying that you're happy to keep working for a racist?' said Macy.

Lia wouldn't meet her eyes but turned again to appeal to Richard.

'If Don Chema got everyone to agree to the idea in principle then would you help?'

'Yes,' said Richard.

Macy shook her head again. In her opinion, if Lia asked Richard to jump into a crocodile-infested swamp he would do it. She was sure Lia knew it too and was simply using it to her advantage.

'Thank you,' said Lia. She reached her arms out to loosely embrace him.

Macy sighed. 'At some point soon you both do realize that it's going to be time to leave?'

She looked out the cottage window towards the hills and the deep green valley that she knew lay behind the darkness. It was such a beautiful place, perhaps it had bewitched them all. Was Lia just seeking solace by staying on the finca? Had the feeling of being useful to Miguel, the locals and the volunteers covered up the pain of her grief?

'I've no idea where to go next,' said Lia, her voice almost a whisper.

'You feel like you couldn't belong anywhere else?'

'I just love being here. Every minute of it.'

'Well, coo-coo-ca-choo, Mrs Robinson,' said Macy.

Lia didn't respond and Macy felt as if she was being too hard on her. She tried again.

'Whatever happens, look at the relationships that have formed out of us being here, as well as the trees that have been planted,' said Macy. 'Home is about having peace of mind with the people around you. So this place isn't the only place in the world you get to call home.'

Lia tried to smile. 'What's your idea of home?'

'That's just it: it's an idea, and until I'm old, I don't want it to just be one thing,' said Macy. 'Every time you live in a new country, you change and learn and adapt and blend your culture into something new. It's a beautiful thing that we should celebrate, whilst maintaining the deepest respect for the indigenous culture.'

'Home is supposed to be the place where you feel like you belong,' said Lia.

'Help me out here, Richard,' said Macy. She was tired and looked forward to crawling into her bed.

'My England home life wasn't exactly a bed of roses, Macy; in fact, it makes this place look like a dream.'

'Home is a place where you can cook breakfast in your pyjamas,' said Macy with a grin. 'You can't do that here.'

'I could but I choose not to,' said Lia.

'Okay, then. Home is where you can place yourself in the moment, maybe with a mug or your favourite slippers, and mentally comfort yourself,' said Macy. She wrapped her fingers around her twenty-year-old mug and held it up to them. 'This goes everywhere with me.'

'Home is your view of the sky at night,' said Richard, 'or somewhere you found along the way, or some place you have yet to find.'

'Bottom line,' said Macy, 'the more adaptable you can be in a world that is impermanent – and trust me, I have learned this the hard way – the better adjusted you'll be, because anywhere can be home.'

'Well, I'm a bit fed up of being so damn adaptable but I know that the rainy season starts next month, so we won't be able to keep things going for much longer,' said Lia.

Macy got up to signal the end of the conversation. Her body was beginning to set like concrete after the record number of trees they had planted in the last two days, in temperatures of over thirty-five degrees. For her, the rainy season couldn't come quickly enough. She looked out the window into the darkness again and was suddenly flooded by another creeping sense of danger.

'You know if you give a wad of money to the *campesinos*, you might be pushing Miguel's buttons in ways he may not appreciate.'

'We won't tell him,' said Lia. It was the way they seemed to deal with everything these days, as if Miguel no longer had ears and eyes of his own.

Macy looked at Richard but his mind was obviously elsewhere. He was staring at Lia, lost in his own world.

'Lia?' said Richard. 'Let's go out for dinner tomorrow, just you and me, in the pueblo.'

Macy could see Lia tense, shifting uneasily as she leaned against the wall. She looked drained and underweight. Fragile. Richard would have to work harder than that to draw her out. Macy didn't want to witness the disappointment she was sure he was about to experience. She quickly excused herself, annoyed that she could still hear the conversation quite clearly from the other bedroom, even with the door shut.

'I don't think that's such a good idea,' said Lia.

Poor Richard, thought Macy.

'Why?'

Lia didn't reply. Macy thought of getting up and going for a walk so she wouldn't have to hear any more but her aching body wouldn't let her. Instead she was forced to think of her own friends and family, most of whom she hadn't had any contact with for the past two years.

'Part of you wants to,' said Richard, his voice slightly muffled behind the wall that separated them.

'It might be a big mistake and then we'd ruin a wonderful friendship,' said Lia. Macy shook her head in frustration. Was the girl stupid? Here was a lovely person, willing to save her from the nights when she was alone and rootless, and who was willing to be there for her whatever the circumstances. She couldn't understand it. It seemed Richard had really flourished on the finca whilst Lia seemed to be turning more and more into the old him the longer they stayed, less willing than ever to take risks or live in the moment.

'Home might be a certain young man who happens to be your friend, Lia! Or the love of your life!' Macy couldn't resist yelling the words before she grabbed her pillow and folded it over her head, holding the two ends over her ears.

Chapter 34

The temperature in the hot season continued to climb and everybody looked forward to the sun dropping behind the mountains each evening, except for Lia. Her imagination, like the temperature, would switch up a gear, turning her skin clammy.

She had always believed that peace and justice were two sides of the same coin. Now she wondered if one could exist without the other. It was difficult to fall asleep at night, even after a whole day spent planting. She imagined Rodrigo creeping up to the cottage in the middle of the night, his machete glinting in the moonlight as he peered through the curtainless window. When she did sleep, it was fitfully. She dreamed that he was coming to get her because she knew what he had done. She even pictured herself dying in the same way Rafael had. She had followed in his footsteps after all, from London to Guatemala, to the city, to the finca and now to almost certain death.

Don Chema called a meeting in the barn. Everyone had quickly and unanimously agreed to him looking after a fund of approximately two month's salary for everyone, to be used exclusively for healthcare emergencies.

Though Julio wasn't given a pay rise, he continued working on the finca and his father received urgently needed medication for a chest infection. Every week one of the volunteers delivered ready-cooked food, and with the few quetzales saved, Julio bought clean bedding and a hammock for his father. Lia discovered that Julio attended AA meetings and quit drinking three years ago, long before he came to work for Miguel.

By the beginning of May, Pavel and Liz were the only two volunteers left. The heat had reduced their numbers more effectively than a cull and everybody was already out in the field that Monday morning, including Richard, Macy and Julio, when Lia arrived for work. The fact that it was International Worker's Day, *Día del Trabajo,* and a public holiday, had no bearing on the finca community.

The first rains had splattered the earth early that morning whilst they still slept, and for the first time in months the ground was moist. Lia recorded the latest logging measurements and walked to the reforesting zone with Don Chema and Tomás.

'It would have been Rafael's birthday next week,' Don Chema whistled under his breath as he viewed the landscape. 'He would have been happy to see all this.'

'I wish he was here to see it,' said Lia. She stared at Richard whose broad, muscular frame seemed to demand so much more of her attention lately. He carried a box of saplings on his head over to the next patch of weed-free earth they had cleared, oblivious to her gaze. He had paid her no further attention since she rebuffed his invitation to go out together, but continued to be warm and kind.

'I'm inviting Richard, Macy, Pavel, Liz and you to my house to celebrate Rafael's life, with us.' Don Chema looked away with the faintest smile on his face and waited for her reply.

Lia felt her breath catch in her throat. It wasn't that they had become good friends just then – they'd learned to like each other long ago. It was the fact that Don Chema now felt comfortable enough to divulge this fact in public by inviting gringos into his home for all to witness. It was one thing to mingle freely with everyone on the finca, but in the pueblo, where Don Chema lived with his family, it was different. The canteens, restaurants and shops were places of segregation. There may not have been signs that banned the *campesinos* from entering, but the prices did. 'Peasants' knew their place, and the landowners and police made sure they kept to them.

Lia paused to gather her thoughts. 'The last thing we want to do is cause trouble. Not so long ago you wouldn't have eaten at the cottage, for fear of reprisals.'

He nodded. 'And now I've shared food from the same table and lived to tell the story. And it's a very good story.' He tried to lighten her mood as she considered the consequences that going to his house might bring. 'We all want you to be there. I'm going to invite Raul too.'

Lia smiled. She didn't need any more convincing. 'Okay, thank you.'

She picked up a hoe, ready to join Richard, when she saw Rodrigo. He never came to help out in the reforesting zone, but today he seemed to have materialized out of nowhere, giving her a sharp shock. He spoke in a hushed voice to Julio, and as she watched, he pointed to her and shook his head.

Julio placed an arm on Rodrigo's shoulder and beckoned Lia over. She shook her head.

'*Estoy ocupado en este momento* ...' she called. I'm busy right now.

She turned away and the pounding in her ears was so loud that she didn't hear Rodrigo walk up behind her until he had tapped her on the shoulder. She startled and turned to face him, her hands exploding with sweat.

'You think you are too good to talk to me?'

She didn't want to give him the idea that he could pressure her into talking to him after months of either being hostile or ignoring her, so she said nothing. It infuriated him.

'You think because you have money and a friendship with the patrón that you can spread lies about me?'

'I don't have any money,' she replied. 'But I have a lot of morality, unlike you.'

She tried to walk away but he grabbed her arm, unwilling to let go even as Lia struggled to free herself, until Julio stepped between them, imploring Rodrigo to stop. Everyone was looking at them now.

'*Está borracho*,' said Julio. He's drunk.

Perhaps her entire time on the finca had been building to this moment, because Lia had finally reached the volatile place where all her pent-up grievances could be let loose.

She rounded on him. 'I choose not to give any of my time to a cowardly wife beater.'

She waited for him to attack, and gripped the hoe as tightly as she could, ready to defend herself.

'*¡Come mierda!*' said Rodrigo with a scowl. Eat shit!

He didn't move or say anything else, just stared at her. It prompted her to continue her assault. She actually *wanted* him to attack her so that she could finally show everyone else how awful and unstable he really was.

'*¡Muy tonto!*' said Lia. Very dumb. '*¡Estoy harto de tus mentiras!*' I'm sick of your lies. She picked up a handful of moist earth and threw it at his bemused and then shocked face.

'There! What an improvement!' She stood back to mock him whilst everyone else stared in silent disbelief. Don Chema was the first to burst out laughing, digging Tomás in the ribs. Tomás fought to keep a straight face but ended up giggling behind his hand and the others soon joined in. Julio was the only person unable to find it funny. She waited to see what Rodrigo would do but he remained silent and then walked away. Julio went after him.

Richard wandered over, grappling to bring his own merriment under control.

'I can't believe that just happened!'

She glared at him. 'I'm sick of the way he's treated me. I don't think he's ever treated you or Macy or anyone else the way he treats me. I've had enough.' Even the level-headed Richard had to admit that Rodrigo had it coming.

Tomás ran off to tell Lola, Marco and Favia what had happened, and within twenty minutes the entire community had stopped work and appeared in the valley, eager to see what else might occur. Every time Lia caught Don Chema's eye he giggled like a teenager, and once her heart rate had slowed, she couldn't help grinning back. The situation was far from resolved though, and before long, Julio was jogging back towards them, grim-faced.

'Rodrigo is demanding that you have a race on the horses so that he can demonstrate what a real man is in comparison to a girl who knows nothing! His words,' he hurriedly added.

Lia gritted her teeth and shook her head, regretting her outburst as she sensed he would never leave her alone now.

'What did you say to him?'

'Only that you personally knew Rafael and believed he might have been involved in his death.'

'What?' she yelled. 'How could you?'

'It's the truth. I kept telling you to talk to him yourself but you wouldn't.' Julio looked down at her as if deeply disappointed.

'I would have in my own time.'

He shook his head and she realized he was right. Her strategy had been to stay away from Rodrigo instead of doing her best to find out the truth. Perhaps Macy had been right when she'd accused her of lacking integrity. She bowed her head.

'This race will sort everything out but you must trust me.'

Julio grinned and she stared moodily back at him, subconsciously wondering if her predicament was merely entertainment to everyone else; or worse, that Julio had hatched some evil plan with Rodrigo to bring her life to a gruesome end. She looked upwards and noticed the sky turning a sombre grey in patches, the only colour she had never learned to like.

'Canela is the fastest horse on this land and I'll give him Piepa to ride. You can't lose!'

Lia couldn't see any way out of it. To refuse would be to show too much weakness. She reluctantly agreed, her breathing becoming once again shallow and shaky. Julio went to tell Rodrigo the news before Lia could change her mind. He returned twenty minutes later to demand that she be at the stables for noon. Lia agreed and waited out the half hour biting her nails, something she hadn't done in years.

'I'll come with you and wait at the finishing point,' said Richard. He put his arm around her and she pressed herself into his chest, wishing she could stay there forever. She caught herself thinking this and immediately pulled away with a frown.

'I need water,' she muttered. If they hurried, they had just enough time to get to the cottage and then to the stables.

Rodrigo was there first, waiting for Julio to finish saddling the horses. He totally ignored her presence. He had wiped his face clean but still had flecks of mud crusted in his hair.

The whole community got wind of the race and turned up to watch. Lia and Rodrigo would start outside the main house where Favia unrolled a line of red and white string across the driveway. They would race all the way to the bottom of the road along the main track that the cars used. Miguel wasn't expected to return from the city for at least a couple of hours, and according to Don Chema, no other cars would be coming in to the finca. Lia hoped he was right; most of the bends on the track were too sharp to see an oncoming car before it would be too late.

As soon as the race started, everyone else would run down the hillside to reach the finish line before the horses.

Julio checked the animals over and told them both to mount. Canela became skittish, picking up on Lia's nerves and dancing around, throwing her head up and flicking her tail proudly behind her. Rodrigo, on the other hand, was confident and egotistical and sat rigidly astride his quiet mare, glaring at her. She cast one last doubtful look at Julio, who nodded encouragement as Canela started twisting and turning her in circles, impatient to run.

On his shout they were to begin. As it came, Canela pressed her ears flat against her head and went like a rocket.

Both horses gathered speed, neck and neck as they raced down the driveway. Lia held her breath and they skidded round the first bend together, hooves sliding against the loose gravel. Piepa's side pressed hard against Lia's right leg. By the time they cleared the second bend she realized how completely out of control she was. Canela had her head to herself, although she was holding the reins. She lowered her body down, twisting clammy hands through the horse's mane, and clung on with all her strength, hanging precariously in the saddle as they galloped on.

By bend number three Canela seemed to ignite with more wild energy and they shot past Rodrigo and Piepa as if on some kind of mission of their own. She became conscious only of the wind whistling past her face as they flew down the road, accompanied by thunderous hoofbeats and Canela's snorting breath. Then the road became straight as they passed Lola and Marco's house, which enabled Canela to gallop at full pelt.

Before she knew it they passed the finish line, and the fleeting image she had of Liz and Pavel leaping to the side of the road was soon forgotten as she wondered how the hell she would get the animal to stop. She tightened her grip on the reins and tried to sit up. Canela responded by tossing her head and veering off to the left of the driveway entrance. She jumped the barbed wire and almost threw Lia out of the saddle. Dislodged, as Canela fled down the embankment, she grabbed a fresh handful of mane and clung like a limpet to Canela's neck until she could leverage her bottom back into place and hook her feet back into the stirrups.

They galloped across a flat field of lush, long grass towards the stream that marked the finca boundary. She had never been there before but was relieved to be off the slippery gravel. She stole a glance over her shoulder. No doubt Rodrigo had been able to slow Piepa to a halt as soon as they had crossed the finish.

She sat up again and felt Canela slowing down. *Thank you thank you thank you*. She couldn't believe she was still in the saddle. Soon they were cantering and then trotting and Lia was able to turn Canela's head towards home.

It was eerily silent. Usually, there would be birds singing, but Lia was grateful for the wind that was picking up and stroking the sweat from her forehead.

She picked up a movement far ahead in her peripheral vision and a tingling of dread in her chest. Rodrigo. He'd found a break in the barbed wire and was directing Piepa through, heading her way. She didn't know whether to pass through the stream towards the shadows of the tall pine trees behind her or wait until he got nearer before making another uncontrolled gallop for it, back towards the finish line. At least she knew they could easily outrun him.

She waited and for once Canela stood stock still. Clouds thickened above them, closing off the light, and the air seemed to whisper a warning.

'*¿Qué quieres?*' What do you want? she called as soon as he was close enough to hear. She wouldn't let him get within ten feet of her.

'To unburden myself,' he replied.

'What?' Her heart sank in the understanding that she had been right all along.

'If the truth is finally told then maybe something good can happen,' he said.

'To who?'

'All of us.'

Piepa took another step towards her.

'Back off, Rodrigo.'

'I won't harm you.'

'You wanted to kill me that one time in the barn.'

'I wanted to tell you to leave this place and to warn you about the patrón, but you never gave me the chance and I didn't know how to tell you something so awful.'

'You've hated me from the word go.'

'I hate everybody.'

He had a point.

'I wanted to encourage you to leave,' he admitted. 'Rafael planned to bring a land rights case against the patrón. He was the only person capable, who could read and write and advance the case on behalf of the community.'

The mourning cry of a lonely fox or *coatimundi* echoed through the trees. She wasn't ready for what he was telling her. She had the sense that everything was about to change forever, again, just like it always did as soon as she was on to something good in her life and the least ready that she could possibly be.

'You'll say anything to protect yourself,' she countered.

'The patrón ordered me to take a package of money to the people who killed him. That was the extent of my involvement.'

The wind rose up a notch, stirring the horses' manes and the long grass. The horses were closing in on each other, almost side by side now, heading back towards the stream and the sound of foaming water. Though his words terrified her, she realized her knees weren't gripping Canela as they had earlier. She was aware of the saddle and the horse's sides, and the stretch in her calf. She could feel Canela's back sway under the saddle as they walked.

He started to sob. The air grew even more suffocating and the low rumble of thunder rolled around them. The first drops of rain fell with a musical chime onto the grass, offering to baptize them both.

'José drove. We didn't know who they were; we were just told that Rafael was finished. We didn't understand what they meant. We didn't even know they were talking about our Rafael. It was impossible for us to warn him in time.'

A sheet of rain swept over them and the musical chime intensified into a whirring drumbeat, threatening to drown the field and all that stood there. They had to shout to be heard.

'How do you know about the land rights case?'

Rodrigo lifted his head to the sky and closed his eyes.

'I asked the patrón what he had done. He said he received a letter from the Association of Maya Lawyers, telling him Rafael had a strong case. He couldn't buy them off. That was all it took. He threatened to fire me if I told anyone and said nobody would believe me.'

She considered his words. He was an outcast, someone who was tolerated but not liked or respected. Rodrigo's family was by far the most malnourished out of everyone on the finca. Although they were financially dependent on him, he often spent his wages on alcohol. It was the close-knit community who, although poor themselves, had kept Lidia and the children going. If Miguel made them leave, they would have nothing.

Lia wiped rain from her eyes and shivered, unable to comprehend how she had been working for someone so evil. He had been responsible for Rafael's brutal death all along. She had wanted to believe that the words of an educated businessman would be more reliable than those of a drunken wife beater.

They were soaked to the soul by the time they crossed the stream to shelter under the nearby trees. His revelations finally came to an end together with the rain. The sun showed itself again, casting beams of light across the meadow. Steam started to rise from the grass and there was an explosion of birdsong from the dripping trees.

Chapter 35

There's nothing like someone else's poverty to kick you in the rear end when you don't feel like there's much to be thankful for, Macy thought, as she got out of the car. They had stopped in what felt like the middle of a maze formed out of tin shacks.

Before she got to Guatemala she could easily outdo most people on any level of sadness, but the longer she stayed, the more she realized that a periodic bout of insanity in an English mental institution was not so bad.

Don Chema's front yard housed a couple of chickens, a *pila* and a washing line stacked with threadbare laundry. It was surrounded by a rotting wooden fence and barbed wire from which more washing flapped. The house consisted of one small rectangular room with bare and crumbling walls. It was poorly lit with one glassless window that was shuttered at night. A naked light bulb hung from the ceiling in the middle of the room. Only much later did she realize that this was a relative sign of wealth compared to other houses in the area that relied on candles.

A table formed an altar in one corner of the room, covered with a white cloth. On display was a photo of Rafael, a loaf of bread and a pineapple. Candles burned on each side and the picture was nailed to a piece of cardboard and framed with freshly picked flowers.

As soon as Macy saw the photo, a hundred secret memories

seemed to seep back into her consciousness of Rafael's booming laugh and the way he'd looked at Lia. She kept getting glimpses of the man who had attacked Rafael, and she finally knew for sure that it was no one she had set eyes on since and most likely wouldn't ever again. The thought brought her comfort. The man she had seen had been skinny and his bushy hair had been pulled into a ponytail at the top of his head. There were more unwanted memories of herself and Richard back in the bar, days later. She sighed and had to look away.

She focused her gaze on the floor next to the table where a collection of ornate wooden masks were stacked beside one another, colourful even in the fading light: a golden and black jaguar, a red and black bull, a blue toucan and many more.

Favia introduced Macy to Florencia, Don Chema's wife. She lacked teeth and shoes and didn't seem comfortable talking to any of the men present, or Raul, but when Macy strained her ears and leaned closer, she realized that she chatted to the women, herself and Lia included; although Lia might as well have been on a different planet. She avoided making eye contact, was jumpy and seemed incapable of staying in one place for more than two minutes at a time.

They had arrived laden with vegetables, fruits, cake and alcohol. All the finca families donated their quota of vegetables from the garden: kilos of tomatoes, spinach, potatoes, chillies, onions and pumpkins. Macy had also taken the liberty of filling a small sack with Miguel's avocados and lemons the night before.

Raul, also without permission from his father, had parked the car outside the Despensa Familiar supermarket in the pueblo and waited with Macy, Pavel and Lia squashed in the back, whilst Richard and Liz ran inside and purchased three chickens, a sack of rice, two chocolate cakes, six bottles of Venado rum and a crate of soda water. After much shuffling around, they managed to load everything and everyone back into the car.

Florencia, Lidia, Favia and Lola washed greens, chopped meat and tended to the fire. Though Lidia was eight months pregnant, she refused to rest and none of the women would let anyone else help. Along with about twenty children, Marco, José, Rodrigo, Tomás, Julio, Carlos and many others from the pueblo dropped by as the late afternoon turned into evening.

Don Chema gave out paper drinking cups filled with a homemade alcoholic brew, but Macy had no difficulty declining his repeated offers. As it got dark, he asked everyone to sit on the floor and the women served rooster, corn tortillas, peas, avocado slices and salad on cut-up pieces of cardboard. She picked up the rooster leg and took a bite, the grease coating her fingers as she reached for the avocado and popped it into her mouth. She couldn't remember a meal more delicious, soft and warm with a thick, hearty taste.

The children were the first to demolish their plates and to look up, hoping for more. They weren't disappointed and *tamales*, with small, dark beans, were peeled and eaten far more slowly and relished with contentment.

Other families came in throughout the meal to lay flowers on the altar, light candles and eat. Once Favia had finished eating, she continued to cook up the rice, chicken and vegetables they had brought, and served it from a smoke-blackened pot, using banana leaves as plates.

Some of the guests brought chairs and stools, which they tried to get the gringos to sit on. They refused as politely as they knew how, not wanting to offend, until the guests finally sat down themselves.

Once most of the food had been served out and eaten by over a hundred people, Don Chema and Lola came out of the kitchen carrying two enormous candles that smelled syrupy when lit. Macy followed them outside, eager to smoke a cigarette away from the cramped room which was hot with human bodies.

A man dressed in white whom she hadn't seen before stood outside. He held rosary beads and incense sticks in one hand and a small brass bell in the other as he walked around a circular mound that hadn't been there when they'd arrived. It looked like it had been made out of earth that had been scraped together. She moved closer to try and see exactly what she was looking at.

Lola turned to whisper conspiratorially to Macy. 'It's made from many things: sugar, *pom*, tobacco, rosemary, lavender, black pepper and *ocote*.'

More than one hundred candles, green, purple, red and blue, were placed precisely in the middle of the mound with the wicks coming together at the centre. Favia appeared beside Macy carrying a tray filled with cinnamon sticks, a jar of honey, sunflower seeds and some sort of tree root.

'What is that?' Macy pointed to the roots.

'Medicine,' Lola replied with a shaky sigh. Her cheeks were wet. 'Today we heal Rafael from the injuries that were inflicted upon him.'

With his photo on the makeshift altar, Macy could once again picture the man who had meant so much to so many people and who had even ended up steering the course of her own life. If they planned to heal him then she wanted to be a part of it.

The man in white stopped in front of her and greeted her with a strange, high-pitched sound in his throat. She had no idea what he was saying.

'He says you would make a good spirit guide,' said Favia.

'That's very kind. Is that what he is?'

'Yes. He's our *Aj Q'ij*,' said Favia.

'You put something in the fire, too,' said Favia, looking to her again. 'It's necessary to continue your own healing.'

'Like what?' asked Macy, looking around.

'Past hurts. Find a stick, a rock, or something symbolic of past hurts.'

Macy hesitated and then picked up a stone, one she had noticed lying on the ground earlier when they'd arrived. Her brother instantly came to mind, an image of him roaring with laughter as he watched comedy on TV at home in London. She had made a point of contacting him once a month until she'd become manic. She counted backwards and realized they hadn't spoken in eight months. In her subconscious perhaps she had cut him off to save him from any further pain and embarrassment she might cause, and yet it felt like a stone she'd tied around her own neck in the process. Worse, he would be worried sick. She planned to call him later that evening.

'Put the stone in the fire and say goodbye to those past hurts,' said Favia, pointing to the ceremonial mound.

Macy did as she was told and Favia walked away with a nod of approval. She felt curiously light on her feet. She stayed where she was as Lola wiped her eyes, sniffed noisily and made her way over to Rodrigo who was coming out of the house, carrying some of the masks. Together they placed the masks in a row in front of the house, leaned up against the wall in prime position to witness the ceremony.

The spirit guide began to chant, ringing the bell and wafting incense around the ceremonial mound. People drifted from the house outside into the shadowy night, squatting in front of the mound or grouping along the side of the house. The children came out to play nearby and a million stars watched over them.

Rodrigo went back into the house and returned, supporting Lidia under one arm, his arm around her shoulders. By some miracle he was still sober. No one knew what had transpired the day of the horse race, only that Lia had returned on her own, white-faced and tight-lipped, a whole hour after the race had finished. She had refused to speak to anyone, even Richard, other than to assure him that she was fine.

Macy had hoped the race would have calmed the tension between Lia and Rodrigo, but nobody could have predicted such an extreme change in Rodrigo's behaviour. He was kind to everyone and Lidia claimed he hadn't touched a single drink. According to Carlos, he had attended every single AA meeting in the pueblo since the horse race. Lia, however, seemed to have taken a turn for the worse, calling out numerous times in restless sleep. Tonight, once again, she merely picked at the precious food placed in front of her, as if she had lost her ability to eat.

Macy watched Richard, Raul, Pavel and Liz pile out behind Rodrigo. With the exception of Raul they were all a little drunk. Born into such a rich family she wondered if Raul would grow up to be just like his father, where wealth accumulation would take priority over the health and happiness of others.

It lifted her own spirits to see Pavel throw back his head and laugh, one arm draped around Liz, carefree and happy. The finca had been his alternative medicine as well as hers, and she suspected he was cured from whatever had brought him there. It wouldn't be long before he and Liz announced their departure: she was sure of it.

The man in white threw something over the mound and with a flick of his wrist, fire began to burn in the centre, bringing Macy back into the present moment. She felt the heat stroke her face and arms as the flames grew in size. Lola took Lia by the hand and led her to the edge of the fire, where she divided a bunch of flowers and gave half to her. They placed the flowers outside the circle in four areas, a gift to the spirits, and Macy began to feel drunk on the beautiful fragrance and colours. As Lola and Lia stood back, others came up and took pieces of the offerings to throw on the fire or decorate the circle.

When it was his turn, Rodrigo walked twice around the fire before throwing eight handfuls of small, round black chips onto the flames. Then he started to sway, rocking his arms backwards and forwards, faster and faster, until he was dancing, as if in a trance, round and round the flames. It was a strange spectacle for someone who was usually so sullen. He was joined by Julio who linked his arm in his, and together they spun and danced in a formation that was slow, graceful and filled with love. Without realising it, Macy had become a part of a ritual that was as old as time itself, and the sense of connection began to overwhelm her.

Don Chema and Lola, Favia and Marco and everyone else paired up behind Rodrigo and Julio and began to sway as one body around the fire as the spirit guide continued to chant. For a moment Macy and Lia were the only ones who weren't moving, and then Richard took Lia by the hand, their hands interlocking as he pulled her up.

Macy considered going for a walk. Collective unity wasn't something she had ever been comfortable around. She wanted to sneak away from this overload of raw beauty before it showed her up for the fraud she undoubtedly was. She still associated togetherness with being forced against her will into a room of claustrophobic crazies. But when Julio took her hands in his and gave a gentle tug, she found her legs getting her up as if she'd been rehearsing for this evening her entire life.

She was familiar with the psychic wilderness that existed between her head and her feet, and she found herself moving in patterns and waves that came to her with graceful fluidity. Renewed and reawakened at the most primordial level, finally, she understood everything Favia had been telling her.

That's it, she thought, closing her eyes to focus. Humanity will fall out of balance whenever it takes from the natural world without giving anything back; every time the earth's resources get taken, a spiritual debt has to be paid in return. She felt a certainty in her heart and opened her eyes again. Suddenly she could relate more closely to her surroundings, to the air she was breathing and the dirt floor that she was dancing on. To Rafael. She had no idea how long they swayed and moved like that, and she didn't notice people donning the masks until she realized she was dancing between an armadillo and a toucan.

At the beginning they had been about seventy people, but as the evening wore on, their numbers dwindled and the chants of the man in white became more noticeable, a lonelier sound echoing into the night. Everyone became tired, especially after midnight, but they all stayed awake, sinking down gratefully onto the earth as the fire died down. Communication became the barest of nods or an outstretched hand on a shoulder, and there was an atmosphere of smoky hallucination as everyone stared into the embers. Clouds snuffed out the moon and stars. Still the man in white murmured prayers and still the bell rang and the incense smoked.

Macy was vaguely aware of someone shouting from the road but paid no attention until she felt Don Chema clamp the mask he'd been wearing over her own face. Just as fast, several of the others removed their masks and placed them upon Raul, Richard, Lia, Pavel and Liz. Macy was already hot and didn't appreciate the claustrophobic, wooden weight of the mask.

A black pickup crawled past the house, window down. Miguel. The car turned around and came back for another view. They sank down, huddled around the fire. She felt a surge of anger as she saw the shotgun pointing towards them from the car. He must have searched them out on the finca, found himself alone and come looking for them in the pueblo.

She searched for Lia and found her sitting next to Richard, arms clasped round her knees. Lia stared back at Miguel and then slowly removed her mask. At least he didn't get out of the car. He looked betrayed and lonely, even with the gun pointed at them. They stared at each other for what felt like an eternity, before Miguel drove on.

Chapter 36

The following Sunday morning the wind howled as if the earth was ending. Lia made sure she was up early, just a few hours after they'd arrived back at the finca. She tiptoed past Macy's sleeping form and closed the bedroom door softly behind her before sliding on her trainers. The grass was shiny, wet with morning dew, and she watched dark clouds form the shapes of monsters, quickly devouring any hint of blue. A storm was coming but her head felt clear, more clear than ever before. The wind slapped her hair into her face and she pulled it back, tying it loosely as she started the walk up to the main house. Nobody stirred from the barn or the neighbouring houses. It should have been a day of rest.

When she got to the kitchen, Miguel sat there alone with his hands wrapped around a black coffee. He wasn't startled by her presence but smiled as if he'd been expecting her. It was a polite and wholly insincere smile. He wore a suit and tie, unusually formal for a Sunday, and chewed a corner of his bottom lip as he looked at her.

'A good party last night?' He stared at her with thinly disguised contempt, his mouth drawn into a tight sneer.

'It wasn't exactly a party,' she began. She was ready to tell him everything.

'Good morning, Lia.' It was Clarisa, strained and tired.

'Good morning, I'm sorry to be in your house so early, and on a Sunday too. I just needed to see Miguel about something.'

'I don't care what it was or wasn't,' said Miguel as if Clarisa wasn't there. 'Things are going to change around here. I don't have the time to talk now.'

'Are you going out?'

'To arrange payment for a wood mill.'

'On a Sunday?'

'I'm paying half in cash and half in wood, which you'd know if you ever bothered to spend any of your time with me. This is the one day I can get the wood out without the police knowing.'

'Is Carlos taking it with you?'

'No.' Miguel's eyes narrowed but he offered no further explanation.

'Last night was a one-off, because you see I knew—'

At that moment Raul walked in, red-cheeked and red-eyed as if he'd been crying.

Raul looked from her to his father and gave her the slightest nod.

'Morning, Raul,' said Lia.

Miguel stood up. 'Remember what we agreed,' he said to Raul, jabbing his finger at him.

'Tomás!' he called.

Tomás appeared in the hallway, slightly wobbly on his feet and rubbing his head. He too looked sleep-deprived and upset. It wasn't surprising, seeing as he had been one of the last people to stop dancing and had probably had the most to drink out of all of them. He didn't acknowledge Lia.

'*Sí*, Patrón.'

'When you've finished cleaning the windows, start on the floors.'

Tomás bowed with difficulty and nodded. '*Sí*, Patrón.'

'And when you've finished that, go and clean the barn.' He jabbed a finger at Lia without looking at her.

'Oh, that's okay, the volunteers do the cleaning there themselves,' said Lia.

'Do it,' he spoke to Tomás again through gritted teeth.

'*Sí*, Patrón.'

Tomás nodded again before scurrying off back down the hall.

'Why is Tomás working on a Sunday?' asked Lia. 'Is anything wrong?'

'Nothing other than it seems you now have greater power and control over my workers than I do.'

Lia took a deep breath and shook her head. 'I don't. We just work together.'

Miguel banged his fist down upon the glass table and Lia jumped. Did he know that she knew? Her mind started to whirl, her breath coming in more shallow and faster, and she reminded herself to stay calm.

'It's because of *you* that they are losing their obedience.'

'Obedience?' She raised an eyebrow as if unsure that she had heard him correctly. 'Giving someone absolute authority over your life? Even when you don't agree with it?' She spoke in her most meek voice and had to look away from him. 'Imagine the moral atrocities that could result from that kind of thinking, Miguel.'

'Everyone must learn respect for authority, and that includes you,' he snapped.

She looked at Raul and then Clarisa. She wanted to tell them to question everything, always, but she didn't dare voice her thinking for fear of pushing Miguel over the edge. His hunched form seemed to seep an acid-like animosity. She couldn't put things off much longer and yet she didn't want to antagonize him.

Clarisa stayed where she was in the hallway with one open hand touching her heart. She shook her head in warning at

Lia, and Lia stared back at her. They shared a mutual smile of empathy. Clarisa turned back to Miguel.

'We won't be here when you come back,' said Clarisa.

'Good riddance,' he snarled. 'I can't trust you in my house.' This was said in front of Raul, who took a step closer to his mother.

Clarisa kept her speech low and steady. 'And I cannot trust you any more. I haven't trusted you for years.'

'Whatever,' he scowled and, scraping his chair back, stood. He dusted himself down and they followed him outside where José waited in the pickup. He revved the engine and Miguel got in, slammed the car door and leaned out of the passenger side.

'Tell Richard I'm expecting him to have dinner with me this evening.'

She nodded as José put the car into drive and they set off down the driveway. She turned back to the house.

Clarisa sighed as soon as they were inside again and sank down to the floor, knees up with her back against the wall. 'That man is toxic. I pray God keeps us all safe.'

Raul sank down beside her and put his arm around her. She hugged him tight. 'Are you sure you won't come with me to live in the city?'

Raul shook his head. 'I really can't.'

Clarisa nodded. She looked up at Lia.

'Please, Lia, try and be responsible. You are all so young and Miguel would never protect you. There have been kidnappings again in the pueblo.' She squeezed her son's shoulder and sighed.

'Things may escalate. It won't be the first time. You know' – she hesitated and glanced nervously outside – 'the deciding factor for me was the way he treated my son and Tomás today. He has forced Tomás to work from five o'clock this morning without food or a break. He keeps yelling at him and threatening to hit him – I don't know why, but he is behaving like a complete tyrant. Raul tried to stop him and he actually slapped my son across the cheek. That's a first, I have to say.'

Lia swallowed and glanced at Raul. He looked hurt and unhappy but there was still a defiance to him in the way that he wrapped an arm around his mother's shoulders and scowled at something distant that she couldn't see.

'I'm going to tell Tomás to rest now that Miguel has gone,' said Clarisa as she got up, 'and then I really must pack the rest of our things and go.'

She and Raul stood up and headed for Raul's bedroom.

When they had gone Lia saw Favia leaving the study with a handful of papers gripped under one arm. Her head was bowed as she wiped tears from her cheeks with her one free hand. On prompting her, she sat down and spoke.

'I'm going to really miss them, that's all. Patrón never used to be like this, so angry and bitter. The rainy season is starting too.'

'I know,' muttered Lia. She didn't want to think about it.

'Patrón was furious when he found out you went to Don Chema's house,' said Favia once she'd blown her nose hard. 'He believes that your first loyalties lie with us and not him. He is scared that you will betray him.'

'But he's *always* known how we've felt,' said Lia. Miguel wasn't the only one who was burdened, she thought with a wry face. Some secrets weren't meant to be kept. The more she'd tried to keep the dreaded knowledge at bay, the more it had risen up in her mind, giving her sleepless nights and eating away at her until she felt as if she was living in a private hell. She'd wanted to tell Richard, Favia, Macy and Lola a hundred times over, but something inside her insisted on hearing it from the king of the castle himself first. She needed to hear him confess. Until then it was as if everything that Rodrigo had told her was unreal; not a lie, but something that was suspended in another time, a place she didn't know how to move on from.

Favia gazed almost impatiently at her and shook her head, wringing her hands. 'Patrón never believed we would become close – close enough for Don Chema to have you of his own free will in his house all night and for all of us to share food together as if we were the same.'

She took a tissue from her cardigan sleeve and wiped her eyes.

'Miguel knows we have eaten together down at the cottage, so why not in the pueblo?' asked Lia.

'This morning he ordered Tomás to go to your house and search it while you were all sleeping. Tomás refused. Do you know what that means? He of all people refused his wishes. Tomás is his most loyal servant.'

'Search for what?' said Lia, reeling in alarm.

'I don't know. Maybe it was simply to test his loyalty.'

'We don't have anything to hide,' said Lia.

Clarisa and Raul reappeared in the hallway. 'He owes money to Carlos again. For the amount of money that my husband has it doesn't make sense that he hasn't paid him.'

'Well,' Lia was unsure what to make of it all, 'we don't keep much money in the house as far as I know.'

Clarisa looked away, her mouth turned down in sadness. 'You've got to be careful. Tomás acts as Miguel's eyes and ears in return for alcohol. Alcohol is the key to his dependency and Miguel holds that key with him.'

Lia nodded. 'I don't blame you for leaving.'

'I'll be able to get on with my life and my children can do the same. Sofía has lost her faith in everything and everyone. Our separation has been the last straw.'

Lia could only nod as she thought of the little girl whose whole world was about to turn upside down yet again. 'I'm sure she'll pull through,' she said.

Clarisa smiled. 'Of course she will. With or without her father I'll make sure of that. It has to be a new beginning for us.'

Lia turned to go but Favia stopped her. 'There's something else.'

'What is it?' said Lia.

'Julio. He's been fired. Patrón has given him and his father twenty-four hours to leave the finca.'

Chapter 37

It was already dark by the time Richard put his shoes on. The wind continued to howl around the cottage and could be heard crashing amongst the trees behind them, threatening to pull them down in its temper. He didn't want to leave the safety of the cottage but had no choice. Lia and Macy had gone to say goodbye to Julio and his father, who were spending their last evening at the stables before hitching to the pueblo early the following morning. Miguel had refused to give them a lift. No one knew where they would go and he couldn't help feeling worried about Julio's father, who was still weak. He jumped as lightning lit up the field outside and imagined he saw a figure walking towards him, but when the next lightning strike came seconds later, all he saw were the trees.

A roll of thunder shook the cottage walls, making Richard's heart quicken. *Pull yourself together*, he told himself. He swung the front door open to meet the storm and was surprised as the door was whipped out of his hand and slammed against the wall. He closed it and walked with his head bent as low as possible to protect his face from the rain which was gathering momentum by the second. At least he had thought to bring a dry set of clothes in a plastic bag.

Though the terrain was now as familiar to him as the teeth in his mouth, he resisted the urge to run. He heard a strange sound close by, like a couple of noisy breaths, and stopped, expecting Macy or Lia to come into view, but there was no one. He struggled on towards the house, fighting against the wind that threw more rain into his screwed-up face as if trying to blind him. He imagined being lifted off his feet or hit by flying debris and he rushed through the front door this time, his shoes still on and muddy water pooling over the floor.

He was about to call for Miguel when he saw him slumped over an empty bottle of whisky in the dining room. Relieved, he turned away and was about to walk back out into the rain when he heard Favia.

'Don Richard, the wind has blown a tree down onto the phone lines. The telephones are not working.'

The news disquieted him. 'Macy has a phone if you need it.'

'Lidia went into labour this morning. It has been ten hours. She needs the doctor. I'm going back to Rodrigo's house to try to help her now.'

She carried in her arms a plastic bag full of papers that she hugged against her chest as if they were treasure. Richard stared after her as she retreated into the black night. She would be soaked in seconds and although Favia was many things, as far as he knew, she wasn't a midwife. His eyes dropped to the sleeping form. The thought of waking Miguel up was abhorrent but they would need to borrow a vehicle if they were to get Lidia to the doctor.

'Miguel,' he called.

There was no response.

He called louder and tapped the slumbering form on the shoulder with growing frustration.

Miguel woke with a start. 'Ah, Richard, you're here, I must have dozed off. Let's have a good drink.'

'I'm sorry, I don't think I can. It's Lidia. She's in labour. Can I borrow a car to take her to the pueblo, please?'

'These people don't do that,' he growled. 'They give birth in their houses.'

'But I think she's having difficulties and there's no medical support here.'

'She'll be fine.' His bloodshot eyes narrowed and a flash of lightning reflected in them.

'Please.' Richard didn't like the sound of his own voice.

Miguel seemed to consider the pleading in Richard's voice.

'Fine, go.'

But instead of letting him go, Miguel grabbed him by the arm and pulled him down into the chair next to him.

'Just so you know, I'm going to withhold everybody's wages for a month,' he whispered, with a voice like acid.

'Why?' asked Richard. The workers would find it impossible to survive, especially as most of the vegetables grown by the project had just been picked and distributed for the ceremony.

'Because of you,' said Miguel. 'And because I don't like the attitudes I've had to put up with recently.'

Richard tried to make sense of his words, temporarily stuck for words of his own. Lia had told him how bad-tempered Miguel had been that morning, but he had put it down to the permanent splitting up of his family. He shook his head. Lia had barely said a word to him in the past week about anything. She'd been withdrawn and he'd been worried about her, but until now he had thought it was because he had gone too far by asking her out.

'Have you got money problems? Is that why you fired Julio?'

Miguel didn't answer.

'I can help you out if you need it,' he pressed on, determined to be helpful. He knew Miguel would be expected to continue to support his family in the city, which would put an extra strain on him. Miguel looked at him in a way that made Richard instantly regret his words.

'I am aware that you have given my workers money. There is no better way to undermine me, Richard, and yet you managed to find a way. You shouldn't have gone to Don Chema's house last night.'

'I'm really sorry,' said Richard. 'I didn't think we would be causing any harm.'

'You've encouraged my workers to believe that they are better than they really are.'

'How?' asked Richard.

'Do I need to spell it out? That you don't belong in a house made of shit?' His face looked red with suppressed rage as he spat the words out.

Richard coughed with embarrassment, unsure of what to say, and glanced at his watch, aware that he needed to be going.

Miguel dangled the pickup key in front of Richard. He went to take it and Miguel lifted it out of his reach.

'Have one drink with me first. We were supposed to have dinner together.'

'I promise I'll come straight back as soon as I've dropped Lidia off at the doctor's and we'll talk this thing out. I assure you it has never been my intention to undermine you and I'll do whatever I can to put things right.'

Miguel nodded, appeased, and dropped the key on the table. Richard swiped it up and stood to go.

'Thank you.' Richard turned on his heels.

'So you'll be paying for her care?' Miguel called after him. 'Making her dependent on you? And what will she do the next time, when you aren't here?'

Richard left the house, his brain numb. He took longer than usual to fit the key into the car lock, unable to stop his fingers trembling.

He steered the pickup to Rodrigo and Lidia's house and found Liz, Pavel and Macy sheltering under a piece of aluminium as the rain still fell in a futile attempt to wash the finca clean.

'What are you doing here?'

Immediately it sounded foolish as Lidia's scream

punctuated the air, as piercing as the thunder that rolled above them a second later. Then he saw the two rucksacks and understood.

'Favia told us you were coming. Can we catch a ride too?' Pavel looked at Richard, his eyes resolute. 'Miguel, waving that gun like an idiot, we can't let it go. It's impossible for us to continue.'

Liz nodded. 'I'm so sorry if it feels like we're running away.'

Richard could only nod, propelled into action as Lidia's scream of wild panic tore through him again. He was grateful for as much company as possible.

'Let's get Lidia into the car as fast as we can,' said Macy. 'Favia asked me to come along too.'

It was the first time Richard had been inside Rodrigo's house. Rainwater poured through the corrugated tin roof into an overflowing bucket, and beyond, Lidia lay writhing on the wet floor on a pile of blankets. Favia held a cloth to her forehead and made the sign of the cross when she saw him. It struck him as something he might have done when he'd just arrived in Guatemala, but not any more. Lola knelt on the opposite side, holding Lidia's hand as she whispered words of support.

'Rodrigo and Marco are looking after the children at my house,' said Lola. Her mouth stretched into a small smile, proud and amazed that Rodrigo had not resumed drinking.

Together they hoisted Lidia, shivering, from the floor and helped her into the passenger side of the pickup. She lay on her left side with her head on the driving seat. Richard took out his dry clothes and spread them as best as he could over her arms and legs.

Pavel and Liz jumped into the back, dragging their rucksacks up behind them. The rain showed no mercy and Richard had to squint as he looked up at them.

'Did you say goodbye to Lia?' he yelled.

They both nodded.

'We gave her a bottle of whisky that we bought last week. For the three of you. To say thanks.'

'I think she's still at the stables,' Macy called out as she attempted to cover her face with her arm. She would probably wait for a break in the rain before making a dash back to the cottage, he thought.

Richard ran around to the passenger side and opened the door to help Favia in. She still had the plastic bag of papers clutched to her chest.

'What are those?' said Richard.

'I don't know yet,' said Favia. She glanced at Lola who nodded before climbing into the back of the pickup next to Macy.

Richard resisted the urge to lift Favia into the pickup, instead holding out his hand, which she grabbed. She was soaked, with water running down her face, and given her age he worried that she would catch a cold or worse. He lifted Lidia's legs so that she could sit down, and placed them in Favia's lap.

Momentarily blinded by a flash of lightning, Richard stopped to wipe his eyes and ran around to the driver's side. He lifted Lidia's head gently as he slid into the car, placing her head onto his lap. She had become silent and her eyes were closed. She was cold to the touch and he didn't know whether it was merely due to the rain. He dreaded the notion of his world breaking apart yet again, shaking his entire belief in humanity. He turned the key in the ignition and hit the accelerator.

Chapter 38

Once at the stables, Lia was thankful she hadn't been blown off her feet or hit by lightning. Hearing her shout his name, Julio peered round the stable door that shielded him and his father from the worst of the lashing rain, and beckoned her inside. She greeted his father and sank down into the hay, ignoring the water that dripped down her body.

'Where will you go?' she asked.

'I have friends in the pueblo,' he replied with a bitter smile. 'They'll take us in until we can sort something else out.'

'Miguel was responsible for Rafael's death,' whispered Lia. She felt ridiculously young and inexperienced next to him, though they were virtually the same age. Her shoulders sagged as soon as she spoke the truth out loud. Somehow Julio got a fire going in the wet air and he set about making them the sweetest coffee she had ever tasted.

Another bitter smile. 'So now we both share the burden. Rodrigo is better for it. He told me the day before he told you. He and José have been silent all this time to protect their families.'

'Why did Miguel fire you?'

Julio shrugged. 'Does it matter?'

Lia took a sip of the syrupy liquid and sighed. 'I've been so blind.'

'You're very different to him,' said Julio. He was serious and then smiled. 'You don't have a moustache or that annoying habit of rolling your sleeves up and saying '*Limonada, por favor,* Favia.'

She considered his words, acutely aware of the everyday privileges that he didn't have, from her British passport, entry visa and ATM card, to the clothes and books she carried. She was different from Miguel, yes, but they both spoke the same language.

Lia lifted her head and met his fiery eyes with her own. 'What a nasty piece of work that man is.'

She wondered at what point Miguel had left the road of empathy and compassion for others. What had he lost from his heart in order to ask another to kill on his behalf?

'Things have been good here for a while.' He smiled. 'We've laughed from our hearts and crossed destinies and defied them. It had to become messy sooner or later.'

He paused and his face burned apple red.

'What?' Lia prompted him.

'I want to do something but the thought of it scares me.' He scowled with discomfort.

'What is it?'

'I was thinking maybe I'll look for a school where I can learn to read and write a little Spanish.'

Lia nodded. 'That's a great idea.'

He blushed again. 'Rafael always said if I learned to read and write, I would change the world more easily. I want to write.'

'I wouldn't be able to speak much Spanish if it wasn't for him,' said Lia.

'Country folk have been led to believe that we are too dumb to learn reading and writing,' he murmured, 'that we are only good for our brute strength.'

'Whoever says that is a liar,' she replied.

'Rafael told me about an organization run by K'iche' people.

I talked to them recently. If my father and I can stay with friends for a few months then I can attend their education programme.'

'I hope you do it, Julio,' said Lia, sitting up with new-found energy. 'I bet Rafael would be smiling right now. How well did you know him?'

'I met him in San José Patula when my father and I were desperate for work. He knew I was good with horses and the patrón was looking for someone. Rafael was always kind and generous towards us.'

'Did he tell you about the land claim he was filing?' said Lia.

Julio shook his head. 'He didn't want to worry everyone here.'

Julio glanced at his father and then looked to the ground. Minutes passed before he spoke again.

'Rafael did talk about the genocide by the military and he was part of a network of activists that supports the survivors in coming forward as witnesses. He had travelled to Panzós, Ixcán and Rabinal and connected lawyers and university people with some of the survivors there.'

Lia nodded and it dawned on her how little she had actually known him.

'He had tattoos on his arm with the names of those places. Is that why? Because of his work there?'

Julio stared tenderly at his father. 'Rafael's parents didn't survive.' He turned back to her and his eyes grew hard again. 'But Rafael was proof that people can revive themselves after immense suffering and grow even stronger. So those tattoos, they were his way of privately honouring the dead.'

Lia nodded. She felt sick with loss and regret.

'Is it true you were there the night he was killed?' asked Julio.

His father convulsed as he erupted into a fit of coughing and Julio jumped up, bringing a plastic mug of water to his lips and waiting until his father was ready to sip it. He helped his father into the hammock and sat close by in the wet hay, rocking the hammock with the gentlest of tugs.

Lia nodded and looked away, biting her lip.

'I didn't know how to call the emergency services,' she said in a small voice, 'and I couldn't stop the bleeding. I was worse than useless.' She closed her eyes and was back there again, the ill-fated bar, a place she had managed to avoid thinking about for months. She watched Rafael, kneeling there but doing nothing to help him. She felt her sense of self becoming bruised again, as if all the good things she once thought she might be destined for were nothing but idealistic dreams that would always end up as rusted and broken as the bolt that was barely hanging from the stable door.

'There was nothing you could have done,' said Julio, with a loud confidence that made her open her eyes and snap back into the present. 'It is what it is, just like this stable, the weather outside and Miguel himself. You have to forgive yourself because the amount of self-blame a human being can put on themselves can ruin them. Don't ruin your life.'

She stared at him. She wanted to believe him.

'Even if you did owe some kind of debt to Rafael, you must know that you have paid it with the reforestation. Anyone who knew him can look out there and know in their heart that he is happy.'

'Not if Miguel is the only person who benefits from those trees,' she said.

'You can't give what you don't have,' said Julio. 'And this land will be here much longer than that man.'

She smiled, feeling lighter. Julio kept talking.

'You and I, sitting here, sharing coffee. It proves we are one and the same, given the chance.'

He looked at his father. 'People with families can't always choose to fight for what is right and true because they care too much for their loved ones and will do anything to protect them.'

She nodded, conscious that the mention of family was something that set her apart from most other people she knew. For once in her life it wasn't a bad thing. She could even use it to her advantage.

'What will you do next?' he asked.

She stood up and paced, up, down, up and down the straw-ridden floor before turning back to him. Her heart thumped in nervous anticipation.

'If you're going to do something that scares you, then so am I. I hope I get to hear from you again too, in the future.'

'You're leaving here?'

'Of course,' said Lia.

He smiled, the warm, relaxed smile he had smiled when they'd first met. She suddenly felt as if she understood him properly and with it, she had got to know herself much better and the worldview forming deep in her psyche. Her body trembled.

'I don't have a family,' she said excitedly. 'No parents and no siblings.' She grinned. 'Usually it fills me with horror to have to tell people that because the last thing I want is pity, or even to be reminded of it.'

Julio sat up, his face expressionless.

'But right now, this second, it's useful.' She shot Julio a sideways glance.

'The last volunteers have left and everyone else has gone to the pueblo. There's something I've got to do that I cannot put off any longer.'

Julio also stood. His father had fallen asleep, lulled by the hot tea he'd sipped, and the rain had finally slowed to a drizzle.

'Be careful,' said Julio.

She nodded.

'You too.'

She turned to go.

Her clothes were still damp and she had taken off her trainers, preferring to squelch her bare toes into the cool earth which had finally been able to drink itself full of water. It was pitch black and she could barely see in front of her but she sensed the air was alive with the gentle beating wings of bats hunting for prey.

Back at the cottage it was darker than ever. A cold dread came over Lia, lifting the hairs on her arms and her back. She shrugged it off, putting it down to the fact that she was shivering, whether from the caffeine or the wet. She needed to change into dry clothes and stepped forward, putting her arms out in front, patting the brick wall as she searched for the light. She was gnawing on the inside of her cheek and stopped herself as soon as she tasted blood. Her fingers located the switch and she squinted in preparation for the flood of light. Nothing. She flicked the switch off and on again. Dead.

Lia continued to shuffle until she was inside the door. Perhaps the bedroom light would work. Seconds later the room was flooded with light and she breathed a sigh of relief. She returned to the entrance and looked up. The bulb was missing. Her heart started to thud against her chest as her mouth dried up.

She cast her mind back. Where had they stored their passports and bank cards? They were the only items in the cottage they absolutely needed. That was it, she thought: on top of the cupboard in Richard's room, locked away in a small rucksack. She marched into the bedroom, turned on the light and looked up. It wasn't there.

Lia searched under the bed, in the drawers and anywhere else she could think of but still couldn't find it. She ran out of the bedroom into the room she shared with Macy and ignored the creepy feeling caressing the back of her neck. Everything looked normal. She avoided looking out of the window into the black night, scared of what she couldn't see.

She changed into a dry pair of trousers and T-shirt, looked around the cottage one last time, and with a frustrated sigh got ready to leave. Pausing at the door, she turned and searched under her bed for the flashlight. It wasn't there. Perhaps Macy had borrowed it. She got to her feet, slid her hand down behind the drawers she kept her clothes in and was relieved to find that the bottle of whisky she had hidden was still there. She pulled it out to take with her.

With a backwards glance she set off to trudge back up the hill, taking a deep breath of the sweet air and holding it, counting to ten – all she could manage as she walked. A half moon lit the path in front for seconds before it disappeared behind a moving mass of clouds. She stared as far ahead as she could, searching for human forms, but couldn't see anyone.

She stopped to look behind her at the cottage one last time. When she turned back she jumped as something wet nudged her leg, but it was only the wet muzzle of the dog-coyote. She felt no fear as it stared up at her before jogging on.

Raul appeared as if from nowhere.

'I said goodbye to Pavel and Liz today. Are you going to leave too?' he asked.

'Yes, we've been talking about it.' She started to explain but Raul cut her off.

'You're all leaving because of my father.'

'Partly,' she replied.

'Will Richard and Macy leave too?'

'I think we all have to go.'

He stared straight ahead, his eyes narrowed although his face remained expressionless. 'I'll be all alone.'

'No you won't,' she said at once. 'The families here are staying and you know they always look out for you. Don Chema and Julio are nearby in the pueblo.'

'My father will kill me if I ever go to Don Chema's house again.'

Lia sighed and wondered what she could say. 'Do what is in your heart. That's all you can do, Raul.'

He remained silent but a flicker of a smile crossed his face and Lia felt her own spirits lift.

'I'm going to keep walking with my dogs,' he said, moving past her down the path.

Lia nodded and watched him stroll away, the three dogs zipping past him.

She had hoped to arrive unseen but a familiar voice rang out from the direction of the kitchen.

'I'm surprised to see you this late.'

'I'm here to explain myself,' she replied. The words were exhaled, threatening to take the last of her energy and bravado as she tried to slow her breathing. She wished Richard was with her. He never seemed to be far from her mind these days, and lately, they'd become more and more inseparable.

'Well, don't just stand there, come in.'

She hesitated before kicking off her shoes which were covered in a thick layer of mud. Miguel looked dishevelled and tired. He grabbed two glasses from the cabinet and was about to take the bottle from her but changed his mind.

'We might as well finish this one first,' he said, lifting a half full bottle of Red Label from the cabinet top.

She waited until he had poured a measure for both of them and sat down and then she raised her glass.

'To the future of Finca San Isidro.'

He repeated her words and took a sip, all the while staring at her.

'Are you scared of me, Lia?' It was as if he hadn't considered it before. He gave her a crooked smile.

'No,' she lied with every shred of her being.

He had his eye on the whisky bottle now. 'Thoughtful of you, and unexpected. I was down to my last half bottle.'

Lia hid a sigh of relief and grinned. Her hare-brained plan only had a chance of working if there was no stash of alcohol in the house.

'Rafael brought me here last year.' She spoke the words ever so softly.

'What?'

She got a ridiculous sense of satisfaction from the shock on his face.

'We met in London and then arranged to meet up again here.'

Miguel wiped his brow and shook his head, his face white.

'It's just you and me now, Miguel.' She took a gulp of the bold liquid and swallowed. 'So, please tell me, what did you do to him?'

She could have been on a movie set where nothing was real. Her voice didn't even sound like hers. Miguel blinked in astonishment.

'What did you do?' she repeated, her voice still soft.

Still he said nothing.

'It's okay, I've accepted his death. Everyone has. I just wanted to hear it directly from you.'

'You've been listening to the Indians again. Rodrigo tell you this, did he?'

'I was in the bar that night too, with Richard and Macy.' She felt no shame in saying the words now.

'Oh my God,' said Miguel. His mouth dropped open.

'Rafael had started a land claim against you, right?' Inwardly she sighed. She wasn't going to get anywhere by being confrontational.

'He was always a troublemaker,' said Miguel. 'Thought he was too good to work for me just because he could read and write.' He spat the words out and took a swig from his glass, and Lia refilled it.

'What happened?' She took another deep breath in an attempt to control herself.

'My children liked him, everybody liked him and listened to his crazy talk of fairness, equality and such nonsense. But I paid for this land, fair and square; that's what he never said.'

He got up, crossed his arms and stalked the length of the dining room.

'He was trying to take *my* land.'

She felt a strange calm settle upon her.

'So what did you do?'

'Look. Who is going to feed my kids if I just sit back and lose land to those Indians? They even have their own lawyers now. Nim Ajpu.' He shook his head in disgust and wiped his hands through his hair before crossing his arms again. 'He had even gained the support of Jorgé Castaño, the mayoral candidate for San José Patula.'

'You introduced him to us and then had him killed, too?'

'Actually, no, it was a coincidence. I don't know who shot him but I can definitely say it was down to his left-wing views. Bloody half-breeds, they're all the same. He had annoyed a lot of good people, you know.'

'So what did you do to Rafael?' She took another sip of the amber liquid, trying to pace herself, but her head was already spinning.

'I made sure he wouldn't come back here.'

'You had him killed.'

Miguel's eyes were like slits when he looked away from her but the fight had gone out of his voice. He looked as if he was suffering from some kind of awful toothache.

'I have the right to defend my property, but don't make the mistake of thinking it's been easy for me. I violated my own moral values and I have to live with that for the rest of my life.'

'I used to think I was in love with Rafael,' said Lia, 'but now I know I wasn't.'

Miguel sighed and for a moment put his head in his hands before looking up at her again with anguished eyes.

'He listened to me and treated me with respect,' she went

on. 'He laughed at my awful jokes. He was an amazing teacher and I didn't even know he was an activist. He gave me ideas to write about and stories to read. He embraced everyone, even you.'

'Look,' said Miguel. 'That man visits me in my head every night, and I think to myself, what other options did I have? Could we have reached some kind of agreement? I didn't ever sit down with him and I regret that.'

Lia sighed. A shiver passed down her spine as she digested all that she had just been told.

'Tomáaaaaas!' Miguel called.

Tomás appeared after a few moments, with the bag that she had been searching for. She stood up to take it from him and Tomás brandished his machete in response, forcing her to sit down again.

Miguel looked pleased with himself. 'I asked Tomás to take these things as surety that you will follow my wishes for two more weeks.'

She looked from Tomás to Miguel and back again. 'Please don't do this.'

Miguel switched to Spanish. 'He will do what I tell him. Won't you, Tomás?'

Tomás gave a strained smile and bowed ceremoniously. '*Sí, patrón*.'

Lia fought the urge to run outside and hide.

'Don't worry, it's very simple,' said Miguel. 'Two more weeks of work, and then I give your things back and you are free to go.'

'Why are you doing this?'

'I won't be going into the city. I will be timing lunch breaks and demanding double workloads.'

It was now or never.

Lia looked at Tomás.

'If you give me my bag back, you can have this bottle of whisky.'

She lifted the whisky bottle from the table and held it out to him.

Miguel scowled. '*Quédate donde estás,* Tomás.' Stay where you are.

Tomás stayed where he was. Lia felt her heart sink.

Chapter 39

The rain had flooded the roads around the pueblo and Macy worried they would get stuck, but they succeeded in reaching the doctor's house without incident and Richard managed a weak smile as he flexed fingers that were stiff from gripping the wheel. She was the first to leap out and help Lola down. Whilst Pavel and Richard waited by the car, Liz, Favia, Lia and Macy supported Lidia, half-carrying her into the doctor's office, a small brick room built at the back of a two-storey house. She was pale and unable to walk but they managed to get her to lie on a makeshift gurney as she wavered in and out of consciousness. The doctor, now a familiar face, quickly wheeled her away, accompanied by a midwife and Favia and Lola following behind.

Macy stood awkwardly next to Richard, fully aware of how much she had relied on Pavel and Liz ever since their arrival on the finca.

'Please let us know how Lidia gets on. We can keep in touch via Facebook,' said Liz with a shiny-eyed smile once she had hugged them both.

'I'm not on there,' Macy replied.

'Neither am I,' said Richard.

The rain had stopped, if only momentarily, and Liz made a note of their email addresses instead. She promised to write.

'Thank you so, so much,' said Macy, looking from Pavel to

Liz and back again. 'There is no way we would have achieved what we did if you guys hadn't turned up.'

'Oh, it's worked both ways,' said Pavel with a shy smile, and Liz nodded in agreement.

'What will you do next?' asked Richard.

'Head to the nearest bar and enjoy a cold beer,' said Pavel. 'Then book into a 4 star hotel, run a hot bath with loads of bubble bath and seduce my girlfriend.'

'Go back to Holland and work there for a while,' replied Liz, digging Pavel playfully in the ribs. 'Save some money.'

They hugged for the last time and Macy watched as Pavel and Liz put on their rucksacks and walked away, hand in hand.

'Every end has a new beginning,' Macy called out and Pavel and Liz turned around once to wave and blow kisses, before they continued trudging over the muddy earth.

Upon hearing the door open again, Macy turned back towards the doctor's house. Lola stood there, hands on her hips, her face grim.

'Macy,' said Lola. 'Do you remember telling me that Rafael's briefcase had been light as if empty? That's because it contained papers. I asked Favia to take all the papers from patrón's desk, bit by bit, as discretely as possible. We have been giving them to the doctor to read to us before returning them.'

Macy nodded. 'You've found something important, haven't you?'

'A petition addressed to the Minister of the Interior, the Secretary of Agrarian Affairs and the Land Fund, signed by various people, and a letter, written by Rafael, requesting that it be reviewed as soon as possible. The petition aims to reassert collective ownership rights over part of the territory known as Finca Santa Isidro which he states was given away by the government, without any consultation process and without our knowledge.'

Richard whistled under his breath and shook his head.

'That was in the briefcase Rafael had with him in the bar the night we met him?'

They looked at each other as Lola nodded.

'The patrón has title deeds to the land, but Rafael also collected statements from some of the oldest families in the pueblo attesting to how long we have lived on the land, which is far longer than the patrón,' said Lola.

Her eyes filled with tears. 'My poor, brave Rafael.'

Richard shook his head again. 'We'd better go back and check that Lia is still okay. I've got a bad feeling.'

Macy agreed, hoping they were wrong but knowing in her heart that she had been right all along. Her mind raced with new possibilities. Should they buy a gun to take back to the finca with them? Something to warn Miguel off when things got heated, as they might well do? She had no idea where they would find such a thing at short notice.

Had they all been living with a psychopath all this time and been totally unaware of the fact? She shuddered, feeling her stomach knot and wishing she could stop time and just think clearly enough to find a solution.

'I think we should find Lia, pack our things and leave straight away,' said Macy.

They got back into the pickup as fast as they could, and Macy prepared for the worst.

Chapter 40

'This is what it feels like to be in control of your own destiny,' said Miguel. He relaxed, his confidence growing with every sip of whisky.

'I just don't understand why you had to go to such extremes,' said Lia.

She suspected she might be swaying in her chair as she spoke, which wasn't a good sign. They'd been drinking for the past hour and Miguel had just opened the bottle of whisky she had brought. Tomás hovered between the kitchen and the hallway, rucksack still in hand, a reminder that she had become Miguel's prisoner.

'You know, in Guatemala you can hire someone to get the job done for less than two hundred American dollars?'

She got up to stretch her legs and, using the table for balance, realized she was probably in more trouble than she had initially thought. She wondered when Richard and Macy would be back. With the stormy weather they would have taken longer to reach the doctor's house and they were also dropping off Pavel and Liz. They might even decide to have dinner there. She sighed. They might not return for ages. She heard thunder in the distance and the rain began to come down hard again.

Lia looked out the window and, squinting, thought she saw movement heading towards the house. Could it be Raul? She sat back down, desperately trying to formulate another plan of action in her head.

'A newspaper report claimed Rafael had been killed by drug traffickers.' She forced herself to laugh. 'Typical media rubbish.'

Miguel looked at her and then smiled. 'That was my idea. Everything gets blamed on the cartels these days, and they don't seem to mind.'

Lia got up again and paced from the dining room to the front door and back before sitting back down, her knees unnecessarily close to Miguel's.

Her head was spinning but she thought she could see Tomás's shadow jutting out from the floor by the corner of the kitchen. They were speaking in English and she knew he wouldn't understand. She couldn't very well switch to Spanish either without making Miguel suspicious. Raul was leaning against the wall near the front door, taking off a new pair of laced boots. She prayed that both would hear her even if Raul would be the only one to understand. She raised her voice as loud as she dared and hoped Miguel was too drunk to notice.

'I don't understand why you couldn't just fire Rafael. Why did you have to hire someone to kill him?'

'Because he wasn't ever going to stop. Stupid Indians, as if they know everything about the land, trying to ruin people like me. He wouldn't stop making trouble.'

Lia nodded her head as if in agreement and sighed. It was no good.

'Papa?' Raul appeared in the hallway, his eyes huge.

Miguel looked up, his face draining to a worried mix of shock and shame. She hadn't thought him capable of such emotions.

'You got someone to kill Rafael?' He had reverted to Spanish and looked incredulous. He turned and ran, barefoot, back into the darkness, his dogs breaking into a run behind him.

Miguel stood up with a look of horror. 'I have to go after my boy.' He stumbled to the door and looked out into the night.

Tomás stepped back into the hallway. He approached Lia and dropped the rucksack lightly at her feet before stepping back again, with tears in his eyes.

'*Lo siento,*' he murmured. I'm sorry. There was no sign of his machete and Lia snatched the rucksack up, before she too backed away from Miguel, wondering what he would do next. She thought he might cry as his eyes swivelled from her to Tomás and back again.

'Get off my property.' His voice rose in height and volume with every word. 'GO. GET OUT.'

She nodded and Miguel lurched out of the door and set off in the dark after Raul. She had come for the truth and received it. There was no other reason for her to stay; and even with the truth, justice would be impossible. She finally understood that.

She heard Miguel yelling for Raul. She turned away from the door and lifted the half bottle of whisky that remained on the table. She thrust it into Tomás's shaking hands.

'*Yo también lo siento,*' she replied. I'm sorry too.

Lia put her shoes on and took the path down to the cottage as quickly as she could, jogging in the slippery undergrowth. She figured she may as well pack. When she had finished she would pack for Richard and Macy, she thought with a shaky sigh.

She was halfway to the barn when she first smelled it, the sweet smell of burning straw. In the night air, the moon gleamed for seconds to illuminate a cloud of smoke spreading over the barn roof, levitating upwards. She watched, unable to move. There was so much smoke billowing that for a moment she was hypnotized, unable to take it in. She could hear crackling and within seconds smoke covered the entire roof.

Had Miguel, in his drunken anger, set fire to the barn? She could think of no other explanation and yet it was an incredible thought. She had no idea how long she stayed rooted to the spot. She finally started to run but skidded to a halt again when she saw Miguel stagger onto the path in front of her. He wailed in a sick panic.

'Have you seen him, my son?'

She shook her head and with a sense of dread pointed at the burning barn. She didn't want to say it in case it made the words true.

'When he's angry or upset, he often spends the night in there.'

Miguel wailed again, a sound that seemed to surprise him. Together they ran towards the flames and Lia dropped the rucksack on the path, far enough away that it would be safe from the fire.

He raced into the smoking barn and Lia followed, forcing her limbs to move. Inside, her eyes began to water, blurring her vision. Flames licked up the walls, illuminating the ramshackle milking equipment, flickering and hissing from the side door across one whole side of the barn.

She looked wildly around, searching for Raul, before climbing up the hatch. She gasped as the newly fitted metal railing burned her palm. The first floor felt like a furnace. The original timbers at one end of the barn smouldered and it would be mere minutes before the fire reached for the straw piled up high at the other end and lifted its ashes skyward.

She pressed the light switch down, out of habit, but the only light came from the fire. Areas of the walls were scorched and blackened but Macy's palapa walls were still intact. She listened for human sounds but heard nothing. In the far corner, lumps of straw already glowed. High above, the original timber beams were black with soot but not yet alight. More and more smoke caught in her throat, forcing her to cough. It was too smoky to tell if anyone was there.

'Raul!'

Miguel appeared next to her. Both were yelling now, and although she understood that on some distant, intellectual level she wasn't responsible for whatever happened next, she still felt responsible. Her head throbbed with the effects of the alcohol and she bit back a sob of helplessness.

'We have to go back, Miguel.' The words came out in a croak. Her throat threatened to close down and the smoke was turning thicker and more bitter each second they remained there. It began to engulf them until it was impossible to see all the way to the end of the barn.

Lia dropped to her knees but it was just as hard to breathe. Her eyes and nose began to stream tears. Her lungs felt as if they were alight.

Miguel came nearer to her, a foot from her face, confused and upset.

'This is all because of you,' he moaned, his face smudged black and contorted.

He dropped to his knees, grabbed her wrist and held it, vice-like.

'He's not here,' she said, twisting her arm to get away from him. He was surprisingly strong. She bent over with the exertion until her nose was touching the wood floor, and coughed until it felt as if she would expel her lungs.

'Go over there and check,' he said.

She looked up. He was pointing towards the end of the barn where the hay bales were stacked. There was no way she would get down there and back without catching on fire or passing out.

'I can't,' she panted, but he refused to let her go.

She got to her feet – anything to make him believe she would do it.

'Okay, I'll go.'

Before she had time to consider it further, Lia lifted her right leg and swung her hips as far round as she could, smashing the ball of her foot into the side of Miguel's face. She hadn't meant to kick him so hard. A wave of dizziness hit her as Miguel released her and fell backwards onto the floor. Her left knee buckled out from under her. Then she was drowning and realized that she must have fallen back down. All she could see was smoke all around her, and directly above, the wooden beams which looked as if they would come crashing down on top of them at any moment.

Lia sat up and put her arms out to try and orientate herself. She could no longer see Miguel, and though she was only a few metres from the barn hatch, she had no idea how to find it. The smoke had grown so thick that she no longer knew which way to turn. She tried to stand but her head swam too much to follow through with the upward effort required.

She was thinking about how she ought to try once more to get up when she felt her wrists encircled once again and pulled out from behind her. She didn't have any remaining strength left to pull away and felt herself being dragged upwards and backwards. Flames started to dance skyward through the roof of the barn. She thought she saw the beams begin to move and a new noise permeated the air, a deep groan which came from the barn itself as it acknowledged its destruction.

She waited with a pathetic curiosity. If she was going to die then they would show themselves; she'd always believed that. She tried to imagine two people, her actual mother and father, walking through the fire to get her. Instead, the only person to appear like a vision was her second mum, precious in the sincerity and love she had always shown Lia. She was laughing and shaking her head at Lia in the indulgent way that she did whenever Lia demanded her attention for something she disapproved of.

She saw Richard, interspersed with snippets of university friends and the faces of volunteers she had met in Guatemala, ebbing and flowing in her vision. What was happening? She shook her head in confusion but felt an urge to live, stronger than anything she had ever experienced before.

She smiled as she suddenly saw her life before her with crystal-clear clarity. There was an art to living that she hadn't ever understood before now; it was a tightrope balance between staying and going. It was one of the most important things people had to figure out for themselves, wherever they came from. It was all very well to name ethnicities and backgrounds when asked, but what did any of that really mean or matter? It was far better to simply understand when to give in and run, and when to hold firm and stand your ground in life. Richard's face appeared again and she felt jolted into a new level of consciousness. He was her very own Richard and he was real! All this time had she simply been blind to her incredible good luck? If she was given one last chance to live, then she was determined to allow her feet to stride forward, in time with his, from this point on. She was ready to abandon everything and start all over, and she would do so as many times as it took for her to get it right. She promised herself that she would be bold enough to step outside of herself and change everything.

The last thing she remembered was the sheer surprise she felt as she took a sharp intake of clear, cool air and saw Richard's shocked face bent over her. The trees creaked and bent in protest as if they were being pulled and torn apart, limb by limb. She was lying on cool, wet grass, watching pine cones fly through the air like ammunition, and somehow she was soaked. She finally understood. She was lying in the middle of another storm and the rain was washing her down. That meant she was outside. Alive. Safe.

Chapter 41

Richard found Lia lying close to the hatch in the barn, and it had been easy to get her out in comparison to Miguel. By the time Raul and Macy found Miguel lying in the centre of the barn and managed to drag him out, he was severely burned and barely conscious.

He was a mess of black, brown and red merged into one ugly colour. His clothes and skin were flayed and charred, and there was no time to get him into the pickup and race him to the doctor. There was not even time to offer comfort, reassurance or forgiveness as he started his final journey to rest. But Miguel offered comfort, remorse and reassurance to his son. He was many awful things but he had always been a devoted father. Raul held his hand until the end.

Raul bent to hear his father's last words and nodded before leaning his cheek to touch his father's. They stayed like that, cheek to cheek, both with their eyes closed tight, holding in their pain as the rain dropped its wet grief upon them. Richard had an immediate flashback to their first night in Guatemala when it was Lia with Rafael, until he'd ended up dragging her away. He wondered if she would ever forgive him for that intrusion.

He knew Lia was going to be all right, though. It was in the strength she used to grab hold of his hand, the way she looked at him and the increasing energy with which she coughed. He didn't know or care about much else.

Macy was the one who took Miguel's pulse. She had started to shiver in the rain and could only nod as she confirmed what he had also been wondering. Miguel was dead.

In the end it was Julio who brought the doctor and broke the spell that Miguel's death had weaved around them. He'd leaped on Canela, ridden bareback to the pueblo in the storm and come back in the doctor's car. They hadn't moved in the time he had taken. How could they, when Raul refused to leave his father's side? There was no way they would leave the boy alone in the dark.

After the doctor had bandaged Lia's superficial burns, which were mainly to her legs, face and arms, he turned to Richard. The thought of even more death frightened him and the doctor looked sombre.

He leaned inches from Richard's ear and grabbed his shoulder to speak in heavily accented English.

'Lidia has given birth to a baby boy. Both mother and baby are doing fine.' He grinned and slapped Richard on the back. 'She has named the baby Ricardo, after the man who helped save their lives.'

Richard fell to his knees and held his arms up in a victory V. Finally he knew what it was like to feel like a hero. Some of the colour began to return to his face – a good thing, because once Macy had taken Raul and Lia into the main house, he was asked to help Julio and the doctor lift Miguel into the back seat of his car. Rich or poor, alive or dead, all were equal when it came to riding in the back of the doctor's car. It was old and battered and the inside was rusty and dirty. The back seats were strewn with disposable rubber gloves, tissues and dirty clothing, which Richard swept onto the floor of the car before they manoeuvred Miguel inside.

Richard wondered who had started the fire. Macy thought it might have been Julio. He had known Pavel and Liz were leaving, and he and his father had also been due to leave the next morning. After years of injustice, who could blame him for setting fire to the barn as an act of revenge? But Julio denied it, saying that he had stayed at the stables with his father until he had smelled burning. Lia thought it might have been Raul in a fit of anger directed at his father, but he too denied it. Lola burned with hatred towards Miguel upon making the discovery of Rafael's papers in his office, and said she would have set both the barn and Miguel's house on fire had she been there, but she had been in the pueblo with Lidia and Favia. Rodrigo, still sober, neither admitted nor denied responsibility, other than to say he had been looking after his children. Privately, Richard believed it most likely to have been him out of anyone. Or perhaps it really had been Miguel after all, receiving a kind of self-administered justice, directed by Rafael's spirit, now healed and freed by his family and friends, in a country that still suffered impunity from the law. They would never know for sure.

The doctor gave Raul a batch of mind-numbing pills that he refused to take. He passed them on to Macy as soon as the doctor had left, taking Miguel with him. Lia and Macy walked with him to the kitchen and Macy insisted on making a brew of hot chocolate mixed with rum. He sat at the head of the table, silent and pale-faced, but he didn't cry. The only thing he said was that his father had admitted guilt and begged for his forgiveness. For all his faults it still seemed so far from what Richard had known of Miguel. He found Clarisa's phone number in the study and succeeded in making contact on the first attempt. Clarisa told him that she was on her way back. Raul remained silent after this last piece of news, leaning forward on the kitchen table with his head on his folded arms until past midnight as he waited for his mother and siblings to return.

Upon her arrival Clarisa asked if he, Lia and Macy would stay on for longer. Macy agreed to stay for a couple of weeks, to support Raul and his family but also to help Rodrigo with the children whilst Lidia recovered from a difficult birth. All Richard wanted to do was pack and leave, and thankfully Lia was more than happy to do the same.

One month later

Dear Macy,

I am so, so deeply sorry for not telling you (and Richard) about Miguel much sooner than I did. The truth is that I wanted to, but I had an even stronger need to stay at the finca until after Rafael's ceremony. It was selfish of me, but that evening at Don Chema's it felt like I was finally able to say goodbye to Rafael. It brought me a sense of peace that I'm not sure I have ever felt before. It's also how long it took for me to figure out that I had to confront Miguel before I could leave. I sometimes wonder, why didn't Don Chema invite Miguel to his house that night? Would he have come? Could everything have turned out differently?

I see now how I idealized Rafael and confused it with being in love with him. He had even told Lola that he was worried he wouldn't be able to live up to my youthful expectations! He'd thrown me what felt like a lifeline when I was finding it hard to survive in London. Perhaps I'd been lonely and a little lost too, and he'd distracted me from myself. He treated me with affection and respect and spoke a language that I found so romantic and beautiful that I wanted to adopt it as my own. I still miss him every day.

It has been a humbling experience to finally understand that just like that land of trees, I am my own home and country. It's up to me to decide whether to love it, embrace it and protect it or not. You have no idea how much you've inspired me. Now I know that home, land and country ... well, the whole thing is just an ongoing, growing story in my head, filled with the people I meet along the way. If that land of trees could talk I sometimes wonder what she would have said to us, with her incredible beauty and tragic past.

Things are going *extremely* well with Richard! We're renting a flat in East London. He's working with his dad and I've got a job working as an Assistant Field Ecologist delivering protected species surveys. I love it, but as soon as we can we will hatch a plan to go to China. I want to learn Chinese! Come and travel with us, please.

Miss and love you.

Lia

Two months later

Dear Lia and Richard,

It was lovely to speak on the phone even if it was mere minutes before we were cut off by the storm, and I'm glad you decided to go back to London for a while. It's really not such a bad place to call your own once you've spent some time there on your own terms.

In reply to you, Lia, I wanted to be angry with you, I wanted to be furious. But I couldn't because I understood why you did it. That night will also stay with me forever. Don Chema didn't invite Miguel to the ceremony because Miguel never attended Rafael's funeral, in spite of Rafael giving Miguel fifteen years of service. It hurt his feelings but even so, he never, ever thought Miguel capable of doing something so evil. Lola and Favia acted on nothing more than female intuition and the fact that I'd told them Rafael's briefcase had been as light as a feather. They were like detectives searching for evidence, and the fact that they found it is probably why you're alive today.

Once Lola and Favia found Rafael's papers they told Don Chema and he called an emergency meeting at Lola and Marco's house. Lola and Favia invited me so I also went to that meeting, and I found out that Rafael had been about to start negotiations for a settlement which would have required Miguel to cede ten hectares of land and retitle it to the community.

Out of respect for Miguel's family everyone (including Rodrigo) agreed not to deliver the papers, to give Clarisa and the family time to grieve. I'm sure it's still something they plan to do in the future if they are unable to negotiate directly with the family. But for now everyone has gone back to work, working just as hard as they always have, in addition to supporting Miguel's family. Rodrigo, Marco and Tomás seem to work around the clock picking and bringing fruits and vegetables to the pueblo to sell, and when they aren't doing that, they continue to repair the fencing around the boundary near to the stream. Rodrigo has been sober for two whole months! His newborn son is adorable.

Julio started a riding school as soon as he received approval from Clarisa and Raul. He already has about fifteen regular students and is happy to split the proceeds fifty-fifty. His father is much better. They moved out of the stables into a new house that I helped to build along with people from the pueblo that Don Chema hired. Even though it's rained every afternoon it only took us a little over three weeks to reach the point where Julio and his father could move in.

Favia is still doing the cooking and cleaning but less of it, and Raul doesn't shy away from making his younger siblings fetch their own drinks. He's assured me that it won't be long before they are making Favia her first cup of tea in the morning. He's doing okay although he's much quieter than before. It's to be expected, I guess.

I've now left the finca and I'm writing this in the pueblo before I take the bus back to the city. From there maybe I'll take a bus to Mexico or head to Cuba.

Sending you both love.

Macy

Four years later

Dear Lia and Richard,

Can you believe it? In five days exactly I will be eighteen years old. Sorry I have taken so long to reply. In between school exams I've been working in the fields. All is okay here and everyone says hello. Julio said he has been too busy to write but you should expect a phone call at the weekend. He has had another piece published, which I attach at the back of this letter.

Life goes on as normal here. Sofía did well in her exams. Alfredo has found his way into the San José Patula football team. Marco takes care of the crop field that you started, and always seems to be producing various fruits and vegetables.

We have now signed the finalized legal documents that give formal land titles in shared ownership to the families that were already here when my father arrived. It includes the land upon which their houses sit, a good-sized piece around each house and part of the reforested land, which has grown higher than a two-storey car park. We have finally stopped all logging. The families agreed to a pay rise and a percentage of the plantation yields, and they are no longer charged for wood or water. Another four families are returning next month, families who say they had no choice but to migrate to the city when my father first came here. No man, woman or child can say that they don't have a fighting chance to make something of themselves if they are a part of Finca San Isidro. In fact, it is our policy that all finca children must go to school.

Once the titles were signed, Tomás, Marco and Lola didn't want to carry on working for the finca. Lola told me that their family used to have a restaurant. She and Marco opened a new restaurant based at your old cottage. They do a very good trade for the workers on the neighbouring fincas as well as those just wanting a change from the food in the pueblo. I grew up on Favia's food and there's nothing better, but the restaurant is a close favourite. Favia, Rodrigo, José and Lidia still work for us but Don Chema is retiring, and we are throwing him a surprise party at the weekend.

I have always felt like an alien in my own country and this continues to be the case, more so the older I get. There has been no land reform around us and I am aware that my family are the only ones to have taken this task upon ourselves. The other landowners who knew my father laugh at me. They tell me that I'm crazy and dishonourable, and it's true that I've lost most of my childhood friends. I am just thankful that I knew Rafael. I hope and believe he forgives my father.

Julio and I work closely together. Occasionally we will breed and sell a horse as part of my father's legacy to ensure that my family and I have everything we need. Don't worry, Canela is still here! I see now how everything has a price, but we could never give her up. Julio says she is the finca's lucky horse.

We are sometimes visited by developers and government officials who want to buy our land. They all know about the 'crazy man-child who gave his land away to the *cholero*'. We are not anti-development, but neither will we entertain anyone offering unethical deals cut between profit-hungry companies and corrupt governments. I will not talk to anyone who thinks they are too good to sit down and consult with the K'iche'. That immediately rules out many, many people! It's everything I hate about my country. The ongoing hatred towards the indigenous and the fact that anyone with a bit of money can buy off the government, the judiciary and the police so easily. Or hire a killer. I never want anyone working for me to feel so desperate that they would do anything for money.

My mother sends you a big kiss and lots of love. You will always be a part of our family. I hope you can come and visit us in the future. I think of my father often, and whatever anyone else says, I believe he would actually be proud of everything I've done. Please give our love to Macy. I'm so sorry she got ill again and we are relieved that she is recovering. I would like to visit London as soon as I finish my studies. Maybe I can come to stay with you?

Hugs, my friends.

Raul

A Growing Movement to Win Land Rights

SAN RAFAEL LAS FLORES – The Peasant Unity Committee (CUC) has announced the successful redistribution of land to 11 indigenous families in San Rafael Las Flores. The families had been evicted by police, military forces and the government in 2013, who forced the Q'eqchi families from their land without notice, destroying their crops and burning their homes, to expand international mining operations nearby.

The families have since become part of a resistance movement in defence of indigenous land rights. In a country with an abundance of fertile farmland, displaced indigenous are being killed for demanding small plots where they can work to sustain their families. In the past year, 83 campesinos in the eastern province have been assassinated for their involvement in a growing peasants' movement to win land rights. Witnesses say land activists are killed with impunity by private paramilitaries hired by plantation owners who have taken over their land.

Criminal collaborators include former members of the military, intelligence agencies and active members of the police who can bribe and intimidate government officials and the judiciary.

More than half a million campesinos in Guatemala are now landless. Several thousand land disputes have been registered throughout the country but with no sign of resolution. Distribution of land has been a source of social conflict ever since the Spanish conquest, with 2% of the population owning 70% of all productive farmland.

Guatemala, a nation of nearly 14 million people, suffers an average of 17 homicides per day, making it one of the world's most dangerous countries. Activists and community leaders continue to risk their lives to defend the land and natural environment against powerful commercial interests allied to loggers, palm oil, biofuel and mining corporations.

By Julio Peyore

Acknowledgements

This story developed out of a period of my life when I travelled from London to Mexico, El Salvador and Guatemala with all my worldly possessions (and a tiny amount of money) in a rucksack. I was young, and it was a hugely important time: 1996, the year the Guatemalan President and leaders of an indigenous rebel group signed a peace treaty, formally ending a civil war that had lasted more than thirty years. The treaty promised to stop the human rights violations that were occurring against the indigenous population.

I ended up staying much longer than planned, in a rural area where I fell in love with this beautiful country in spite of her tragic and painful history. I met many affected families and saw at first hand how the installation of brutal, authoritarian regimes, funded and trained by the USA's merciless CIA, continued to impact on rural communities.

I also saw the impact that deforestation was having on rural communities. And I know that the more we deforest land across the world, the more we reduce the planet's natural ability to produce the clean air that we breathe. Trees also prevent erosion of the nutrients in soil, and flooding, and provide a home for what's left of our wildlife. So today, please, go out, get a tree and plant it!

After I left, I continued to follow the news, read academic treatises on the country and kept in touch with people there.

In Guatemala it takes real guts and fire in your belly to oppose deforestation, land grabbing, hydroelectric power or dirty mining activities. You are likely to be persecuted and could even be killed with impunity. Through the eyes of an indigenous activist, the land is sacred and to be protected. It's a crime to strip the land of trees or pollute the water. Hence the land conflict continues, in spite of the peace treaty.

I have many people to thank, starting with my mum, dad and brother. Without them, I would never have gone to Guatemala. Thank you for giving me the opportunity to see so much of the world and call more than one place home. I'd also like to thank Sunil Puri and our daughter, Jeevika, for their precious love, encouragement, kindness, wisdom and belief in me. For that alone I consider myself the luckiest person alive, and without them, this book would not have been written.

I'd like to thank Eddie and Gail Benevides, with whom I stayed in Bermuda, for being so kind and giving me the space to work on early drafts. I'm also grateful to old friends such as Kully Kaur for offering to read the first three chapters and providing such helpful feedback. When you live far away from your oldest friends, you honour them whenever you can, so thank you also to Elaine, Parul, David, Dalia, Prity, Haddy, Myriam and Hasina for your positive words and for being part of my journey.

It was the kind words and editorial assistance from Liz Garner that gave me the boost and guidance I needed to keep going to the end. I am also grateful to Nicky Taylor for her eagle eyes, patience and generosity of spirit.

Where would I be without friends in Phuket? Sterling, Noni, Jasmine, Maciek, Rebecca, Catlin, Paul and James, your spontaneity and expertize in café culture ensured many working hours were fairly exchanged for entertainment, laughter and togetherness. Without Jack, Laki, Pook, Ulf and everyone else I've met at Yoga Republic, I'm sure my body and brain would have ground to a halt years ago. Thank you for being such inspiring, strong individuals.

I'm also so thankful to David, Max, Cheryl, Beau and everyone at Life Education International – without you guys, life as I know it would not exist.

This book is dedicated to the people of Guatemala, particularly indigenous activists and those trying to leave due to violence, poverty and persecution. I am hopeful that one day soon, mainstream society will recognize that if we continue to allow the world's natural resources – timber, oil, gas and minerals – to be taken from lands occupied by indigenous people, against their better judgement, we do so at our own peril. As we destroy the natural world, and obliterate our remaining indigenous people and their ancient knowledge, so too do we destroy ourselves.